PRAISE FOR *AN AGENT IN PLACE*

"*An Agent in Place* is all a thriller should be—intricately plotted, suspenseful, and convincing in its details of protocol and intrigue."

—*The Washington Post Book World*

"The action takes place in Moscow, and Mr. Littell . . . seems to know every street there. He gives us some vivid characters, a lot of action, a wonderfully detailed plot and, as a bonus, a splendid idea of how life is actually lived in Moscow in these tumultuous days."

—*The New York Times Book Review*

"Littell has constructed a complex, intelligent and gripping drama which has the additional merit of being almost entirely plausible."

—*Daily Mail*, London

"Veteran of the genre Robert Littell has struck pay dirt with *An Agent in Place.*"

—*San Francisco Chronicle*

Robert Littell's thrillers are distinguished by intelligence and grown-up writing."

—*The Times*, London

"If you enjoyed *The Russia House*, you'll find some of the same kind of pleasures here."

—*Chicago Tribune*

A fine Cold War tale from Robert Littell."

—*Daily News*, New York

"Every war needs a historian/novelist, and the Cold War is no exception. . . . Littell is both prescient and savvy regarding the Soviet power structure, and we are left feeling that it is not over yet, and it could happen again."

—Nelson DeMille, author of *The Charm School* and *Gold Coast*

"A subtle, ironic, sometimes passionate study of loyalties played out in the shadow of latter-day cloak and dagger, with characterisation to match the complexities of the plot."

—*The Literary Review*, London

W9-CHO-931

An Agent in Place

Robert Littell

BANTAM BOOKS
NEW YORK • TORONTO • LONDON • SYDNEY • AUCKLAND

AN AGENT IN PLACE

A Bantam Falcon Book

PUBLISHING HISTORY
Bantam hardcover edition published October 1991
Bantam export edition / April 1992
Bantam paperback edition / October 1992

FALCON and the portrayal of a boxed "f" are trademarks of Bantam Books, a division of Bantam Doubleday Dell Publishing Group, Inc.

ISBN 0-553-29965-4

Published simultaneously in the United States and Canada

Bantam Books are published by Bantam Books, a division of Bantam Doubleday Dell Publishing Group, Inc. Its trademark, consisting of the words "Bantam Books" and the portrayal of a rooster, is Registered in U.S. Patent and Trademark Office and in other countries. Marca Registrada. Bantam Books, 666 Fifth Avenue, New York, New York 10103.

PRINTED IN THE UNITED STATES OF AMERICA

OPM 0 9 8 7 6 5 4 3 2 1

For Lew Gillenson . . .

*If the past and the future really
exist, where are they?*

—St. Augustine

*. . . the past is rotting in the future—
A terrible carnival of dead leaves.*

—Anna Akhmatova, "Poem Without a Hero"

An
Agent
in Place

The first threads of plot *I was able to discover date back to the summer of 1986. According to a security log I was not supposed to see, four people whose names would not have meant anything to the general public gathered around a table in a basement room of the Pentagon. The table was metal and covered with frayed green felt, the room windowless, stuffy, remote. This was the first session of a shadowy Pentagon organization listed innocuously as an Intelligence Support Activity. The group had come into existence during the Carter presidency to deal with the Iranian hostage crisis. When the crisis ended the Support Activity had been disbanded—but it had remained on the books. It had been resurrected several months before the first session by some middle-ranking Pentagon officers who were intrigued by the fact that the group, which was not associated with the Central Intelligence Agency or the Pentagon's Defense Intelligence Agency, was outside congressional oversight parameters. Intriguingly, it was also outside White House oversight parameters, inasmuch as it did not require a presidential "Finding" to set the wheels*

in motion. Few in Washington were even aware of the Support Activity's existence; of those who knew, only a handful had an inkling of how it was funded or who was in charge.

Fitting the odd pieces of the puzzle together, I learned that the Intelligence Support Activity's budget was buried in the Joint Chiefs' contingency fund under the heading "Transportation, miscellaneous." The person in charge was a marine colonel attached to the long-term planning staff of the Joint Chiefs.

As near as I can determine, there were subsequent meetings, exploratory in nature, through the rest of '86 and all of '87 and into the winter of '88. The discussions revolved around a series of carefully honed written questions devised by the group's éminence grise, a soft-spoken, poker-faced one-time aide to the President's National Security Advisor, about where the American military establishment was headed. It was headed, everyone agreed, for disaster. "There is nothing more pathetic," the marine colonel is supposed to have remarked (in a comment that summed up the general mood of the group) "than a warrior without an adversary." As the winter of '88–'89 waned, there was a general consensus that something had to be done. The question was, what? By the time the cherry blossoms along the Potomac had burst into flower, the group was kicking around scenarios, exploring alternatives, checking and rechecking the givens, agonizing over the unknowns. I have it on unimpeachable authority that what was inelegantly billed as the "shit-or-get-off-the-pot session" was held in June 1989.

At one time or another I have worked with two of the four men in the room, played poker with the third and done some serious drinking with the fourth. I have a pretty good idea of how they operate. I think I know their weaknesses and their strengths; I think I know what their faces look like when they hesitate or plunge. Which is why it wasn't difficult for me to reconstruct this pivotal meeting, to figure out who said what. The Support Activity's nuts-and-bolts specialist, a fat man in his early fifties who went by the name of Marlowe, would have been the one to kick it off. "Suppose we go over it once more," he might have suggested. Knowing Marlowe, he would have loosened a very loud tie and unbuttoned the top button of a very wrinkled shirt. "What is the best that could happen?"

"The best that could happen," the retired CIA Deputy Director, who supplied the Support Activity with its operational expertise, would have explained patiently, "is that Ironweed will succeed. It is drastic surgery, I grant you, but the situation is desperate."

The marine colonel, who managed to look military even when he turned up in civilian clothing for a regular Wednesday night poker game, might have remarked, "In a manner of speaking, the operation is what our German friends would call an Endlösung—a final solution."

I can imagine Marlowe eyeing the group's éminence grise with his icy eyes and noting, "Henry here has not given us the benefit of his thoughts yet."

The éminence grise would have been sucking thoughtfully on the stem of a dead pipe. In his middle seventies, his hair silky white with age, he had started what his colleagues invariably referred to as a "long and distinguished career" as a young OSS field agent armed with a poison pill and one-time pads coated with potassium permanganate so they would burn quickly if he had to destroy them in a hurry. Those were the days, he liked to say, when Americans still had qualms about reading other people's mail—qualms, he made it clear, he had never shared. A former head of the Pentagon's Defense Intelligence Agency, he was known to be prudent to a fault. Without his assent there was no chance of the Intelligence Support Activity giving the green light to what had become known as operation Ironweed.

"My obsession in life," the man with the white hair would have reminded everyone, "is damage control. We propose to play with fire. I want to be absolutely sure there is no possibility of our getting burned."

"Which brings us to the next logical question," Mar-

lowe, a former Prague station chief for the CIA, would
have observed. "What is the worst that could happen?"

I can see the retired CIA Deputy Director removing a
pair of bifocals and massaging his eyelids with his thumb
and third finger. "I have been involved in a great many
schemes in my time, but this one is by far the most imagi-
native, and the most compartmented, I've seen. It is textbook perfect from every point of view. Assuming we give
him the go-ahead, the agent charged with carrying out
our instructions won't have the vaguest idea whom he is
working for or what Ironweed is all about, and thus will
be incapable of compromising it, or us. As a matter of fact
the only ones who can fit all the pieces of the puzzle together are inside these four walls. That's about as tightly
held as an operation can get." He looked directly at the
man with the silky white hair, whom all of them considered the Godfather of the plot. "To dot the i's and cross
the t's: The worst that could happen is the Russians will
not react the way we expect, and the plot won't succeed.
But even then they will not be aware that it was a plot."

The others in the room would have exchanged looks;
there was really nothing more to be said. They had approached the problem from every possible angle, antici-
pated every conceivable snare, weighed and reweighed the
risks. An agent had been painstakingly selected, discreetly
briefed by Marlowe (who had passed himself off as a State
Department security consultant), and dispatched to
Prague to await the coded signal ordering him to launch
Ironweed. If they were going to bite the bullet, the moment to do it was obviously now.

At this point the man with the silky white hair might
have shrugged. I can see him screwing up his eyes, something he always did before he plunged. I can hear him
saying: "What the hell. Let's take a crack at it."

1

"Welcome to Mother Russia."

There were traces of cynicism where such things were usually to be found—at the corners of the eyes, in the pitch of the voice, on the curl of the lips. As if he knew something the others didn't; as if they wouldn't be amused when they discovered it.

"Welcome to the emotional hardship post known as the American Embassy."

He scrutinized the three people who had squeezed into his cubbyhole of an office. "My name," he went on, rubbing the ball of an oversize thumb against the side of an oversize nose, "is Immanuel Custer. The few friends I have call me Manny. You can call me Mr. Custer. I have the dubious distinction of being the embassy security officer. The purpose of today's session is . . . vaccination—"

"Against?" Miss Harkenrider asked anxiously. She had been brought to Moscow to teach grammar to the children of American diplomats attending the embassy's junior high school. The last thing in the world she had

expected was to be invited to attend a security briefing.
What a story it would make when she wrote home.

Savoring the moment—for Manny, startling the titulars
of diplomatic passports came under the heading of indoor
sport—he quietly announced, "Against the Russians who
will certainly try and tempt you to betray your country."

The three people in the room, two women and one
man freshly posted to the Soviet Union, resisted the urge
to look at each other. If they had they would have burst
out laughing. Who was this political Neanderthal guarding
the chastity of the American enclave in Moscow? Hadn't
he heard of the political prestidigitator the Russians referred to as the Great Helmsman and the resident Americans had taken to calling the Great Houdini? Hadn't he
heard of *glasnost* or *perestroika*? Didn't he know the Cold
War was a sun-bleached bone that historians gnawed on
every now and then to sharpen their academic teeth?

Manny read the expressions of disbelief on their faces.
He had seen similar reactions every time he briefed new
hands. They memorized a couple of Russian slogans and,
as far as they were concerned, the Cold War was over.
Peace in our time. The only thing missing from the picture was Chamberlain's umbrella. The embassy security
officer coughed up a guttural laugh from some remote
corner of his ulcer-prone stomach. The sound conveyed
dry irreverence, which was Manny Custer's preferred pro-
tective coloring. Most of the time his irreverence amused
more than it offended. But there were moments when he
lost control, when his mood slipped across a frontier into
outright insolence. Which accounted for the pile of am-
bivalent fitness reports in his service record. Which explained why he had been denied promotions someone
judged purely on performance would have merited.
Which also explained why the current assignment was his
last posting before early retirement.

Moscow, embassy wags proclaimed gleefully, was going
to be Custer's last stand.

"You are probably thinking," Manny was saying, "that I
am treating possibilities as probabilities in order to cap-

ture your attention." His bushy eyebrows arched their backs like two lazy cats as another mocking laugh bubbled to the surface. "Consider this: Every word spoken here is being beamed through hidden microphones to those antennas on the roof across the street"—with a toss of his head he indicated the window, the city, the enemy—"and from there into the ears of some bilingual *techint* comrade in an overheated office at the Komitet Gosudarstvennoi Bezopasnosti, better known by its initials, KGB."

The man sitting on a folding chair between the two women, a diplomat in his early thirties with disheveled dark hair and the alert, watchful eyes of someone too rational to be passionate about anything, cleared his throat. "In other words," he said so guilelessly that Manny understood he was being baited, "Big Brother is watching us."

A faint smile found its unaccustomed way onto the security officer's lips. He let his gaze stray idly over the desk cluttered with service records and telexes and hastily scribbled notes to himself, over the paint peeling like sunburned skin from the office wall, over the battleship gray safe with the collection of paperback detective novels stacked on top, over his bookcase crammed with security manuals and bound State Department biographies of Soviet leaders, over the faces of the three who had turned up for the obligatory security briefing. Manny had the knack of scrutinizing people as if they held no secrets for him, which prompted those who didn't know him well to conclude that he was indifferent to the world around him. The truth was less complex. He was far from indifferent; he disliked it intensely. "Orwell got it all wrong," Manny said presently. "He completely misunderstood the nature of the totalitarian regime. It was never Big Brother who was doing the watching. It was a psychotic father figure who sometimes went by the title of Tsar and sometimes Secretary General of the Communist Party. Whatever."

Manny glanced at the service records on his desk, noted the young diplomat's name: It was Benedict Bassett. A newcomer to the diplomatic corps, divorced, the

father of a six-year-old son, Bassett had distant Russian
roots and spoke Russian fluently. He had been stationed
in Prague for four months before being posted to Moscow. The four months struck Manny as curious. Most diplomatic tours lasted two years; many three. Manny, who
collected details the way other men collected lint in their
trouser cuffs when trousers still had cuffs, made a mental
note to find out what eggs Bassett had hatched during his
stay in Prague. And why the tour had lasted only four
months.

The other woman, Esther Easley, a stenographer re-
placing a secretary on maternity leave, asked, "Who is this
Orwell? And what is his connection with the American
Embassy in Moscow?"

"Mr. Custer here is warning us that walls have ears,"
observed Ben Bassett, as if Manny's remarks needed to be
translated into English. Bassett angled his head and eyed
the security officer. "That's what it boils down to, isn't it,
Mr. Custer?"

"A little bird is whispering in my ear," commented
Manny. "He's saying you and I don't talk the same language." He shrugged a heavy shoulder to indicate that he
would not let their failure to communicate affect his appetite or his bowels. Reaching into a desk drawer for Xerox
copies of his standard security briefing, he handed one to
each of them. "Read through this when you have a moment. It lists some elementary do's and don'ts. Kindly sign
on the dotted line to indicate you have digested the contents and stick it in my mailbox downstairs."

The grammar teacher examined the sheet. "Are these
rules something we should learn by heart?"

"Security isn't so much a matter of rules as common
sense," Manny said. "Vary your daily routine. Don't talk
shop outside the shop." He looked pointedly at Bassett.
"Contrary to what some of our colleagues think, walls really do have ears. The KGB still has roughly two million
employees on its payroll, and it has to keep them occupied. Don't accept letters or packages from Russians you
don't know, and think twice about accepting them from

Russians you do know. This kind of thing happens all the time. Just yesterday a Russian woman buttonholed one of our political officers in a store and tried to get him to accept a sealed envelope. He quite rightly refused. Don't deal on the black market. Don't order a Sony video recorder from Finland as a favor for a Russian friend even if you sell it to him at cost; nobody will believe you didn't trade it for an icon. I certainly won't. Whatever else you do, don't fall in love with a Russian. The KGB has been known to plant what they call a 'swallow' and we call a 'dangle' in the path of unsuspecting diplomats, who can then be blackmailed. Give me a written report of anything that smells like a compromising situation. If you have any doubts report it and let me decide. If you need something from the Russians—a maid, a language teacher, hotel reservations for a visiting relative, whatever—get it through the General Service Office downstairs. You want Bolshoi tickets, see the folks in the Community Liaison Office. The two of you"—Manny indicated the two women "have white badges, which means that everything above the sixth floor of the embassy is off-limits. Your green badge, Mr. Bassett, authorizes you to go anywhere in the embassy, up to and including the communications bubble, but you'd better have a reason for being there. Also, unlike the ladies, who are being housed in the New Office Building complex around the corner, you'll be living in a compound across the street from the Hotel Ukraine on Kutuzovsky Prospekt, which means you'll be more exposed. Your neighbors are mostly African diplomats, but there will be several Russians—and everyone understands they are there to report on what you do and who you do it with."

Bassett, who had been skimming Manny's photocopied sheet while the security officer was talking, pulled an expensive fountain pen from the breast pocket of his sports jacket, uncapped it and resting the sheet on Manny's desk, scrawled his name at the bottom. "Is it all right if I leave this with you now?" he asked.

An amused smile pulled at the corners of Manny's eyes

as he accepted the sheet. The truth was he found Bassett's irreverence refreshing. In his experience most young diplomats panted like lapdogs at the feet of their masters; a ball only had to be tossed to send them scampering off to fetch it. Bassett didn't come on like a careerist; he appeared indifferent to the exigencies of the embassy pecking order and protocol. Custer liked that about him. "You'll have one other neighbor at the Kutuzovsky compound you'll be interested in," he informed the newcomer to the embassy with a playful grin.

"Who?"

"Me."

2

Needles of icy air pricked Viktor Prosenko's cheeks as he waited in front of the apartment building for his car. He stamped his feet, he pulled the sheepskin collar of the worn greatcoat around his neck, he drew the flaps of his astrakhan over his ears, he flailed his arms against his sides, he cursed his driver for a scoundrel and a nitwit and vowed, not for the first time, to send him packing no matter what excuse he offered. God knows why he put up with Zenkevich, who ground the gears when he shifted and regularly siphoned gasoline from the tank to sell on the black market. God knows why he put up with living in Aeroport when he could have had, for the asking, ninety-five square meters in a prewar building off Dzerzhinsky Square, a three-minute stroll from the Center.

Viktor expelled a lung full of air and watched the vapor billow around his face. He put up with Zenkevich because Zenkevich had once been hit by an assassin's bullet intended for him, and he felt guilty about it. He put up with living in Aeroport because Ekaterina left him no choice; because she preferred one of the cooperative apartments

11

on Red Army Street between the Dynamo Stadium and
the Aeroport metro stop, with hundreds of writers and
actors and critics and directors for neighbors (and, not
incidentally, potential lovers), to the "dull desert of a military compound" (her words, repeated often enough for
Viktor to have committed them to memory) inhabited by
the Komitet Gosudarstvennoi Bezopasnosti people closer
to the heart of the city.

There was still no sign of his limousine. Zenkevich was
exaggerating this time. Viktor toyed with the idea of retreating into the lobby, but abandoned it. The *babushka*
holding fort at the table inside the door would take it as a
sign of weakness; would smile to herself at the fragility of
a grown man who could not tolerate a dose of Russian
winter.

Viktor's thoughts drifted back to the winter of '45. He
had been sixteen at the time, but had lied about his age to
get into the Army before the war ended. The winter of '45
had been colder than this winter, his boots had been thinner, he had had only an Army cloth cap on his head and a
rough woolen scarf over his ears, and fur-lined sniper's
mittens scavenged from a corpse frozen in the ice of a
German river they had crossed. (He still wore the much
mended sniper's mittens in winter, a sign, no doubt, of
nostalgia for the simpler days when he had been able to
fight his enemies.) Thinking back, Viktor remembered
that spit had frozen before it hit the ground during the
winter of '45, but he could not recall ever suffering from
the cold. But then he and his comrades had had other
things to occupy them—there was Berlin's Reichstag dead
ahead and the savage house-to-house, hand-to-hand combat to get there.

How times had changed! Now he worried about a wife
twenty-two years younger than he was openly flirting with
her Jewish lover during a dinner at the Actor's Union, or
the fact that she seemed to have more rehearsals than
usual and they seemed to last longer than usual. One
night, with half a bottle of garlic-and-dill–flavored vodka
under his belt, Viktor had worked up the nerve to ask her

what her lover had that he lacked, but she had only laughed the laugh that always made her sound on the bitter edge of hysteria. "He knows how to make me forget, Viktor," Ekaterina had said. "You make me remember." Her voice slipping into the octave she normally reserved for melodrama, she had arched her carefully plucked eyebrows and had added, "I hope you are not having second thoughts about our *arrangement.*"

What could he do? Trot off to her father, Viktor's mentor, not to mention his superior in the chain of command, with tales of . . . what? Infidelities? Treasons? The old general would wave his deformed hand in the direction of the Kremlin. (He suffered from a disorder called Dupuytren's Contracture, a gradual curling of the fingers; catching their first glimpse of the general, newcomers to his service invariably thought they were being summoned.) "My daughter's transgressions are trivial compared with the infidelities, the treasons out there," he would mutter in a voice gravelly with age. And producing a bottle of imported bourbon, he would change the subject so abruptly Viktor's shoulders would droop under the weight of the things that had been left unsaid.

A horn shrilled at the corner. Zenkevich, at last! Viktor could see him flinging open the door of the black Zil and waving frantically over the roof of the car. Imagine a chauffeur *waving* at a lieutenant colonel of the Komitet Gosudarstvennoi Bezopasnosti as if he had forgotten his laundry on the backseat! Viktor rolled his head from side to side in frustration as he delicately picked his way over the icy sidewalk toward the limousine.

Zenkevich, bareheaded, his tangled hair flying off in all directions, his enormous ear lobes beet red, was holding open the front door when he got there. (Viktor had begun his military career as the chauffeur of a general who always rode next to the driver out of a sense of egalitarianism; he did the same.) "The comrade colonel won't believe what happened to me this morning," Zenkevich sputtered as he slid behind the wheel. Gunning the motor, grinding gears, he steered the limousine past an or-

ange-and-yellow trolley and headed between enormous
banks of dirty snow down Leningrad Prospekt toward the
center of Moscow. He stole a glance at Viktor's frozen
cheek muscles. Almost shouting so he could be heard over
the roar of the car's heater, which was turned on full blast,
Zenkevich launched into an account of how his wife's
sister-in-law had complained of excruciating stomach
cramps; how the ambulance sent to fetch her to the clinic
had skidded into a fire hydrant; how his wife's brother had
phoned in panic from a booth when a second ambulance
failed to arrive; how Zenkevich, knowing the comrade colonel would understand that it had been a matter of life or
death, had driven his sister-in-law to the clinic in the comrade colonel's limousine where, at this very moment, she
was probably being operated on for a burst appendix. "In
my shoes—" here Zenkevich groaned to indicate he was
suffering pangs of conscience at having kept the colonel
waiting in the −24° temperature—"wouldn't the comrade
colonel have done the same?" So saying, he plucked a
leather-covered flask from the bulging pocket of his overcoat and offered it to his boss, his role model, above all his
meal ticket.

Viktor, who was convinced that *homo sapiens* func-
tioned more efficiently if they kept a reasonable amount
of alcohol in their bloodstream at all times, unscrewed the
cap and, tilting back his head, took a healthy swig. "Cognac," Zenkevich noted as he spotted the color seeping
back into the colonel's cheeks. "Imported from Paris,
France. Three stars. I still have the bottle in the trunk
compartment—the comrade colonel can count the stars
himself if he doesn't believe me."

"I accept your apology," Viktor murmured, wiping his
lips on the back of a sniper's mitten.

"And I wholeheartedly offer one," Zenkevich shot back
eagerly. He hadn't hoped to squirm off the hook so easily.

Viktor treated himself to another mouthful of
Zenkevich's black-market cognac, produced in some basement still, no doubt, and poured into bottles scavenged
from garbage bins behind the hotels that catered to for-

eign tourists. He felt a pleasant warmth in his stomach. "Did you know, Zenkevich, that if it had not been for alcohol," he informed his driver, "Russia would be a Moslem country to this day?"

"How is that, comrade colonel?" Zenkevich asked. He ran the windshield wipers to clear away some slush.

"Didn't they teach you anything in school? It was the Tsar Vladimir who rejected the Moslem faith and converted to Christianity because alcohol was forbidden by Moslems, and who could survive a Russian winter without alcohol?"

"Who?" Zenkevich agreed enthusiastically.

"Nowadays," Viktor went on glumly, "we need alcohol to survive the summers as well as the winters, but thanks to our bureaucrats"—thanks to the Great Helmsman, he thought, but it was not the kind of insight he dared share with a chauffeur—"not enough of it is available. In the sense that everyone in Russia drinks less than they need to, everyone in Russia can be said to be on the wagon."

Zenkevich was impressed by the colonel's logic. "I never looked at it like that," he admitted.

In the street, a traffic policeman wearing several layers of clothing and moving with the awkwardness of a stuffed doll, waved a white baton, stopping traffic. A mob of workers spilling out of the railroad station, their faces obscured by frayed collars and hand-knit scarfs, swarmed across the intersection in front of the Zil. After a while the traffic light turned green. The policeman waved his baton and shouted for the workers to stop crossing, but they kept coming, a herd of mindless bulls plunging on, heads bent against the cold, against the authority of the policeman too, grimly pressing forward as if they were walking across an ocean bottom in lead-weighted shoes without the slightest desire, so it seemed to Viktor, to get where they were going.

It dawned on Viktor, observing the scene unfold in front of his windshield as if it were an allegorical play, that the Great Helmsman and the clever young men around him didn't know about the chaos that lurked in the heart of the heart of Mother Russia. The last thing the country needed was *perestroika,* or restructuring. Let the Great Helmsman restructure rents, which were last raised in 1928, or the price of bread, which had been the same since 1954, and he would wind up with a bloody civil war on his hands. The unrest in Azerbaijan, in the Ukraine, in the Baltic republics, in Armenia, in Uzbekistan, in the Donets Basin, would be nothing compared to it. The insurrection that had ousted Russia's last Tsar and had led eventually to the Bolshevik revolution had started with bread riots. Couldn't the Great Helmsman see that he was trifling with disaster when he talked of *glasnost,* or transparence? There were things the masses were better off not knowing. Nobody dared speak of it openly, but the absolute necessity of keeping the masses on a short leash was something that Stalin, for all his excesses, had intuitively grasped. Nowadays this was an unfashionable, even dangerous, point of view, but more and more people were coming around to it. Viktor remembered the old general turning up a radio in his corner office one day and pulling his son-in-law over to the window and pointing with his withered fingers to the word *Perestroika* splashed across a huge banner draped over the facade of the toy store diagonally across the street from the Center. "The Frenchman de Tocqueville had a theory about the French revolution," the old man had muttered. "He noticed the oppressed masses had not revolted until the oppression was lifted a bit and expectations were aroused. What do you think, Viktor? Will our *norod,* our dark masses, get a whiff of the Great Helmsman's stew and take to the streets for their dinner? Will they dine on us?" Then, to Viktor's utter astonishment, the old general had breathed a word that, if overheard, would have gotten the speaker and his auditor instantly transferred to some frozen timber collective in the reaches of Siberia. "*Pamyat,*" he had murmured. "*Pamyat* is our flame. We must fan its embers for the sake of the Motherland. When it is burning bright we will use it to incinerate the kike-intellectuals who are ruining us."

Gunning his engine, honking his horn to intimidate the

workers crossing against the light, Zenkevich succeeded in nosing the car through the mob. A few minutes later he pulled up on a narrow side street behind Detsky Mir, the toy store across Dzerzhinsky Square from the massive KGB center. "Will the comrade colonel be needing me again during the day?"

"The comrade colonel will not be needing you," Viktor said, "but that does not mean you are to cruise around picking up private fares."

Zenkevich, who had been Viktor's driver in Kabul in the early 1980s until the assassin's bullet aimed at the colonel had punctured one of the chauffeur's lungs, managed to look hurt. "I was planning to get the comrade colonel's car greased and oiled at a new private garage near the Exhibition of Economic Achievements," he said. "I heard of some Kazakhs there who use German motor oil," he added, as if it were a critical detail.

Viktor knew from long experience that his driver was impervious to sarcasm, but he mumbled something anyway about how he would appreciate Zenkevich being there at six o'clock if his sister-in-law's state of health permitted, and started for the delivery entrance to the toy store. He went down one flight, pushed through a pair of swinging doors marked "Absolutely no one admitted" and walked the length of a narrow, well-lit corridor. A uniformed militiaman sitting behind a table at the far end leapt to his feet and snapped off a smart salute at Viktor, who flashed his red identification booklet and leaned over to sign the register. The militiaman inserted the register in a slot so that a camera could read the signature. There was a moment of silence, then a bell rang once and the door next to the table clicked open. Viktor continued down a long brilliantly lit white-tiled tunnel, had his signature and identity booklet checked once more at the subterranean entrance to the Center, then headed down the marble hallway toward the elevator and his fifth-floor office.

His secretary, a prematurely gray-haired middle-aged woman who had also been with him in Kabul, was laying

out dossiers on his desk when he arrived. "My God, it's
hot in here," Viktor noted as he flung his greatcoat over
the back of a chair. "I take it the thermostats in the radiators still have not been adjusted." He eyed the pile of
dossiers suspiciously. "What world-shaking events are
waiting in ambush for us today?" he wanted to know.

The secretary, whose name was Evgeniya Leonovna,
handed Viktor a file thick with overnight cables as he settled heavily into a padded swivel chair. "There was a time
when you were known as the house optimist, Colonel
Prosenko," she remarked.

Viktor removed his eyeglasses and began cleaning the
lens with the tip of his tie. "The peasants have a saying,"
he told her. "An optimist is someone who does not know
enough." He hooked the glasses back over his ears and
started reading the first cable. It contained the latest gos-
sip from a KGB *stukach,* or stool pigeon, in the Politburo
secretariat; according to the *stukach,* the Great Helmsman had been overheard telling a visiting regional Communist Party delegation that he was going to institute a
system of annual fitness reports for everyone holding positions of importance in the government. Promotions would
be based on performance, not on whom you knew or how
long you had been in the Party. Those who did not pass
muster, the Great Helmsman was reported to have promised, would be pensioned off to make way for younger,
more dynamic people.

Evgeniya Leonovna, who harbored a secret vision of
herself as the colonel's doting adopted daughter, placed a
glass of strong tea on Viktor's desk and stirred in a spoon
full of her homemade confiture. Viktor swiveled toward a
window, heard the chair squeak under his weight, wondered why something as simple as getting a handyman in
the Center to oil a squeaking chair or turn down a radiator
so that his office did not feel like a sauna seemed beyond
the realm of possibility. He stared morosely out the window, then focused on the window as he noticed the lacelike crystals of snow etched onto the outside of the panes.
It reminded him of the embroidered white curtains that

had been in his room when he was a child. He reconstructed the room in his head, effortlessly placing objects in their proper places. He enjoyed reconstructing the past; he liked it when things were in order.

Things were far from tidy in the Great Helmsman's Kremlin. Fitness reports today, God knows what other capitalist innovation tomorrow. In fact the Great Helmsman was slowly dismantling the Party, which was the bulwark that protected Russia from its own worst instincts. And he was slowly dismantling the KGB along with it; he had already disbanded the Center's Fifth Directorate, which was responsible for unearthing ideological subversion—as if there were no more ideology and no more subversion. Anyone who got in the Great Helmsman's way, anyone who argued the merits of leaving things as they were, quickly found himself posted to some Siberian wasteland. Even the old general, Viktor's father-in-law, felt powerless to stop the tide of reform. "I am looking forward to my pension," he once confided to his daughter in Viktor's presence, "but the way things are going, I very much doubt whether the ruble will buy as much when I get it, whether in fact there will be anything on the shelves to buy."

Having stirred the confiture into the tea, Evgeniya Leonovna edged the saucer toward Viktor. He bent his head to savor the aroma, then lifted the glass and began sipping the sweetened tea as he shuffled through the cables. Each one produced in him a snort of derision, an angry shake of the head. There had been a street fight the night before in a Moscow suburb; youths from the Lefortovo District armed with chains and iron bars had attacked Armenian refugees living in a dormitory behind a textile factory. The so-called progressive faction in parliament had called for the Great Helmsman's ouster on the grounds that his program of reforms was not ambitious enough. There had been tumultuous meetings of separatists in the Baltic region who were claiming that the secret 1940 Hitler-Stalin pact ceding these states to Soviet Russia was null and void. There had been work stoppages in the Ukraine, talk of a general strike in Kazakhstan, skirmishes between marauding groups of Armenians and Azerbaijanis in Baku, riots in Lithuania and Estonia, an attack on a police station by stone-throwing miners in the Donets Basin. Some Azerbaijani Shiites had been arrested while building bridges across the Araks River to create links with their "brothers" in Iran. Not to mention what was happening in Poland and Hungary and East Germany and Czechoslovakia and Bulgaria. Reading the overnight cables morning after morning had led Viktor to an ominous conclusion: The Union of Soviet Socialist Republics, created by the blood and sweat of the visionary Bolshevik revolutionaries of 1917—Viktor's father and mother had been in the front ranks—and defended by the blood and sweat of subsequent generations of Bolsheviks—Viktor himself had been in the front ranks—was coming apart at the seams. And there was absolutely nothing Viktor could do about it.

The telephone on the desk rang once. Scowling at a photograph of his wife set in a silver frame—it had been taken while they were honeymooning at a Black Sea resort eleven years before—Viktor reached for the receiver. His appointments secretary was on the line, reminding the colonel that the section chiefs of Department One had arrived for the regular Wednesday meeting. Viktor, who was the head of the Second Chief Directorate—the internal counterintelligence component of the KGB responsible for intelligence and counterespionage against all foreigners in the Soviet Union—had been astonished to discover, when he returned from Kabul in the mid-1980s to take over his new responsibilities, that the men who ran the various sections of Department One, which kept track of American diplomats, were barely on speaking terms. His first official act had been to replace them with new people and convene a regular weekly meeting in order to coordinate the activities of Department One's sections. In the space of a year, thanks in large measure to this coordination, Viktor had organized the first successful penetration of the American Embassy in Moscow in decades. It happened this way. Section Three, which routinely kept track of Russians who came in contact with American diplomats, had reported that several members of the embassy's marine guard contingent had Russian girlfriends. In short order Section One had dangled a swallow before one of the marines, and he had been hooked. After that it had been child's play for the case officers of the first section, which was responsible for recruiting and running Americans, to blackmail the marine into giving them after-hours access to some of the embassy's restricted areas. The penetration would have reaped even more secrets if it hadn't been for the embassy security officer, an old pro named Custer. He had noticed a dropped stitch, had tugged on it and unraveled the sweater. The swallow had been identified, the marine had been whisked off to a court-martial, the leak had been plugged.

The section heads, settled in seats around Viktor's coffee table, exchanged small talk while Evgeniya Leonovna distributed glasses of tea (she did not put out her confiture, preferring to keep it for Viktor). When she had slipped discreetly out of the office, Viktor nodded at the young officer who was in charge of Department One's third section, a captain with tobacco-stained teeth and a distinctly pear-shaped face that conveyed infinite innocence. His mother had died the week before, and he was dressed entirely in black, with a black arm band on the sleeve of his black jacket. His lips were compressed in an appropriately mournful expression. Producing a sheet of paper stamped "Very Secret—no distribution outside of Second Chief Directorate," the captain, whose name was Boris Frolov, began to read, in a droning monotone, the list of known contacts between Russians and American diplomats the previous week. The usual writers and directors and editors and artists had had the usual lunches and dinners and drinks with the usual cultural affairs officers; there had been far too many contacts for the operatives in the third section, working under strict budget restraints, to keep track of. Given his meager resources, Frolov had had his people focus on the more curious contacts.

A woman had accosted one of the embassy's political

affairs officers while he was shopping at the diplomatic gastronome and had tried to get him to accept a sealed envelope. He had politely, but forcefully, refused. Questioned afterward, the woman had claimed to be sending news of her father's death to a brother who had emigrated to America; the letter in question had in fact been addressed to her brother and described in detail the father's death from cancer. The woman was not employed in a sensitive industry, and was not considered to be in the possession of secret material.

Some prostitutes working the underpasses that led to Red Square (who regularly reported any contacts with foreigners to the third section) had been picked up by two Americans whom they took to be military attachés. But when the ladies had been shown photographs of all 128 males attached to the American Embassy, they had failed to identify their clients.

A young woman speaking Russian with what seemed like an American accent had buttonholed a Soviet journalist at a party and offered to trade a Sony Walkman for an icon. Word of this had caused a stir when the journalist said he thought he had seen the woman at a recent American Embassy reception. A rendezvous had been arranged and the woman had been photographed in the act. Her photo had been given to the ID team in Section One, who identified her as an Australian au pair girl working for a Canadian diplomat. The icon had been retrieved, the young woman had been conducted to the frontier and expelled.

"Slim pickings," Viktor noted gloomily. He had been hoping for more—the opening gambit of an intricate espionage game, perhaps—if only to take his mind off Ekaterina's endless exploration of infidelity; if only to divert him from the festering boil that was poisoning the Soviet body politic and ruining the morale of its defenders.

Frolov shrugged his shoulders in reluctant apology. It was not his fault if the political climate lulled Russians who would ordinarily have fallen over each other reporting contacts with Americans into believing that the Cold

War was over. On top of everything there was the seasonal element to contend with; in midwinter most contacts tended to take place indoors, out of sight of people who might still be inclined to report these things to the KGB.

"Another reason to look forward to the end of winter," Viktor commented dryly. The section chiefs nodded appreciatively. Viktor turned his attention to Andrei Krostin, the painfully thin captain who ran Section One. Krostin, who wore a thick hand-knit sweater under his sports jacket to render his thinness less conspicuous, spoke, as he always did, without notes. Absently stroking his neatly trimmed blond beard, he led off with a detailed description of the activities of Charles Inkermann, the CIA station chief at the American Embassy: where he had gone, whom he had seen, what he had said to his wife in the privacy of their bedroom. At one point during the week Krostin had suspected he was on to something important when he eavesdropped on Inkermann telephoning two Russians from a public booth; the calls had been traced to two members of the Central Committee noted for their reformist tendencies. Both men had been "interviewed" (in the current political atmosphere, the Center no longer "interrogated"), both had sworn they thought they were dealing with a cultural affairs officer trying to set up appointments for a visiting *New York Times* columnist.

Krostin wound up his presentation with a brief description of the various Americans who had touched base at the embassy during the week: There had been several congressmen and their staffers on a junket, a Congressional Budget Office accountant presumably checking the embassy's books, a delegation of Pentagon aides coming to meet their Soviet counterparts, a handful of visiting journalists, a small army of tourists exhilarated at having traded blue jeans for black beluga caviar. Oh, and there was one other thing. Three new diplomats, two females and one male, had reported to the embassy since Viktor's last weekly session. The first woman was named Esther Easley, age forty-eight, on temporary assignment replacing a stenographer who had been sent back to the United

States on maternity leave; Easley was married and her husband, a teacher, was expected to arrive in Moscow at the end of the month. The male diplomat's name was Benedict Bassett. He was single, divorced, thirty-three, a low-level housekeeper for the embassy's Arms Control Inspection Team. Bassett had come to Moscow directly from a four-month tour at the American Embassy in Prague. He had been looked over by the Center's Czech friends while he was in Prague. A swallow had actually made a pass at him, but nothing had come of it and Bassett, a loner who didn't make friends easily, had been written off as an unlikely candidate for blackmail. The third new diplomat was Sabine Harkenrider, age twenty-eight, single, on permanent assignment in Moscow to teach grammar to the American children in the embassy school. Of the three new arrivals, she clearly had the most potential for Krostin and his colleagues in Section One. She was plain looking and single—the archetypical profile of someone who could be seduced by a KGB operative. Because she lived and worked inside the embassy compound, the problem would be to get at her. Chances were she would be coming out, it was hoped before spring, to go to the opera or ballet, or participate in one of the embassy-organized cross-country ski trips. Krostin proposed to take a closer look at her then.

"About this Bassett fellow," Viktor said thoughtfully, "the four-months' stint in Prague strikes me as a curiously short tour of duty."

"I noticed that too," Krostin agreed. "As a precaution I have instructed our people in Prague to try and discover what he was doing there, and most especially why he was reassigned after only four months."

"Is that it?" Viktor asked.

"I have one other thing that will interest you," Krostin said. He reached into his leather briefcase for a transcript of Custer's security briefing to the three new diplomats. "Here is what he told them." And he read the words that his microphones had recorded. " 'Consider this,' " Custer had lectured the newly arrived diplomats. " 'Every word spoken here is being beamed through hidden microphones to those antennas on the roof across the street, and from there into the ears of some bilingual *techint* comrade in an overheated office at the Komitet Gosudarstvennoi Bezopasnosti, better known by its initials, KGB.' "

Krostin looked up with something akin to a leer in his eyes. "How do you think he found out about your office being overheated?" he asked Viktor.

With a snicker, Frolov remarked, "Perhaps he is listening to us listen to him."

For the first time that day Viktor managed a smile. He had never met Custer face-to-face, but he had read dozens of transcripts of his conversations—so many that he thought he could detect the insolence in Custer's tone as he baited the ambassador, or badgered newly arrived diplomats with his talk of vaccination, or argued with Inkermann, the CIA station chief who, in a strange twist of fate, had been Custer's superior before Custer was kicked out of the CIA. The truth was that Viktor harbored a grudging respect for Custer—he liked his impetuous orneriness, his imperturbable professionalism, his I-don't-give-a-damn style of dealing with people above him as well as below him in the chain of command. "Custer is not listening to us listen to him," Viktor told his section chiefs. "He is *imagining* us listening to him. He is the last of a breed, one of those who figures out what the other side is doing by deciding what he would do if he were in their shoes."

Viktor turned his head to take another look at the lacelike crystals of snow etched onto the outside of the window panes. This time the sight tripped a vision, not of his childhood, but of the corpse frozen into the ice of the German river back in 1945. The body had been that of an unshaven Wehrmacht soldier, bayoneted to death—by Viktor. Something had coursed through Viktor's veins the day he killed the German that he later learned to identify as adrenaline. It was then that destroying an enemy had become his habit, a high to which he was still addicted. Now, in the overheated stillness of his office, his voice came drifting back over his shoulder. "Custer is on his last roll. He thinks that a man needs an enemy to validate his masculinity; to give to all intercourse an urgency that comes only when you confront the possibility that it may be the last. He understands that pretty soon there will be no enemies left, and no Cold War to fight."

Even as he described Custer, Viktor understood that he was describing himself.

3

She was introduced by the chairlady as the last dissident; the last person in the Union of Soviet Socialist Republics to hold views so outside the now broad mainstream that the male establishment, puritanical to its corrupt core, refused to permit what she wrote to be published. Her subject, around which she wove spiderwebs of poems, was women: their dread of male violence, their incredible courage in the face of it. Her poems boldly explored the no-man's-land of women's sensuality; explored their hunger to be physical with the people to whom they were mentally attracted, to be emotional with those to whom they were physically attracted. The chairwoman, a stout woman with a pince-nez clipped onto the bridge of her nose, leaned closer to the microphone. "It is an honor for me," she whispered, her voice husky with emotion, "to welcome to the House of Architects auditorium the woman many of us consider to be the spiritual heir of our beloved poet Anna Akhmatova. Please salute Zinaïda Ivanovna Zavaskaya."

The two hundred or so women packed into the folding

metal chairs of the drab auditorium, the eighty or so others lining the walls, burst into enthusiastic applause. The
chairwoman signaled toward the wings for the poet to
make her entrance.

Stepping out from behind the fire curtain, Aïda glanced
furtively at the audience as if she mistrusted the entire
proceeding. She was one of those rare individuals who
took no pleasure from the stir she created when she
walked into a room, but she could not prevent it. Big-
boned, well-proportioned, somewhere in her early forties,
she had ample hips and wide shoulders and a broken,
badly set nose alive with freckles. Her mouth was generous, her lips thick, her eyelashes huge, her hair bound in a
dirty-blond braid that tumbled halfway to her waist. Enormous, melancholy eyes were her most distinctive feature;
Aïda had a way of looking at people so intently she appeared to be committing them to memory. The first time
the poet Akhmatova, by then an old woman, had peered
into Aïda's gray eyes, she had announced that they conveyed an animal's innocence, which she cheerfully de-
fined as an innocence capable of killing, but never for
pleasure. As for Aïda's clothes, they were in complete dis-
array; there seemed to be a riot of colors and textures and
forms pulling her in different directions. (It wasn't that
she didn't care; she did, but not enough to spend time and
money and energy to put herself together in what passed
for a coherent style.) A 1930s pillbox hat with an enormous white feather spiked through it was planted
squarely on her large head. Across her shoulders she had
flung a threadbare fox neckpiece with a marble-eyed
shrunken fox's head on one end. The fox was worn over a
quilted satin jacket, which in turn was worn over a faded
purple sweatshirt with "What needs restructuring is the
relationship between women and men" embroidered in
Russian across the chest. On one of her long, strong fingers she wore a ring that had been given to her by
Akhmatova only days before her death because, so the
poet had said, Aïda "understood the wind better than human speech." Set into the ring's beaten silver was a wedge

of agate, a stone that according to Akhmatova was supposed to banish fear. (Aïda dearly loved the ring, but did not believe in miracles; she still lived in terror of losing poetry.)

Now, with the frayed hem of a thick, black, much-mended ankle-length skirt swirling around the tops of her fur-lined galoshes, Aïda strode across the stage to shake hands with the woman who had introduced her. Turning toward the audience, she fitted a pair of perfectly round steel-rimmed eyeglasses onto her nose, spread some papers on the lectern and studied them until the applause died away. She glanced at a tiny watch on her wrist. Manufactured in Poland, it had been constructed so that the hour and minute hands ran counterclockwise. "If time ran backward," her Polish friend had said when he gave her the watch as a joke, "you could go back in time and undo the future. You could fix things so that things did not need to be fixed." Smiling at this conceit, Aïda made a mental note of the time and looked up abruptly at her audience.

"I will read for one hour, no more, no less," she announced. "I say this so that those of you who are new to poetry readings do not have to worry about me droning on beyond your lunch break." There was an appreciative titter from the crowd. "If you are bored, or have errands to do, or prefer a sandwich to a poetry reading, feel absolutely free to leave. I will not be offended. I have a thick hide. To be a poet in Soviet Russia, to have been a poet in Tsarist Russia for that matter, a thick hide is only slightly less essential than a gift for images. But that's another story. Or is it? In any case, I will try to give you some background on each poem I read—try, in other words, to set it into time for you. And I will read each poem twice in the hope that I will be saying more than one listening can get at."

Flashing a self-conscious half-smile, Aïda reached up to toy with a tiny mother-of-pearl earring. "So: Let us plunge together into poetry. In the late 1970s the bosses, ignoring the fact that I was pregnant, locked me up in the Serbsky Institute for the Criminally Insane. There was no trial, no sentence, only an administrative decision that Mother Russia would be better off if there were one poet less in circulation. They kept me locked up for a relatively short time—two months, six days, nine and a half hours—but it seemed to me like an eternity. When I refused to cooperate I was held down and given injections of sulfur, which caused my body temperature to shoot up five degrees. All you can do in such circumstances is toss and turn in bed in an endless search for a position that does not hurt. I do not remember ever finding one. When you first arrive at this so-called institute you are invited to fill in a questionnaire. It was this questionnaire that inspired the poem I am going to read. The questions were a humiliating invasion of privacy, something like being subjected to a gynecological examination by a drunken veterinarian. I like to think that my interlocutors were not prepared for the answers I gave. So: Here is the poem. I call it 'Q and A.' "

And peering through her granny glasses at a scrap of paper she did not really need, Aïda began her recitation in a brittle, high-pitched voice.

When did you lose your virginity?

To a man or to a woman?

Resist the temptation to answer a question with a question. Can you describe your arrest?

The police were very polite. They brought me tea with cakes. When I had finished, one of them cleared away the cup and saucer and punched me in the nose. Another fitted on a surgical glove and inspected my anus.

What do women want from men?

Their dreams and their cocks.

Why their dreams?

We are the ones who make the day work—we shop and cook and clean up afterward and

remember everyone's birthday and bring in a
second salary and rear the children and brew herb
tea and watch our weight and make love and
make babies. We do not have time to dream.

Why their cocks?

To suck on.

What is in it for you?

The object of intercourse is intimacy.

You think you will know men better if you
suck their cocks?

I think I will know myself better. Sensuality
is not for the faint of heart.

Are you afraid of losing your sanity?

I am afraid of losing my insanity.
I am afraid of losing poetry.

What is in the shortest supply in the Motherland?

Smiles.

What is in the greatest supply?

Shrugs.

Shrugs?

Shrugs. Yes.

You are full of shit.

That is not a question.

I will rephrase it. Did anyone ever tell you you
were full of shit?

Many times.

Do you agree?

What I am full of is unshed tears.

Inebriated with poetry, Aïda read the questions and answers a second time to an utterly still audience. Then, suppressing a shiver, she drew a deep breath, as if she were purging a painful memory. The poem seemed to have cast a spell on the assembly; no one dared to applaud for fear of being irreverent. Shuffling through her papers, Aïda selected a second poem. "I do not do this in any particular order," she remarked. "I invent it as I go along. In this respect a poetry reading imitates life."

Aïda forged on, explaining the source of each poem, then reading and rereading it in a deliberately flat, undramatic voice. She wanted the words and the spaces between them to convey the moods and meanings, and not her tone; she detested films in which the music told people how to feel. The women in the crowded auditorium, stunned by the audacity of the overt sexual references, mesmerized by what they took to be the echo of their own secret voices, hung on her poems in rapt attention. Reciting one of her older poems, Aïda forgot a word. Several women who obviously knew the poem by heart called it out to her. Some of the women in the audience could be heard sobbing after she read a poem describing an abortion in such clinical detail that everyone understood it had to be autobiographical. Dozens of heads nodded in agreement when Aïda, in eight barbed lines, noted that the KGB had not been disbanded; that its agents, the great majority of whom were men, were even now copying down the names of those who wrote subversive poetry, as well as those who listened to it.

With the hour almost up Aïda glanced at her wristwatch, shuffled her papers, looked out tiredly at the audience. "The last poem I will recite is one I stumbled across last night when I was reading through notes I made years ago. Like most of my poems, it has never been published. I had not set eyes on it for years, so it took me a while to figure out where it sprang from. Eventually it came back to me. I wrote it during the period of stagnation, as our current helmsman calls the Brezhnev years. The poem was inspired by three propositions. The first proposition states that even in the worst of times, and God knows we have had more than our share of the worst of times, sex has been a sanctuary; a place we could retreat to where the state and its police could not follow. The second proposition states that women, like men, have a garden full of lust; but unlike men, we understand that the body can keep people apart as easily as it can draw them together, and that in any case it is never neutral. The third proposition states that women have a central dilemma about which men know nothing, namely how to give yourself freely while holding part of yourself back; how, in other words, to be lusty and lucid at the same time. So: I call this poem 'Geography.'"

And she began to read again.

> *Beating the air, she lighted*
> *like a butterfly*
> *on the leaf of his lip,*
> *her longitude*
> *to his latitude.*

> *Beating the air, she drifted away*
> *before he could get a fix.*

There was an incredible stillness as Aïda finished reading the poem a second time; as if the women in the audience, barely daring to breathe, had penetrated to the eye of a storm. A ripple of applause spread across the auditorium. Then the women were standing and clapping rhythmically and stamping their feet. The floor shook. The chairwoman rushed onto the stage to pump Aïda's hand. Blushing self-consciously, Aïda smiled and nodded her thanks. Some of the younger women in the crowd swarmed forward to thrust copies of Aïda's only published book, a thin volume of poetry titled *Stranded*, up for her to sign.

"You were wonderful," one young woman called.

"Where would we be without your voice?" another cried.

Worn out but exhilarated, Aïda crouched and scratched her name in bold letters across the title pages.

THE POSTPARTUM LETDOWN that invariably followed her poetry readings had gripped Aïda when she stopped by the office of *Novy Mir* an hour later to correct the galley proofs of two recent poems and pick up a check from the editor who was proposing to publish them. "If I didn't know you better," the editor, Joseph Mikhailovich, told Aïda, eyeing her cheeks flushed with color, "I would think you were wearing makeup. Let me guess. Either you were outdoors too long or you have been reading your poems to unwashed women in a windy hall."

"Both are true," Aïda said. "I walked over from the House of Architects." She hiked herself onto a radiator to soak up some of its warmth.

The editor, whose long flowing beard and fervent eyes left him looking more like a Russian Orthodox priest than a man of letters, watched as she fitted eyeglasses over her slightly disjointed nose and started to read the proofs. He was toying with the idea of raising a delicate subject. "If you would tone down the feminist rhetoric and remove the word *cunt* from the third poem you submitted," he finally remarked, "I might be able to get that one published too."

Smiling faintly, Aïda looked up. "And what is it about the word *cunt* that makes it inappropriate for a poem?" she asked innocently.

"I was trying to be helpful," the editor said defensively. He had been tempting fate to bring it up, but the damage was done.

From the rehearsal studio on the floor below came the muted sound of a soprano practicing scales. Aïda gazed at the editor scornfully. "I suppose I should be more grateful. I suppose I should crawl across the floor for the crumbs you throw my way every few months."

"It is not a question of being grateful, but respectful."

"I wholeheartedly agree," Aïda retorted hotly. "More respect is what is needed here. Not only for people, but for poems. Most especially for poems that use what you may think of as dirty words to explore clean subjects, in this case the proposition that if two people were left on earth, one would invade the other, which is what you are doing to me now."

"I show respect for your poems by publishing some of them," the editor muttered in a voice laced with irritation.

"Some of them!" Aïda exploded. She flung her head back and blew out air between her lips in a perfect imitation of a horse whinnying. Several junior editors, attracted by the whinny, gathered outside the open door of the office. The editor scraped back his chair and came around to plant himself in front of the desk with his arms folded across his chest. Aïda noticed what appeared to be caviar stains on his beard and on the lapels of his checkered sports jacket. The sight provoked her. "So: What *would* happen if your readers came across *cunt* in print?" she inquired sarcastically. "Would the earth quit rotating on its axis? Would the polar ice cap melt? What hypocrites you all are. It is prudes like you who refused to publish stanzas from Pushkin's *Tsar Nikita*, who even now think Nabokov went too far with *Lolita*. Admit it, Joseph Mikhailovich, you are afraid of crossing some Party line, afraid of offending some male chauvinist cog in the Bolshevik wheel."

For a moment the only sound in the room was the hollow ticking of the wall clock. "When will you get it into that virago's skull of yours that there is no Party line anymore," the editor lectured her, raising his voice, tapping a forefinger against his own skull. "Our poets should be the first to understand this, the first to support those who are risking everything to bring a human face to Socialism."

Aïda slid off the radiator and, producing some cheap tobacco and paper from the pocket of her blanket-lined overcoat, proceeded to roll a thin cigarette; as a young girl she had worked for eighteen months in a cigarette factory in central Asia, and had never lost the knack. "The business of poets," she said as her fingers worked the tobacco onto the paper, "is to permanently position themselves to the left of the official line. During the Brezhnev era we stood for *glasnost*. Now we must stand to the left of *glasnost*—it is clearly not ambitious enough if it cannot live with the publication of a poem that contains the word *cunt*." She licked the edge of the paper and threaded the cigarette closed and thrust it between her lips. "You would not happen to have fire?" she challenged, her eyes boring into his, and it was clear from the angle of her chin, from the slight smile on her trembling lips, that she intended the double meaning.

Shaking his head in frustration, the editor thumbed a lighter and held the flame to the tip of her cigarette. "How is it we always end up arguing when we are on the same side?"

"I suppose the answer is that we are not on the same side."

The minute hand on the wall clock lurched forward with a resounding click that sounded like a lock closing. Aïda checked her wristwatch against the clock. Joseph Mikhailovich shrugged in exasperation. "Spare me your feminist song-and-dance routine," he said scornfully. He caught a glimpse of the editors eavesdropping at the door and turned on them in anger. "Don't you have anything better to do than stand around gaping in hallways?" He stalked over and kicked the door closed so hard Aïda thought the opaque pane of glass in it would shatter.

She exhaled a lung full of foul-smelling cigarette smoke. "You should be opening doors, not closing them, Joseph Mikhailovich. You know the story about Pasternak on his deathbed—he kept mumbling the same thing over and over, but nobody could figure out what he wanted. Finally someone deciphered it—he was asking for the door to be opened."

That was too much for the editor, for whom Pasternak was a hero, an icon, a god. "What is that supposed to mean?"

"Poetry is a moving target. Poets too. You have to stalk both of them. In other words, Joseph Mikhailovich, it means whatever you want it to mean."

"What a cunt you are!"

Aïda produced a mocking half-smile. Though the editor could not have known it, the person she was mocking was herself; another battle had been won, another war lost.

Breathing heavily through his nostrils, flicking imaginary specks of soot from his lilac shirt, Joseph Mikhailovich retreated to his fortress behind the pile of manuscripts on the desk. "You ambushed me," he complained. He threaded his fingers through his long beard, absently working out the knots. "That is the thanks I get for going out on a limb and publishing your poems."

Aïda grew bored with the game. "If you really want to help me," she observed quietly, "you can pay me for the two poems you have accepted."

"You know the magazine's rules," the editor told her. "We pay on publication, not on correcting galley proofs."

"You are so hot to restructure the country," Aïda replied wearily, "why don't you start by restructuring the magazine's rules?" Suddenly she felt overwhelmed by a persuasive sense of despair. She had too many nagging problems, too much on her mind, too many people dependent on her. Everyone took her strength for granted. They did not understand how fragile she really was, how easy it would have been for her to fold her tent and run for the hills, leaving her son and her father and her future ex-husband and all the women's groups to fend for themselves. They did not understand how close she came at times to crossing that delicate threshold where dying seemed easier than living. Stubbing out her cigarette against the wall in a corkscrew motion and flicking it into a wire mesh wastebasket, she tucked her eyeglasses away in a plastic case and gathered her belongings. "Thanks for nothing," she said as she started toward the door.

The editor noticed the droop to her shoulders. "How is Saava doing?" he called after her.

Aïda turned back at the door. "Saava is, thanks to God, all right. It is the world that is sick."

The editor smiled in grudging agreement. "Come by

tomorrow at six," he muttered. "I will see what I can do about getting you paid for the poems."

Aïda stared at the editor briefly, nodded as if she had confirmed some obscure observation on the human condition and left.

Housekeeping for the "Seven Dwarfs" (the in-house epithet for the seven officers assigned to the Arms Control Implementation Unit) consumed most of Ben Bassett's time and all of his patience. He shuttled between the unit's shabby warren of offices, located immediately under the embassy's cultural affairs section, and the General Services Office, to the left of the main entrance and the marines guarding it. There were train and hotel reservations to be booked through the *Upravleniye po Obsluzheniyu Diplomaticheskoyo Korpusa,* better known to American diplomats in Moscow as the UPDK, and pronounced "Updik." There were car pool Chevrolets to be reserved, gasoline coupons to be bought, the office burn bag to be disposed of, a visiting fireman from the Pentagon to be shepherded around town. A supply of Pampers had just arrived in the weekly shipment from Stockman's Department Store in Helsinki and had to be delivered to a woman whose husband was off inspecting Soviet missile sites in central Asia. The unit's Xerox machine had broken down. Again. The toilet in the office bathroom was backing up into the bathtub. (The embassy had been an apartment building in a previous incarnation, which explained why many of the bathrooms were equipped with bathtubs; the apartment building had been constructed *after* the Bolshevik revolution, which explained why the plumbing banged when it worked, which was rarely.) It took Ben three-quarters of an hour to track down the embassy's resident plumber, and another fifteen minutes to convince him that the situation was desperate. By the time Ben got around to collecting his mail in the administrative section, he was wilting with fatigue. He was reading the announcements on the bulletin board ("All those who agree there is too much salt in the commissary salads, put their John/Jane Hancocks below") when a woman tapped him on an arm.

"Hi, Ben," she said.

"Oh. Hello."

"Sabine Harkenrider?"

"I remember your name," he lied.

"How are you getting on?"

Ben laughed under his breath. "I'll survive. What about you?"

Sabine rewarded him with a shy smile and Ben decided she wasn't nearly as plain looking as he had first thought. "The junior high facilities at the New Office Building are first rate," she told him. "I came to this job from a New Haven ghetto. For me, having shades on windows is sheer luxury. But the kids here are a bit snooty. The main topic of conversation is the latest killing they made on the black market—they seem to be able to get just about anything in exchange for jeans and sweatshirts." Sabine studied the bulletin board, and reached up to add her name to the list of those interested in participating in a cross-country ski outing being organized by the embassy's Weight Watchers the following Sunday.

"You don't look like a Weight Watcher," Ben remarked.

"I don't look like one because I am one." She glanced at Ben inquisitively. "Do you watch your weight? Do you ski?"

"No on both counts."

Sabine, fanning the ember of the conversation to keep it alive, said, "You and Mr. Custer didn't hit it off too well the other day."

Ben shrugged. "He ran true to type—he's still fighting the Cold War. It's pathetic." In fact Ben regretted having baited the embassy security officer. He should be steering clear of people like that and keeping a low profile.

"I don't follow politics," Sabine remarked. "I suppose it's because I don't really understand what motivates someone to become a politician."

"Power."

"That's what everyone says. Power." She shook her head. "There's got to be more to it. It's like saying a businessman is only motivated by money. I don't believe that."

She waited for Ben to respond. When he didn't she said, "Well," and smiled at the ground. She started to walk away, then turned back. "There's a happy hour over at Sam's Lounge in the New Office Building at four. Come on by, Ben. I'll buy you a drink."

Ben thought: The last thing I want to do in Moscow is get involved with an American. He said something about having to see someone at four fifteen. "Another time maybe."

"Sure. Another time." Turning away, she smiled again and then laughed out loud. Ben thought he detected a note of pain in her laughter. He wondered if he had reopened an old wound—or inflicted a new one.

HE DID HAVE an appointment at four fifteen—with Charlie Inkermann, the Central Intelligence Agency station chief at the embassy. At ten minutes past the hour Ben took the elevator to the ninth floor, had his green badge checked by a marine with a plump baby face crawling with acne, then walked up one flight to the tenth floor and made his way down the hall, past the defense attaché offices, past the deputy chief of mission's office, to a door with only a number on it. He knocked and stuck his head in.

A young secretary in a flaming red miniskirt was filing documents in a metal cabinet. She waved him into the room. "We're expecting you," she said cheerfully. She threaded a steel bar through the drawer handles and secured the bar with a combination lock at the top and activated the electronic alarm. Drifting over to her desk, she gave Ben the kind of frank once-over that women wearing flaming red miniskirts get from men. "I'm Mehetabel Macy," she announced breathlessly. "You're probably asking yourself, what kind of name is Mehetabel? The answer is, it's biblical—it means 'beloved of God.' It makes you wonder, doesn't it? I mean, if I got posted to Moscow, imagine where the ones who aren't beloved of God get posted!" She held up a hand when Ben started to say something. "You're Mr. Inkermann's four fifteen. That's what I'll call you from now on no matter what time I see you—you'll always be our four fifteen." Eyeing Ben, she stretched across her desk and flicked a lever on an intercom. "Your four fifteen is here, Mr. Inkermann."

An impatient nasal whine filtered back over the box. "Send him on in."

The secretary uncoiled herself from the desk and opened one of the four doors giving off her outer office and lazily stood aside. Ben got a whiff of lilac perfume as he strolled past her into a murky inner office. As the door closed behind him, cutting off most of the light, he had the peculiar weightless sensation that comes when you plunge to the bottom of a lake. What light there was seemed to mingle uncomfortably with shifting shadows. Gradually his eyes grew accustomed to the darkness and he began to make out the CIA station chief. A short, meaty man with strands of hair slicked back in an only partially successful attempt to cover a bald spot, he was sitting at a bridge table illuminated by a low desk lamp, manipulating something with his stubby fingers. When Ben approached he saw that Inkermann was fitting tiny stanchions onto a model of a warship. "Right with you," the station chief mumbled without looking up. He dabbed some Super Glue onto the end of another stanchion and delicately stuck it into place. Peering at the model through a magnifying glass, Inkermann said, "You're looking at a World War Two Sumner class destroyer named the U.S.S. *John R. Pierce*. She's the one that stopped the first Russian freighter off Cuba when John Kennedy quarantined the island during the missile crisis." Inkermann contemplated the model of the ship with something akin to nostalgia. "I had the great good fortune to be serving on the *Pierce* at that historic moment in time." Tearing his eyes away from the model with reluctance, he angled the desk lamp so that it illuminated his visitor. "So you're Bassett," he growled. He didn't offer to shake hands.

Ben appeared startled to hear Inkermann pronounce his name out loud. "Just the other day," he noted wryly, "Mr. Custer warned us that walls have ears."

"Custer's an asshole," Inkermann snapped. Gesturing with his head for Ben to take a seat, he walked across the room to a very cluttered desk and settled into the wooden swivel chair behind it. "Fact of the matter is some walls have ears, some don't. These particular walls don't." He reached over and switched on a desk lamp with a green shade. "This office was constructed by Seabees. The windows have double panes to prevent lasers picking off voice vibrations. The venetian blinds are always closed. Neither the Russians, nor your coworkers in the embassy for that matter, will know you've been up here. If there's one thing we're meticulous about, Bassett, it's tradecraft. You will have noticed that my secretary referred to you as my four fifteen. That's because her space is not considered one hundred percent secure." Inkermann, who was trying to give up smoking, planted a plastic cigarette between his thick lips and started to work it in his jaw. "I was told you were with Army Intelligence. I was told you could do no wrong. I was told that was all I would be told. By my superiors in Washington. By you."

Inkermann observed his visitor with thinly disguised hostility. He was not tickled at the idea of someone freelancing out of his shop. Some sort of operation was obviously under way. For the station chief to be cut out of the chain of command was not unheard-of, but it was rare. To Inkermann it meant one of two things: Either he wasn't completely trusted, or the operation in question was especially tightly held. He hoped to hell it was the second, but worried himself sick that it was the first. Still, Inkermann liked to think of himself as a team player, and a professional; he liked to say that he only had to be given a compass heading for him to set sail. So, swallowing his pride, he asked, "What can I do for you?"

Ben supplied the station chief with a verbal shopping list. He would need the sealed attaché case that had been sent to him in the diplomatic pouch. He would need a room to himself; it didn't have to be big, but it had to be secure. He would need a safe and a shredding machine and a burn bag. He would need access to the station chief's backlist of enciphered Sensitive Compartmented Information Cables—a category so secret the messages were always BIGOT listed, which meant that the addressee controlled dissemination and all copies were numbered. Oh, he had almost forgotten his last but not least. He would also need the station's cipher logs.

"Anything else?" Inkermann asked with a thin smile.

Ben indicated with a quick shake of his head that that would be all.

Inkermann asked him how far back he wanted to go in the cable files. Ben said he planned to start with 1967. Inkermann wanted to know what hours Ben would be working. Ben said he would hold down his housekeeping job to keep his cover intact, and work on the cables nights, weekends. When Inkermann observed that it would take months to work through the station's Sensitive Compartmented Information Cables, Ben only shrugged.

As Ben was leaving Inkermann asked him, "Just as a matter of curiosity, has Custer been briefed about you?"

Ben said, "Nobody but you has been briefed about me. Not the ambassador. Not Custer."

Inkermann said, "The marines checking green badges on the sixth floor keep a log. Custer might find out you've been coming up here. You'd better have a story ready."

"One of my housekeeping chores for the Seven Dwarfs involves enciphering their status reports to the Pentagon. If Custer asks I'll tell him you loaned me a safe to keep my ciphers in, and a table to work on when I encipher."

Inkermann heaved himself out of his chair. "He won't get a different story from me. You can count on it."

Ben could have said, "I am." But he wanted to put some maneuvering room between himself and Inkermann. So he said, "We are," knowing Inkermann would notice the "We" and draw the appropriate conclusion.

He did.

5

Tuesday was not one of Viktor Prosenko's better days. His gout had acted up again, causing his big toes to swell, obliging him to hobble when he walked. The gout was the result, according to the Center doctor who examined him, of having downed several liters of a very bad year of a very bad Georgian white wine the night his wife left for a Moscow suburb. She was "on location" to film an episode for a television soap opera. Viktor was haunted by his vision of the "location." If he knew Ekaterina, she would be spending most of her nonworking hours in a king-size double bed in the local hotel, and she would be sharing it with her lover, the seedy Yid hustler half Viktor's age who liked to tell anti-Soviet jokes at cocktail parties.

To make matters worse, Viktor's doting secretary, Evgeniya Leonovna, had slipped on a patch of ice in front of her apartment building, spraining her left wrist. She had phoned up in tears to say she would be out for two days and to remind him where she kept the homemade confiture for his tea. The plump secretary dispatched from the Center's pool of temporaries reeked of what the old hands

46

around the building called "Stalin's breath" (a mass-produced perfume), could not even spell the Center's name correctly, and brewed the worst glass of tea Viktor had ever tasted, one that no amount of confiture could save. On top of everything she whined.

She was whining over the telephone now. "There's a Captain Kruchtin out here—"

Viktor could hear his irritated chief of section correcting her. "My name happens to be Krostin, not Kruchtin."

"Kruchtin, Krostin, whichever," the secretary whined into the phone. "He wants to know if he can have a minute of your time. What do I tell him?"

"You tell him you are sorry you mispronounced his name. You tell him to come straight in."

"I would offer you a glass of tea," Viktor told his section chief when he had been admitted to the office, "but you might never drink that particular liquid again if I did."

Krostin, as usual, came straight to the point. "I may have stumbled onto something interesting," he told Viktor. He had been scanning snatches of conversation picked up by a microphone buried in the wall near the bulletin board in the American embassy's administrative section. One of the three newcomers to the embassy, the woman named Harkenrider, had been overheard inviting someone named Ben to have a drink with her at the embassy lounge at four. (Krostin divined that the Ben in question was the Arms Control Unit housekeeper, Benedict Bassett, because of a reference in the conversation to the briefing they had both received from the security officer, Custer.) Bassett had begged off, saying he had to see someone at four fifteen. As Viktor would see, the mention of a four fifteen appointment was significant. Later in the afternoon a microphone imbedded in the wall of the outer office of the CIA station had picked up the secretary informing Inkermann that his four fifteen had arrived. "She never uses proper names because they worry about bugs," Krostin explained. "She always refers to visitors by the hour of their appointment."

Viktor was beginning to see what his section chief was driving at. "You think this Benedict Bassett had an appointment with Inkermann?"

"Inkermann's response to his secretary over the intercom came across loud and clear. He said, 'Send *him* on in.'"

"Him," Viktor repeated thoughtfully, reaching down to massage a swollen ankle.

Krostin put into words the obvious question. "What business could a housekeeper for the Arms Control Implementation Unit have with the CIA station chief?"

A light appeared in each of Viktor's eyes. "If it really was Bassett up there," he told Krostin, "it could mean he is more than a housekeeper."

For the first time since his wife had gone off "on location," Viktor's imagination conjured up something other than the vision of her chalk-white body spiking itself on the circumcised penis of an alcoholic Jewish hustler in a cheap hotel room. "By all means, let's put Bassett onto our Priority Target List," he instructed Krostin. "Don't stint. I want Section Three to assign an entire team to him. If this Bassett is really more than a housekeeper, we are starting out with the great advantage that he does not know we know. Let's not lose it by being overeager or unprofessional."

Viktor swiveled in his chair and contemplated the thick ribbons of snow slanting across his field of vision toward the street below. For a delicious moment he savored the illusion that the snow was perfectly still and he was rocketing up through it. A pensive smile etched fault lines in his weathered cheeks.

The sensation of being, at long last, in motion caused Viktor's joints to tingle from something other than gout.

6

The moment Aïda started up the narrow staircase, feeling her way in the pitch darkness because the light bulbs had burned out and replacements could not be found, she knew she had lost the race to be the first to use the communal kitchen. The pungent odor of cooked cabbage filled the stairwells and grew more intense as she mounted. On her floor, the fifth, it was overpowering. Aïda would have liked to get Saava's dinner started and the boy to bed at a reasonable hour, but she had been held up by the lines at the gastronome on the ground floor of the building next door. The shelves had been almost bare when she arrived, but that had not stopped people from queuing. There had been seven lines, actually—one for the frozen sardines that were so small the man behind her had claimed they were minnows, a second for the runty potatoes studded with eyes that had sprouted, a third for the loaf of dry black bread, a fourth to pay for everything, then another round of queuing to hand in the stamped slips and retrieve the items. Now, fumbling at the end of a long day to insert the skeleton

key in the lock, Aïda felt drained of energy, of hope. Her
feet might have been made of lead. Her heart also. She
pushed open the door, forced what could pass for a smile
onto her face and called out, "Saava, it's me. It's Aïda
come home at last."

Saava came bounding down the corridor into Aïda's
arms. He planted a wet kiss squarely on her lips; Aïda
loved it that at eleven he had no inhibitions about being
physical with his mother. Grabbing her hand, he tugged
her past the kitchen, where the woman who shared the
apartment was grating cooked beets into a meatless
borscht, toward the bathroom. "Aïda, come see what
Vadim is up to," Saava cried in a voice pitched high with
excitement.

The boy pulled Aïda along the hallway crammed with
cartons of books and valises packed with summer clothing, past the communal refrigerator, into the long, narrow
bathroom that managed to smell of sewage no matter how
often it was disinfected. Vadim, who was filling a large jar
with rust-colored water trickling from a bathtub tap,
raised his eyes and flashed a lopsided grin in his wife's
direction. Aïda's future ex-husband (he categorically refused to get a divorce until he could move into a penthouse apartment overlooking the Moscow River; and he
couldn't do that until the present occupant obtained legal
custody of her son so that the two of them could emigrate
to Israel) had the gaunt, pinched face of a lapsed alcoholic; his eyes, dark peach pits sunken into his skull,
bloodshot from the liters of cheap vodka he consumed
daily, were fixed in the permanent squint of someone
about to make a sales pitch. The skin on the back of his
hands crawled with warts. From time to time his entire
body trembled like a leaf caught in a current of air. There
were moments when Aïda wondered what Vadim's mistress saw in him. There were moments when she had
difficulty remembering what she had seen in him.

"He says we will all get drunk and go to America,"
Saava announced gravely. "He says the streets there are

paved with discarded Sony Walkmans, some of which can still be made to work."

"I have no desire to go to America," Aïda said. "I am perfectly satisfied to be here." She turned on Vadim. "Why do you put foolish ideas in his head?"

Vadim, who had spent the afternoon drinking retsina with a diplomat friend just back from Athens, slurred his words as he answered. "And what is so foolish about going to America? It is a place where ideas are run up flagpoles. Their Madison Street leads the world in advertising. Chances are they could use a creative Russian Jew who has experience pitching products nobody wants to buy."

Aïda regarded the jar in the bathtub. "So: What is it you are concocting?"

"I got the recipe from my taxi driver who got it from a chemist from Uzbekistan. You mix in rice, you mix in sugar if you can find sugar, saccharine if not, you mix in some fruit—I found a peasant selling dried peaches at the central market. Don't ask me what I paid for them because if I told you, which I won't, you would physically assault me. You mix it all up in a jar, you add beer, you add warm water, you cover the jar with a rubber surgeon's glove. As the mixture ferments, the glove inflates. When all the fingers are sticking up, 'the Great Helmsman's Greeting,' which is what the cocktail is called, is ready to drink."

"Why do you bother when you have enough money to buy all the alcohol you can drink on the black market?" Aïda demanded.

"I do it because it is illegal," Vadim explained. "I plan to present a bottle to the deputy vice minister in charge of the state advertising budget."

Saava asked Vadim, "What does it mean, ferment?"

Vadim turned off the tap, fitted the rubber glove over the lid with a rubber band and carefully lifted the jar out of the tub. "Ferment is what happens when something rots."

"Like when Communism ferments?" Saava asked brightly.

Vadim snickered. "Where can I put the jar so it is in the dark?" he asked Aïda.

Aïda went back into the corridor and hung her coat and fox fur on a hook. Vadim, carrying the jar with the rubber glove attached as if it were a lid, trailed after her. "While you were busy buying your dried peaches," Aïda asked over her shoulder, "did you by any chance find meat for supper?"

"To tell the truth, I didn't look. If you want I could phone up my taxi driver and have him bring us something from a restaurant."

"Luckily I found some sardines," Aïda told him as she kicked off her galoshes and fitted her feet into fleece-lined bedroom slippers.

"I think I would prefer meat."

"If you wanted meat you should have thought about it when you were paying a small fortune for fruit at the central market. Imagine buying fruit in winter!"

Vadim followed her into the room that served as a living room and Aïda's bedroom. It was furnished with a narrow wooden bed covered with a bright Uzbek shawl, an armoire with mirrors in the doors, a round wooden table that Aïda used as a desk when meals were not being served, makeshift shelves overflowing with books and manuscripts and magazines, and three faded oil paintings hung, the way Russians always hang paintings, high on the wall. "Money," Vadim muttered, looking around for a place to store his jar, "is not my problem. In any case, buying fruit in winter is a *poetic* gesture. You of all people should be able to relate to that."

"Poetry is food for the soul. Saava also needs food for the stomach." Aïda, sorting through the mail piled on the round table, tossed the typewritten envelopes behind the radiator with the others already there; it was a matter of absolute principle with her never to open typewritten envelopes or read typewritten letters. She settled into the only decent chair in the room to take a look at the handwritten note postmarked Leningrad. The letter turned out to be from the head of the Pushkin memorial committee;

he was offering to pay her way to the city she called Peter (after its founder, Peter the Great) and everyone else called Leningrad if she would agree to read some of Pushkin's poems at the gathering marking the anniversary of the poet's death in February.

Vadim shoved aside a pile of Aïda's books and squeezed his precious jar onto a shelf in the armoire. Quite pleased with himself, he started recounting the latest joke. "Speaking of meat, did you hear about the woman who stands on line for two hours? When she finally reaches the counter she asks the salesman for meat. He tells her"— Vadim couldn't keep from smirking at his own joke— " 'Here we have no fish. Next door is where they have no meat.' "

Aïda didn't laugh. "Why is it always the woman who stands on line in your jokes?"

Vadim shook his head in disgust. "Where's your sense of humor?" he muttered under his alcoholic breath, and wobbling unsteadily, he staggered toward the room he shared with Saava.

Tears of frustration, of outrage, welled up. As always Aïda resisted the urge to weep. She had lost what sense of humor she still had somewhere between the center of Moscow and the Maritime Station, Rechnoi Vokzal, the last stop on the Gorkovskaya metro line; jammed into the subway car, swaying with the motion of the train, she had felt a hand rub against her buttocks. Twisting around, she had slapped the fat man squeezed up against her. He had bellowed in surprise and had accused her of being mentally deranged. The other passengers had stared at her as if she was. Maybe they sensed something she didn't. It was true that she could not remember the last time she had burst out laughing; the last time she had found some one or some thing funny. Humor seemed to have been squeezed out of her life. What was funny about scavenging for rubles to make ends meet? Or queuing week in, week out for the pills that her son needed to remain alive? Or living with a filthy rich future ex who could afford meat but forgot to buy it. Where was the humor in spending a

small fortune to buy peaches in winter? Her future ex had
probably paid twenty rubles for them. For twenty rubles
she could have bought two chickens on the black market,
three if they were small ones.

Aïda heaved herself out of the chair—she felt as if she
could have sat there forever—and knelt down next to the
mint geranium she left on the floor so that it would catch
the beams of sunlight during the day, the beams of moonlight at night that knifed between two tall buildings across
the street. Was an occasional beam of sunlight or moonlight nourishment enough for a plant? Was one small
plant clinging to life nourishment enough for a poet?

Reflecting on the poetic possibilities of the riddle, she
made her way along the corridor to her father's tiny bedroom. She opened the door the width of a finger and
looked in. As always at this hour Ivan had taken up the
vigil that would last until dawn; in the metallic moonlight
seeping into the room she could just make him out, sitting
in his wicker chair drawn up to the double windows with a
layer of cotton on the sill between the two panes to absorb
moisture, staring silently into the night, scratching absently at the hair as thick as broom bristles on his chin,
lost in thought; lost in fear. His right hand would be on
his cane, Aïda knew, ready to tap out a staccato message
of alarm on the floor if they came. At the slightest sound
from outside—a car door slamming, a cat screeching, the
whine of brakes—his heartbeat would quicken and he
would lean forward anxiously. Although Aïda could not
see his eyes she could imagine them; they would have the
wild concentration of someone who had spent a lifetime
waiting. Two lines of Akhmatova's leapt into her head.

> . . . *faces fall apart,*
> . . . *fear looks out from under the eyelids*

Was she missing the humor of the situation, she wondered?

At supper Saava, pulling a face, gulped down his pills,
then again asked Aïda to explain why grandfather Ivan

slept days and stayed awake nights; again Aïda told him he was too young to understand. How old would he have to be, Saava wanted to know. Twelve? Thirteen? Maybe when you are thirteen, she told him. Thirteen, he said gloomily, is too far away to touch. Vadim, sucking noisily on the head of a sardine, snorted. Me also, I'm too far away from thirteen to touch it, he said. He started to laugh, but stopped when he saw that Aïda was not amused. She turned back to Saava and asked him what he had studied in history class that day. When he told her she said no, no, it did not happen at all like that even if your textbook says it did, and scraping the last bits of fish from the sardine's skeleton onto Saava's plate, she proceeded to set the record straight. Stalin had not been the wise war leader pictured in the textbook. He had failed to heed warnings that the Nazis planned to attack. The Air Force had been caught on the ground and destroyed. The Red Army had suffered dreadful losses, had been driven back to the gates of Moscow. Stalin himself had panicked and disappeared for ten days. If the tide of war had eventually turned, it had been due more to the courage of the Russian soldiers and their determination to defend the Motherland; it had been *despite* Stalin, not *because* of him.

Lying in bed later, Aïda found herself straining to catch sounds from the street. She tried to picture herself bursting into spontaneous laughter at some sight, some comment, but the image eluded her. She wondered if fear could be passed like a virus from one person to another; she wondered if she had been infected by her father. She wondered if she would infect Saava.

There was a scuffing sound at the door leading to Saava's room. A stain of light spread on the floor as the door swung open. Vadim padded across the room in his bare feet and sank down on the edge of the bed. In the darkness he groped under the blankets, under her nightdress, and began to run his fingers along the inside of her thigh. "Remember how it used to be between us?" he whispered hoarsely.

Aïda was sorely tempted; she did have a garden full of

lust and would have welcomed taking momentary refuge
in the sanctuary of the sex act. Vadim must have sensed
her hesitating because he became bolder, working his
hand up to her pubic hair. "Relax," he whispered. "Enjoy
it." He leaned toward her until his face was hovering
above hers. She got a whiff of the liquor on his breath.
Suddenly the idea of being kissed by his alcoholic lips
killed whatever desire she felt. She pushed his hand away.
"It is out of the realm of possibility," she murmured.

Vadim wrenched his hand out from under the blanket
as if it had been burned. "What a cunt you are, Aïda!" he
muttered angrily, and smothering a belch in the sleeve of
his bathrobe, he lumbered back toward his room to crawl
into bed alongside Saava.

Aïda sat up. Her breath came in pained gasps. "There is
more to me than cunt—" she called after him in the fierce
whisper that people in communal apartments used when
they argued. Before she could say anything else the door
clicked closed, erasing the stain of light on the floor.

Sinking back onto the pillow, Aïda let her lids drift
closed over her eyes. In her mind's eye the stain of light
lingered, increasing in intensity. The absence of darkness
did not annoy her. It reminded her of the white nights she
dearly loved in Peter. She encountered a vision of her
father staring unblinkingly through the double panes into
the night, and began to put words to the images that had
been orbiting each other in her head.

At first light, the trolleys grinding up the hill.
We pressed against each other, whispering.

By the bed, a canvas satchel stuffed with tea,
A collected works, paper, pencil, a photo of me.

How can you be sure? I asked.
It was the way he looked at me.

How did he look at you?
As if I were transparent.

In the street, the whine of brakes.
His body, stiff against mine, embraced the sound.

We are into morning, I said.
If they have not come by now . . .

Try to get some sleep, I said.
I pulled the cover over his head.

You do not need to do that, he said.
The memory of a white night had overpowered light.

1

From the moment Ben Bassett's foot touched Russian soil, places and people and things he had never set eyes on seemed hauntingly familiar. His father's father (the "Russian roots" of Ben's service record) had warned him it would be like that; had warned him that he would have the impression of reliving an incarnation; had warned him that he would feel Russia pulling at him, like gravity, through the thick soles of his L.L. Bean hunting boots. Now, wandering on a narrow, slush-filled back street behind the Bolshoi Theater late one afternoon two weeks after his arrival in Moscow, stopping to buy a handful of hazelnuts from a vendor wearing tinted plastic ski goggles, he thought he could hear his grandfather laughing, with that peculiar stifled sound that was half-cough and half-cackle, at the riot of emotions raging in his grandson's head.

Ben had been weaned on things Russian: The dry self-mocking humor; the tendency to laugh in undertones so as not to attract attention to yourself; the use of dignity as a kind of armor; the use of alcohol as a kind of palliative.

It was at the knee of his grandfather that Ben had learned about the intricate declensions that gave to the Russian language a suppleness few tongues matched; about the vastness of the steppe that gave to the Russian soul its dread of unordered space, of unstructured existence; about the coldness of the Russian winter that gave to the Russian heart its morbid conviction that life was essentially tragedy. In his youth Ben's grandfather had been caught up in the idealism of the Revolution; had fought in one of Trotsky's mobile Red Guard battalions during the Civil War; had become disenchanted when a rude Georgian peasant named Iosif Vissarionovich Dzhugashvili (better known to the world by his underground name, Stalin) manipulated his way to power on the death of Lenin in 1924; had stowed away on a steamer bound for Istanbul and points west one jump ahead of the Cheka agents hunting him as an "enemy of the people"; had wound up, ancient before he was old, operating a projector in a Bronx motion picture theater. Even on his deathbed, with a death rattle tickling the back of his throat, the stories had continued to gush out of him. Ben remembered being struck by the fact that they had no beginning and no end, but unraveled in a long coil of narrative that broke off only when the ancient heart ceased to beat.

Was it possible, Ben wondered now, making his way past a peasant woman in a thick quilted Army greatcoat peddling clumps of parsley, that it was his turn to pick up the thread of his grandfather's narrative? One way or another he too would have a story to tell—though the number of people he could tell it to would always be extremely limited.

Turning off Petrovka into a warren of streets behind the Bolshoi, Ben had to step into the gutter to avoid a group of giggling girls in short skirts and bright tights walking on ice-skate blades covered with rubber sheaths. On the spur of the moment he decided to test his tradecraft. Before leaving Washington he had been given a crash course by Army Intelligence field agents, and elaborately briefed by a nuts-and-bolts type with credentials identifying him as a

State Department security officer. The nuts-and-bolts
man had discouraged him from practicing tradecraft in
the streets of Moscow, first because Ben (according to the
field agents) was not very adept at it, then because his
failure to spot anyone following him might mean that the
Russians had assigned one of their crack teams to him;
employing teams that made use of women and even children as well as men, that constantly shifted the point
agent, that sometimes trailed targets from in front rather
than from behind, made it virtually impossible to pick up
the tail.

Ben paused to look at a display of hockey sticks and ice-
skates in the window of a sports store, and used the window to study the street behind him. As far as he could
observe in the accumulating darkness, no one on the
street appeared to take the slightest interest in him; no
one turned away or changed his or her trajectory; no one
stopped suddenly to window-shop in front of another
store; no automobile pulled over to the curb and parked
with its motor idling.

From somewhere overhead Ben heard the quicksilvery
ripple of a soprano voice skating back and forth across
scales. Stepping back off the curb and looking up, he
could make out the large windows of a second-floor rehearsal studio. Someone played a few chords on a piano.
Then, with the piano accompanying her, the soprano began to sing the opening measures of a well-known aria.
She stopped abruptly. The piano repeated a phrase twice.
The soprano tried it again without the piano. A man's
voice could be heard exhorting her. "You are swallowing
vowels," he cried. "Spit them out." The singer attempted
the phrase again. It was apparently satisfactory because
she went back to the beginning, and with the piano accompanying her, continued on past the phrase.

Under the rehearsal studio a big-boned woman pushed
through the double doors leading to the street. She stood
for a moment with her coat open, her gloves off and
tucked under an armpit, counting with naked fingers a
wad of rubles. Ben was instantly alert to her. He had

never seen anyone quite like her in Moscow—or anywhere else for that matter; in this incarnation or any of the previous incarnations his grandfather insisted he had had. She looked as if she had walked off a 1930s movie set. Planted squarely on her large head was a pillbox hat with an enormous white feather spiked through it. Around her neck she had flung a threadbare fox neckpiece with a shrunken fox's head on one end that stared out at the world with unblinking marble eyes, almost as if it were stalking the hunter who had shot it. The fox in turn was draped over a worn cloth coat lined with what looked like a green Army blanket. The slush-stained hem of a thick ankle-length black skirt appeared to foam around her galoshes as she stamped her feet to keep them warm.

Apparently satisfied with the count, the woman stuffed the money in a coat pocket and pulled on her gloves. She must have become aware of the singing coming from above because she angled her head up and cocked an ear, then backed over to stand near Ben and listen. The soprano voice broke off. A male voice straining to reach an octave above its normal range demonstrated the phrasing. The soprano attacked the passage several times without the piano, then with it. Ben turned to the woman and said, in Russian, "*Tosca*. Act two, scene two."

Without taking her eyes off the windows of the rehearsal studio, the woman shook her head. "*Turandot*. I do not know the act. But there can be no discussion. I would recognize it anywhere."

Ben asked, "Are you a singer?"

The woman slowly turned her head toward Ben and studied him, her eyes as fixed as those of the fox peering from her shoulder. Then she said in a tone that did not invite him to continue the conversation, "In a manner of speaking, yes."

Ben became aware of the broken, badly set nose. Curiously, the deformation only made her more sensual. He tried out a smile on her, but it didn't dent the wall of indifference behind which she seemed to be barricaded.

"If you are a singer," he challenged her, "can you explain what pushes human beings to sing?"

The woman sniffed at the imbecility of the question. "What is it that makes a bird sing?"

Ben retorted, "Only a sky diver can know what makes a bird sing."

The woman half-smiled as the image struck her, then burst out laughing. To Ben's ear the laughter sounded rusty, as if it hadn't been used in a long time.

The woman appeared to inch out from behind her wall of indifference. "You speak with some kind of an accent," she noted.

"I am American."

"Is this your first visit to Kuchkovo?"

"What is Kuchkovo?"

The woman seemed quite pleased with herself. "That is the original name of Moscow. It tickles the Slavophile in me to use it."

Ben said, "I am not a tourist. I should tell you right off that I work at the American Embassy. I am a very junior diplomat."

The woman surprised him by switching to English. "I have never before now recountered someone from the other side of the looking glass. I must admit that America does not fascinate me the way it fascinates others. I have heard it spoken that the only original American contribution to world culture is the banjo."

Ben answered in Russian. "You are forgetting the rocking chair," he said good-humoredly. "And baseball."

She laughed at this. "You speak Russian good for a foreign person. You speak it like me. Well, not exactly like me." She smiled self-consciously at her English. "Almost like me."

"Your English is as good as my Russian," Ben said. "Where did you pick it up?"

"In prison," she replied, measuring him to see what effect her reply would have. "I once shared a cell with a Hungarian origin lady that formerly instructed the English grammar for the children of Hungarian diplomats.

She had a Russian husband who got into what you with your love of clichés call heated water. I have nothing against clichés, mind you. Clichés are dead poems. When the Hungarian origin lady defended her Russian husband, she got also into heated water. In this prison she to me recited English poems. In exchange I to her recited Russian poems. Mostly but not always Akhmatova, some Pushkin, some Mandelstam."

Above their heads the soprano reached for a high note and missed. The woman with the broken nose winced. She and Ben exchanged conspiratorial smiles; more of the wall behind which the woman was barricaded crumbled. She studied Ben frankly, then asked, "So: Are you a sky diver?"

"In a manner of speaking, yes."

This made her laugh again. "It does not change the fact that what she is singing, though not very well, is *Turandot*, and not *Tosca.*"

"You want to bet?"

The woman switched back to Russian. "You are very sure of yourself. I do not think that is such a good thing in a man. To be less sure is to be more open." Angling her head, she half-smiled again at the idea of taking him down a peg. "What is it you would have us bet?"

"If I lose I will buy you a cup of coffee and a piece of cake. If you lose you will buy me a cup of coffee and a piece of cake."

The woman was clearly tempted. Above their heads the soprano broke off again as her teacher demonstrated the phrasing of still another passage. The teacher and the soprano repeated the passage in chorus. In the street the white feather piercing the pillbox hat quivered in the icy evening currents of air. The woman came to a decision. "Not coffee, but hot wine. Not cake, but finger sandwiches."

Ben, surprised, nodded; he hadn't expected her to agree. She nodded in return, and disappeared through the double doors into the building. The soprano's voice stopped in midphrase, and for two or three minutes the

piano and the soprano were both silent. After they re-
sumed the woman with the fox around her neck reappeared on the street. She walked directly up to Ben and
regarded him with her characteristic half-smile that had
very little to do with humor and a great deal to do with
nervousness. "*Tosca,* act two, scene two," she said.

She turned on her heel and started to walk off, then
stopped to look over her shoulder. Seeing Ben's uncertainty, she called, "A bet is a bet" and motioned with her
head for him to follow her. He fell into step alongside her.
They passed the peasant woman selling parsley and
rounded the corner.

"Where are you taking me?" Ben inquired.

"There is a café called the Druzhba on the corner of
Petrovka and Kuznetsky Most, at the Petrovka Passage."

They walked in silence, pushing through a swarm of
teenage girls with painted eyes and rouged cheeks standing in front of a store window watching a Russian rock
singer on television. Further on they had to detour
around workmen digging up a segment of sidewalk with
jackhammers. When they were far enough away from the
jackhammers to make themselves heard, Ben commented
that he found Moscow incredibly noisy. If cities were
quiet, the woman remarked, people would not live in
them. Explain yourself, Ben insisted. Contrary to what
our sociologists tell us, she said, the real reason people
congregate in monstrous warts we call cities has little to
do with economics and a lot to do with loneliness. Noise
provides evidence that we are not alone.

Ben asked her what she thought of *perestroika.* The
woman said she thought it was a fine thing as far as it
went. The trouble was that it did not go far enough; it did
not go to the root of the problem, which was to define the
role of the Communist Party in a society that had been
ruined by the Communist Party. She had read an American novel called *Catch* something or other, she said.
Catch-22, he prompted. That was it, she said. *Catch-22.*
We Russians have our own catch-22. Under Stalin, under
Khrushchev, under Brezhnev, policy was set at the top

and everyone fell into line. Now the policy set at the top is that policy should not be set at the top. It would be funny if it were not a matter of life and death. But it was. A matter of life and death. There was a time bomb ticking away in the Soviet Union, she told him. The current bosses justified their reforms by pointing to the terrible condition of the economy. It was only a matter of time before their enemies—prominent among them, the ultraright-wing anti-Semitic nationalist Circle that went by the name of *Pamyat,* or Memory—cited these same conditions as proof that the reforms were not working. Ben asked her what would happen then. She shouldered through a line of people queuing at a kiosk for waffles stuffed with frozen strawberries. An old man who thought she was trying to get in ahead of him insulted her, but she ignored him and strode on. Ben made his way around the end of the line and caught up with the woman who had lost the bet. He repeated his question. What would happen when *Pamyat* cited the economic conditions as proof that the reforms were not working? The woman hiked a shoulder in irritation; on her neck the fox's head nodded in eager agreement. *Perestroika* would give way to *perestrelka,* she said. Did he know the word? *Perestrelka* was Russian for shoot-out. Some people will start shooting at other people.

Ben wanted to know what she would do if that happened.

The woman breathed out into the cold air. A cloud of vapor swirled around her face. "I will duck for as long as such a thing is possible," she announced. "But violence is a circle. I will certainly end up wounding someone."

With Ben trailing after her, she pushed through a revolving door into the Druzhba Café, stamped the slush off her galoshes on a worn doormat and strode past the coatroom into the crowded, noisy, smoke-filled café. Looking around, she spotted a free table and went over to claim it. Settling onto the metal chair with a sigh of relief, she pulled off her gloves, loosened the fox fur around her neck and opened the buttons of her coat. Ben sat opposite her and unbuttoned his sheepskin overcoat. A waiter in a stained black dinner jacket delivered two drinks and a plate of sandwiches to the next table, then turned to them. "Two glasses of hot wine," the woman ordered. "And a plate of liverwurst sandwiches."

Ben said, "My name is Benedict, which is the long version of Ben."

The woman reached into the pocket of her coat, came up with some paper and tobacco and began to roll a thin cigarette. "Mine is Zinaïda Ivanovna. My son shortened Zinaïda to Aïda, which is what my friends call me."

Ben watched her moving fingers, fascinated by their dexterity. "I will call you what your friends call you. If you have a son you must be married."

When Aïda saw that Ben expected an answer, she said with a trace of irony, "That is not a question."

Ben watched her fingers work the tobacco onto the paper and deftly roll it. "Are you married?"

"In a manner of speaking, yes."

"Every time I ask you something you reply 'in a manner of speaking.'"

Aïda licked the paper closed and struck a match with her thumbnail and held it to the tip of her cigarette. She filled the air with a haze of unpleasant-smelling smoke before she replied. "I am married—and I am not married," she said presently. "Which is to say I have a husband, but Vadim, which is the name of my future ex, has a mistress with whom he is madly in love. He and I are only waiting for him to move out of my apartment to get divorced."

"What prevents him from moving out right away?"

"He has his heart set on moving into a penthouse overlooking the Moscow River. Before he can do that the woman who lives there must get legal custody of her son so they can emigrate to Israel. The logistics of life in Moscow can be complicated." Aïda smiled bitterly. "It is the complications that save us. If we did not have them, if life were relatively simple, if you could buy a pair of stockings without queuing on three lines and move out of an apartment when you wanted to get divorced, there would be time to *think*. And then where would we be?"

Ben wanted to know how she had met her husband.

"You ask a great many questions," Aïda noted.

"That is the usual way of starting a friendship?"

Clearly annoyed, she dragged on her cigarette, exhaled a perfect ring of smoke and watched it lose its form as it drifted away. "What we have," she said, "is not a friendship. We made a bet. I lost, so I will buy you a glass of warm wine. That will be the beginning and the end of our relationship."

The waiter returned and set two glass mugs of hot red wine on the table, along with a plate of small sandwiches. Ben wrapped his fingers around his glass to warm them. "I would still like to know how you met your husband."

Aïda shrugged quickly, stubbed out her cigarette in an ashtray and started eating a sandwich. She spoke with her mouth full. "So: We were both of us students at Lomonosov University on the Lenin Hills. In order to make money to buy books I found a part-time job washing windows in office buildings. One day I was washing a window and Vadim suddenly appeared on a scaffold washing the same window from the outside."

Ben sipped his wine. He relished the warmth in his throat. "What was it that attracted you to him?"

"His sense of humor. His Jewishness. His insolence. His courage even. He would say the most scandalous things about the bosses, even with other people around. He had the knack of passing off as a joke things that were deadly serious. The day I met him he pressed his face to the window, flattening his nose. He wrote on the glass backwards in soap, 'Will you marry me?' I shook my head no. So he wrote, 'Will you at least sleep with me?' Unlike most of the boys I knew, Vadim did not beat around the bush. I wrote back on my side of the window *mozhet bit*— maybe. He did a jig on the scaffold. That is how I always imagine him—doing a jig on the scaffold twelve floors above the street."

"How long were you married before you had your son?"

Aïda sipped her hot wine, then brought the glass up to warm her cheek. "Vadim is not the father of my son," she said softly.

Ben waited for her to go on.

"Why do I tell you all this?" She shrugged. "I had a friend who became a lover . . . he was a wonderful friend, a wonderful lover . . . he was an editor . . . he died of old age . . . at thirty-two." A film of tears transformed Aïda's eyes into mirrors. She half-smiled at a memory. "He spoke Russian with a Polish accent and lisped. He left a message on his telephone answering machine. 'I talk before the beep, you talk after,' is what it said. After he died I phoned up two or three times a day for weeks to hear his Polish accent and his lisp. One day I called and found that his voice had been replaced by the recorded voice of his widow. 'What do you want?' is what it said. What I wanted was him. It was on that day that I recorded his death in my journal."

"What did Vadim say when you gave birth to a son who was not his?"

"Vadim and I had long since stopped being lovers and become comrades. About Saava, he was very chic. He always treated him as if he were his own son."

"What happened between you and Vadim? What went wrong?"

"He retained his insolence, but lost his sense of humor. In order to make people laugh he was reduced to telling jokes." Aïda smiled wistfully. "It is not possible"—she slowly shook her head and repeated the phrase as if she were reminding herself of a fact of life—"to survive in Russia without a sense of humor."

Nibbling on one of the sandwiches, Ben noticed that a young woman sitting alone at another table was glancing furtively at his companion. The young woman, gathering her courage, scraped back her chair and approached their table. She offered a ball-point pen and a small notebook to

Aïda. "I am a great fan of yours, Zinaïda Ivanovna. Would you give me an autograph?"

Aïda scribbled her name in the notebook. "I will treasure this for the rest of my life," the young woman announced with great seriousness. Half-bowing, she backed away from the table.

Ben, flustered, asked, "Are you famous?"

Aïda laughed. "Pasternak said to be famous is indecent," she replied. "To answer your question, I am slightly indecent."

"What kind of things do you sing?"

"I said I was a singer in a manner of speaking. What I do is rummage in the debris of language. I listen to silence. What I am is a poet."

Ben was impressed. "If I knew your family name, could I find your books?"

"I had one collection published years ago, but it has long since gone out of print. I have been told that one of those new private publishing houses is ready to bring out a collected works, but I will believe it when I see it. I do translations of poems, always from the American, always by women poets—Emily Dickinson is my special passion. Some of my less controversial poems are occasionally taken by journals. When you met me I had come from collecting money for two poems being published by *Novy Mir*. I am often invited to read my poems. I never refuse. What fame I have comes from that."

Aïda popped another sandwich into her mouth and washed it down with a gulp of wine. Ben asked, "What is it about your controversial poems that makes them controversial?"

Aïda thought about this. "They are about the one subject still taboo in Russia despite *glasnost* and the new openness in the press, and that is sex. My point of view, it goes without saying, is feminist. I am all for liberating men from the straitjacket of the Party, but I want also to liberate men from the straitjacket of the penis, and women from the straitjacket of men. My future ex claims that I am the founder and only member of the tiniest splinter group in the Soviet Union, which is to say the feminist movement."

Ben said, "How did you become a feminist? How did you become a poet?"

Aïda raised a hand and signaled the waiter to bring the check. "I did not *become* a feminist or a poet," she explained impatiently. In her experience men usually made the same mistake. "I have always been a feminist and a poet. God planted the seed of feminism within my body when He created me. As for poetry, everyone in Russia is a poet in the sense that, for the last seventy years, everything really important has been said between the lines. Even as a small child I was mesmerized by the spaces between the lines, between the words, which is what I meant when I spoke about listening to silence. Poetry is what is hidden in the spaces between the lines, between the words."

A blizzard of snow was falling on Moscow when they pushed through the revolving door to the street. Aïda, accustomed to the weather, wrapped her fox tightly around her neck, pulled on her gloves and turned to leave. Ben, squinting into the snow, shouted over the storm. "Can I see you again, Aïda?"

She turned back. "That is simply not possible."

"Why?"

Flashing a wistful half-smile, Aïda studied the ground, stamped her feet on the thin layer of sanded ice, then raised her eyes to gaze directly into Ben's. Flakes had caked his brows, turning them white. She had a vision of what he would look like as an old man. "My life is complicated enough," she called over the storm. "I do not want to complicate it further by sleeping with an American, and a diplomat to boot."

Ben was not prepared for her bluntness. "I was not proposing that we sleep together. Only that we meet, that we get to know each other."

"I am as direct as Vadim in things that concern bodily functions," Aïda announced. "You are interested in my body, or at least the body you have imagined under all

AN AGENT IN PLACE

these layers of clothing. I have a garden of lust of my own, which means I am not uninterested in your body." Peering into the pupils of his eyes, two points of darkness in a sea of olive green, she was struck by their feverish alertness. For some reason his eyes seemed familiar. "Your head seems relatively interesting too. If you propose another meeting and I accept, what would it be for except to get involved? The sex act, the act of sex, is what we both have in mind. Why pretend otherwise? So: We would meet again, we would circle each other for a suitable length of time, hunting for points we have in common— 'What a coincidence we both love *Tosca*!'—in order to create the illusion of a connivance. You would use every trick in the book to convince me that you were not violent so that I would not be afraid to collaborate in what is essentially a violent act."

"If you really believe all that," Ben shouted, "why did you come with me today?"

"I came with you because you made me laugh," she called. "You will have guessed by now that I have not laughed in a long time." She sniffed at the air, testing the coldness in her nostrils, then shivered and hugged herself, almost as if she were holding herself together. It dawned on Ben that it was her body language, more than her body, that accounted for her incredible sensuality. "There is another reason I agreed to come with you," she added, elevating her chin a notch. One of the whimsical smiles that Ben was starting to recognize appeared on her lips. "I love the American accent. I love to hear the language of Emily Dickinson spoken as she might have spoken it."

Squinting into the falling snow, Ben studied her broken nose alive with freckles; he decided to memorize one thing about her every time they met—if they ever met. He shouted, "I can make you laugh again."

Aïda turned her head into the blizzard and closed her eyes, savoring the icy crystals that melted on her lids. Presently she turned back to Ben. "I would be lying if I said I was not tempted." She offered her hand. "Thank you, but no thank you."

An old man with a scarf wound over his mouth and nose walked between them going toward the revolving door. As soon as he was past Ben grasped her hand in both of his. He noticed traces of what looked like tears on her cheeks, then realized they were melted crystals of snow. Suddenly he felt himself spiral out of character. A flash flood of words that he might have spoken in a previous incarnation gushed out before he knew what he was saying. "I hope to Christ we do not meet again!"

Aïda was stunned. What he had said, the ardor with which he had said it, the mystery hidden in the spaces between his words, pierced her chest, and she found herself short of breath. Everything that had gone before had been conversation; seduction. But his valediction had cut to a marrow, bared a nerve. She searched his eyes for the meaning of his cryptic announcement, but all she saw was a feverish alertness amid the traces of a riot of emotions. Accepting his fervor with a delicate smile that for the first time mounted, like a tide creeping in, as far as her gray animal eyes, she snapped a sliver of ice from the revolving door and sucked on it, then leaned forward and brushed her blue lips against his. Before he realized what had happened she had spun away from his clumsy effort to put an arm around her and plunged into the freezing Kuchkovo night.

Adrift on the steps in the suddenly silent storm, Ben watched her white feather vanish among the giant clots of snow drifting lazily through the yellowish beams of street lights.

AïDA CROUCHED NEXT to the wicker chair, feeding broth to her father a spoonful at a time, wiping with a kitchen towel the drops that spilled down the stubble on his chin. Ivan's eyes were riveted on her as he ate. When he had finished, she set aside the bowl and picked up a plate of kasha mixed with small bits of fatty sausage. The old man pulled his head back. "Eat some of it," Aïda whispered. "It is good for you."

Barely moving his lips, he said in a rasping voice, "Do

not lose any part of your body if you can avoid it." He held out his trembling fingers for her to see. The tips of all of them were scarred, deformed, twisted, the nails missing. They had been pulled out, his fingers had been crushed, by NKVD interrogators. "These are not my fingers," the old man said matter-of-factly. "Mine were quite different."

Aïda looked out of the window so he would not see her reaction. She remembered the riot of emotions on the face of the strange American she had met that day; she wondered what secret had pushed him to hope they would never meet again. His eyes had seemed so familiar. It suddenly came to her where she had seen them before. The American reminded her of her Polish lover—they both had a wall of lucidity that had to be razed before you could get at their lust.

Images wheeled in her brain. She discovered words to describe them.

> I have hung on words you left unsaid,
> Been moved to tears by tears you left unshed,
> Caught your heart's ache through the snow's storm,
> As proof I tender—my iced lips for you to warm.

Putting her emotions into poetry made her better able to control them. She turned back to her father. "What about a homemade yogurt to finish off the meal?" When he did not refuse, she began feeding him yogurt by the spoonful. Between swallows he summoned a disturbing memory. "You were a very small girl at the time," he told her. "Not more than five or six. When we rented the room to him we had no idea he had been a White Russian, and an admiral. How could we have been expected to know such a thing? They moved in, the admiral, his wife and his wife's sister, only she wasn't his wife's sister, she was his mistress and they were a *ménage à trois* as the French say, all old, all gray haired, one of the women hobbling on crutches with her face painted, the old admiral scurrying around like a rat trying to find food for them to eat or coal for them to burn."

"I remember them very well," Aïda reminded her father. "It was the first time in my life I had ever seen a woman use makeup. The one who claimed to be his wife's sister spent hours every day painting her lips to look as if she were pouting, painting her eyes to look wide and innocent. Once, when I was eleven, I decided to paint my lips with Mercurochrome in order to look like her. When you came home and saw what I had done you slapped my face. Then you scrubbed it."

"They had somehow been overlooked," Aïda's father droned on, "the old admiral, his wife, the sister who was not a sister. But one day they came and took all three of them away in a bread truck that was not a bread truck. For me it was the beginning of the end." He shook his head again and again, trying to figure out how he had allowed it to happen.

Aïda wiped her father's chin with the dish towel and got up and set the empty yogurt cup on a table. "I remember I stuttered when I was a child," she said. "The woman on crutches, the one with the eyes made up to look innocent, used to imitate my stutter to tease me. 'Zinaïd-d-d-da's c-c-come b-b-back,' she would say. The day they took her away she was stuttering for real. 'G-g-god prot-t-t-tect us,' she cried. I remember thinking she had taken my stutter with her. So: I never stuttered again."

From the street came a muffled shout, then the sound of a car door slamming. The old man strained forward, taut in his wicker chair. "Have they finally gotten around to me?" he whispered. He scraped the chair closer to the window and peered into the night that had settled over the city like a lid. Aïda was reminded of two lines from the Irish poet Yeats:

> *When one looks into darkness*
> *there is always something there.*

She came up behind her father. Through the double panes of the window she could see two men tying a couch onto the roof of a small automobile. She rested a hand on her father's shoulder, felt his muscles relax under her touch.

"Good night to you, Father," she said, knowing that he was just starting his vigil; that the night, like the thousands that had gone before it, would be anything but good for him.

8

Flashing what Manny took to be a government-issue smile, Miss Macy thumbed the lever on the intercom. "Your nine o'clock is here, Mr. Inkermann," she announced.

Manny Custer realized that his daily briefing session with the CIA station chief had gotten off to a sour start (again!) when he heard Charlie Inkermann's testy nasal whine spurt over the tiny speaker. "He is ten fucking minutes late," the voice complained.

"What kept you?" Inkermann growled as Manny, casually kicking the door closed behind him, ambled into the shadowy inner sanctum with its sealed venetian blinds. "In case you have not remarked on it, I run a taut ship."

Inkermann slouched in front of a Teletype machine, the bald spot on the top of his head flashing an indecipherable Morse message as it caught the light from a flickering overhead fluorescent fixture. He scanned the printout, letting the paper uncoil through his stubby fingers, pursing his lips and whistling quietly through them as he took in an item that annoyed him. To Manny's ear it sounded like a kettle coming to a boil.

It was not the first time he had heard this particular kettle approach boil. Their paths had first crossed in the late seventies when Manny returned to the Company's home base in Langley, Virginia, after two back-to-back tours in Turkey; with the help of two Cossack smugglers working out of Rostov-on-Don, twins known in the trade as the Brothers Karamazov, he had run more than two hundred agents across the Soviet Union's heavily guarded southern frontier. Even then Inkermann—at Langley, Manny's immediate superior in a long-range intraoffice project evaluating second-echelon Soviet leaders—had liked to say he ran a taut ship, though his idea of a taut ship was to set impossible deadlines and mutter salty obscenities (learned, Manny suspected, while rowing for Harvard) when they were not met. The few grudging words of praise that escaped his lips were invariably sprinkled like salt in open wounds. Things had come to a head in 1979 when Manny flatly refused Inkermann's order to water down his written assessment of a new candidate member of the ruling Politburo named Mikhail Gorbachev, whom Manny saw as a potential Dubcek-like reformer. Inkermann, intent on delivering a more pessimistic evaluation that would support the case for an eternally belligerent Soviet leadership and higher military and intelligence budgets, forced Manny to resign. Manny had made a number of diplomat friends during his years abroad and was quickly picked up by the State Department Security Office and posted to Bonn. When the ambassador there was transferred to Moscow he had invited Manny, whom he admired as a no-nonsense security chief who would not tie an embassy in knots looking for security violations, to tag along with him. When the current ambassador came on board he had inherited Manny, by then something of a fixture in Moscow, along with the furniture. Judging from the fitness reports he filed on Manny, he seemed to prefer the furniture to an outspoken security chief who said precisely what he thought.

Delicately running the palm of his hand over his slicked-back hair, Inkermann lowered himself into the swivel chair behind the desk. Out of the corner of an eye he watched Manny pull over a chair and sink into it, his legs stretched out and crossed at his thick ankles, a great expanse of sickly white skin visible above his socks, his hands clasped behind his head, his sports jacket parted like a curtain, the shirt buttons straining in their holes against a swelling stomach, the expression on his martyr's face as arrogant as ever. "The ambassador's wife is going straight up the wall over the piano-string caper," Inkermann said. He rummaged in an oversize in-basket that looked like a compost heap and came up with a handwritten note, which he waved at Manny. "She says she's sure the F string didn't break by accident. She says the Russkies knew she had personally invited the piano player. She says they somehow sneaked one of their agents into Spaso House before the concert and weakened the string so that it would break when he started tickling the ivories. She says that it was all part of a scheme to humiliate her husband, the ambassador, and discourage cultural contacts. She says what are you doing to make sure it doesn't happen again?"

Manny snickered. "I could always post an armed marine next to the piano twenty-four hours a day."

Inkermann eyed Manny suspiciously. "How can you be positive the Russkies didn't break the string? I mean *glasnost* or no *glasnost*, our friends over at the KGB are still drawing their paychecks. For all we know they have an entire section that does nothing but try to figure out how to annoy the ambassador's wife."

Manny said, "You're not serious."

Inkermann announced gravely, "If the ambassador's wife is serious, I am serious."

"I examined the piano string under a magnifying glass," Manny said tiredly. "There was no sign of it having been clipped or filed."

"You are an expert on such things, I take it."

"We are going to look goddamn silly shipping a piece of piano wire off to Washington for analysis."

"How come you never show up at the Spaso House concerts or lectures?"

Manny brought the back of a hand to his mouth and suppressed a yawn. "The Russians have a word for people like me. It's *nekulturni.*" In his most condescending voice he added, "That means uncultured."

"I don't need a translation," Inkermann remarked stiffly. "I took the same Foreign Service Russian course you did." He plucked a pen from a holder and printed "Action" on the top of the note from the ambassador's wife. Then, reading out the words as his pen scratched across the paper, he wrote, "Custer will personally supervise preparations for all Spaso House cultural events as well as be present at these events."

The station chief scrawled "Ink" for Inkermann in the upper-right-hand corner of the letter and tossed it into an oversize out-basket. "From this moment in time on," he informed Manny, "whatever goes wrong at Spaso House happens on your watch. You check the piano before a recital, you check the slide projector before a lecture. You start tomorrow. Some Russian or other has been invited over to read poems. You check the microphone to make sure it's working, you check the radiators to make sure they're hot, you check the drinks to make sure they haven't been spiked, you check the toilets to make sure they flush. You never know, Custer. Someone with your sensitivity could wind up liking poetry."

Manny, never one to let his emotions show, took shelter behind a thin smile. "Whatever," he mumbled. Inkermann, who as chief of station was in overall charge of embassy security, had already reduced him to warning new arrivals that walls had ears, to spinning combination dials after working hours to make sure the safes had been properly locked. Now he was trying to humiliate him further, to push him into retiring before his tour was up. Manny took a grim pleasure from hanging in; from surviving.

If Moscow was going to be Custer's last stand, at least he would go out in style.

KUCHKOVO (AS AÏDA CALLED MOSCOW) was shrouded in soot-like dusk by the time she reached the Kremlin hospital not far from what she referred to as Trinity Square (the old name for Red Square). Wiping the slush off her galoshes on the pages of *Pravda* spread on the linoleum floor immediately inside the revolving door, she joined the queue that stretched the length of a dirty-gray corridor, rounded a corner and continued on past the bank of elevators, only one of which was in working condition. No matter how many times Aïda waited on line here—and she had queued once a week every week for the past six years—she never grew accustomed to the odors. Some weeks the corridor reeked of urine or vomit or ether, but most of the time the stench of disinfectant was so sharp it overpowered the other smells, stinging her nostrils, bringing tears to her eyes. Still, nobody who was fortunate enough to be on the line ever uttered a word of complaint —about its length, about the odors. For at the end of the long, dim corridor was the door to the hospital pharmacy, and the unsmiling white-coated women who distributed Western prescription drugs to those well connected enough or rich enough or lucky enough to have the appropriate authorization.

Aïda had the appropriate authorization—a sheet of paper that had been folded and unfolded so many times it felt as soft to the touch as an old handkerchief. It had been obtained for her by her future ex-husband, Vadim, the same way he had found the apartment with a separate bedroom for her son and another for her father, the same way he had wangled her the six-day cure at a rest home in the Crimea when her nerves were about to give out; the same way he got whatever he wanted: By getting people to return the favors he had done for them, and when that did not work, by paying in American dollars or British pounds or French francs. When Vadim was sober, Aïda's attempts to express gratitude always irritated him. "The less said the better," he would reply, waving her thanks away with an embarrassed sweep of an arm. "Russia is a rat race. I just happen to be the fastest rat in town. Ha!"

At the window up ahead, a white-haired woman whom Aïda recognized as a regular in the corridor was arguing shrilly with one of the white-coated pharmacists. "How can that be?" the woman cried. "My daughter has been taking this drug for three years. Without it she will need cataract surgery."

The pharmacist, a cranky time server with several steel teeth glistening in her small, tight mouth, shrugged listlessly. "I fill prescriptions if the drug in question is available. If not, not. You got a complaint, take it up with the administrators."

When Aïda's turn finally came she carefully unfolded the letter of authorization and held it up for the pharmacist to read. "Has his weight changed?" the pharmacist asked in a bored voice. She glanced at the wall clock to see how long it would be before the night shift came on.

Aïda said, "It is the same as it was last week, thirty kilos. His dose is two point five milligrams multiplied by his weight."

"I can read," the pharmacist commented sullenly. She disappeared behind the shelves crammed with imported drugs. Aïda caught a glimpse of her spilling pills onto a glass tray and counting them out with a spatula. The pharmacist returned a few moments later with a small brown paper satchel filled with pills. She shook a ball-point pen to start the ink flowing and filled in a gummed label, then licked the gummed side and slapped it onto the satchel.

Aïda read the label, which said, "Purinethol, 75 milligrams of 6-mercaptopurine, to be taken orally at supper each day." A tide of relief swept through her chest; the devil could be kept at arm's length for another seven days. "You are sure you gave me enough for the week?" she asked. She forced a smile onto her face, hoping it would keep the pharmacist from becoming irked by the question.

It didn't. "If you don't have confidence in the service

here you can always take your business elsewhere," the pharmacist muttered. She stared arrogantly into Aïda's face, knowing there was no place else to go in Moscow for foreign prescription drugs. Aïda lowered her gaze, counted out five one-ruble bills from a small purse and laid them soundlessly on the counter.

Scooping up the rubles, the pharmacist looked over Aïda's shoulder and called, "Next?"

9

The room Inkermann put at Ben's disposal, one of four giving off the outer office, had been used as the CIA station's storage area. Most of the contents had been removed before Ben arrived, but one entire wall was still piled high with cartons of ribbons for the station's IBM typewriters. It was standard operating procedure to discard used ribbons in burn bags at the end of every workday so there would be no traces of the secret messages or reports that had been typed up. The fact that the station budgeted more for typewriter ribbons than for all other office supplies put together never failed to astonish the accountant from the Office of Budget Management who audited the books.

"How do you manage to spend $10,180 a year on typewriter ribbons?" he would ask the station chief.

"Easy," Inkermann would answer, his pudgy face totally devoid of human expression. "We use IBM ribbons instead of tinsel on the office Christmas tree."

Ben had to smile when Inkermann's secretary, Mehetabel Macy, told him the story by way of apologizing for the boxes of ribbons in his cramped quarters. "We wouldn't want our four fifteen to be uncomfortable," she said with exaggerated sweetness. She lingered with her back against the jamb of the open office door, her skirt hiked up on her thighs, her long legs crossed at the ankles, one toe suggestively dipping in and out of a suede shoe.

"As long as there's room for a table and chair," Ben assured her, "I'll get by."

She held out an index card to Ben. "The top number is the code for the electronic lock on the door," she explained breathlessly. "The bottom one is for the safe. Don't change either of them—if, God forbid, anything were to happen to you, we would want to be able to get our hot hands on your little secrets."

Ben took the card. "Thanks." He stood gazing at her until, with a birdlike flutter of her narrow shoulders, she pivoted on a heel and headed for her desk. "For God's sake," she called, "don't be bashful about asking me if you need anything." She seemed to give the word *anything* a special twist.

Ben looked around at what the half dozen agents assigned to the station called the "ribbon room," then went to work. He set out the station's cipher log on the small metal table, along with the thin notebook that had been in the sealed attaché case shipped to him from Washington, and started to plow through the station chief's backlist of enciphered Sensitive Compartmented Information cables for 1967.

Brushing off Miss Macy's flirtatious forays ("Well, if it isn't our bashful four fifteen slumming on the tenth floor!"), Ben managed to spend an hour a day most weekdays, and an hour and a half a day most weekends, in the ribbon room. It was slow going—but it was meant to be slow going. Following very precise instructions, he was careful to get Ironweed off to an unhurried start. "It's essential not to rush things once you're in Moscow," the nuts-and-bolts man had warned him at the last briefing session before he left for his first posting in Czechoslovakia. "You want to take your sweet time working through the cables."

Late one Saturday afternoon, after spending a boring hour and a half in the ribbon room, Ben headed for the New Office Building around the corner from the embassy to see if the thermal underwear he had ordered from Finland had arrived. A blast of arctic air hit him as he left the embassy; the cold seemed to invade the folds of his sheepskin overcoat. Two Soviet militiamen, their collars up, their ear flaps down, their cheeks burning from the subzero temperature, nodded stiffly when he passed. The last brittle beams of midwinter sunlight were grazing the rooftops as Ben picked his way along the sanded street. A vendor wearing tinted plastic ski goggles had set up a makeshift stand on the corner and was selling hazelnuts by the handful to people waiting for the trolley. A dozen peasant women in thick quilted overcoats tied with rope belts, their heads hidden in washed-out shawls, were half-heartedly chipping away at the ice in front of a drab government building. Seeing the sparks of ice flying off in all directions brought back to Ben the bizarre gesture of the woman who rummaged in the debris of language, who listened to the silences in the spaces between words. In his mind's eye he recreated the contours of her broken nose alive with freckles, saw her sucking on the sliver of ice, felt her blue lips brush lightly against his, watched her white feather disappear amid the falling crystals of snow.

Ben had relived the brief encounter a dozen times. There had been something about her that was both haunted and hunted. She had been beaten down by the system (he remembered her story of having learned English in prison), but had managed to achieve a measure of nobility by continuing to war against it. Was she, like him, an aficionado of lost causes? Would this have been one of the points they found in common if they had taken the trouble to search? There were moments when he bitterly regretted letting her slip out of his grasp; slip out of his life. There were other moments when he really hoped to Christ they would not meet again.

Inside the New Office Building, Ben thumped his feet
on a mat to get the slush off his boots. There was a hint of
frustration in the enthusiasm he invested in the gesture.
Shaking his head to clear away the vision of Aïda, he
looked up to find himself face-to-face with Manny Custer.
"There was this Frog, name of Voltaire," Manny said in a
lazy drawl that he slipped into whenever he was afraid of
sounding too highbrow. "He was on his deathbed, so the
story goes, so it was told to me, and some priest was trying
to talk him into denying the devil. And this Voltaire character, you know what he went and told the priest? He told
him"—Manny didn't try to cap the mocking laugh that
seeped from his lips—" 'This is not the time to make enemies.' "

Ben was at a loss and his expression showed it. "Why
are you telling me this?"

Manny shrugged a heavy shoulder. It had been a long
week and it was not over yet. "I thought you would read
the story the same way I do."

Ben grinned. "You mean, as if there is ever a time to
make enemies?"

"Whatever," Manny agreed. "I'm on my coffee break,
only I don't drink coffee. Come on. I'll break a golden rule
and buy you one for the road."

Except for a couple of code clerks and the man who ran
the embassy's automobile pool, Sam's Lounge, down the
wide hallway inside the New Office Building, was deserted. Sliding his bulky body into a booth, Manny called
to the bartender, "The usual scotch on the usual rocks,
followed by the usual chaser, huh?"

"Two," said Ben.

"Two usual scotches on the usual rocks, two chasers,"
repeated Manny.

When the bartender had set the drinks on the table
Ben said, "You're right, of course. About it always being
the wrong time to make enemies. I'm sorry if I rubbed
you the wrong way at that security briefing of yours. I
know you have a job to do. On the other hand, you seem

to treat *perestroika* and *glasnost* as if it were all a Communist plot to lull us to sleep."

Manny massaged his pitted nose with the side of his glass. "If I remember right, you are a Russian speaker. You know the word *peredyshka*?"

"Breathing space," Ben said.

Manny shook the ice in his glass so that it tinkled musically. "You want my opinion, what the Russians are after isn't *perestroika,* but *peredyshka.* The economy is an unholy mess. They're buying time to put their house in order. After which the Cold War could—I don't say will, I say could—start up again." Manny knocked back the rest of his drink. "You want evidence? Your *glasnost* and your *perestroika* notwithstanding, the KGB as far as I know is still doing business at the same stand."

"So is the CIA."

"And so am I."

"So nothing has changed?"

Manny pushed his empty glass to one side and attacked the chaser, a mug of pale beer. "What I think is: Until all this *perestroika* business irons itself out one way or another, we have got to be careful not to let down our guard. The Russia I know and don't particularly love is a country where anarchy lurks just under the surface—along with thirty-eight thousand nuclear warheads." Ben tried to interrupt, but the embassy's security chief raised his voice and plunged on. "I know what you're going to say. You're going to say, what about all the reforms. Look, nobody knows if these reforms are for real. Even assuming they're for real, nobody knows if they can work. What we do know is there's a lot of folks out there"—Manny let his voice sink into a husky stage whisper—"on both sides of what used to be called the Iron Curtain, right, waiting for the Great Houdini and company to fall on their fat faces. Me, I don't think he's going to be able to turn the ball game around, but I'm all for giving him a fair shot at it."

Squinting at his guest, Manny drained his mug of beer. Ben realized the security officer had had more than one

for the road. "Listen," Manny continued, wiping foam off
his lips with the back of his hand, "I was one of the first to
say that the Great Houdini had the makings of a reformer,
and I got into hot water for saying it. I might not want to
come right out and admit it in so many words—hell,
changing colors isn't easy for an old cold warrior like me
—but in my own way I'm even rooting for him. What the
hell? Your average Russian is as nice as your average
American, and they sure stored up points in heaven
knocking off the Nazis. I remember reading somewhere
that ten out of every thirteen Germans killed during the
war bought it on the Russian front. So they earned their
chance, that's what I say." Manny leaned across the table
and winked at Ben. "But take a tip from an old pro, Mr.
Bassett. Keep your powder dry."

Manny leaned back and rubbed the ball of his forefinger around the rim of his mug several times, then, sighing,
checked his watch. "Jesus, I got to go." He tucked several
bills under the empty mug. "I'm off to baby-sit some poet
at Spaso House," he said, sliding out of the booth, pulling
his overcoat and fur hat after him.

"Is there a reading?" asked Ben.

"You have a soft spot for Russian poets, Mr. Bassett?"

"I have a soft spot for Russian poetry," Ben retorted.

"I have a feeling you're full of soft spots." Manny
hovered over Ben, his head cocked, eyeing him suspiciously. "Tell me something, Mr. Bassett. What is it you
really do at the embassy?"

Ben's pulse stirred. "I keep house for the Seven
Dwarfs."

"That being the case, what brings you up to Inkermann's bailiwick so often?"

Ben forced a grin onto his face. "You really do keep
your ear to the ground."

"The marine who checks your green badge on the ninth
floor writes your name in a log."

"Part of my housekeeping chores include enciphering
status reports," Ben explained. "I can't store the ciphers
downstairs because it's a white-badge area, so Mr. Inker-

mann loaned me the use of his ribbon room. It has a safe, and a table to work on."

"The housekeeper before you didn't do enciphering. The Dwarfs had one of the code clerks in the bubble working part-time for them."

"I kill two birds with one stone. Less strain on the budget."

"You never told me you were trained in ciphers."

"You never asked."

Manny, suddenly very sober, studied Ben and grunted. "That is correct. I never asked. But I am asking now."

"I was trained by Army Intelligence in the manly art of enciphering and deciphering. Why all the questions?"

Coughing up a belly laugh, Manny thrust his arms into the sleeves of his overcoat and hiked it onto his shoulders. "Just keeping my powder dry."

AïDA GLANCED AT THE HANDS that ran counterclockwise on her tiny wristwatch. She had intended to stop when the hour was up, but something she preferred not to examine too closely was pushing her to read one more. "Do I have time, do you have patience, for a last poem?" she asked the fifty or so Americans gathered in the ballroom of the ambassador's official residence, Spaso House.

"By all means," the ambassador, who spoke fluent Russian and was translating her poems into English, told her. Miss Harkenrider, sitting on a folding chair in the first row, started clapping rhythmically, and the other women in the audience took it up. Aïda adjusted her round steel-rimmed eyeglasses. The Americans in the ballroom settled down. Shuffling through her papers, Aïda found the poem she wanted—some lines scratched on the back of a napkin—before she knew she was looking for it, which reinforced the sensation she had of going through motions that were predestined. Her eyes fixed on the napkin, she said a few words about the poem. The ambassador asked her in what sense she was using a particular Russian idiom, and when she told him, he repeated the gist of her remarks in English. "She describes this poem as a freshly

plucked plant, so fresh that you will be the first to hear it.
She says the act of listening to a poem is what gives it life.
Rather than tell you more, she invites you to interpret the
poem into life." He turned to Aïda expectantly.

She had spotted him the instant he appeared, pushing
through the double door at the back of the ballroom halfway through her first poem, his long sheepskin overcoat
(every detail engraved itself on her brain) still on but
open, a hat, a scarf, a package wrapped in brown paper
tucked under an arm, his dark hair, disheveled the one
time she had seen him, flattened from having worn the
hat, his lips parted in astonishment (so she imagined, so
she hoped) at seeing her again. He had stood next to a
heavyset man who kept scowling at his wristwatch after
every poem. His back was against the wall, his body taut.
His eyes, riveted on hers, seemed to put an unspoken
question.

The poem would be her answer.

She recited it in Russian in a still flat voice, letting the
spaces between the words convey the emotion she hoped
was there. After she had read it a second time, the ambassador—who had been scrawling a rough translation on a
yellow note pad—looked up and said in English, "I don't
think I'll be giving away the plot if I tell you this is a love
poem. I hope I can do it justice." And he translated it into
English:

> I have hung on words you left unsaid,
> Been moved to tears by tears you left unshed,
> Caught your heart's ache through the snow's storm,
> As proof I tender—my iced lips for you to warm.

When the applause died away people began drifting
over to the long table covered with zakusky and bottles of
Georgian wine. With the ambassador trailing in her wake,
Aïda plowed through the group like an icebreaker (so it
seemed to Manny Custer, watching from the wall) and
helped herself to several wedges of toast covered with
caviar. A group gathered around her. The ambassador of-

fered her a glass of wine and raised his own glass to her. "To Russian poets," he declared, "who kept the flame alive."

Aïda thought about this. "Some did, some did not," she replied dryly in her accented English, "but I must anyhow drink to your toast because I am thirsty."

The Americans around Aïda laughed. The cultural attaché who had invited her asked, "Aside from the fact that one is composed in English and the other in Russian, do you see a difference between American poetry and Russian poetry?"

Aïda noticed Ben at the edge of the group. He let his eyes drift up in their sockets to indicate what he thought of the question. Aïda, feeling the irresistible pull of a conspiracy, fought the urge to respond with a laugh. "American poetry," she told the cultural attaché, her face serious, her eyes dancing with amusement, "wants to be horizontal, which is to say it treats people as if they were beautiful items in one of those postal order catalogues published by your Mr. L. Bean. The result more often than not is poetry who skates on the surface of thin ice. Our Russian poetry wants to be vertical, which is to say it runs risks, it plunges to the heart of the belly of the whale, it explores how people live and love, and how they die."

"Did my translations capture the verticality of your poems?" the ambassador inquired.

"The poetry, whether vertical or horizontal, is what's usually lost in translation," Ben commented over the heads of those in front of him. Several of the embassy people, Manny Custer among them, turned to stare at him. "I mean," Ben added, looking at everyone but Aïda, "how can you translate the spaces between the words."

"I don't see what the spaces between the words has to do with poetry," the ambassador objected sourly.

"That's where the poetry is," Ben insisted.

"That is more or less how I would describe it," agreed Aïda. She and Ben exchanged looks. "In the spaces between the words is where you must hunt for the poetry."

The ambassador, glancing from Aïda to Ben and back,

said, "American poets may be skating on thin ice, but our critics are plunging—how did you put it?—to the heart of the belly of the whale."

Aïda got into a long discussion with the ambassador's wife about the feminist movement in Russia, or more precisely the reasons why there was none. When she looked around for Ben, he had disappeared. Helping her on with her coat later, the cultural attaché offered her a ride home in an embassy car, but Aïda said she preferred to take the metro and the attaché—aware that many Russians still did not want to be seen getting in or out of an embassy car—didn't press her.

The night was crystalline cold as Aïda headed back along the peripheric toward the Gorki Street metro stop and the train that would take her to Rechnoi Vokzal at the end of the line and her rendezvous with Vadim on the boat. Several blocks from the embassy a figure materialized out of the darkness. One instant she was alone, the next Ben was walking in lock step beside her. "How do you know about the Bean catalogue?" he asked as if he were picking up the thread of an interrupted conversation.

"It is because of my future ex," she said. She tried to keep her voice from betraying her excitement; it had been a while since her pulse had been set to throbbing by the presence of a man, as opposed to an idea. "Vadim is what we call an operator—he has a dozen irons in a dozen fires. So: Every now and again, against my will, he insists on offering presents to my son. Last year on Saava's name day Vadim gave him one of Mr. L. Bean's catalogues, God only knows how he organized it, and told him he could have one thing in it. Saava agonized over the choice for a week. He made up his mind a dozen times only to change it at the last moment."

Ben slipped his arm through hers. "The first time I saw you I wanted to make love to the body I imagined under all those layers of clothing," he said. "Only when you had disappeared into the storm of snow did it dawn on me that I could fall in love with you."

She could feel his elbow pressing against her rib cage. For once in her life she was at a loss for words. "My son settled on a red knife with many blades that the catalogue said was used by soldiers in Switzerland," she continued. Her breath came in shallow gasps. "There was even a magnifying glass in it, though what a magnifying glass was doing in a knife I do not know."

"Did you hear what I said?"

She looked at him. "I heard what you said, yes. If you want to sleep with me you can come right out and say so without confusing lust and love." The dimple under her lower lip trembled. "Without confusing me in the process."

"I want to sleep with you—and more." When she didn't reply, Ben muttered, "For Christ's sake, say something."

Smiling the bittersweet smile that always appeared on her face when she quoted lines from Akhmatova, she recited:

> You have come ten years too late—
> I am glad to see you all the same.

Inside the metro station, Ben pulled off one of his gloves and inserted a five-kopeck coin in the turnstile. "Where are you taking me?" he asked Aïda.

"Anywhere," she murmured. Moving as if in a dream, she pushed through the turnstile. Inserting another coin, Ben pushed through after her. "Anywhere is where I will go with you," he declared with such intensity only a fool would have doubted his sincerity. As Russians racing for trains jostled past on either side, he peeled off her glove and grasped her hand in his and started to memorize it— her fingers were long and lean and rough, her nails cut short, her knuckles chapped. On her middle finger she wore a ring of beaten silver with some kind of stone set in it. "It is agate," she answered his question before he asked it. "It is said to banish fear, but so far it has not worked."

Caught in currents of Muscovites, they found themselves on a long escalator plunging into the earth. Ben descended to the step below Aïda and turned to face her.

Their eyes were on the same level. "What are you afraid of?" he asked.

Everything around Aïda seemed a blur. Only Ben remained in sharp focus. Studying his eyes, she was struck again by their feverish alertness; by their lucidity. Responding to his question, she offered an answer that had the texture, the tone of a sigh. "I am terrified of dying," she told him, "and weary to the bone of living. I am afraid of losing poetry. Of losing my son. Of losing my insanity, which in a manner of speaking is the source of my poetry." A half-smile saturated with pain appeared on her face. "I am afraid of hoping. Of desiring. Of giving myself without holding part of myself back." Waiting for a train to pull into the station, she shivered from something other than the cold and hugged herself. Leaning against him, she pressed her lips to his ear and whispered, "I am terrified of being loved and terrified of not being loved."

With Aïda leading the way, they got off at the last stop and headed toward the river through a narrow park sandwiched between clusters of apartment buildings. Neither spoke; there seemed to be too much to say. They passed under the arched entrance of the Maritime Station and made their way down the middle of a long road, with the shadows of woods on either side, until they came to the edge of the river and the fifteen or so sparkling white passenger ships tied up in twos to the pier. The ships were alive with lights, and humming with the sounds of motors and generators. The walkway was thick with ice and the footing was precarious. They held onto each other, and exchanged smiles when Aïda slipped and clung to Ben's arm to keep from falling. At the end of the pier several dozen automobiles and taxis were parked in front of a brightly lit ship with the name *Maxim Gorki* printed in large block letters on the hull. Many of the cars had drivers waiting in them, and motors running so that the heaters would work. In front of the gangway Aïda turned to Ben. "Vadim is a great capitalist," she explained quickly. "He and some of his friends leased the *Maxim Gorki* from the State under a new law intended for farmers who want to rent land, and turned it into a cooperative restaurant." She indicated the parked cars. "It has become a hangout for the new rich, the ones who, like Vadim, can squeeze money out of stone."

Ben followed Aïda through a door amidships into the ship's dining area. Inside the door a blast of warm air hit them. An emaciated teenage girl tottering about on high heels she was not accustomed to took their coats. From somewhere beyond a thick crimson curtain came the mournful whine of a gypsy violin playing Hungarian dances. A man with the pinched face and sunken eyes of an alcoholic pushed through the curtain and seized Aïda by the elbow. "You were supposed to be here at seven," he hissed.

"This is Vadim," Aïda started to say, but her future ex was already steering her through the curtain into the dining room. "He is waiting for you," he said under his breath. "In theory the deal is done. He has agreed to publish a book of your poems and I have agreed to add a sun porch to his *dacha* in Repino. Only, I ask it of you as a friend, be polite to him."

The lighting inside the restaurant was subdued and it took a moment before Ben could make anything out. He trailed after Aïda and Vadim, past booths crammed with men and women talking in undertones. The tables were heaped with piles of steaming blinis and two-kilo tins of black beluga caviar and bowls of cream and bottles of vodka and champagne and wine. Two waiters in black trousers and white shirts pushed past carrying trays heaped with fruit, something Ben had only seen in the special gastronome that supplied food to diplomats. Aïda reached for Ben's hand and pulled him toward a round table next to a floor-to-ceiling window in the far corner of the room. Outside, streaks of light from the docked boats skidded off the ice-covered surface of the Moscow River.

A fat man with a Chaplinesque mustache on his upper lip half-rose out of his chair at the sight of Aïda. The woman sitting next to him, dressed in a black lace dress that exposed half her bosom, grabbed the end of his tie to keep it from falling into a bowl of cream. The fat man reached for Aïda's hand and lightly grazed the back of it with his lips, which looked as if they had been rouged. "Vadim has told me a great deal about you," he confided in a silky whisper.

He sank back into his chair as if the effort to get half out of it had exhausted a reserve of energy. Vadim snapped his fingers. Waiters appeared with two more chairs, place settings and long-stemmed glasses filled with champagne.

Vadim plunked himself down next between Ben and the publisher, grasped the stem of a glass with shaking fingers and proposed a toast. "Now that we are all here, let us drink to private enterprise and your new publishing project."

The fat man flattened his mustache with the side of a finger. "My *maison d'édition* is honored to be charged with the publication of the poems of the legendary Zavaskaya."

"How many?" Aïda challenged.

The fat man cast a quick, dark glance at Vadim, then looked back at Aïda. "How many what?"

"How many poems are you prepared to include in the book? And how many books are you prepared to print?"

Vadim groaned. The fat man said, "The number of poems in the book must depend on the length of the poems, as well as the size of the type we decide on. As for the press run, we were thinking of something in the neighborhood of five thousand. How many poems were you planning to offer us?"

Smiling grimly, Aïda announced her terms. "Fifty poems. Set in ten-point type. With an appropriate amount of white space around the poems. In an edition of not less than twenty-five thousand copies."

The woman sitting next to the fat man nervously stuffed a blini into her mouth and washed it down with a mouthful of champagne. The publisher leaned back in his chair and pulled air in through enormous nostrils. His stomach seemed to bloat until it pressed against the edge of the table. "Fifty poems is out of the question," he said flatly. "We are a new publishing venture. Where would we get paper for an edition of fifty poems? Twenty, if the layout is tight, twenty-five even, is within the realm of possibility. In an edition of ten thousand."

"Forty poems in an edition of fifteen thousand is my absolute limit," Aïda said.

The violinist started to draw near the table, but Vadim waved him off. "Assuming that the numbers are negotiable," he said, "what are the other stumbling blocks?"

Aïda caressed the stem of her champagne glass. "There is the question of the quality of the paper. There is the matter of who has the final say on the selection of the poems."

The publisher's eyebrows slithered up on his forehead and remained there. He said to Vadim, "You led me to believe that I would be able to exercise editorial judgment when it came to the selection of the poems. You likewise led me to believe that Madame Zavaskaya was willing to tone down some of her more outrageous images—"

The stem of the champagne glass splintered between Aïda's fingers as she roared, "Outrageous images!" Conversation in the dining room, the whine of the gypsy violin, broke off. Heads swiveled. Sucking on a finger from which blood trickled, Aïda asked sarcastically, "So: If you consider the images in my poems so outrageous, what pushes you to publish them?"

Vadim shot a look at the violinist, who immediately started playing again. The fat publisher scraped back his chair and slowly levered himself to his feet. "My dear Vadim, thank you for a most delightful supper and the great pleasure of your company. Perhaps you can iron out the details with Madame Zavaskaya, in which case we can put our heads together at a later date."

Followed by his dinner companion, the publisher waddled down the aisle toward the door. Aïda reached for a bowl of cream and would have flung it at his broad back if Ben had not taken hold of her wrist.

Vadim started laughing. "Aïda is no *dzhentlman*," he

informed Ben. "Assuming you have aspirations in that direction, you will find her easier to live with if you let her act out her frustrations."

Ben was amused by the whole scene. "Thank you for the advice."

Still shaking with anger, Aïda reached for her tobacco and paper and began to roll a thin cigarette. "At least you will not have to build a sun porch for the bastard," she told Vadim.

A waiter reached over Aïda's shoulder with a lighted match and she sucked the cigarette into life. Eddies of dense smoke masked her face, which was still crimson with anger.

Vadim edged his chair nearer to Ben's. Kneading the warts on the back of his hand already raw from scratching, he said, "I could not help but notice you speak Russian with some kind of peculiar accent."

Aïda said, "He is an Israeli come to lead the Jews, you foremost among them, out of Russia to the Promised Land."

"For me," Vadim retorted, "America, not Israel, is the Promised Land." He eyed Aïda's new friend as if he were a potential client.

Ben said, "I am American."

Vadim's beady eyes blazed with interest. "Ah, an American!" he said in English. "I been to America the beautiful once. Too many years ago. America the beautiful is a country where people have one point eight children per family. That's quite a feat, having one point eight children! I myself prefer zero point zero children per family. Don't misunderstand me. I take the view that there is nothing wrong with children that not having them can't cure." He stopped talking long enough to smother a belch in his hand. "I was a member of a delegation who visited your famous Madison Street. You look like a man of the world. You have probably heard of Madison Street. That's where they run ideas up flagpoles and salute them."

Vadim snapped off a drunken salute as he downed the rest of his champagne. Clutching the bottle by the neck, squinting as he took aim, he sloshed more champagne into his glass, then leaned toward Ben. "Among my other business interests, I happen to be in the advertising game myself," he plunged on, slurring his words, batting his bloodshot eyes, rolling his head from side to side in his eagerness to make his English understood. "Only in Russia the ad game has a peculiar twist. Things which are well made are never advertised. They don't need to be. As soon as they go on sale word spreads, lines form, the item sells out in hours, even minutes. The advertising executive's job is to push the products that are *badly* made, that nobody will buy even if you sell them at a gigantic discount. Listen, a week doesn't go by without me being taken to warehouses to inspect mountains of coats without buttonholes, galoshes that aren't waterproof, electric heaters without heating coils, gloves that fit only left hands, belts without buckles, bicycles without pedals, wheels with defective spokes, fishing reels that don't rewind, bottled vinegar seasoned with dead ants. If an item has no selling point I make it sing. I try image advertising, which leaves people feeling good about the product. But in Russia none of the techniques I learned from Madison Street work, because everyone knows that if a product is advertised it means it is badly made and not selling. It's not as if people don't pay attention to advertisements. They pay a lot of attention. They watch advertisements in order to know what not to buy."

Aïda tried to interrupt. "I do not think Benedict is very interested in advertising."

"I am not talking about advertising," Vadim insisted. "I am talking about a sociological phenomenon." He scraped his chair still closer to his neighbor until their knees were touching. "I got into hot water during the period of stagnation, which is our usual euphemism for the period that precedes the present, for proposing an ad campaign to sell Marxism-Leninism to the masses. I ran the idea up a flagpole and they almost ran me up the flagpole after it. I am not making it up. This is not alcohol inventing. It's me talking what really happened. My bosses said to me I was trying to sabotage Marxism-Leninism by advertising it, since everybody would jump at the conclusion that if it was advertised there must be something wrong with it."

"The whole thing was Kafkaesque," Aïda remarked. "He barely talked them out of packing him off to Siberia for anti-Soviet activity."

Vadim peered into Ben's face. "You know the difference between a Communist and an anti-Communist?" he demanded. "A Communist is someone who has read Marx and Lenin. An anti-Communist is someone who has understood Marx and Lenin! Ha!"

"You have had a long day," Aïda told her husband in a comradely way. "You ought to go home."

But Vadim, once launched, was unstoppable. "I got another idea which is maybe worth millions," he confided to Ben with a smirk. "It's a campaign to advertise the most perfect product in the universe—the vagina. You look like a man of the world. You have probably heard of the vagina. Picture it: You start with a celebrity endorsement from someone with a high Q, maybe the first lady, maybe the Great Helmsman himself. Think of the verbatims you would get back when the masses out there heard him pitching its tangy odor, its soft furriness, its bittersweet taste." Smothering a hoarse laugh in the palm of a sweaty hand, Vadim suddenly turned morose; his eyes almost disappeared into his skull. "Except if the vagina was advertised everybody would assume it was a lousy product. It could mean the end of cunnilingus in Mother Russia. Ha! Maybe what we should do is leave oral sex to word of mouth." Exploding with glee at the play on words, Vadim flailed his raw hands around his head as if he were swatting mosquitoes.

"Trying to follow a conversation in English makes my head spin," Aïda announced after her future ex had finally stumbled off, leaning on the shoulder of the emaciated girl to keep from falling. "Vadim means well. His problem is that he enjoys playing more than scoring, he likes the journey more than the getting there. He is eternally along for the ride."

The dining room was beginning to empty. Calculating rates of exchange on an abacus, the emaciated girl was busy making change in dollars and pounds and francs and marks. Ben said, "It is difficult to imagine you falling in love with the Vadim I met tonight."

Aïda inspected the spot of coagulated blood on her finger. "Like everyone else," she told him, "Russians have multiple personalities. They show different faces to different people. The Vadim who pressed his face against the window and wrote in soap 'Will you marry me?' was not the Vadim you met tonight. There was a core of fearlessness, of gallantry, to him back then that could not be concealed by a torrent of glib cynicism. He joined the system and reduced it to *ad absurdum*. It is still there, that core, but it is hidden under layers of bruises and warts, physical and mental." She ran her fingertips lightly over the back of Ben's hand, examining a childhood scar. "You have not been in Russia long enough to understand that there are two realities, two sides to every personality and every situation. Two sides to Russia itself. Everything is exactly as it seems—but the opposite is also true. You have heard of our poet Voznesensky? One of his better poems deals with this phenomenon. It is called 'Antiworlds.'" Staring off into some middle distance, she resurrected several lines.

> *Long live antiworlds! They rebut*
> *With dreams the rat race and the rut.*

Ben asked with a curious smile, "Do you think there are two sides to me?"

Aïda appeared to exchange knowing looks with the fox at the end of her neckpiece. "Jung said somewhere that we are all trailed by a shadow self that is less inhibited by conventional morality than the so-called real self we present to the world. My pet fox, whom I call Pandora after the famous box which, when you opened it, had hope inside, has two sides to her. Why should you be different? Why should I, for that matter? The self I show to the

world would have flung a bowl of cream at that bastard of
a publisher. My shadow self, which I repress, could have
plunged a knife in his back."

The restaurant was empty now except for Aïda and
Ben, and the waiters clearing tables and setting out fresh
linen and silver. Yawning, the gypsy violinist fitted his in-
strument into a case, tucked it under his arm and, nibbling on a folded blini stuffed with caviar, headed for the
exit. Absently fingering a knife, Aïda examined a vertical
stripe of her face in the blade, then turned the blade to
examine the horizontal stripe of her eyes. Still looking at
herself in the knife blade, she said with sudden intensity,
"What you told me on the steps the other day about hoping we would never meet again"—she looked suddenly at
Ben—"it struck me as the most honest thing any man has
ever said to me. But why did you say it? What was behind
it?"

Ben's thoughts raced. It was not too late to get to his
feet and leave. But he was caught in the web of her anger,
her passion, her sensuality. He could feel a lust for life
radiating from the pores of her body. He wanted to push
the limits of intimacy to extremes with her; he harbored
the irrational desire not so much to penetrate her as to
take refuge in her. Looking at her now, it was hard to
imagine she had ever been young. No innocence remained, not a trace, in her eyes, in the melancholy half-
smile that created a fan of tiny wrinkles at the corners of
her mouth, in the dimple under her lower lip that trembled slightly with—what? Uncertainty? Fear? Fear of
fear?

Her question hung in the air between them. She was
waiting for an answer. "Through the snow's storm," he
said finally, "I caught *your* heart's ache. It frightened
me."

The skin around Aïda's eyes stiffened in disappointment. "I barely know you," she commented softly, "but I
can already tell when you are not cutting to the bone.
There is more to it than that. There is more to you than
meets the eye. One day you will tell me a truth as intently

as you did outside the café. I hope I will believe you when you do."

The emaciated girl brought word that, because of the extreme cold, Vadim had sent his taxi back for Aïda. He rented it by the year, paid whatever was on the meter at the end of every week, claimed that the arrangement was more convenient than owning an automobile and having to hunt for motor oil and gasoline and spare parts. Its engine idling, the taxi was waiting for them when they came down the gangway. Aïda was surprised to find a driver she did not know behind the wheel and said so. "Dmitri has the flu," the driver, who had enormous beet-red ear lobes, explained. "I am a friend of a friend."

"You trust him," Ben said in English, indicating with a flick of his head the back of the taxi driver.

Aïda answered in English. "He is driving Vadim's taxi," she said simply.

During the short ride back to Rechnoi Vokzal, Ben told her about his Russian roots; about his grandfather's warning that he would feel Russia pulling at him like gravity through the soles of his shoes; about majoring in Russian studies at university; about the master's thesis he wrote comparing Stalin before and after the suicide of his wife, Nadezhda. Aïda asked Ben if he had ever been married and he nodded yes. She asked him if he had any children. He nodded yes again. "A boy," he said. "His name is Felix."

She said, "You must miss him," but he only stared out the window at the branches of the trees weeping under the weight of the ice clinging to them.

She touched his arm. "How old is he?"

"He was six in January."

"That makes him a Capricorn," she noted. "My Saava is also a Capricorn. So am I. We are a family of Capricorns."

"Me, I'm an honorary Capricorn," the driver called over his shoulder. "That's what the wife says. It's because I always finish what I start, is why she says it."

At Rechnoi Vokzal, the taxi pulled up in front of the door of a shabby apartment building. Aïda looked up at her father's window, imagined him sitting rigid in his wicker chair, straining to see whether the car that had stopped in front of the building was filled with militiamen. Ben asked in a hushed voice, "Is this where you live?"

Aïda nodded. "We have three rooms on the fifth floor."

"Can we spend the night together?"

"Act as if I am not here," the driver said.

Aïda switched to English. "We will spend the night together," she told him, "but not this night. It would not be prudent. I share the flat with a woman whose husband's brother is a militia officer. Also there is my son, Saava. How would I explain you to him?"

"When? Where?"

"I am invited to read at Pushkin's apartment in the city I call Peter and others call Leningrad on the anniversary of the poet's death. I am going there by night train Monday. Vadim will arrange everything—train tickets, a compartment to ourselves, a place to stay in Peter. You have only to make yourself free. Is such a thing possible?"

Ben slipped a hand under her fox fur piece and grazed the skin on the back of her neck. She turned and they sat there with their foreheads touching. Switching back to Russian, Aïda said, "I read recently where the Egyptians believed that two holy fish swam before the prow of the sun god's ship to guide it clear of shoals. The story must have made a deep impression on me because it explains the origins of a dream I had last night. In my dream I was swimming ahead of a glistening white ship with a strange flag flying from the mast, indicating it came from a distant country. I was naked and could feel the warm water slipping along the length of my body in an endless caress. Then, suddenly, I saw that I was swimming through a tangle of reefs that left razorlike scratches on my skin. Bleeding from dozens of cuts, I leapt half out of the water to warn the ship that it was heading toward the reefs. A man on the deck, who may or may not have been you, watched me through binoculars because I was naked, but he either did not understand my warning or chose to ignore it. Just when the ship was about to go aground on a reef, I woke up."

"How do you interpret your dream?"

"I took it as a portent, though I was not sure of what." Aïda laughed under her breath. "Maybe I should pay more attention to portents." Then, her lower lip trembling, she repeated the word *maybe* in a harsh whisper.

"Maybe you should," Ben agreed.

Aïda pulled her head back and examined his face for clues. Finding, once again, a riot of emotions, she pushed roughly against the door and fled toward the entrance of the building.

The driver glanced at the retreating figure of the woman. "You win some, you lose some," he observed philosophically. He twisted around in his seat and reached back to offer Ben a leather-covered flask. "Cognac," he said with a twinkle. "Imported from Paris, France. Three stars. Did you know it was the Tsar Vladimir who rejected the Moslem faith and converted to Christianity because alcohol was forbidden by Moslems, and who could survive a Russian winter without alcohol?"

"I didn't know that," Ben admitted. So as not to offend the driver, he took a sip from the flask before handing it back.

Gunning the motor of the taxi, grinding gears, the driver headed toward the center of Moscow. "How could you know about Tsar Vladimir," he said to his passenger, "you being an American and all?"

Ben sank back into the seat. "How did you know I was American?"

The driver cackled. "I may not speak American, but I recognize it when I hear it."

10

In a dilapidated hunting lodge tucked away in a thick stand of white birches off the Moscow-Kiev highway, eighteen high-ranking officers and former officers of the Komitet Gosudarstvennoi Bezopasnosti were winding up a meeting that had started in the afternoon and dragged on until the early hours of the next morning. Some of the members of the Circle's "Directorate," as the group styled itself, had made their way from the far reaches of central Asia and eastern Siberia for the session. The thick wooden peasant table around which they sat bore the ruts and furrows of the thousands of cutlets that had been hacked away from the bone on its surface. On this particular night the table was littered with half-empty bottles of mineral water and empty dinner plates and ashtrays brimming with cigar and cigarette butts. At two A.M. an electric cuckoo clock on the wall struck the hour; a small wooden grizzly bear wheeled into view on the clock's face and reared up on its hind legs several times before disappearing into the bowels of the clock. Distracted for a moment by the grizzly, the participants turned back to hear the end of a story.

"I was told it happened during a meeting of the Soviet of People's Commissars right after the Revolution," a man with sickle-shaped sideburns was recounting. "Lenin slipped a note to Felix Dzerzhinsky asking how many counterrevolutionists were actually in prison. Dzerzhinsky jotted down the number 15,000 and passed the note back. Reading it, Lenin screwed up his face in what Dzerzhinsky took to be a sign of displeasure, and marked an X next to the number 15,000 to indicate he had read it. You have surely heard the story before?"

"No, never."

"Absolutely not."

"Finish it."

"When the meeting broke up, Dzerzhinsky retrieved the paper and noticed the X next to the '15,000.' He immediately issued orders for the prisoners to be shot."

"Good riddance to bad rubbish," the old general chairing the meeting remarked in a gravelly voice. He waved a deformed hand to dispel the smoke that had seeped into the room from the joints of a wood-burning stove. "Dzerzhinsky understood the adage, 'Impossible to make an omelet without cracking eggs.'"

"It is a lesson our present crop of leaders has forgotten," noted the retired Party ideological commissar from Uzbekistan.

"It is not possible to govern a country as vast as Russia once you have lost your nerve," agreed a younger man whose photograph had appeared in *Pravda* two days before above an article announcing that he had been purged from the Central Committee secretariat.

"For all his talk of *glasnost* and *perestroika*, the Great Helmsman has committed a great many blunders," Viktor Prosenko, the Directorate's newest member, chimed in. "He lost Eastern Europe for us. He opened the road to German reunification and the creation of a Fourth Reich. He slashed military budgets, leaving us at the mercy of the Capitalists, who henceforth will negotiate from

strength. He undermined a planned economy without
providing a workable alternative. He opened the door to
the dismantling of the Soviet Socialist Union through se-
cessions. He abandoned the constitutional clause giving
our Communist Party the monopoly of power and opened
the door to the dismantling of the Party through so-called
free elections."

"If he were a paid agent of Capitalism," declared the
head of the Directorate's Siberian cell, "he could not have
done more to undermine all we have fought for, all we
have sacrificed for."

"He has raised expectations," the old general said. "He
will be vulnerable when the masses understand that he
has not delivered on his promises. We must bide our time,
consolidate our strength, meticulously prepare the terrain
for the return to the *status quo ante* when the pendulum
swings in our direction."

The representative from Leningrad went around the
room passing out tiny glasses filled with home-brewed
apricot liquor. Everyone stood and looked at the old general, the Directorate's *éminence grise*.

"To *pamyat*," the general announced solemnly, raising
his glass. "Our time will come."

"To *pamyat*," echoed the others. "Our time will come."

Throwing back their heads, the eighteen members of
the *Pamyat* Directorate tossed off the burning alcohol.

DRIVING BACK TO MOSCOW on narrow back roads that were
unlikely to be patrolled, Viktor watched the headlights
sweep across the dirty white bark of the birches at each
curve. The old general, his head nodding with drowsiness,
slouched next to him in the passenger seat. The more
Viktor saw of the general, the more he was impressed by
the resemblance between him and his daughter, Viktor's
wife, Ekaterina. They were cut from the same bolt of
cloth, this father and daughter. They had the same way of
flaring their nostrils when they sneered, the same plodding sense of caution, the same willingness, when they

thought the odds had shifted in their favor, to fling caution to the wind and gamble.

"Where are we?" the old man mumbled in the shadowy darkness of the car.

"We will hit the ring road in another five or seven minutes," Viktor replied. He shifted down and rounded a curve and shifted up again. "What do you think the chances are that the pendulum will swing in our direction?"

The old man pulled an enormous handkerchief from a jacket pocket and smothered a hacking cough in it. Out of the corner of his eye, Viktor could see his slight body heaving even after the sound of coughing had ceased. "Fifty-fifty," the general finally managed to mutter. Thinking out loud, he added, "It was Stalin who formulated the rule of thumb that an enemy had to be eliminated politically before he could be eliminated physically. That is the essence of our problem—how to eliminate the Great Helmsman politically. How to discredit him in the eyes of the masses so that his physical elimination will pass almost unnoticed . . ."

The mother-of-pearl lights from the first in an endless string of suburban housing projects flickered invitingly on the horizon ahead. "How?" Viktor inquired.

But the old man's head had sagged heavily against his chest. Had he dozed off, Viktor wondered, or was he avoiding a question to which he had no answer?

EKATERINA, WHO SLEPT with plugs in her ears and blinders over her eyes, didn't stir when Viktor tiptoed into their bedroom. The clock on his side of the double bed, visible in the light coming from the open bathroom door, registered five to four. He undressed quickly in the bathroom, opened the medicine chest to hunt for some dental floss, shook his head at the number of jars and tubes (most of them manufactured in the West) his wife had managed to accumulate. It occurred to Viktor that the greater danger posed by the Great Helmsman was that he might succeed; that he might bring the West, with its skin lotions and hair dyes and face-lifts and eyeliners and nail polishes and vaginal deodorant sprays, to the East. Russian airwaves were already polluted with the noise of Western rock music. Young girls who two decades before would not have been seen in public in anything except skirts now strutted around in obscenely tight blue jeans. Young men let their hair grow to their shoulders. Back in the fifties the militia would have carted these long-haired hooligans off to the local station house and sheared them like sheep. Now good-thinking people shrugged, as if young women in tight jeans and young men with shoulder-length hair were the wave of the future. What the *Pamyat* Circle was fighting for, Viktor grasped, was nothing more or less than the purity of the Russian soul. He had not mustered as much enthusiasm for a cause since he had lied about his age to get into the Red Army during the Great Patriotic War. He had put his life on the line for Greater Russia then; it was only fitting that he do so now.

Viktor padded on bare feet into the bedroom and stared down at the still body of his wife, folded into a fetal position under the electric blanket (manufactured in Germany). He knew she slept naked and for a fleeting moment he was tempted to slip under the sheets alongside her, glide a hand between her thighs, press the erection that was forming at the mere thought of her nakedness into her buttocks. But he understood from bitter experience that she would whine at him for wakening her before she had had her nine hours of beauty sleep, would sulk for days, would disappear for "auditions" or "dubbing" to punish him. For the last several years the sexual activity that could be coaxed out of her had only been available on her terms. All that would change when she discovered that he had joined her father in the glorious struggle for the soul of Russia; when that struggle was crowned with success; when he was rewarded for his contribution to *Pamyat*, as the old general had hinted, by being named head of the Komitet Gosudarstvennoi Bezopasnosti.

·   ·   ·

TICKING OFF ITEMS IN HIS REPORT, Frolov's usual droning monotone was filled with eddies of exhilaration. "I had a man selling hazelnuts," he was saying. "I had a woman selling parsley, I had seventeen people on foot all told, I had three teams in radio cars, I had a photographer hidden in a bread truck." He pushed a sheaf of enlarged photographs across the table to his chief. The one on the top of the pile, dark, grainy, showed Bassett and the Zavaskaya woman walking arm in arm under a street lamp, deep in conversation. "It is only the beginning of February," Frolov complained, a frown distorting the pear shape of his face, "and I am already over the limit on my first quarter budget."

"We will find the money," Viktor said impatiently. He tapped the photograph with a forefinger. "What makes you think they had never met before?"

"My operative covering them inside the Druzhba Café recognized her and went over to their table to ask for an autograph."

"She was taking a big chance," Viktor commented.

"It was a natural thing to do, and thus within our guidelines," Frolov insisted. "As she was leaving she heard the American ask the Zavaskaya woman if she was famous. This indicates that he did not know her personally or by reputation, that it was a first encounter."

"If it was their first meeting," Krostin, his head nodding eagerly, asked, "how do you account for her kissing him on the steps outside the café?"

"They had been talking intently for several minutes," Frolov said. "One of my people pushed past them into the café. He overheard the American telling the Zavaskaya woman that he hoped they would never meet again. The kiss came immediately after he said this and was a reaction to his words. The way I interpret it, he was smitten with her, but realized that, as an American diplomat involved in some sort of secret work at the embassy, he could not afford to get involved with a Russian woman."

"How do you explain the second meeting, then?" Viktor asked.

"I am at a loss to explain it," Frolov admitted. "We were not tapping her phone line at that point, so we have no idea whether he invited her to read her poetry to the Americans at Spaso House, or it was a simple coincidence. We have no idea what happened inside Spaso House between them. We do know that they left separately, that he joined her, as if by prearrangement, several blocks from the embassy. We do know that they descended into the metro station together, talking intently. We know also that they sat and talked late into the night in the restaurant on the boat, though we do not know what they talked about. And then, of course, we know precisely what was said in the taxi afterward."

"From the tape recorder in the pocket of my driver, Zenkevich."

Frolov took Viktor's comment as a criticism. "You made a point of saying that the American must not suspect he was under surveillance. I had run out of faces that would be new to the American and the Zavaskaya woman. So I accepted your driver's standing offer to work overtime."

"I was not complaining," Viktor said.

"When the Zavaskaya woman quit the taxi," Krostin said, "there was no more talk of not seeing each other again?"

"Quite the contrary," Frolov said. "On Zenkevich's tape, you hear the American asking if he can spend the night with her. And you hear her response, which is in English. She says she will arrange it when she goes to Leningrad for the Pushkin business."

"Which brings us to the Pushkin business," Viktor noted. "We have three days in which to prepare the ground. This ought to give us enough time to find out which sleeping car they will be in and plant a microphone in it. Frolov, you are to take personal charge at the Leningrad end—lay on as many teams as you need without worrying about the budget. Bring people in from Kiev if you require fresh faces. Needless to say, I will want photographs."

Making his way down the corridor to deliver an initial

report to the old general, Viktor turned to Krostin. "Were you able to find out what the American did during his four months in Prague?"

Krostin shook his head. "As he was a bachelor, our Czech friends routinely dangled a woman under his nose —a former ballerina, I was told, with a lean body and jet-black hair down to her waist. Apparently he never batted an eyelash. What he did during his tour at the embassy remains a mystery."

"What about the Zavaskaya woman?"

"She lives with a husband, a father, a son." Krostin stopped talking as they walked past a group of younger officers chatting around a water cooler. Looking at the officers, Viktor was struck by the gloomy paleness of their faces, the absence of a gleam in their eyes, the lack of any note of excitement in their voices. Morale at the Center was at an all-time low, recruiting (Viktor knew from the old general) was lagging, officers were dying or retiring or simply quitting faster than the Center could replace them. A casual stroll through the labyrinthine corridors of the massive building revealed dozens of offices sitting empty. Slowly, inexorably, the KGB was being reduced to a shell. Only a startling triumph could reverse the slide into oblivion.

"The Zavaskaya woman's husband is known to you," Krostin continued in the same dispassionate tone. "He goes by the name of Vadim. He is the one you had us work up a dossier on two years ago." Viktor glanced quickly at his section chief, but Krostin's face revealed no hint of smugness. "You will remember that this Vadim," Krostin continued, "is in the business of advertising, but seems to be something of a wheeler-dealer on the side. He owns a *dacha* at the edge of a lake near Zagorsk. He is said to have a vast amount of cash available, some of it in hard currency. He hires a taxi by the year and pays the driver partly in rubles, partly in dollars; it was this driver your man Zenkevich was standing in for. The notary registry lists Vadim as a part owner of that cooperative restaurant on the boat. According to the lady who shares the apartment with the Zavaskaya woman, she and her husband have not slept together for years. The Zavaskaya woman has been heard to say that she and her husband are planning to divorce as soon as he is able to move into an apartment of his own."

Viktor stopped before the thick oaken door leading to the old general's outer office. "What have you got on the father and the son?"

"The father is old and confined to his room. In the early fifties he was a member of Stalin's personal bodyguard, but was expelled from his Interior unit when it was discovered that he was harboring a White Russian admiral. He was questioned several times by one of our interrogators, but refused to confess to anti-Party activities. Because of the heavy case load at the time, the procurer never got around to arresting him. When Stalin died in 1953, the affair was quietly dropped. As for the son, he is age eleven, and has some sort of medical problem—I am still trying to find out exactly what it is."

Krostin lowered his voice to a whisper. His pointed blond beard fluttered with excitement. "Aside from those marine guards, we have not had an American diplomat become seriously involved with a Russian woman for decades."

"We must play them both as an angler would play a salmon," Viktor cautioned. "We must give them plenty of line, let them run with it. Only when they are seriously hooked can we begin to reel them in."

In the old general's inner sanctum a few minutes later, Viktor informed his father-in-law, "I think we may be onto something big."

11

At one fifteen in the morning, the night train for Peter
(as Aïda called Leningrad) crept out of the old station on
Kalanchevsky Square (her name for Komsomol Square)
and, shunted one way, then another, meandered through
a tangle of tracks etched in the shimmering blanket of
snow covering the marshaling yard. As the long train
rounded the first great curve, Ben—his forehead touching
the icy pane of the compartment window—could make
out a shadowy figure standing on the lower step at each
door in the cars ahead and behind. Each of the figures
swung a hurricane lamp back and forth in a signal of de-
parture. As the train straightened the chain of lights
blinked out. Gradually the tracks narrowed from fifteen
abreast to ten to five to two. The train, swaying rhythmically underfoot, picked up speed. Fields of snow stretching to a penumbra slipped past. Aïda, gazing out the
window next to Ben, her arm draped lightly over his
shoulder, said quietly, "We are being squeezed out of
Moscow like dental paste from a tube." As she spoke her
breath fogged the pane. With the tip of the finger on

which she wore the agate ring she reached up and wrote a message on the fogged glass. It said: "Lucidity must yield to lust."

Ben turned and pulled her to him and felt the softness of her breast against his heart. Then his lips touched hers and lust, mounting like sap from the soles of his feet, asphyxiated what was left of lucidity. After that he lost track of the sequence in which things happened. Had her clothes fallen away from her body before or after he lifted her, weightless, off the ground and buried his face in her chest? Had she whispered something about settling like a butterfly on the leaf of his lip before or after she shook free the dirty-blond braid that tumbled halfway to her waist and brushed his body with her loose hair? When had he become aware of odors—the rich ripe snow-soaked wetness of his sheepskin overcoat swaying from a hook on the back of the compartment door, the sour staleness of the hot air coming from the heating vent, the sweet acidity of her secretions? Was it before or after he pushed her onto her stomach and breathed disjointed declarations of eternal lust into the sweat-damp nape of her neck? When had he become aware of sounds—the almost human voice of the ties echoing under the wheels, her half-gasps that were transformed into half-moans when she exhaled, the shrill whistle of the wind when she lowered the window and let it snow onto her feverish face and breasts? Was it before or after the pace suddenly changed from the wild flight of electrons to the slow wheeling of galaxies?

At length, breathing hard, they backed away from each other like two prizefighters between rounds. She nicked a tangerine with a fingernail and peeled away petals of skin while Ben memorized the soft rise and fall of her heavy breasts. She handed him wedges of tangerine. Sucking on a wedge herself, juice trickling down her chin, she said, "Akhmatova once spoke of a moment of happiness so intense, she wanted to carry it with her, like baggage, through the rest of her life. For me this is such a moment." She held up a warning palm. "Above all do not spoil it by feeling you need to respond."

Ben whispered, "For me too this is such a moment. I swear it."

Kneeling on the bunk, her weight on her heels, her eyes fixed with an animal's intensity on his, she parted her thighs and reached with the last wedge of tangerine to perfume the lips of her vagina. Murmuring a line of Akhmatova's—

And I was bold and bad and gay

—she sank back as he came toward her.

In the early hours of the morning the train crawled across a flat, still winter wasteland. In the train Aïda and Ben raised the shade and stood naked at the window staring out at a distant cluster of one-story wooden houses lost in the black snow-encrusted landscape. From one chimney a thin pencil line of silver smoke spiraled into the sky. Aïda toyed with the ring on her finger. "This is Dostoevsky's Russia—the Russia of the yellow light of oil lamps, of mirrors in walnut frames, of rustling skirts."

They were still peering out of the window when the train jerked to a stop at a small station illuminated by naked electric bulbs strung on wires between poles. Steam from the engine scoured the deserted platform. From somewhere up ahead came the sound of a trainman testing the brakes with an iron bar. Pulling out of the station, the train crossed a rusting railroad trestle spanning a frozen river and sped on through vast stretches of birch forests. In the compartment Ben and Aïda stretched out on the cot, their foreheads touching, their limbs braided as her hair had been braided, whispering and dozing and making love, and whispering and dozing again.

SHUFFLING AWKWARDLY THROUGH the crowded rooms of Pushkin's flat at No. 12 Moika Quay in backless felt slippers fitted over his L.L. Bean boots, Ben was hard pressed to keep up with Aïda. Her fox furpiece flying like a pennant from her neck, her head high, her eyes shining, she skated on her own slippers through knots of people, shaking hands, pecking at cheeks, exchanging greetings with the poets and poetry lovers gathered to celebrate the anniversary of Pushkin's death at the hands of the Frenchman D'Anthés. Reaching back, she grasped Ben's wrist and pulled him into Pushkin's library. "After the duel," she told him, "they carried him back here and laid him out on that couch. This was his favorite room. The Turkish saber on the wall was a memento of the Caucasian campaign. The figure in the portrait there is the poet Zhukovsky. The inscription is well known—'To the victorious pupil from the vanquished master.' Townspeople, hearing Pushkin had been wounded, mounted a vigil on the quay outside. Every day at noon the doctors would write out a medical bulletin and post it on the front door. Pushkin suffered excruciating pain for forty-six hours. Just before the end he was heard to say, 'Life is finished. It is difficult to breathe.' When his heart stopped beating, one of his friends opened the face of the clock and stopped time. You can see the hands are still set to the hour, to the minute of Pushkin's death—two forty-five in the afternoon." Aïda's lips grazed Ben's ear and she whispered, "So: Pushkin thought that lovers constructed walls of words to shut themselves off from the world, that they communicated in a shorthand of coded phrases and glances and touches, that the absence of a look when there should have been one became a secret message. Shall we build a wall of words to shut ourselves off from the world, dear heart?"

Before he could answer, a stout woman who seemed to know Aïda elbowed her way through to her and planted a moist kiss on each of her cheeks. "I only came because I heard Zavaskaya was reading," she gushed. The woman eyed Ben curiously. "Aren't you going to introduce me to your friend?" she demanded with a sly smile.

"No," Aïda said flatly.

The woman seemed to find that funny. "You are a queer bird, Aïda Ivanovna."

In a corner of the library an elderly man was helped to climb onto a metal chair. "Friends," he called in a feeble voice. The people crowding into the rooms quieted down. "We are come together," the old man announced, "as we do every year on the tenth of February to pay homage to our beloved Pushkin—the poet who could 'burn the hearts of men with the Word'—on the anniversary of his death. This year, as every year, the words of Pushkin's friend V. Odoevsky float in the air." The elderly man shut his eyes and angled his head toward the ceiling as he quoted. "'Our poetry's sun has set! Pushkin has died, died in the prime of life.' We will begin by observing a minute of silence at two forty-five, the moment of his death. Then we will have his verses read by several of our poets."

A man with alcohol on his breath edged closer to Ben and whispered in English, "Is this your first time at one of these things?"

Aïda, suddenly alert, angrily asked, "Why do you talk to him in English?"

The man looked agitated. "I only thought . . ."

Before he could finish, Aïda was pulling Ben away.

"What's the matter?" he whispered to her.

"I do not like the look of him," she whispered back. "I do not like it that he spoke to you in English without knowing you."

Ben glanced over his shoulder. The man who had addressed him in English had melted into the crowd.

The poetry readings began immediately after the moment of silence at two forty-five. Aïda was the third to read. Climbing on the metal chair, gazing out at the sea of faces, she recited Pushkin's unfinished poem "Ezersky," which ended with the lines:

> Where in the tower-room long-forgotten
> Grass grows as in a wilderness.

After the ceremony, Aïda took Ben to see the two rooms in flat 44 of Fontannyy Dom where Akhmatova had spent the last days of her life. Staring at the day bed in the small room, Aïda said softly, "It was here, in this room, that she gave me the agate ring. She was as white as a sheet . . . stretched out on that bed. I was fifteen at the time . . . to me, it seemed like a gift from a goddess."

As the afternoon waned, Aïda and Ben wandered for hours arm in arm through the endless halls of the Hermitage, pausing only in front of the half dozen paintings that she said nourished the soul as well as the eye. Afterward, they took tea and cream-filled cakes in a new cooperative café off Nevsky Prospekt that Vadim had discovered on a business trip the previous month. There was a band and a small dance floor. Leaning across the table, Aïda asked Ben in English, "Are you dancing as well as you are fucking?"

Flustered, he said, "You are the first woman on this planet to suggest that I am a good lover."

She switched to Russian. "We are all good lovers when we make love to people we love."

A middle-aged man sitting at the next table leaned toward Ben. "Excuse me, but I could not help overhearing you talk in English," he said in heavily accented English. "I been to Texas, America, to study the techniques of oil drilling. If you think Americans talk funny, you should hear the Americans who are also Texans."

Ben, to be polite, asked, "When were you in Texas?"

"Ah, too long ago," the man responded. "I would give five years of my life to be able to visit Texas again. Their cowboys say things like 'whody' or 'howdy' in place of 'how do you do.' They got rifles in their cars and throw empty beer cans out the window when they are driving from one place to another." The man pulled a small jar of instant Maxwell House coffee from his jacket pocket and stirred a spoonful of it into a cup of boiling water. He looked at Ben. "You are American, no? Can I offer you and your friend a cup of genuine instant American coffee?"

The band began playing a foxtrot. Before Ben could accept, Aïda pulled him onto the dance floor. Holding her in his arms, he could feel the tenseness in her body. He drew back slightly to look at her, but she avoided his eyes. "The absence of a look when there should be one is a secret message," he reminded her.

Her eyes flicked up. Ben was startled to see that they were brimming with fear. "What are you afraid of?" he whispered.

"Of losing poetry," she whispered. "Of losing you. So: Once my father was summoned to the KGB for questioning. He was instructed to bring my mother and me with him. I must have been four or five. The three of us sat across the desk from an officer in uniform. He had shiny gold stripes on his shoulder boards. On the desk was a shiny golden ruler and a jar of instant coffee, which was something I had never laid eyes on until then. He was stirring a spoonful of it into a cup of boiling water as he questioned my father. When we left, my mother and father walked ahead, talking intently. I followed behind them, past the wrought-iron fence that surrounded the KGB building, tapping the golden ruler against the fence. My father heard the *tap-tap-tap* and saw the ruler and understood I had stolen it from the officer's desk. He slapped me hard across the face and snatched the ruler away from me. That night he punched a hole in the ice on the river and dropped the ruler through it. Since that day" —she finished the sentence with a line from one of Akhmatova's poems—" *'every sound frightened and tortured me.'* "

"It was the sight of the instant coffee that brought back the memory."

"It was also the face of the man. It was him speaking English to you."

Ben tried to reassure her. "Times have changed," he said. He wondered if it was true; he wondered if they had changed enough.

In the hotel room that Vadim had organized for them, they stood gazing out at the Neva. Jagged chunks of blue-gray ice drifted downstream on the outgoing tide. Ducks skidded to a stop between the ice floes and bobbed like

corks in the murky water. The battleship *Aurora*, which
had led the assault on the Winter Palace during the Bolshevik Revolution, sat imbedded in ice next to a pier below them, blanketed in snow. Icicles dripped from the
ship's frozen rigging. A cold haze hung over the city like a
shroud, obscuring its spires and domes, making it seem as
if time in this northern latitude had slowed. Aïda remarked absently, "Mandelstam once said that living in
Peter was the same as lying in a coffin, but I never saw
that side of it. Peter was Akhmatova's lover. *'Our separa-
tion is illusion,'* she once wrote.

> You and I cannot be parted,
> My shadow is on your walls,
> My reflection, in your canals . . .

Aïda turned and caressed Ben's lips with the back of
her hand as she recited the last two lines of the poem.

> The sound of my steps in the Hermitage halls
> Where I wandered with my love . . .

She kissed the corners of his mouth and then his lips.
"We are a perfect couple, dear heart. I am poetry, you are
prose. In a few hours poetry and prose will stand naked at
the open window and observe the sunrise. Prose will discover what poetry knows: how the barbs of white light
slant in at an abrupt angle, evidence of what I call the
city's northness. Prose will discover the odor of the sea's
surf breaking out there beyond the perpetual fog, as salty
as human tears."

Ben's fingers undid a button of her shirt and his hand
slid under it to the soft rise of her chest. "Would you leave
Russia if you could?"

"Never!" she shot back, startled by the question. "I am,
like Akhmatova, a guest upon the earth. I have many
times asked myself why I was invited here. And I have
discovered the answer—to compose poetry. It is because
I accept this destiny that I also can be a lover and a

mother. If I were to leave Russia I would lose my sense of soil. I would lose poetry. If you were to oblige me to leave you would lose prose." She smiled solemnly. "We would no longer be a perfect couple."

In an almost inaudible voice he said, "Eventually I must go away from here."

Her chin rose imperceptibly. "If you are Russian," she informed him, "you associate happiness with pain; you follow your heart until it breaks."

12

Viktor, slouched in a front row seat of the small screening room, could hear the old general wheezing through his sinuses one row behind him as the first images flashed over their heads onto the screen. Frolov narrated from the projection booth in his usual droning voice. "Subjects are seen here boarding *voiture* four of the night train for Leningrad," he intoned over a microphone. On the screen, the American Bassett, almost lost in an ankle-length sheepskin overcoat, handed up two small valises to Aïda, then glanced over his shoulder in the direction of the camera, which he obviously did not spot, before clambering after her into the car. The camera zoomed in on Aïda, her face glowing with excitement, smiling into Ben's eyes. "The Zavaskaya woman," Frolov continued, "can be seen carrying an *avoska* filled with tangerines—"

The old general clicked on the microphone next to his seat. "Where the hell did she get tangerines this time of year?" he wanted to know.

"The train reservations, the tickets, the tangerines, the

hotel in Leningrad were all organized by her husband," Frolov replied.

"If he can figure out how to get his hands on tangerines in February," the old general remarked sourly to Viktor, "maybe we ought to employ him."

"The Zavaskaya woman and the American Bassett shared sleeping compartment nine," Frolov narrated. "We had a microphone planted under the floor boards of the compartment, but once the train started moving all conversation was drowned out by the noise of the wheels."

The old general tapped Viktor on the shoulder with his withered fingers. "Hell of a place to put a microphone," he muttered in a gravelly voice. "Next thing you know they will be planting them in the bottoms of toilets. All conversation will be drowned out by the noise of the flushing."

On the screen the scene shifted. An engine with a large red star on the front was entering a small deserted station illuminated by bare light bulbs strung on wires between poles. Judging from the darkness it must have been before dawn. As the train drew to a stop, steam from the engine swept the length of the platform. The camera zoomed in through the steam to the window of a compartment. Two figures could be seen staring out at the station. Both were stark naked. The woman, slightly taller than the man, was toying with a ring on her finger. "The fact of their nakedness is the first conclusive evidence," Frolov was saying, "that they had actually copulated."

"Copulated," the general muttered in Viktor's ear, "is a fancy way of saying they screwed like rabbits."

The image changed again on the screen. There were several quick unfocused shots of Ben trying to keep up with Aïda as she plunged through the crowded rooms of Pushkin's apartment, then a shot of Aïda climbing onto the chair and reading her Pushkin poem, and another of Ben, lost in a sea of people, looking around absently, as if he expected to spot someone he knew.

"This last footage," Frolov explained as a new series

appeared on the screen, "needs no narration. We were able to install a two-way mirror near the bed in their hotel room. As they copulated with a light on, the images are of excellent quality."

"Now that's more like it," the old general muttered to Viktor as the first shot swam into focus.

On the screen the Zavaskaya woman, naked, could be seen hovering with total concentration over the American's organ, luring it in increments to erection with her eyes and breasts and hands and lips and tongue, then carefully impaling herself on it. Watching from his seat in the darkened screening room, Viktor felt the blood stirring in his groin. Ekaterina had made love to him like that when they first met on the Black Sea; had hovered over him like a haruspex, summoning erections as if they were spirits that needed to be enticed back from the dead. On the screen the Zavaskaya woman, her long hair trailing behind her, suddenly arched her spine, then slumped languorously forward across the body of the American.

Viktor reached for his microphone. "I think we have seen enough to get the idea," he told Frolov. Instantly the screen went white and the overhead lights came on. Twisting around in his seat, Viktor told the general, "What you have seen is the expurgated version. The footage of them making love in the hotel room goes on for three and a half hours. We have shots of them strolling through the halls of the Hermitage. They tried to keep their hands off each other in public, but wound up touching at every opportunity. We had a man planted at a table next to them in a café engage them in conversation. He concluded that they were clearly lovers in full hormonal flight. The American was overheard telling her that she was the first person to suggest that he was a good lover. The Zavaskaya woman was overheard replying, 'We are all good lovers when we make love to people we love.'"

"Full hormonal flight," the old man muttered. "That is an interesting way of putting it."

"That's an accurate way of putting it."

"When?" the general demanded.

"When?" Viktor did not understand the question.

"When will you spring the trap?"

"Ah. The trap. Soon."

VIKTOR'S WIFE, EKATERINA, fresh from her bath, her hair wrapped in a white towel, settled snugly onto a corner of the couch, her legs tucked under her body, her arms holding closed the white terry cloth bathrobe whose belt had been misplaced by the maid. Viktor fitted the tape into the video recorder and sat down next to her to work the remote control. As the first images appeared on the television screen, Ekaterina almost purred with curiosity. "The woman is exquisite," she declared in a throaty growl. "Who is she?"

Viktor's failure to respond only stimulated her even more.

In recent years he had, on occasion, brought home cocaine, pornographic films, even some gadgets confiscated from a Japanese businessman caught *in flagrante delicto* with a prostitute—whatever came to hand that could rouse her from the lethargy she fell into when he proposed sex. Reaching behind her, he slipped a finger under the collar of her bathrobe and began to lightly massage the nape of her neck. Touching his lips to her ear, he whispered his pet name for her. "Katya, Katya, my own Katya." He knew the videotape was having an effect on her when she did not lean away.

On the television screen a train could be seen pulling into a deserted station. Then the camera zoomed in through the steam and came to focus on two naked figures in the compartment window. Ekaterina breathed, "Tell me at least if they are spies?"

"The fact that we went to all this trouble to photograph them speaks for itself," Viktor told her. He began to ease the robe off her left shoulder.

The shots of the woman working on the man's organ with her hands and breasts and mouth and tongue appeared on the screen. "Oh, oh, oh," Ekaterina whimpered, languorously raising an arm so Viktor could slip it out of the sleeve. Half-covered, half-naked, her mouth gaping open, her pale skin shimmering in the light from the television set, she stared at the screen. When the woman in the film arched her spine, Ekaterina arched hers. When the woman slumped forward onto the man, a gasp escaped from Ekaterina's throat and she slumped forward too—into Viktor's outstretched arms.

SABINE HARKENRIDER BUTTONHOLED Manny as he emerged from the post office carrying a batch of letters. Her face was deathly pale, her tone was urgent. "Mr. Custer, you did say if we had any doubts we should report it and let you decide."

Shuffling absently through the letters, Manny singled one out. It was from an old buddy who was the embassy security officer in Prague. He looked up from the letter into Miss Harkenrider's troubled eyes. "Decide what?" he asked.

"Decide if it was a compromising situation," she explained.

Manny steered her into a corner. The letter he was aching to get at would have to wait until he dealt with Miss Harkenrider. "Maybe you should start at the start," he suggested.

"I hope you won't think I'm hallucinating. The last thing I want to do is make a fool of myself . . ."

"Only tell me what happened."

"It's this way. I've been going every Sunday on the cross-country ski outings organized by the Community Liaison people. The Sunday before last I was lagging behind the others and a Russian . . . a Russian man . . . a young Russian man actually, skied up alongside me and started to talk to me."

"So far," Manny commented, "it does not sound too ominous."

"He was talking in English," Miss Harkenrider stiffly informed Manny.

"What did he want?"

"That's just it. He wanted me to meet him in Moscow.

He said he had been following me for several Sundays, waiting for an opportunity to speak to me." She lowered her voice to a whisper. "You warned they would try to plant someone—I forget the expression you used."

"A dangle?"

"That's it. A dangle."

"And you think this young Russian was a dangle?"

"You don't understand. Last Sunday he was there again. I skied off from the group to attend to a bodily function. The next thing I knew he was skiing alongside me. To be perfectly honest with you, Mr. Custer, he made what we usually refer to as an obscene proposal."

"You were quite right to tell me about this," Manny said. "Here's what to do. Give up cross-country skiing for a while. If the man tries to contact you again, let me know immediately."

"You think he will?"

Manny hiked one of his heavy shoulders. "Whatever. If he really is a KGB dangle, chances are he'll turn up. If he was just someone who wanted to meet an American, he'll stick to the woods and the cross-country skiers."

Manny could see the color flooding back into Miss Harkenrider's face. She grabbed his hand. "I certainly feel relieved now that I've told you what happened."

"Come back to me if you spot him again," Manny said.

Turning away, he looked again at the letter. It had arrived in the morning's diplomatic pouch. "Immanuel Custer—Personal and Confidential." Manny slit open the envelope with a fingertip, plucked out the letter and snapped it open with a shake of his wrist. It began, "Manny, old fart."

So you're making your last stand in Moscow. I imagine you, a smoking Colt in each of your paws, surrounded by Injuns howling for your scalp. Knowing you, I don't envy the one who gets close enough to take it. Re your question: He was as much a mystery here as he seems to be in your neck of the diplomatic woods. He was supposed to be housekeeping but

seems to have spent most of his time in a room put at
his disposal by your former employer. Doing I don't
know what. As to why he hi-hoed off after four
months, your guess is as good as mine. Probably better. Sorry I can't be more helpful.

Back in his cubbyhole of an office, Manny reread the
letter, then ripped it into tiny pieces and let them flutter
down into the burn bag. From long professional habit he
appreciated the need to limit access to secrets on the basis
of a need to know. Still, there was more here than met the
eye. If Bassett was working out of Inkermann's tenth-floor
bailiwick, it could mean that Inkermann was up to something. With *glasnost* in full flight, there had been a general
hold on operations that could embarrass the Great Houdini. Was Bassett working for the Company? Was the
Company ignoring the "hold" order? Was Inkermann
free-lancing?

The truth was that Manny detested Inkermann. He had
always seen the relationship between them as a confrontation between old money and no money; between someone
who had been driven to all-male private schools by a
chauffeur (in Manny's view, this kind of thing scarred you
for life) and someone who had ducked under the turnstile
and taken the subway to public school.

Manny's instinct told him that the Bassett mystery was
worth solving. If he could discover what he was up to, and
it turned out that Inkermann was involved, he might be
able to take Inkermann down a peg or two before Custer's
last stand ended and he was shipped off to early retirement. The possibility tickled him. Opening a small refrigerator stashed under a table in the corner of his
cubbyhole, he pulled out a bottle and the ice tray. Settling
back in his wooden chair, contemplating the usual scotch
on the usual rocks, he switched into the lazy drawl he
used when he was afraid of being taken for an intellectual
and uttered out loud the formula from Samuel Beckett
that inspired him every time he ran into a stone wall.

"I try," Manny growled. "I fail. I fail better."

13

Slowly, inexorably, their lives entwined like shoots of ivy twisting their way up the bark of a tree. Through February and early March they managed to steal several hours together every two or three days. Once, Aïda took Ben to the Novodevichy Cemetery to show him the statue of Stalin's young wife, Nadezhda Alliluyeva, next to her tomb. Nadezhda's marble nose had been chipped off by souvenir hunters. Since then the statue had been covered with a plastic case to prevent vandalism. A light rain the previous night and then a sharp drop in temperature had left the plastic case coated with a thin film of ice, making it appear as if Nadezhda herself were being held prisoner in a block of ice. "We are all of us prisoners in blocks of ice," Aïda remarked when Ben pointed it out to her.

Strolling between tombstones jutting like buck teeth from the ground, pausing to read the inscriptions on Gogol's and Chekhov's and Mayakovski's, they made their way back to the entrance of the cemetery. Aïda waved a hand in the direction of the Moscow skyline. "The Tsar Peter, sometimes referred to as the Great, sometimes not, humiliated Kuchkovo when he moved the court to Peter in seventeen hundred something. The Kuchkovo I love is a jilted woman who has never recovered from the insult."

Ben slipped his arm through Aïda's. "I am a jilted man. Maybe that explains my affinity for the city you call Kuchkovo and I call Moscow."

"There is another explanation," she told him. "I copied a wonderful line into my journal. It came from a book by the English writer Durrell . . . about how a city becomes a world when you love one of its inhabitants."

Ben regarded her strangely. "Do you think I am in love with you?"

The freckles on Aïda's face appeared to be dancing as she offered him one of her whimsical half-smiles. "Of course you are in love with me." After a moment she murmured, "Being apart is like not having a dose of a drug you are addicted to." She breathed out in frustration, creating a cloud of vapor that shrouded her face. "What would the Americans do to you if they found out about us?"

"When I arrived in Moscow, the embassy security officer warned us not to fall in love with a Russian."

"But what would they do?" Aïda insisted.

Ben shrugged. "We would have to pay the piper," he said in English.

"Who is this piper and what is he being paid to do?" Aïda asked.

" 'Pay the piper' is an expression. It is better if the Americans don't find out."

Aïda digested his answer. At length she said, "Maybe we should see less of each other."

Ben grinned. "Maybe we should see more of each other."

As March progressed they did manage to meet more often: Half a dozen times in a dingy room in a ramshackle hostel that Vadim rented by the year for the use of his out-of-town "clients," once in a church that was being restored, once in the dressing room of an actress friend of Aïda's while she was on stage performing, several times in out-of-the-way workers' canteens, once in Aïda's apartment when the woman who shared it had to hurry off to Kiev to care for her ailing mother and Vadim was off with his mistress.

Together with Saava, Aïda and Ben went weekends to Vadim's wooden *dacha* on a hill overlooking a lake near Zagorsk. The first weekend at the *dacha* was Saava's first encounter with his mother's new friend. Everyone was appropriately edgy during the ride out in Vadim's taxi. "Stop biting your nails," Aïda snapped at her son.

"I'll stop biting my nails when you stop smoking those awful cigarettes," Saava shot back.

"Maybe this wasn't such a good idea," Ben whispered to Aïda.

Although Ben didn't admit it, he had mixed feelings about the boy. It was one thing to become involved with Aïda, and quite another to deal with someone who inevitably reminded him of his own son, Felix. For Ben, it was like tearing open a wound on which a scab was just beginning to form. Following Aïda's advice, he waited for Saava to come to him. The first weekend the boy seemed to resent the intrusion. He hung back, observing Ben out of the corner of his eye, circling him, edging closer at each pass—but always keeping his distance. "I don't understand why you need new friends when you have old friends whom you know already," he told his mother when they were back in Moscow.

The second weekend, Saava started to come out of his shell. Clearly intrigued by the new man in his mother's life, he watched in silence as Ben rolled a giant snowball down an incline to make it bigger. Eventually curiosity overpowered timidity.

"Is it true what Aïda says about you being an American?" he called from the porch.

Ben looked up from the snowball and nodded. "Have you ever met an American before?"

"Hundreds of times," Saava called back. "Also French. Also English." Saava advanced to the bottom step and squatted. "Aïda said I shouldn't talk about you to anyone but Vadim. She said she wants to keep you a secret."

Ben winked at the boy. "I'm keeping you and her a secret too."

"So: Have you ever seen a real American cowboy? The kind with beautiful boots and a six-shooter?"

Ben kept pushing the snowball through the snow. "The ones with guns only exist in movies."

Saava took in Ben's answer with wide, serious eyes. He gestured with his chin toward the snowball. "What are you doing?"

"I'm making a snow woman."

That made Saava giggle. "Everyone else makes snow men."

"Snow women are prettier than snow men," Ben called. He looked up. "I could use some help."

The boy shrugged. "I never made a snow woman before."

"Come on, I'll show you how."

When the snow woman—with pebbles for eyes and a small cucumber for a nose and straw for hair and two wedges of orange peel for a mouth and two coconut shells for breasts—was finished, Saava stepped back to admire it. "What if we put Aïda's funny hat and scarf on her," he suggested.

"Good idea," Ben agreed.

Some time later Aïda, who had gone down to the lake to saw slabs of ice for the *dacha*'s icebox, came over a rise carrying the ice wrapped in a towel. When she caught sight of the snow woman, with her 1930s pillbox hat on its head and her threadbare fox neckpiece over its shoulders, she howled in delight. "That is the most elegant snow woman I have ever seen," she exclaimed. "Does she have a name?"

"She is called Benedictovna," Saava said, converting Ben's name, in the Russian style, to its feminine equivalent.

Ben flung an arm over the boy's shoulder and pulled him closer. Feeling Saava's thin body against his side, Ben glanced up at the sky so that Aïda wouldn't notice the tears glistening in the corners of his eyes. The last time he had stood with an arm over the shoulder of a boy, he had been with Felix, waiting for the flight that would take his son back to his mother after a school holiday.

Later, at lunch, Saava scraped his chair up on the same side of the table as Ben's. "I'm cutting down on biting nails," he told his mother.

"I'm cutting down on cigarettes," Aïda announced.

"Spending weekends together wasn't such a bad idea after all," Ben remarked.

IT WAS DURING THE WEEKENDS at the *dacha* that Ben and Aïda discovered what Aïda called the miracle of morning love-making—an achingly gentle coupling before either one was fully awake, when the real world mingled with vaguely remembered dreams.

Evenings she would weave her spiderweb of poems . . .

> *Softly into the center of me you came,*
> *I don't know when.*
> *What difference would it make?*
> *You became (before I knew you were there)*
> *The heart of the matter.*
>
> *I want to laugh more often now,*
> *I don't know why.*
> *What difference would it make?*
> *You don't have to identify emotions*
> *In order to have them.*

. . . and murmur fragments from Akhmatova's . . .

> *There is a sacred line in human intimacy*
> *That love and passion cannot cross—*

. . . as they lay on a bearskin in front of a roaring fire. When Saava was safely asleep in the *dacha's* only bed-

room, they would begin the fierce search for ways across
the line that Akhmatova said could not be crossed.

Some afternoons they joined the blond peasant boys,
with rope belts knotted around the waists of their gray
knee-long, blanketlike coats, ice-skating on the frozen
lake. Their bodies angled forward from the waist, their
hands clasped behind their backs, their coattails flying,
the peasants etched great figure eights into the ice, then
warmed themselves beside a roaring birch fire crackling at
the lake's edge.

One Sunday, with Saava in tow, Ben and Aïda trudged
across fields of shin-deep snow, past clusters of thatched,
whitewashed huts set on either side of a single wide un-
paved street, into Zagorsk, which Aïda called by its original name, Sergiev. There they threaded their way through
a mass of pigeons, past the gleaming white Church of the
Assumption where Ivan the Terrible stopped to pray after
killing his son, past the mausoleum of Boris Godunov, to
the Church of the Holy Trinity. Inside, a young priest
with a flowing beard and long dark hair parted in the
middle lay prostrate on the ground, his forehead pressed
to the cold stones. "He is being ordained," Aïda whispered as a barrel-chested Orthodox priest sent chants spiraling up with the incense toward the image of Jesus
staring down from the golden dome, and the old women,
their heads buried in black shawls, responded in feeble
chorus. "He is marrying the church."

The idea seemed to preoccupy her. Making their way
back across the fields toward the *dacha,* she asked, "So:
Explain if you can how is it you desire many, but love only
one?"

"What makes you think I desire many but love one?"
Ben teased.

Saava had run ahead following the paw prints in the
snow of a rabbit. Aïda stopped in her tracks. Her eyes
teared. In an instant the tears were transformed into tiny
crusts of ice, making her look ten years older. "I acknowl-
edged I loved you before you asked," she reminded him.
"I permitted lust to obliterate lucidity; I gave myself

freely without holding part of myself back. I told you that you loved me before you admitted it to yourself. Why do you play games with me now?"

Ben apologized profusely. "I have not yet grown accustomed to your directness," he explained. He scooped up a mitten-full of snow and rubbed it against her lips, then clumsily tried to kiss her, but she avoided his embrace. He pulled back. "I never before met a woman who exposed herself the way you do," he said awkwardly. "To answer your question: If we desire many but love one, it is probably because desire and love do not have as much to do with each other as we thought."

"I esteem your answer," she said simply.

Up ahead Saava called across the snow, "Come look, Ben. I have discovered the rabbit hole."

The third weekend at the *dacha* Ben turned up with a present for Saava that he had ordered from Stockman's Department Store in Helsinki. He could see he had made a serious mistake when he spotted the look on Aïda's face as he handed Saava the box. The boy glanced at his mother, and only when she reluctantly nodded did he tear the paper away. His eyes bulged as he pulled a fleece-lined denim jacket from the box. Casting dark looks in Ben's direction, Aïda told the boy, "It is too important a gift to accept." There was a burst of ardent pleading from Saava. Aïda took the boy's hand and led him into the bedroom. Ben could hear Aïda trying to reason with Saava, and the boy's muffled crying. When the two returned Saava held out his hand. In it were half a dozen lapel pins. "He will accept the gift," Aïda told Ben, "if you in turn will accept two pins from his collection." Ben carefully selected two pins from Saava's hand, one depicting the Battleship *Aurora,* the other, Vladimir Lenin.

Stretched out on blankets in front of the fire that night, Aïda said, "Please do not do that again. I do not want him to grow up admiring America for its blue jeans."

In late March the first faint thaw filled the Moscow air. Within hours vendors appeared on street corners selling small brown bags filled with vegetable and flower seeds.

Watching a long line of people waiting patiently for seeds, Ben took stock. The KGB had either not noticed that he was having a love affair with a Russian woman, or if they had noticed, the political climate was such that they were in no position to do anything about it. No one had confronted him with compromising photographs and demands for information. He was still putting in a full workday housekeeping for the Seven Dwarfs, and an hour or so in Inkermann's ribbon room.

Which left enough time for him to meet Aïda.

MANNY CUSTER, PASSING BEN in the hallway one afternoon, noticed a faraway look in his eyes. The embassy security chief noticed something else too—two buttons pinned to the lapel of Ben's jacket, one depicting the Battleship *Aurora*, the other, Vladimir Lenin.

WATCHING VIKTOR'S LATEST FOOTAGE in the KGB screening room, the old general leaned forward and drummed his withered fingers against his son-in-law's shoulder.

"When?" he demanded in a voice gravelly with impatience.

"Now."

14

The woman who lived in the penthouse over the Moscow River had finally gotten legal custody of her son and departed for Israel. Vadim had moved in the afternoon of the day she moved out. Tipsy from vodka and enthusiasm (he liked to quip that a man should change wives and jobs and apartments as often as he changed underwear), he came around the next morning with divorce papers for Aïda to sign. Afterward he half-jokingly (half-seriously) invited her to consummate the divorce. When she politely but firmly refused, he invited her to what he described as the next best thing: Lunch in the revolving restaurant atop Moscow's needlelike television tower. To mark what was after all an important turning point in both their lives, what could be more appropriate than to break bread in a "turning" restaurant? he said. He ordered champagne and blinis and caviar and cream, and began to regale her with the latest jokes.

"Socialism," he said, biting into a blini dripping with caviar and cream, wagging his head with laughter before he reached the punch line, "is the longest and most painful path from Capitalism to Capitalism!

"Remember the Great Helmsman's campaign to cut down on the consumption of alcohol?" he asked, splashing more champagne into both their glasses. "At the height of it two Russians are queuing for vodka. When their turn comes they discover there is none. One of the Russians complains that the trouble with the Great Helmsman is he is a teetotaler. The second Russian"—Vadim tilted back his head and tossed off another glass of champagne —"the second tells his friend, 'Look on the bright side. He might have been celibate.' Don't you get it, Aïda? If he were celibate we would all have to give up sex! Mind you, contrary to the conventional wisdom, it would not be a catastrophe, giving up sex. We would still have our assholes to scratch when we felt the urge for a satisfying physical sensation."

Aïda knew from experience that Vadim was only trying to goad her into an argument. For once she refused to rise to the bait. She felt slightly dizzy, though she didn't think it was because of the champagne. The restaurant atop the tower made one complete revolution every forty minutes. Kuchkovo sprawled below them like a toy city in a museum. She could see Opekudin's statue of Pushkin and the planetarium and the corner where the Tverskaya (the original name of Gorki Street) turned into Leningrad Prospekt. She could even make out the building at the university on Sparrow Hills (now Lenin Hills) where she had been washing windows when she met Vadim. An image came to her. Thinking that it might one day form the nucleus of a poem, she committed it to memory. The image was of the restaurant sitting perfectly still atop the tower and Kuchkovo rotating beneath it like a record on a giant turntable at the rate of one revolution every forty minutes.

The dizziness persisted when Aïda stepped out of the elevator after lunch. Glancing at her watch gave her an idea, and she slowly unwound herself in a counterclockwise direction. Closing her eyes, she imagined that she was going back in time to undo the future—to fix things so that things did not need to be fixed. Sure enough the dizziness passed. The gesture tickled Vadim, who offered to give her a lift in his taxi. "You are dizzy from love," he told her when they had settled in the backseat of the cab he rented by the year. "It is the American who is making your head spin."

When Aïda failed to respond, Vadim elbowed her in the ribs. "Admit it, Aïda. I have not seen you like this since you fell for that Polish critic who lisped. You are crazy about the American. But you are playing with fire. Even with all this *glasnost* crap they bandy about, there is no place for you and your American in Russia. I know you better than you know yourself, Aïda. When he leaves he will invite you to go with him, but you will refuse, even if it breaks your heart. Remember the poem you underlined in red and left on my pillow the day I suggested we emigrate to Paris?"

Smiling at Vadim's unerring ability to pierce to the core of a problem, she whispered Akhmatova's lines:

> *I heard a voice call . . .*
> *'Leave your remote and sinful country,*
> *Leave Russia behind for ever . . .'*

Nodding, Vadim finished the poem in chorus with her.

> *I covered my ears with my palms . . .*

VADIM DROPPED HER OFF in front of the Kremlin hospital and she joined the queue winding down the corridor toward the hospital pharmacy. The stench of vomit was overpowering and Aïda pulled the fox fur up over her nose to filter the air she breathed. When her turn finally came, she carefully unfolded her authorization and held it up for the pharmacist to read. "Please, his dose is two point five milligrams multiplied by his weight. His weight is thirty kilos."

Instead of turning back toward the shelves brimming

with Western drugs, the pharmacist noted the number on Aïda's authorization and started rifling through the green index cards in a cardboard file box. She finally came up with the card she was looking for and pulled it half out of the box. The steel teeth in her mouth flashed malevolently as she looked up and with callous indifference announced, "Your authorization for Purinethol has expired."

Aïda's heart started hammering against her rib cage. Her knees began to give way and it took all her concentration to remain on her feet. "Such a thing is not within the realm of possibility," she protested. She suddenly realized that she had spoken the words in her head, that they needed to be repeated out loud. "Such a thing is not within the realm of possibility!" she cried shrilly.

But the pharmacist was already peering over her shoulder and calling, "Who's next?"

"You obviously do not understand," Aïda told the pharmacist in a whisper so controlled, so strained, that her voice did not strike her as familiar. "My son must have these pills . . ." It occurred to her that the pharmacist might not have seen the piece of paper that had been folded and unfolded so many times it felt soft to the touch, so she held it up again. "I have an authorization . . . Purinethol, seventy-five milligrams of 6-mercaptopurine a day . . . signed, with an official seal . . ."

The floor under Aïda began to wheel and she clutched the edge of the counter to keep from falling. Had Kuchkovo started rotating under her feet, one revolution every forty minutes, like a record on a turntable?

Behind the counter the pharmacist reached for a telephone. "Either you make way for the next person," she warned Aïda, "or I will summon an orderly."

Aïda backed away from the pharmacy door. Walking as if in a dream past the women queuing, past the hall clock that had stopped working many years before, her right hand on the wall to steady herself, she came to a door marked "Administration." She pushed through it into an office. Five women were busily preparing bills with the aid of abacuses. The clatter of the wooden beads broke off abruptly as the women became aware of the intruder, her hair disheveled, the head of her fox piece trailing along the floor. For an instant Aïda thought she was back in the metro and the fat man who had rubbed her ass was staring at her as if she were mentally deranged. Images of buzzards ripping entrails out of decomposed corpses flashed through her brain. She flailed an arm to ward off a buzzard and shouldered through another door into an inner office where a gray-haired man in a white smock was fitting dentures into the jaw of a skeleton. It occurred to Aïda that she had somehow managed to slip across a frontier into a world of madness. "I have a written authorization—" she cried out, waving her handkerchief-soft scrap of paper as she stumbled toward the man in the white smock. "His dose is two point five milligrams of 6-mercaptopurine multiplied by his weight, which is thirty kilos."

And then Aïda was down on her knees begging in disjointed sentences for medicine, and the man in the white smock was stabbing at an intercom, and two young men in white shirts and white trousers and white shoes were pulling her roughly to her feet and propelling her down a corridor and feeding her into a revolving door and then spinning it, expelling her from the building.

A blast of icy air brought her back to the terrible reality of who she was and where she was and what had been denied her. Cramps stabbed at her intestines. An elderly woman came up to her and buttoned her coat and wound the fox piece around her neck and put a comforting arm around her waist. "When everything else fails," the woman whispered, "you must turn to God."

"God has abandoned Russia," Aïda retorted bitterly.

The woman did not argue. "Do you have someone you can call?" she asked. "Someone who can come and get you?"

"Vadim," Aïda muttered to herself. "He organized the authorization. He will fix things so I can have another one."

"Are you all right now?" the woman asked anxiously. "Can you manage?"

"Yes. Yes. You are very kind."

Squeezing Aïda's fingers, the woman smiled up at her. "There is a God," she whispered. "There is also His Son. There are also His faithful servants, of whom I am one."

The woman disappeared into the hospital. Still feeling shaky, but concentrating on the absolute necessity of finding Vadim, Aïda started toward the street. A black Zil limousine was parked at the curb directly in front of the hospital. Aïda noticed that both the back door and the front door were open. Men wearing identical belted raincoats stood next to the open doors. "Zinaïda Ivanovna Zavaskaya?" the taller of the two politely inquired when Aïda came within earshot.

"Yes."

The man stepped forward and took a firm grip on her elbow. "You are invited to come with us," he said as he steered her toward the waiting limousine.

Taking refuge in a kind of delirium, convinced that Vadim must have rented the limousine by the year, Aïda permitted the two men to fold her into the backseat.

THE WINDOW SHADES HAD been pulled down, the lights turned off, her granny glasses fitted over her eyes, the tape inserted in the video machine. Sitting with unnatural stiffness on a straight-backed wooden kitchen chair directly in front of a television set, Aïda stole a glance over her shoulder. The four men in the room were staring over her head at the television. She turned back and watched the silent image swim into focus on the screen. Unbelievably, a naked woman could be seen bending over something that looked like an erect penis, caressing it first with her heavy breasts, then drawing it delicately into her mouth. Why were they showing her a pornographic film? The last time she had been arrested they had been more straightforward in their efforts to humiliate her. One man had lined up her face with his left hand and punched her in the nose with his right. Then they had folded her over like a napkin, torn off her undergarments, kicked her legs apart so that the doctor who had pulled on a surgical glove could insert a finger in her anus. On the television screen the woman seized the penis with her hand and carefully fitted herself onto it. Aïda wondered what it would be like to see herself copulate. The few times she had made love with a woman she had been able to catch glimpses of herself in a mirror set against the wall next to the bed. She remembered thinking when she had been making love with the American in Peter that she would have liked to see a film of it; would have liked to watch the coupling and uncoupling from several points of view.

On the television screen the woman arched her spine, causing a cascade of long hair that seemed vaguely familiar to spill behind her.

And then Aïda recognized the hair, and the gesture, and the woman.

A stifled scream tore from her throat as she wrenched her head to one side. Akhmatova's acid voice reverberated in her brain, repeating three lines over and over as if a needle had been stuck on a record.

> All has grown confused . . .
> I cannot discern
> Who is man and who is beast . . .

The man who seemed to be directing the interrogation nodded at one of his colleagues, who shut off the video machine and the television set and switched on a lamp that played directly into Aïda's face. She lifted an arm to shade her eyes and tried to make out the dark figures circling like buzzards around her chair. "How did you get such a film?" she demanded, and immediately regretted it. What did it matter how they had gotten it? She tried to stop her hands, her knees from trembling but could not locate the muscles that controlled them. She tried to regulate her breathing, but even that was difficult. What air she took in came in little sucking gasps.

She had been infected with fear by her father. She was permanently frightened.

A hand materialized out of the darkness to offer her something. "It will not bite you," a sarcastic voice said when she hesitated. "Take it."

Aïda felt something almost weightless being placed in her palm. Squinting, she held it up to the light. It was a small brown paper satchel with a gummed label that read, "Purinethol, 75 milligrams of 6-mercaptopurine, to be taken orally at supper each day." Her fingers locked around the satchel and she clasped it to her breast. The hand appeared out of the darkness again to pry her fingers from the satchel and remove it.

Several minutes passed before Aïda could find a voice. Her lips, her mouth were bone dry. "What game are you playing with me?" she whispered huskily. Her head was reeling with possibilities—they wanted to have sex with her in return for Saava's weekly ration of Purinethol, they wanted her to denounce someone as an enemy of the people, they wanted her to stop writing seditious feminist poetry . . .

"How long have you been sleeping with the American Bassett?" someone inquired from the shadows.

The question propelled Aïda across another frontier; she suddenly found herself in the wintry world of her father's nightmares, where you are beyond fear because the thing you are most afraid of has happened. It dawned on her that she was being tested by what she called her Muse and others referred to as God. With this realization, her hands, her knees ceased trembling and she recognized as her own the voice she summoned to respond to the insolent question of the interrogator. "So: Times have not changed that much after all," she said, articulating each word. "You want me to give him up in exchange for the pills."

"We do not want you to give him up. We want you to continue to see him."

"We want you to continue to make love to him," a second man added.

"We want you to go on sucking his cock," a bored voice remarked.

Aïda retorted with a sneer, "Only someone from a Gestapo could make a natural act of sex sound vulgar."

"Everyone who has seen the film agrees," the same bored voice commented. "You fuck like an animal."

Aïda, wounded, cried out, "Everyone who has seen the film!"

"It is in great demand at the office," the bored voice explained.

"The object of intercourse," Aïda moaned, "is intimacy, not entertainment."

"Either you want the pills or you do not want the pills!" snapped the man directing the interrogation.

"I want them," Aïda said tiredly. "But I cannot, I will not lie to the American."

Two of the shadowy figures retreated to a corner of the room and conversed in undertones. Aïda heard one of them snicker. She asked, "Can you turn this light off?"

No one bothered to reply.

The man directing the interrogation strolled back and circled Aïda's chair. His voice came out of the darkness from different directions, making Aïda feel as if she were still in the rotating restaurant. "We do not ask you to lie to him," he explained. "We want you to tell him the truth. Tell him about the pills. Tell him about the film. Tell him about us."

Someone pressed a two-day supply of Purinethol into Aïda's hand. "You have forty-eight hours to bring us what we want."

15

Ben felt a storm raging in the lobe of his brain that
produced emotions. His toes, his fingertips actually tin-
gled. The pulse drumming in his ears almost drowned out
the wild words spilling from her mouth.

Almost, but not quite.

They were standing in an overheated room in the Pushkin Museum, but her lips were as blue as the day she had
sucked the sliver of ice in front of the revolving door of
the Druzhba Café. He explored her face for some sign of
how she was taking it.

She was taking it as if it were the end of a world.

So the KGB had been watching him after all. He had
assumed that if the Russians got wind of the love affair, he
would be the one to be blackmailed. It had never occurred to Ben that they would try to get at him through
her; get at her through her son. She ran out of words and
sighed and turned away from a window and stared so
intently at an enormous Bonnard still life that Ben suspected her of committing it to memory; as if, once memorized, she could seek refuge in it.

Ben broke the spell with a question. "Why does Saava need medicine?"

There was a fruit orchard in the Bonnard. Aïda reached out to brush her fingertips against the trees. A matron in a shapeless brown sack of a dress that buttoned down the front called sternly from across the room, "It is not permitted to touch the paintings."

Aïda's hand drifted back to her side. "He has acute lymphoblastic leukemia," she said dully. Her throat was bone dry and aching. "Remission was induced by an American drug named Purinethol, which blocks the multiplication of white blood cells. That is what leukemia is— the proliferation of abnormal white blood cells." She noticed a splash of bright red on a Matisse canvas across the room. With sudden intensity she whispered, "Akhmatova says somewhere that only blood smells of blood."

"How can you think of poetry at a time like this?"

"When the world was stark raving mad, a handful of poems saved Akhmatova. It is what can save us, dear heart."

His thoughts racing ahead, he breathed in deeply and breathed out deeply and said, "After what has happened, is there still an 'us' to save?" and waited for an answer he discovered, to his surprise, he was afraid to hear.

"I do not blame you for what has happened, Benedict. I do not love you less because of it."

"Oh, God," he muttered. He was suddenly struck by the staleness of the air in the room. He glanced at the window, longing to throw it open, to feel the blast of cold air sweep through the museum. He looked quickly at the matron, thought he heard her stern warning in his ear. "It is not permitted to touch the windows either."

He was not sure if she had actually spoken or he had imagined it.

He looked around tensely. Four French tourists were studying a Vuillard near the entrance of the room. A teacher was lecturing to a group of teenagers gathered around a statue in the adjoining room. Ben steered Aïda over to the next painting, another Matisse alive with colors and textures. "I could get you the pills," he whispered.

She shook her head. "I thought of that but it won't work. They said if you do not give them what they want, they will cancel my Kuchkovo residence permit and pack Saava and me off to some remote village in central Asia where you cannot even buy aspirin. They will find an excuse to expel you from the country. The white blood cells will proliferate and Saava will die."

Ben kneaded his lower lip with his teeth, thinking hard. "You said they showed you a film. What kind of film?" When she failed to respond he shook her elbow. "What was on the film?"

"Us. In Peter. In the hotel room."

He wondered how they had done it without his noticing. Probably by shifting the point agent, trailing him from in front, planting microphones, listening to conversations, getting wind of their plans in time to install cameras behind two-way mirrors. "Of us in the hotel room?"

"We were . . . engaged in an act of sex . . . in a sex act. We were making wonderful love."

Ben remembered the act of sex, the sense of miracle with which it had been suffused. He remembered every time they had made love, could close his eyes and reconstruct each sex act in his brain, could feel the cool curve of her skin beneath his palm. . . . Shaking away the vision, he asked, "What about Vadim? He got you the original authorization. You told me he had connections. Maybe he can get you the pills—"

"I was with Vadim when I left the message for you at the embassy. He made several phone calls, but his sources have all dried up. He said he thought I was in over my head."

"Maybe they're bluffing. Maybe if we sit tight—"

"Forty hours from now I will have no more pills to give to Saava!"

The group of teenagers filed into the room and formed a half circle around the Bonnard. Ben took hold of the sleeve of Aïda's coat and pulled her into the next room. "Tell me again what they want?"

"So: They said something about seven dwarfs. They said you would know what that meant. They said something about wanting an itinerary."

Ben stared at the Matisse in front of his face. Details leapt from the painting; shades of color, brush strokes that trailed off to nothing, the thickness of the paint, its texture. It seemed to him he had never looked at a painting in his life as he was looking at this one; he felt as if he were participating in its creation, as if the paint were still wet. Turning back to Aïda, talking in a whisper, he started to unravel the mystery of who he was for her. "I work for the Arms Control Inspection Team. They are the ones who go around the country inspecting factories and military bases and missile sites to make sure the Russians live up to the disarmament agreements they sign. Inside the embassy they are called the Seven Dwarfs. I keep records and submit expense accounts and run errands for them. I don't have access to secrets."

"Could you get your hands on an itinerary?"

After a moment Ben nodded.

"What would the KGB do with it?"

"The whole logic of on-site inspection depends on the Russians not having advance notice of which sites will be inspected."

"You mean the Russians could cheat." When Ben nodded again Aïda covered her eyes with a hand. "Saava is condemned if we do not give in to them. And we are condemned if we do."

"Why do you say we are condemned?"

"The day we met I told you violence was a circle. Oh, Benedict, don't you see it? We will duck for as long as such a thing is possible. Then we will begin to wound each other."

For an instant Ben almost regretted going back on his "I hope to Christ I never see you again!" "Look," he said. "I'll find something inconsequential for you to pass on to them. It will buy us time. There has to be a way out.

Maybe when they see how low on the diplomatic ladder I am, they will back off rather than risk an international incident."

Even as he tried to reassure her, she spotted in his eyes something that made her shiver—a fiery lucidity, a feverish shrewdness, almost as if he had expected this to happen; almost as if he were scheming. From a long intimacy with fear, she understood that he was not frightened.

It was his lack of fear that terrified her more than anything else.

It HAD BEEN A WHITE night for Manny Custer. Making his rounds at the end of the previous workday, he had punched in the door code (the embassy security officer guarded copies of all door codes and safe combinations in his own safe) and let himself into the deserted political section on the eighth floor. Looking around for classified documents that might have been left out on desks, he had absently twirled the dial of a safe. To his surprise the dial had stuck and the heavy door had clicked open. The assistant political attaché who had locked it for the day had forgotten to give the dial an extra twirl. Manny had posted a marine next to the open safe and had summoned the assistant political attaché back from a cocktail party in the Hotel Peking. The ambassador and the deputy chief of mission had been notified, along with the CIA station chief, Charlie Inkermann. They had all hurried back from a reception for some visiting fireman from the House Armed Services Committee to assess the seriousness of the breach of security. With Manny, the ambassador, the deputy chief of mission and Inkermann breathing down his neck, a very miserable assistant political attaché had conducted an inventory of the documents in the safe. Nothing was missing, but as Manny felt obliged to point out, this didn't guarantee that unauthorized eyes hadn't gotten a glimpse (or a photograph) of some NOFORN or ORCON text in the safe. Manny spent several hours filling out and filing a top secret "Breach-of-Security" report, which concluded that because the safe was in an area of the embassy where access was strictly controlled, the likelihood of an actual penetration was negligible.

Manny's assessment did not get the assistant political attaché off the hook. The same night the safe was found unlocked, the ambassador appended a scathing note to his fitness report that more or less insured that the current tour in Moscow would be his last.

"Another career bites the dust," Inkermann commented to Manny when the two met for their daily briefing the next morning. He ran the palm of his hand over his slicked-back hair, smoothing it down over the bald spot. "You want my opinion, I think the ambassador would have been just as happy if you had locked the safe yourself and finished your rounds."

Manny swallowed a yawn. "The drill is standard operating procedure. You find a safe open, you post a guard, you notify the ambassador, you get the custodian of the safe to do an inventory, you file a Breach-of-Security report."

Inkermann tapped a lead pencil on his blotter. "You knew from the marine log nobody had been up there."

Manny, his hands clasped behind his head, watched the point of Inkermann's pencil drumming on the blotter. Inkermann noticed him watching and stopped. Manny said, "The object isn't to screw some dumb assistant political attaché. The object is to make sure it doesn't happen again. In ten days every diplomat in every embassy around the globe will have heard about the ruined career and started spinning the dials of their safes to make sure they're locked." He shrugged again. "Whatever."

The station chief reached into his in-basket and let the folds of Teletype paper slide through his thick fingers. He came to the item he was looking for. "Your sand's running out, Manny. Your replacement's due in sometime next week. You'll overlap him a month to show him the ropes. Then we'll throw a bash for you at the Praga Restaurant and give you a wristwatch with an inscription citing your long and distinguished career, and drive you to the airport. Have you thought about how you're going to spend your retirement?"

A gleam appeared in Manny's eyes. "Maybe I'll read books. Maybe I'll write them."

"You'd never know we were on the same side all these years."

"Were we?"

Inkermann shook his head in disgust. Manny uncoiled in the chair. "I've been meaning to ask you something . . ."

The station chief stuck a plastic cigarette between his lips and began to gnaw on the end of it. "Ask quick. I have a nine thirty due any minute."

"It's about Benedict Bassett."

"Yeah. So?"

"It's about him working out of your ribbon room."

"You'll dirty your ear keeping it to the ground one of these days."

"You got to admit it's curious—a housekeeper who locks himself more or less regularly in your ribbon room. So what does he do?"

Inkermann was beginning to enjoy the conversation. "For all I know he masturbates over pictures he stores in his safe."

Manny didn't laugh. "Bassett claims he is enciphering status reports for the Seven Dwarfs using ciphers he keeps in the safe you gave him. But I don't think that's it."

"Why not?"

"I checked the outgoing log in the communications bubble. Bassett does turn up with an enciphered message from the Dwarfs from time to time, but it would hardly take him"—Manny pulled an envelope from his breast pocket and looked at some notes he had jotted on the back of it—"nine and a half hours, which is how much time he spent up here last week, for example, to encipher the five messages he sent."

"Maybe he is a slow worker," Inkermann suggested.

"Maybe what he's really doing is working for the Company," Manny said.

"He's not Company," Inkermann said flatly.

"Then again maybe he's working for you and you're free-lancing."

Inkermann stood up to indicate the meeting had come to an end. "Like I said, your replacement will need a four-week overlap, after which you'll be on your way stateside. You should consider this formal notification of an impending transfer of responsibilities and prepare the appropriate paperwork."

Heading for the door, Manny said, "Thanks for your help."

"Anytime," Inkermann called after him. He couldn't contain a snicker as he added, "Only ask if I can do something for you."

"Whatever," Manny muttered before the door slammed.

THE LAST TIME MANNY'S NOSE had been atwitch he had caught one marine covering for another who should have been on duty, but (as things turned out) was being dined and wined and sexually ensnared by a luscious Russian swallow. The discovery had led to the foiling of a Soviet operation to penetrate the embassy.

Waiting now near the mailboxes inside the main entrance of the embassy, Manny felt his nose atwitch again. It was true that he spent most of his waking hours treating possibilities as probabilities, true that he spent most of his nonwaking hours converting probabilities into nightmares. But what embassy security officer didn't? Imagining that every case was the worst case was an occupational disease. He reminded himself that he had only another month or so to go before whatever happened would happen on someone else's watch.

The thought gave cold comfort to an old pro like Custer.

At six twenty he caught a glimpse of Benedict Bassett hurrying through the courtyard behind the embassy and handing his burn bag to the wiry technician who tended the incinerator. Moments later Bassett waved to the marine on duty at the checkpoint on his way out of the front door of the embassy. Manny quickly pulled on his knee-length ski parka and ambled after him. He caught up with Bassett in the street.

"Well, Mr. Bassett, looks as if we punch the same clock for once. Where are you off to?"

Ben seemed rattled. "I was going to walk over to the Metropole and grab a drink at the hard-currency bar before heading home."

"Mind if I keep you company part of the way?" Without waiting for an answer Manny fell into step alongside Bassett. "I'm heading down Gorki to a gastronome I know not far from Red Square. They sell pickled herrings from the Baltic that remind me of my wife's herrings. She used to pickle them herself. I lost the recipe when she died."

Their heads hunched forward, their hands plunged into their coat pockets, Manny and Bassett trudged past a peasant woman in a thick quilted Army coat peddling clumps of parsley. "They're an amazing people, these Russians," Manny was saying in a lazy drawl. "A Tsar like Peter the Great could build a city like Leningrad to open a window to the West, and then murder his son. A Tsarina like Catherine the Great could flirt with eighteenth-century French liberalism, and then murder her husband."

"They say there are two sides to Russia," Ben remarked. "Everything is exactly as it seems—but the opposite is also true. Voznesensky wrote a poem on the subject called 'Antiworlds.' " He glanced sideways at the security chief. "You obviously like the Russians or you wouldn't have bothered to learn their history."

"I like them, but I don't trust them, Mr. Bassett. I will break bread with them and let them divide the loaf in two, but, as the peasants say, I want to have first pick." Manny shrugged. "Whatever."

They came abreast of a fishing supply store. "Are you an angler, Mr. Bassett?"

"An angler?"

"A fisherman?" He steered Ben over to the window. "Come on, let's window-shop for a minute. The Russians make some fine lightweight casting rods. If you go out

into the countryside, you can pick up some homemade
flies that will knock your eye out." Manny seemed genu-
inely interested in some of the rods and reels in the window, pointing out which ones were for rivers and which
for surf. When they started down Gorki again Manny said,
"It was right after the Bolshevik Revolution that Lenin
posed the question: What should you give starving people,
fish or fishing rods? Do you have an opinion, Mr. Bassett?"

"Both."

Manny had to laugh. "You're avoiding having to make a
choice."

"I suppose I am."

They came to the gastronome, which had a long line
winding out the door and down the sidewalk. "Here's
where our paths part," Manny said. "Thanks for your
company."

"You did most of the talking."

Manny smiled thinly. "And you did the right amount of
listening."

Ben, trying to hide his relief that Custer was not going
to tag along with him any further, strode off down Gorki
and soon disappeared in the crowd. Manny watched him
go, then ambled away from the queue and headed for the
nearest metro to return to his apartment in the complex
across from the Hotel Ukraine on Kutuzovsky Prospekt.

TINKLING THE USUAL ROCKS against the sides of a tall glass
containing double the usual scotch, Manny stared out the
window at what he could see of the city. Below, droves of
dark figures bundled in layers of clothing were cutting
across the dirty snow of Kutuzovsky Prospekt, which was
laced with the tracks of tires. A dirty yellow motorcycle
with a dirty yellow sidecar attached to it made its noisy
way up the street, backfiring every few meters. On the
other side of the wide boulevard, long lines of shoppers
snaked back and forth across the sawdust-covered floors
of brightly lit stores which, Manny knew, had next to
nothing piled on the thick glass shelves. Manny's eyes

focused on his own reflection in the window and he caught sight of the grim smile of satisfaction playing on his lips.

It was true what they said about him collecting details the way other men collected lint in their trouser cuffs when trousers still had cuffs.

Item: Walking away from the embassy with Bassett, Manny had observed out of the corner of his eye the peasant woman in the thick quilted Army coat selling parsley. He had seen her raise a bouquet of parsley as they passed; had seen a young woman carrying an airline bag detach herself from the queue and fall into step twenty paces behind them; had seen her turn a shade too quickly to window-shop in a store selling used spare parts for automobiles when he and Bassett stopped in front of the store selling fishing rods. She had probably noticed Manny glancing nonchalantly over his shoulder, had probably realized that she did not look like someone who would be window-shopping for used spare automobile parts, because she had removed her fur hat and lowered the ear flaps and replaced the hat on her head. Moments later she had peeled off down a side street as a dirty brown sedan pulled over to the curb across Gorki. A tall man wearing an overcoat with a fur collar had gotten out. He had strolled down Gorki parallel to them for a time, then he too had peeled off to be replaced, if Manny's instinct was accurate, by a young couple with their arms around each other's waists.

Manny, who had organized his share of surveillance operations during his back-to-back tours in Turkey, recognized professionals at work when he saw them. Either he or Bassett was being followed by some very experienced folks who were going to a lot of trouble and expense to keep the surveillance from being noticed.

Item: Heading for home, Manny had doubled back on the metro line, had lingered inside the station near Kutuzovsky Prospekt, had entered a liquor store near the Hotel Ukraine and had ducked out of a back door and circled around through an alley to the street to see who might be waiting for him.

No one had been waiting for him. Which meant that it was Bassett, and not Manny, who was being followed.

Item: Wandering through the embassy's New Office Building earlier that week, Manny had come across a package on the floor outside the Post Office from Stockman's Department Store in Helsinki addressed to Benedict Bassett. Checking the master invoice posted on the bulletin board, Manny discovered that Bassett had ordered a fleece-lined denim jacket. What was intriguing was the size: 11.

Item: During a routine check of the embassy's telephone logs, Manny had noticed a message for Bassett. "Please can he meet Z in front of Pushkin Museum at 4," the message had read. "Just Z?" Manny had asked the operator who took the message. "If she had left a name I would have recorded a name," the operator had retorted in annoyance. "She?" Manny had asked. "She," the operator had confirmed. "Was this female Z American?" Manny had inquired with exaggerated politeness. "Not sure," the operator had replied. "She spoke very slowly and her English was very precise. To tell the truth, I couldn't tell if she had an accent." Manny had read out the message in the log. " 'Please can he meet Z in front of Pushkin Museum at 4.' Are you sure she didn't say 'the' Pushkin Museum?" "If she had said 'the Pushkin Museum' I would have written 'the Pushkin Museum,' " the operator had answered testily.

Item: Manny was no grammarian, but he understood enough Russian to know that there were no articles in the language. And he had noticed that Russians speaking in English tended to drop the definite article, to say, for instance, "Pushkin Museum" and not "the Pushkin Museum." Which meant that if the operator had really recorded the message word for word, the chances were that the Z who wanted to meet Bassett was a Russian woman speaking English.

Manny coughed up one of his guttural laughs that had

no trace of mirth. It turned into a dry hacking cough. He had had a department physical before being posted to Moscow. A Foreign Service doctor had scared him into giving up cigarettes after having smoked two packs a day for thirty-five years. Gradually, the coughing subsided. The doctor, Manny remembered, had tried to get him to give up alcohol too. He was glad he had resisted. Nursing the double scotch, staring into the accumulating darkness, Manny began to sketch the outline of a theory that would account for the various specks of lint in his trouser cuff. The result was too crazy to be convincing. Then he re-membered a shrewd observation he had come across in a book the previous summer. It had been made by the physicist Niels Bohr to a young colleague.

"Your theory is crazy," Bohr had said. "But not crazy enough."

16

During his lunch break the next day, Ben hurried over to the Praga Restaurant for a buffet in honor of one of the Seven Dwarfs being reassigned to Washington. "Can't say I'm sorry to be passing the baton," the Dwarf, a marine captain, cheerfully told his replacement, a Navy lieutenant commander named Pierce whom Ben had picked up at the airport the previous week.

"How long were you stationed here?" the lieutenant commander asked.

"Eighteen months, two weeks and four days, which is eighteen months, two weeks and four days too long." The other Dwarfs and their wives nodded grimly in agreement.

The marine captain's wife plucked a wedge of toast covered with salmon from a tarnished silver tray carried by a passing waiter. "Whatever else you do," she advised the wife of the lieutenant commander, "do not set foot in one of their hair dressing emporiums—unless of course you want to wind up with hair like this." She threaded her fingers through her bleached silver curls, which were stiff and weathered. "Their permanents tend to be really permanent."

The ambassador, working on his fourth vodka, beckoned to Ben. "If you give me the watch I'll put our friend out of his misery," he told him in an undertone. Ben handed him the gift-wrapped package he had had flown in from Stockman's. The ambassador clanked a knife against the side of a vodka bottle. "Ladies, gentlemen, if rank has its privileges, surely one of them is that I get to deliver the official 'Thank you and Godspeed' to our colleagues heading for sunnier climes." He turned to address the departing marine directly. "Captain, you have performed a tedious assignment with competence and perseverance. You have been an adroit referee at our Little League baseball games. You have been a congenial companion at Sam's happy hours. But the thing for which you will be most remembered is that you took all comers to the cleaners at the regular Thursday night poker game."

Manny Custer, who never missed a pour if he could help it, raised his glass to the marine captain. "To paraphrase Winston Churchill," he muttered in a voice that originated at the back of his throat, "never before have so many owed so much to one man. Whatever."

The Dwarfs and their guests laughed amiably. The ambassador, pulling a face because he had been upstaged, offered the gift-wrapped package to the departing officer.

"Something tells me it's a wristwatch," the marine captain announced as he tore off the wrapping. He opened the box and pulled out a stainless steel Rolex and held it aloft. Everyone applauded.

"Read the inscription," the ambassador's wife called.

The captain held the back of the watch up to the light. "To R.M.W. from his friends in Moscow."

Everyone applauded again. The marine captain took off his own watch and strapped on the Rolex. "Well, now, I want y'all to know how much Helen and I . . . ."

On the fringe of the crowd, Ben glanced at his own watch, then quickly left the reception. He raced down the steps to the cloakroom and handed his stub to the woman behind the counter. She came back a moment later with his hat and sheepskin overcoat. Getting into his coat, he brushed against a woman with a broken, badly set nose alive with freckles. Her enormous eyes were dark with fear. She clutched a bright fringed Uzbek shawl that was draped over the shoulders of her coat.

"Excuse me," Ben said very softly.

The woman smiled nervously as he backed away from her. When he had disappeared through the restaurant's front door, Aïda felt around in the folds of the shawl and found the sealed envelope he had slipped there. She dropped it into her handbag and hurried out of the building into the street. Half an hour later she pushed through a door into a prewar apartment building on the Lenin Hills. Stopping at each stairwell to make sure she was not being followed, she climbed to the sixth floor, where it was possible to cross into another wing of the building, then descended a staircase that reeked of urine to the third floor and rang the plastic bell next to the door with the number 310 on it.

The door opened almost instantly, as if she had been expected. A pear-faced young man with tobacco-stained teeth, wearing an overcoat and a thick knit scarf wound around his thin neck, pulled her inside the apartment and pushed the door closed behind her. "You have the material?" he demanded.

Aïda noticed immediately that the room was unheated. It was lit by a single bulb dangling from the ceiling. There was a large mirror on a wall next to a closed double-door and a television set in a corner—the one on which she had been shown the film clips of her making love to Benedict. Near a kitchenette there was a wooden table covered with squares of Formica, along with half a dozen wooden kitchen chairs, no two of them alike. A kettle at full boil was whistling on the stove in the kitchenette. "Do you have the pills?" Aïda asked.

The man produced a small brown paper satchel from his jacket pocket. Staring at it, Aïda backed toward the door.

"Don't be a fool," the man told her, as if he had been reading her mind; as if he had recognized in her wild eyes the beady stare of a bird about to take to the wing.

Aïda pulled Ben's envelope from her pocket, but could not bring herself to give it to him; could not bring herself to cross the threshold. The man solved the dilemma by stepping forward and snatching it out of her fingers. He weighed the envelope in his palm, then slit it open with a fingertip and extracted a single sheet of paper, which he proceeded to read. Apparently satisfied, he tossed her the paper satchel filled with the pills. Her fingers working frantically, Aïda opened it and counted them. Pulling the shawl tighter around her shoulders as if it were some sort of armor, she reached for the door knob.

"Your son will run out of pills Wednesday night," the man warned her. "Return here between three and four in the afternoon two days before. And do not speak of this to anyone."

Aïda turned back. She was a head taller than the man with the tobacco-stained teeth, and for an instant she imagined herself crowding him against a wall and pounding his head into it. The image faded and she said, "Will you give me more pills?"

"We will tell you what we want in return for more pills," the man informed her.

THE SHEEPSKIN COLLAR of his soul-warmer turned up around his neck, the flaps of his astrakhan spilling over his ears, Viktor pushed through the double doors into the room moments after Aïda had left. Captain Krostin appeared behind Viktor and started to prepare a pot of tea. Frolov handed Viktor the sheet of paper that he had plucked out of Aïda's fingers. Nodding, Viktor read it, then reached out to shake Frolov's hand. "I watched the whole thing through the mirror," he told him. "You worked the Zavaskaya woman beautifully."

"What the American gave us, of course, is worthless," Frolov said.

"That was to be expected," Krostin called from the kitchenette.

"His idea of an itinerary," Frolov remarked, "is a list of regions they plan to visit. Without dates."

Krostin lined up three kitchen tumblers and spooned a lump of store-bought confiture into each. "How does the colonel take his tea?" he asked Viktor.

"Dirty, like dishwater," Viktor replied. Frolov, normally very reserved, actually cracked a smile. "The important thing," Viktor continued, putting an arm over Frolov's shoulder, drawing him toward the table, "is that he gave us the list instead of going to the security officer, Custer."

Krostin rinsed the teapot with boiling water to warm it, then spilled out the water, added four teaspoons of tea and filled the pot with the rest of the boiling water.

They talked shop for several minutes. There were bills to be paid out of contingency funds, surveillance teams to be rotated into and out of Moscow, a report to be drafted for the old general. "What a stroke of good fortune it was —the boy having leukemia and needing those pills," Krostin commented. Viktor sank tiredly into a seat at the table and produced a package of dry biscuits from his overcoat pocket. He passed a couple of biscuits to both of his young section chiefs. Krostin half-filled the three glasses with muddy tea. Viktor said something about having been joking when he said he took his tea dirty, like dishwater. He stirred the tea until the confiture dissolved, then gripping his glass at the rim, brought it to his mouth and noisily sipped it.

Krostin watched him anxiously. Viktor took another sip. "I seriously believe this is the worst glass of tea of my life," he said.

A shadow of a smile played on Viktor's face as he made the announcement. The head of the KGB's Second Chief Directorate did not look as if he were suffering.

17

They met briefly the following afternoon in a stuffy café on the Arbat crowded with workers from a nearby canning factory, but spent most of their twenty minutes together looking over each other's shoulders. Now that they knew they had been followed, it seemed as if everyone who took an interest in them, as well as those who didn't, was a KGB agent. Huddling over two cups of watery coffee set on a tiny round table, Ben memorized the fear glistening in Aïda's eyes as she told him what had happened in the apartment that she referred to as Gehenna and he called a safe house. She had recognized the voice of the man who had opened the door; he was the one who had sneered in a bored voice, "You fuck like an animal" the first time she had been brought there. Yes, he had appeared satisfied with the information Ben had provided; yes, he had given her enough pills to see Saava through Wednesday night; yes, he would supply more pills—but only when she supplied more information. "Dear heart," she groaned, "where will this end? And what will become of us if I oblige you to betray your country?"

He had no answers to offer her, either in the café that afternoon or later in the week when they spent the night together (Vadim was taking care of Saava and Aïda's father) in an apartment of a friend of Aïda's who had gone off to Sochi. Aïda, looking drained, looking older, went through the motions of frying some liver that Ben had bought in the diplomatic gastronome (she had set aside two portions for her father and Saava). But when it came time to eat she discovered that she had lost her appetite. For the food on her plate. For the physical assault on the sacred line that Akhmatova said could not be crossed. For life in general. "So: It is difficult for me to believe this is really happening," Aïda told him. She was lying in his arms on the bed. Her long dirty-blond hair was bound in a braid and both had kept their clothes on, as if they were afraid to expose their naked bodies to some hidden camera.

Ben, for his part, seemed alternately moody and optimistic. There were moments when he disappeared so completely into his thoughts that Aïda had to repeat his name several times to get his attention. The few times Aïda pressed him, he claimed to be hopeful that they would be thrown back, like small fish, after she had delivered three or four of his envelopes; the people who were blackmailing them would realize how limited Ben's access to secrets really was and drop the penetration operation. Aïda half believed him; half believed it would end the way the nightmares she could never remember ended: With her sitting up abruptly, in a cold sweat, surprised and relieved that it had only been a bad dream.

The next morning, in a chilly factory auditorium, Aïda read some of her poems to several dozen women in blue smocks. Two days later she gave another reading to a group of women in white smocks in the operating amphitheater of a suburban clinic. Both readings went badly. Her mind wandering, her fingers drumming against the edge of the lectern, she recited her verses without enthusiasm, forgot lines, started to say something about the origin of a poem only to lose the thread completely and wind up staring blankly at the audience. The women in the amphitheater shifted uncomfortably in their seats, exchanged looks, whispered among themselves. After the second reading Aïda took the subway across town and delivered a new poem to the editor at *Novy Mir,* who asked if something was wrong when she agreed, without arguing, to delete the expression "menstrual cycle" from it.

At her apartment that evening Aïda watched Saava doing his history homework on the kitchen table. "Is it so, Aïda, that the United States of America's President Truman said America would support whichever side was losing in order to make the Great Patriotic War drag on? That he sent military supplies to us while we were losing, but began sending them to the Nazis when we started winning?"

Aïda, her mind elsewhere, regarded Saava absently. She didn't have the energy to set him straight. "Eat what's on your plate and go to your room," she mumbled.

Later, unable to sleep, Aïda quietly opened the door of her father's room and looked in. Saava was on his knees next to the wicker chair, arranging the quilted blanket so that it covered his grandfather's old Army trousers as he sat, motionless, staring out through the double panes of the window. "What is it you are waiting for all these years, Granddad?" she heard the boy whispering.

The old man brought a mutilated hand up to rub the stubble on his chin. He cleared his throat and said, very clearly, "Cossacks."

"Cossacks?" When the old man did not reply, Saava, his eyes wide with wonder, asked, "Did you ever see any?"

"It's us, the Cossacks."

"Us?"

The old man grunted. "Us."

Back in her room, Aïda pulled a chair over to the window and settled into it to look out at the street. She saw a man emerge from a building carrying a small dog under his arm. He set it down in the gutter and gently nudged it with his foot until it relieved itself against a tire. She heard the motor of the last bus of the night pass the intersection down the block. She watched a car pull up across the street and leaned her forehead against the cold pane when nobody got out. She could feel the tenseness in her forehead; a migraine must be lurking behind her lids. Finally a woman emerged from the car and, waving gaily to the driver, darted into the building. The car pulled slowly away from the curb. Aïda, relieved, rocked back into the chair. A hollow silence, in which the lack of sound seemed to reverberate, settled over the deserted street. In the silence Aïda heard a distant voice pose a question. It was only when she formulated an answer that she discovered the conversation was taking place in her head.

Describe your latest arrest.

They did not actually arrest me. There was no tea, no cakes. They sat me in a chair and showed a film of me fucking like an animal.

What conclusion did you reach?

The object of intercourse is blackmail.

What is in the shortest supply in the Motherland?

Light bulbs. Soap. Toilet paper. Hope.

What is in the greatest supply?

Dead leaves.

Dead leaves?

Dead leaves. Yes.

I am not sure I follow you.

. . .

*Do you think it is possible? To love a man
so much you begin to hate him for complicating your life?*

*I am afraid of running out of unshed tears.
I am afraid of losing poetry.*

You are avoiding the question.

*So: I am not avoiding the question.
I am avoiding the answer.*

GOING THROUGH THE MOTIONS of housekeeping, Ben showed
the ropes to the wife of the new Dwarf. He guided Mrs.
Pierce through the peeling embassy corridors so she
would know where to go for gas coupons or Bolshoi tickets. He arranged with the General Services Office for a
maid and a Russian language teacher. He signed her up
for the video rental club in the New Office Building. He
took her over to the embassy's warehouse to pick up a
toaster and a microwave oven and an electric blanket. All
the while his thoughts raced.

He had hoped to meet a Russian woman in Moscow,
hoped even to be able to have an affair with her. But he
had not been prepared for Aïda; had thought the bitter
wounds inflicted by his divorce, the loss of custody of his
son, would give him a working immunity on the off
chance he came across someone like her. What was it
about her that touched a nerve in him, that pulled at him
the way Russia itself pulled at him through the thick soles
of his shoes? Before he had slept with her—before he had
gotten to know the part of her that was bold and bad and
gay—he had thought her haunted and hunted, but he saw
now that there was more to her than that; much more.
Ben was beginning to understand that being a poet in
Russia involved more than writing poetry; that the language of her body had everything to do with what she
discovered in the spaces between words.

.   .   .

THE MEETING HAD BEEN jokingly billed as a very mini summit. The case had become important enough so that the old general himself presided. Viktor, his toes tingling with gout, sat on one side of the long oak table, with his two section chiefs, Frolov and Krostin, downstream. The two senior analysts attached to the general's secretariat faced them across the table.

"We operated under the usual ground rules," the junior of the two analysts, a middle-aged woman named Olga Glebova, was explaining to the general. She had a pinched face and bulging eyes and a nest of stiff bleached blond hair teased up on her head. She spoke with excruciating slowness, as if words were stones set in a stream and she was fastidiously stepping from one to the other to get across without wetting her feet. "Which is to say, we were not told where the documents came from. We were instructed to evaluate them without reference to origin." Peering through the lower half of octagonal bifocals, Glebova studied her handwritten notes as the general's withered fingers tapped out the passing seconds on the table.

Glebova found what she was looking for. "The documents were apparently acquired, as you know and we guess, in four batches. In batch number one unnamed people in groups of twos or threes are going by train or by plane or by car to various regions of the Soviet Union. They will stay in these regions for periods ranging from two to five days. By matching this very sketchy information against intercepts from microphones planted in apartments—"

Glebova's colleague, the senior analyst N. Fillipov, grew impatient and finished the sentence for her. "—we were able to establish that batch number one is actually a rough itinerary for the seven members of the American Arms Control Implementation Unit."

The general leaned forward. "But does it tell us anything we did not know before?"

Fillipov, a stony-faced man wearing a three-piece, pin-striped suit of Hungarian manufacture one size too tight for his pudgy, middle-aged body, shook his head very delicately, as if he were afraid to dislodge his carefully groomed, prematurely gray locks. "Our service has been predicting the itinerary of the American inspection teams since they began functioning—sometimes from things the inspectors said to their wives, sometimes from the clothing or guidebooks they purchased, sometimes from the train or plane schedules the unit's housekeeper was overheard requesting from the travel section on the first floor of the embassy." Fillipov arched bushy white eyebrows, which jutted like awnings over his eyes. "Take for instance the last trip mentioned in the so-called itinerary you gave us. One knew about their intention to visit the ballistic missile sites in the Kara Kum desert since the wife of the inspector in question was overheard telling her husband that Khiva was famous for its handwoven rugs and asking if he could bring back several. One also knew that the trip was scheduled for late April when the wife was overheard during a long-distance telephone call advising her mother-in-law that the last week in April was not a good time for her to visit Moscow."

"The material identified as batch number two," Glebova picked up the thread in her plodding, precise style, "is made up of disjointed scraps of writing in American English. In places sentences are fragmented, in other places even the words are fragmented. From this we have concluded that the batch represents material recovered at random from an American embassy burn bag. There are two mentions of dwarfs, which means the material almost certainly comes from the embassy's Arms Control Implementation Unit, since, as you know, the seven American arms control inspectors—"

"—are humorously known as the Seven Dwarfs," Fillipov finished the sentence for her. "Once again the material tells one nothing that one did not already know—details of the office expense account, references to the kind of film and lenses they use when they take pictures on their inspection tours, translations of excerpts of articles on military matters clipped from our journals, a garbled scrap that could be part of a summary of the monthly estimate of our missile readiness. Nothing to set one's heart to quaking here."

"Batch number three," Glebova waded on, "is the service record of the lieutenant commander who recently replaced the marine captain on the Inspection Unit."

Fillipov swallowed a yawn. The general cast a look in Viktor's direction, as if to say: Our two analysts are so excited about the gold mine of information you have come up with they are having trouble staying awake. "The service record of the lieutenant commander," Fillipov droned on, "duplicates information that our Washington embassy worked up on him when he was named to the Moscow post. The lieutenant commander comes from a small village in western New York State named Alfred. His biography was published in the local newspaper."

"Which brings us to batch number four," said Glebova. "This batch consists entirely of lists of names of staff members at the American embassy."

"I can tell you that this item stumped us for a week," Fillipov admitted. "We considered every possibility: that the names were divided according to security clearances, which of course would be interesting to us; that the lists showed who was permitted access to different parts of the embassy compound; that they showed a breakdown of housing assignments; that they represented the duty officer shift for nights and weekends."

Across the table Viktor scraped back his chair loudly enough to indicate he was tiring of the game. Fillipov got the message. "The lists," he said, "represent the teams in the embassy's bowling league."

The old general, wheezing from a sinus attack, dropped an orange-colored pill into a glass of mineral water and watched it drift to the bottom and dissolve. With a nod from Viktor, his two section chiefs and the two analysts gathered their notes and slipped out of the room. "It is as plain as the nose on your face," the general muttered as soon as the door had closed, "that we can learn more by reading the *New York Times*." He stirred the bubbling

water with the back of a spoon and drank off the discol-
ored liquid in one long gulp. His large Adam's apple
worked against the wrinkled skin of his neck as he swallowed. "It seems to me," he went on, settling back into his
chair, breathing through his mouth, "that you are running
a very big risk for very little compensation. This Bassett is
nothing more than a housekeeper without access to important information. If he takes it into his head to go
crying to his security people, his lords and masters in
Washington will raise hell. We will be caught in the cross-
fire between the Americans and those of our bosses who
have lost the appetite for combating international Capitalism. Unless you have some compelling arguments that I
have not heard, I am of the opinion that the American
should be cut loose and the operation discontinued."

Viktor cleared his throat. "Bassett is more than a housekeeper."

The general eyed his son-in-law. "What makes you
think so?"

"We know he had an appointment with the CIA station
chief soon after he reported for work at the embassy. We
have reason to believe he has been up to the station almost every day since." Viktor reminded the general how
the Center's microphones had overheard the secretary,
Miss Macy, referring to Bassett as "our four fifteen" the
first time he went up to see Inkermann; how she continued to greet someone she tauntingly called "our bashful
four fifteen" almost daily.

Assuming it was Bassett, what was he doing on the
tenth floor, the general asked.

"I wish we knew," Viktor admitted. "Our microphones
record him in the station's outer office greeting the secretary Macy. We hear her make a remark about 'our four
fifteen slumming on the tenth floor' or some such thing.
We hear a door being opened and closed."

"He sees Inkermann?"

"The secretary Macy always announces Inkermann's
visitors over an intercom. Except for Bassett's first visit,
she has never announced him. My guess is that he is going

into another of the station's rooms. An hour or so later he can be heard emerging from the room. There is usually more banter. The secretary Macy can be overheard hinting she would not mind being invited to dinner or a film. Bassett always begs off. Often it is because he has a rendezvous with the Zavaskaya woman."

Viktor could see that the old general was torn between his instinct for caution and his instinct to gamble. He turned his chair so that he was facing his father-in-law. "We have never before been able to penetrate the embassy's CIA station," he said, masking his excitement behind a facade of professionalism. "If we could get our hands on evidence that the CIA is taking advantage of the climate of *glasnost* to run operations against us, it would strengthen the hand of those of us who think the reforms have weakened the Motherland."

The general immediately saw what Viktor was driving at. "*Pamyat* could profit."

Viktor nodded carefully.

The general's eyes narrowed. "What do you propose?"

"We want to turn the screw. We want to put more pressure on the Zavaskaya woman. We want her to put pressure on Bassett. When the ground has been prepared, we will invite him to the safe house for an interview."

"You want to debrief him?"

"We want to find out what he does during those daily visits to Inkermann's station on the tenth floor."

The fingers of the general's left hand slowly curled of their own accord. Viktor took the gesture for a summons to gamble.

18

Squeezed into a corner behind a life-size bronze statue of a nude woman with three eyes and three breasts, Ben reread the lines scrawled on the back of the envelope that Aïda had slipped him.

Do you think it is possible? To love a man so much you begin to hate him for complicating your life?

I am afraid of running out of unshed tears.
I am afraid of losing poetry.

You are avoiding the question.

So: I am not avoiding the question.
I am avoiding the answer.

Rising on his toes, peering over the heads of the Muscovites swirling through the gallery in search of champagne or *zakuski* or each other, he made out Aïda, backed up against a mosaic, the stem of a champagne glass in one hand, a hand-rolled cigarette in the other, surrounded by a gaggle of men whom she kept at arm's length by exhaling bursts of foul-smelling smoke in their faces. She had on the same 1930s pillbox hat with an enormous white feather spiked through it that she had been wearing when he met her under the windows of the rehearsal studio a lifetime ago. Ben needed to be alone with her; to breathe declarations of eternal lust into the nape of her neck, to swear to God that he had not set out to complicate her life. Shouldering through the mob milling around some People's Artist's latest oeuvre, a tractor compressed into a package the size of a small trunk, Ben tried to catch Aïda's eye, but she turned away without noticing him to hear what her ex-husband was saying. "Read the history books and weep," Vadim announced gleefully, waving so wildly with a champagne glass that half its contents spilled onto his corduroy jacket. "Karl Marx had pleurisy, bronchitis, carbuncles, asthma, inflamed eyes, a diseased liver, a swollen spleen, migraine headaches, chronic insomnia, chronic diarrhea, ingrown toenails, decaying teeth and an itching anus probably caused by worms. Freddy Engels had a weakness for wine and women and spent more feeding his horse than Karl earned writing for the *New York Herald*. And these are the people who gave us Communism!"

Aïda drained the last of the champagne from her glass. She was looking around for a place to set it when she spotted Ben. He gestured with his head for her to follow him. Pushing past a sculptor who was ranting drunkenly about how events were moving so rapidly you had to run to be an *arrière garde,* she made her way to the cloakroom and collected her blanket-lined overcoat and fox neckpiece. She found Ben waiting on a landing outside the main hall. He started down a corridor ahead of her, opened a door, checked to see if the room was empty and pulled Aïda inside. Kicking the door closed, he pressed her body back against a wall with his own and found her lips in the darkness and kissed her so hungrily and so long that she had to struggle free in order to breathe. They clung to each other for several minutes.

Ben finally whispered, "You hate me for complicating your life."

"I should not have given you the poem."

"If you don't hate me, why did you avoid the answer?"

"I love you, Benedict. I only wish I had never met you."

"Aïda—"

There were footsteps in the corridor. Someone could be heard pausing in front of the door. Barely daring to breathe, Aïda and Ben held on to each other, listening. The footsteps retreated down the corridor.

"Your message frightened me," Ben told her. "How are you?"

She remembered how the peasants responded to such a question. "Better than tomorrow," she said with a dry laugh.

"Are things that bad?"

"Dear heart, I swore to myself I would not tell you, but I must. The last time I delivered your envelope, he only gave me two-thirds of the dose."

Ben didn't understand. "Two-thirds of the dose?"

"Saava is supposed to take seventy-five milligrams of 6-mercaptopurine a day. He only gave me enough for fifty milligrams a day."

"They made a mistake," Ben said quickly. Even as the words crossed his lips, he knew it had not been a mistake.

Slipping out of his arms, Aïda moved over to a window almost opaque with grime and fumbled in her sack for tobacco and paper, then decided she did not want to smoke after all. Ben came up behind her. "Did you ask him why he gave you fifty milligrams?"

She said very quietly, "He wants to see you, Benedict."

"Me."

"He wants to talk to you."

After a moment he asked, "About what?"

Aïda shrugged. "About the other twenty-five milligrams."

Ben suddenly became aware of the beat of his own heart. He had been wondering when they would get around to him. "He wants to see *me* about the twenty-five milligrams?"

"So: He said he was holding out on Saava because you were holding out on him."

"I gave him whatever I could get my hands on."

She shrugged again, but in a particularly apathetic way, as if hiking her shoulders required more energy than she had available.

Gripping her fox neckpiece, Ben pulled her around so that she was facing him. "I cannot do it," he whispered intently. "There would be no hope of getting out from under if I did—it's one thing if they have films of us making love, it's another if they have a film of me talking to the KGB."

Aïda nodded grimly. It was the answer she had expected.

There was a rush of footsteps in the corridor. A woman could be heard whining, "For God's sake, Leonid, not here!"

"Where?" a male voice demanded.

"Where you like, but not here. What if my husband or your wife saw us leave together?"

When the two people outside the door had departed, Aïda whispered, "We cannot remain here."

Ben thrust an envelope into Aïda's fingers. "This is for tomorrow's session in the safe house." He suggested they meet at five thirty the next afternoon at a workers' canteen on Krasnaya Presnya that they had been to before. "Give me a few minutes' head start," he told her. He checked the corridor, then turned back to plant a quick kiss on her lips before he ducked out of the room.

AT THE CANTEEN THE NEXT day Ben bought two coffees and two stale doughnuts and settled at a table in the back. Twenty minutes went by without a sign of Aïda. Another twenty minutes passed. He fed some kopecks into a pay phone outside the canteen's toilets and dialed her apartment. He let the phone ring for several minutes before hanging up.

Returning to his apartment, he sat in the dark nursing a tall bourbon and flicking with the remote control device from one television channel to another. On one channel a member of the Central Committee known for his conservative views was being interviewed outside the Kremlin wall. In the background the chimes from the Kremlin clock could be heard tolling the hour. "He has opened the door to an orgy of chaos," the Central Committee member was telling the journalist who thrust a microphone in his face. "Only the Communist Party that Lenin created has the force, the experience, the discipline to bring the country back from the brink." The speaker shook his head in disgust. "Our masses will one day wake up to the fact that he is not the patriot he makes himself out to be. I only hope it will not be too late."

Ben flicked past two stations running cartoons to another where a team of mobile journalists were interviewing a woman who had gone into the hospital complaining of a urinary infection and had been operated on for appendicitis by mistake. "Our system of Socialist medicine has broken down," the woman told the interviewer as the camera zoomed in on the stitches on her abdomen. "All the restructuring in the world is not going to save things. In the old days someone would have been put up against a wall and shot."

"If you were in charge, would you order the execution of the doctor who made the mistake?" the journalist asked.

"Absolutely," the woman responded without hesitation. "If we make an example of him, others will do their jobs properly, that's what I say."

The remarks came back to Ben several days later as he sat staring at Inkermann's cipher logs in the tenth-floor ribbon room. It was true what Manny Custer had said about chaos being right under the surface of the Russia he knew and didn't particularly like. It occurred to Ben that the Russians played with chaos and violence the way someone might toy with a loose tooth in his mouth, working it back and forth with his tongue, taking a certain amount of pleasure from the pain. This attitude explained the gleam of pride in Aïda's eyes when she told him, "If you are Russian you associate happiness with pain; you follow your heart until it breaks."

Had she reached the point where her heart had broken? Had she stopped following it? He had not heard from her in the three days since she failed to show up at the canteen. He had phoned her apartment a dozen times —had even risked calling from his office—but nobody had answered.

He had to know. So much depended on it.

After work that night Ben went through the motions of trying to throw off anyone who might be following him. He mingled with the rush hour crowd in the metro, then at the last instant darted onto a train heading for the last stop. At Rechnoi Vokzal, he lingered inside the station reading tear sheets of *Pravda* tacked up on a glassed-in bulletin board until everyone had gone. Emerging from the station, he meandered through a housing project, climbing over rusting gas pipes that honeycombed the ground, coming up behind the shabby building in which Aïda lived. The paths in the area were deserted. He circled around to the front of the building, spotted a light in her window on the fifth floor. Entering the lobby, Ben pressed the button lighting stairwell B on his right, but it didn't work. Feeling his way up the narrow steel staircase, he tried to walk softly, but his footsteps seemed to echo through the building. Through his head, too. On the fifth floor he pushed through a fire door with a round hole where the knob and lock had been. He put his ear to Aïda's door and heard the faint notes of what he took to be recorded chamber music. Taking a deep breath, he knocked. After a while he knocked a second time. He heard footsteps approaching the door.

A woman Ben had never seen before opened it and peered out at him.

"I am a friend of Aïda Zavaskaya," he mumbled in Russian.

The woman bellowed, "Aïda!" Leaving the door ajar,

studying the visitor with undisguised curiosity, she retreated toward her own room.

The chamber music broke off abruptly. Aïda appeared
at the end of a dark, narrow hallway. She did not look as if
she were surprised to see him.

Ben closed the front door and walked over to her. "I
had to come," he told her. "I must know whether you
have stopped following your heart."

With Ben trailing after her, Aïda shuffled into her
room. She went over to the door that led to Saava's room,
pulled it partly open and stepped aside. Ben brushed past
her and looked in. The room was illuminated by a dim
night lamp with a red shade. A poster of a famous Russian
rock singer was tacked to the wall over a desk. In the bed
that he had shared with Vadim, Saava, twitching in his
sleep, lay curled up in a ball. Only an arm and his head
were visible above the two blankets and the flowery Uzbek shawl that Aïda had flung over his thin body. His
breathing seemed regular but shallow. For a moment Ben
imagined he was seeing his own son, Felix, curled up in a
ball in his bed, his thin body draped with the flowery quilt
that had covered Ben's grandfather the day he died.

"I took him for his monthly blood test yesterday," Aïda
whispered. "The results were . . . not good. The blood
count . . . the liver function . . ." Her shoulders
heaved in despair.

Ben murmured, "Oh, God!"

Aïda closed the door softly. Shuffling across the room,
she sank dejectedly onto the edge of the bed. "Saava vom-
ited up his dinner tonight. He is so listless, as if he has no
energy. He is paler too." She appeared to be talking to
herself. "I must move him into the sun. . . ."

Ben towered over her. "What happened when you gave
them the last envelope?"

"The one with the tobacco-stained teeth read what was
in it and laughed. He gave me another paper satchel.
There were only enough pills in it for twenty-five milligrams a day."

Ben sat down heavily on the bed next to her. "Do they still want to see me?"

Aïda shrugged. The answer was obvious.

Ben put an arm around her shoulder. "Okay," he said.

"I have lost my way," Aïda mumbled. "I no longer know what is right and what is wrong in this business."

"How do you contact them between meetings?"

"I call a number. A man answers. I ask to speak to the man who lost his keys. How many keys? the man asks. I give him a number corresponding to the hour of the rendezvous. He says I must have the wrong party and hangs up."

"Arrange a meeting for six tomorrow night."

"Are you sure you want to go through with it?"

Now it was Ben's turn to shrug, as if to say, what choice do I have?

Aïda let her head settle onto his shoulder. "I thank you for this thing you do, Benedict."

They sat on the bed, motionless, listening to each other breathing. Ben pushed her gently down on the bed and started to unbutton her blouse, but she turned her head to one side. "No," she said dully. Seeing the hurt look on his face, she said softly, "Dear heart, to make love one has to concentrate on not concentrating. You see the problem?"

Later, after Ben had left, Aïda regretted they had not made love. She had been a fool to discourage him; she yearned for the weight of his body on hers. She heard a scraping of knuckles on her bedroom door. Thinking he had come back, she ran over in her bare feet and pulled it open.

The woman who shared the apartment was standing there. "I forgot to give you your mail," she told Aïda.

"Many thanks, Nadezhda," Aïda said, taking the letters.

"You do not mind I used the kitchen first?" the woman asked. "My Vladimir had been off to the factory gymnasium lifting weights and was dying of hunger."

"It makes no difference," Aïda said, trying to press the door closed without being too obvious about it.

"Have I seen him somewhere, the man who came by before? A writer? A painter? He seemed to speak with an accent."

"He is a friend." Aïda put more pressure on the door.

"By the way, Zinaïda Ivanovna, your Saava by mistake used some butter that belonged to me. I would not mention it except that butter is hard to come by these days."

"How much did he take?"

"Ten grams at least."

"I will pay you back next time I find butter," Aïda promised. She pushed on the door and managed to shut it this time.

Shuffling through her mail, she added the two envelopes that were typewritten to the pile of unopened mail behind the radiator. The third envelope, which had been addressed by hand, she slit open with a fingernail. Inside was a sheet of paper with a crude drawing of a tombstone on it. Under the tombstone was a caption: "Your poetry is dirty like your mind. Do everyone a favor, go get murdered!"

Crumpling the paper in her fist, sinking to her knees next to the potted mint geranium in the middle of the room, Aïda came a hairs-breadth away from offering herself the luxury of shedding some of her unshed tears. But she was terrified that if she started to cry she would never be able to stop.

THEY MET IN THE BACK OF the workers' canteen on Krasnaya Presnya late the following afternoon. Aïda was already installed at a table, gazing at some wedges of salami without seeing them when Ben pushed through the crowd at the counter and found her.

She searched his face as he pulled over a chair. "Do not go to them," she said. She rested a hand on his arm. "I will tell them you have changed your mind."

"I have a plan," he told her.

Her face was a mask; she did not dare let herself hope. "A plan?"

"I have figured out a way to put an end to their blackmail."

"Is such a thing possible?"

"I will make them an offer they cannot refuse."

Her heart sank. It did not exist, the offer that could not be refused.

"Trust me," he said.

She pushed a piece of paper across the table. On it was scrawled the name of a metro stop, an address, a stairwell letter, an apartment number. "So: Gehenna is on the Lenin Hills," Aïda hoarsely observed. A bitter smirk deformed the lips Ben had once found so sensual. "Who would have dreamed it was so near?"

19

Emerging from the metro station, Ben brushed past a beggar who had one foot in a dirty plaster cast. She was propped up on a pre-Great Patriotic War wooden crutch planted under an armpit, and held in her free hand an empty paint bucket into which passersby dropped coins or uneaten sandwiches. Suddenly Ben could hear the half-cough, half-cackle of his grandfather in his ear. In Russia, the old man was warning, the best that passing someone carrying an empty bucket could bring was bad luck. The superstition was so deeply ingrained in Ben's psyche that he was tempted to retrace his steps, to take a different way out of the metro.

Especially today, he would have liked the omens to be auspicious.

He pulled out the scrap of paper with the name of the metro stop, the address, the stairwell letter, the apartment number scrawled on it, got his bearings, started up a hill that led to the university. Halfway up he came to a pre-Great Patriotic War apartment house. It had been built in a style the Russians had taken to calling Stalin Gothic, which essentially meant massive, elaborate, distinctly pretentious, faintly ridiculous. He found stairwell C, which had recently been given a fresh coat of battleship gray and smelled it, climbed to the sixth floor, crossed over into another wing of the building, descended a staircase that reeked of urine and rang a plastic bell next to the door with the number 310 on it.

A pear-faced young man with sloping shoulders and tobacco-stained teeth pulled it open. He was wearing an overcoat and had a thick knit scarf wound around a thin neck. "Please come in," he said pleasantly, as if Ben had turned up for nothing more ominous than a session of root canal. "The apartment is not heated so you would probably be better off keeping your coat on."

There was a wooden kitchen table covered with squares of Formica in the middle of the room. Four ordinary straight-backed kitchen chairs were placed around it. A naked electric bulb dangled from the ceiling above the table. The man with the tobacco-stained teeth appeared from a kitchenette carrying two tumblers and a bottle of vodka, which he placed on the table. Looking around, Ben noticed a large mirror on one wall next to a closed double door. Circling the kitchen table, he spotted a television set on another straight-backed chair in a corner of the room. "I suppose the television over there is the one on which you showed the film of her fucking like an animal," he told the man with the tobacco-stained teeth. Ben sat down on one of the straight-backed chairs. "Do you come up here weekends and run it for your friends? Do you jerk each other off while you are watching it?"

The skin on the pear-shaped face tightened over the cheek bones, erasing any suggestion of innocence. Repressing his annoyance, the man seated himself on a chair directly across the table from Ben. "I can understand that you are agitated," he said. "I wish to point out that we have no desire to harm you. We can work things out so . that your compatriots never become aware—"

Ben leaned forward. "Tell the truth, when you were

watching the film, didn't you imagine yourself making love to her? The answer is written on your face. But you must know that she would never make love with someone like you—your beady eyes, your sallow complexion, your coarse skin, your bad breath give you away. You are a worm."

Frolov kept a tight rein on his emotions. "Perhaps a glass of vodka will calm you," he remarked, reaching for the bottle.

Ben intercepted his hand. "I will not drink with you. I will not talk with you either." He gestured with a snap of his head toward the mirror on the wall. "I will only drink with him. I have an offer to make, but I will only make it to him."

Frolov was losing control. "You are in no position to dictate—"

Ben caught the sound of the double door opening behind his back. Smiling insolently, feeling as if he had won the first round, he kept his eyes fixed on the man with the tobacco-stained teeth.

Frolov looked over the shoulder of the American, then without comment stood up and left the room. The double door could be heard closing. A heavyset man, wearing a worn greatcoat and carrying an astrakhan hat and a pair of mittens, sat down in the seat that had been vacated. He placed the hat and the mittens on the table. "It is one of my pet theories," he informed Ben as he poured two shots of vodka flavored with dill and garlic into the tumblers and pushed one across the table, "that *homo sapiens* function more efficiently if they keep a reasonable amount of alcohol in their bloodstream at all times." He tilted back his head and downed the vodka in one gulp. "It is another of my pet theories," he went on, setting his tumbler on the table sharply, wiping his lips on the sleeve of his greatcoat, "that people who are ostensible opponents—you will have noticed I do not employ the word *enemies*—can find a common ground, namely self-interest. Drink up, Mr. Benedict Bassett, and let us begin the search for this common ground."

Ben remembered Aïda telling him, at their first meeting, "We would circle each other for a suitable length of time, hunting for points we have in common in order to create the illusion of a connivance." He raised his tumbler and took a sip of vodka. The alcohol burned his throat. "Who are you?" he asked.

"Who I am should be evident from the fact that I am sitting across the table from you in this room."

Ben tried to sound sarcastic. "You must have a name."

"Of course I have a name. But I am certainly not going to reveal it to you. If the Americans ever accuse us of trying to turn a diplomat into a penetration agent, we will deny it as the ravings of a wild imagination spurred on by people in high places who want to bring back the Cold War. You will describe meeting me in a safe house, but you will not find my photograph in the albums your Central Intelligence Agency keeps of known KGB agents. For all intents, I do not exist." Viktor shook his large head amiably. "If it will make this conversation easier for you, by all means call me Viktor. That is as good a name as any."

Viktor measured Ben with a cold eye. His tone became noticeably crisper. "The material contained in the five envelopes your friend delivered to us is completely useless."

Ben gnawed on his lower lip. "I could have told you that when you started blackmailing her."

"We would not have believed you."

"I am only a housekeeper," Ben insisted.

"For the members of the Arms Control Implementation Unit," Viktor said. "Known in the embassy as the Seven Dwarfs."

Ben appeared startled that the Russian would know such a detail. "My access to secrets is almost nonexistent," he whispered.

"Judging from the material you gave us, this would seem to be the case. You mentioned to my colleague that you were going to make us an offer."

Ben took a deep breath. "I have given the matter a great deal of thought. Since the material I have access to is useless to you, I propose to give you something else in its place."

Viktor blinked encouragingly. "What would that be?"

"Me."

"You?"

Bending forward, Ben argued his case with great intensity. "It is no secret to you that I am in love with Zinaïda Zavaskaya. I want to live with her. I want to ask for political asylum in the Soviet Union."

Viktor sucked in his cheeks in surprise. "You want to *defect*?"

Ben nodded eagerly. "Exactly. I will defect and collaborate with you in any way I can."

Viktor leaned back and scrutinized the American. "It is an intriguing idea, you defecting. But there can be no question of anything of the kind. The relationship between your government and mine has gone too far down the road of *détente* for either side to put up with a defection. We would not grant you political asylum. We would have you examined by a psychiatrist, who would pronounce you mentally unstable. Your American friends would welcome the diagnosis and return you to a secluded hospital in the States for prolonged treatment. There is every possibility that your offer to defect would never be made public. Of course, your lady friend and her son would be sent far away so as not to run the risk of her complicating matters. Unfortunately for the boy, there would be no possibility of obtaining special medicines where he was sent."

Noticing the forlorn expression on Ben's face, Viktor raised his hands, palms upward, as if to say: You will have to do better.

Ben got up and walked over to the mirror and studied himself in it. He wondered who was on the other side staring back at him. Viktor's superior, probably. He wondered how much they knew about what went on in the embassy. The time had come to find out. He strode back to his seat and drank some more vodka before asking Viktor, "If you don't want me and you are not satisfied with the scraps I can get my hands on, where do we go from here?"

"Where we go from here," Viktor said carefully, "is I ask you questions and you give me answers."

"What kind of questions?"

"Explain, please, how is it, if you are only an embassy housekeeper, you possess a green badge, as opposed to the more usual white badge?"

Ben hesitated long enough for Viktor to understand that he was uncomfortable with the question. "Part of my housekeeping chores involve running errands for the Dwarfs—the Arms Control inspectors—in areas of the embassy restricted to the holders of white badges."

"The Central Intelligence Agency station on the tenth floor, for instance."

Ben's pulse throbbed. So they did know what went on in the embassy after all. He stared at Viktor without answering.

"Mr. Charles Inkermann's office, for instance."

Ben started to protest, "I have never set foot in—" but Viktor's fist slamming down on the table cut him off in midsentence. The tumblers, the vodka bottle, the astrakhan, the mittens danced on the tabletop. "Let things be very clear between us," the Russian declared in a harsh whisper. "Push me too far and I will duck like a spider back into my hole in the wall and you will duck back into yours and we will never meet again. And the Zavaskaya woman can go to hell for her Purinethol."

Viktor cleared his throat several times, as if something were stuck in his gullet; as if anger were a bone that could be coughed up. When he spoke again his voice had returned to its normal conversational pitch. "What were you doing in Mr. Inkermann's office at four fifteen in the afternoon one day soon after your arrival at the embassy? What brings you up to the Central Intelligence Agency station for an hour or so almost every afternoon?"

Ben avoided Viktor's eyes. "As part of my housekeeping chores," he said very softly, "I encipher status reports from the Dwarfs to their counterparts in Washington. I can't keep the ciphers downstairs because it's a white badge area, so I went up to Mr. Inkermann to see if he could give me a table to work on and a secure place to store my ciphers."

"And he agreed?"

Ben nodded.

"It would have been more logical to try and obtain space in the communications bubble."

"I heard it was crowded up there. I heard they couldn't even keep their cigarettes in the safe, they were so short of space."

Viktor removed his eyeglasses and exhaled on each lens and wiped them with the tip of his tie. Then he hooked his eyeglasses back over his ears and thrust himself to his feet. Across the table Ben rose to face him. Viktor said, "Have the Zavaskaya woman bring us copies of the enciphered messages and the plain language texts, as well as the cipher keys. If the material is sufficiently interesting, we will give her the pills she needs."

Ben said, "Enough for seventy-five milligrams of 6-mercaptopurine a day?"

Viktor only said, "I knew if we worked hard enough at it we would find that common ground of self-interest."

When the front door of the apartment had closed behind Ben, the old general, teetering with excitement, barged through the double door into the room. He went directly to the mirror and stared at himself in it. "When he peered into the mirror," he called to Viktor, "I could have sworn he was looking through it. I could have sworn he could see me." Turning to his son-in-law, he said, "Congratulations, Viktor. You were right about him being more than a housekeeper. Yesterday he gave us itineraries. Today it is ciphers. But what will he bring us tomorrow?"

Viktor, relieved that the session had gone so well, started to pour himself another shot of vodka. "Tomorrow he will offer us secrets from Inkermann's heart of darkness."

·   ·   ·

MANNY CUSTER'S REPLACEMENT, a bright-eyed, balding FS3 whose toughest posting to date had been as embassy security officer in Ottawa, turned up the first thing Monday morning at Custer's cubbyhole of an office. "Pulled in Saturday morning," announced Leo Hurlburt, pumping Manny's hand, levering his lanky body onto a folding chair. "Between me and Moscow," he plunged on, "it was love at first sight. Got an eyeful of the Kremlin, saw St. Basil's onion domes, even caught the changing of the guard in front of old Vladimir's tomb." Surveying with obvious distaste the books and pamphlets spilling from Manny's shelves, the dossiers spilling from his in-basket, Hurlburt muttered something about having had a room in Ottawa as big as Manny's office just for overcoats. "Don't get me wrong," he quickly added. "Man doesn't live by creature comforts alone. Ran into your Mr. Inkermann at Sam's Saturday, by the way. Seems like a straight shooter. Spoke highly of you. Wished me luck. Don't guess as how I'll need it, what with the Cold War being over and all. Probably had more security headaches a week in Canada than I'll see here in a month of Mondays."

Rubbing the side of his large, pitted nose with the ball of his thumb, Manny treated Hurlburt to the standard security briefing, ending on the business of the embassy walls having ears. The talk of hidden microphones, of antennas across the street, had the desired effect. Leaning toward Manny, Hurlburt asked in a whisper, "You really think they can hear every word we're saying?"

Manny let his bushy eyebrows dance knowingly. "When the Marx and Lenin you see on those billboards in Red Square are Groucho and John, we won't need an embassy security officer. Right now we're still dealing with Karl and Vladimir. And it's business as usual for the roughly two million employees still on the KGB payroll. For us too. Whatever."

Did Manny have any reason to suspect the embassy had actually been penetrated? Hurlburt asked.

Manny's head shook once. No. He had no reason to suspect the embassy had been penetrated.

In fact, Manny had an uncanny feeling, bordering on certitude, that something was not kosher at the embassy.

Item: Nosing around the travel section on the first floor, Manny had learned that the Russians had suddenly relaxed travel restrictions. It was no longer necessary to give seventy-two hours' advance notice for trips within the USSR. Surprisingly, even the Arms Control Implementation inspectors were not being held to the seventy-two-hour rule. Even more startling, the Russian UPDK, which made travel arrangements for diplomats, was coming up with train and plane and hotel reservations in place of the usual excuses.

Item: A highly placed official of the KGB had taken the deputy chief of mission aside at a reception and warned him that one of the several assistant economic attachés at the embassy had been dealing regularly on the black market, trading Western currency for icons. The official made it clear that the KGB did not want to embarrass the embassy or the Americans by filing charges. The icons were returned to the Russians and the offending diplomat was quietly packed off to the States on the next flight out.

Item: One of the Arms Control Inspectors, returning from a tour of a missile repair facility near Kharkov, had had his briefcase stolen during a stopover in Kursk. The local militia was routinely notified. Manny had assumed that because the briefcase contained classified material, the KGB was behind the theft. Twenty-four hours later a foreign ministry representative delivered the inspector's briefcase to the embassy, claiming it had been recovered by the local police in Kursk. Manny didn't believe a word and shipped the sealed envelopes in the briefcase to the FBI labs in Washington for elaborate tests. The results came back two days later: According to FBI specialists, the seals had not been broken, the contents had not been compromised.

Years before, during a stint in Washington between foreign assignments, Manny had worked on a CIA case study of embassy penetrations. The study had concluded that the Russians were most dangerous when they seemed to be the least active; that they went to great lengths to convince the Americans they had not penetrated an embassy in order to protect a current penetration.

His feet up on his desk, his usual scotch pressed thoughtfully against his cheek, Manny considered variations on a theme. The Russians might have relaxed travel restrictions, for instance, so that a penetration agent would be free to travel and meet with them. They might have reported the icon scam instead of trying to blackmail the attaché in question because they wanted the Americans to let their guard down. They might have returned the Arms Control Inspector's envelopes unopened because they already knew what was in them.

In short, the more the Russians looked as if they were not interested in penetrating the embassy, the more Manny's large, pitted nose twitched.

AT THE FIRST HINT OF FIRST LIGHT, Aïda's father, Ivan, leaned his weight on his cane and heaved himself to his feet. He walked stiffly across the room to the armoire, removed a cardboard box from the top shelf and carried it over to his bed. Lifting the lid, he pulled out his old parade trousers with the red stripe running down the side of each leg, and his old parade blouse with the Interior unit's insignia on each shoulder. From a metal box he pulled his medals from the Great Patriotic War (Hero of Socialist Labor, Order of Lenin, an assortment of red and gold ribbons, coin-size medallions with hammers and sickles and profiles of Lenin) and pinned them in rows on the blouse over the breast pocket. Slivers of sandalwood had been put in the box to protect the trousers and blouse from moths, but they had not done the job—there were finger-size holes in several places in the fabric. The old man toyed with the idea of getting needle and thread and patching the holes, but then decided he didn't have time. With an effort he struggled into the trousers, which were high-waisted and held up by suspenders, and the blouse, which he buttoned up to his unshaven chin. The starched collar bit uncomfortably into the soft skin of his neck. He

turned to the armoire and looked at himself in the mirror
on the door.

Studying the Army trousers with the red stripe down
the side of each leg, the blouse buttoned up to the neck,
caused the old man's emaciated chest to swell with pride.
He had worn the uniform from the end of the Great Patriotic War until the day the KGB interrogator, using a
cheap pliers, had pried the nails out of his fingers and
then crushed his fingers, one by one, in a vise. When Ivan
had obstinately refused to confess to being a member of a
conspiracy against Comrade Stalin, he had been sent
home, his fingers wrapped in blood-stained gauze, to
await the outcome of the investigation; to await his inevi-
table arrest as an enemy of the people.

Now, after thirty-seven years, he had grown sick of
waiting. He had to know if there was a warrant for his
arrest, if they were going to come for him that night,
arriving in a delivery van with the word "Bread" painted
on its panels so that nobody would know prisoners were
inside when it rolled through the streets of Moscow.

Ivan forced his swollen feet into the black parade boots
and laced them up. Running his fingers through his thin
gray hair, he took his worn leather wallet with his identity
card from a drawer and put it in his breast pocket. How
could they process him if he could not prove who he was?
Easing open the bedroom door, he listened for a moment
to make sure that Saava and Aïda and their neighbors,
Nadezhda and her weight-lifting husband, were all still
asleep. Then carefully keeping his cane from banging
against the corridor walls, he tiptoed out of the apartment.

Shivering from the cold, he queued with a host of shadowy figures for the bus that ran parallel to the river toward the center of Moscow. When it pulled up, he
clambered on board and thrust his chest full of medals
into the driver's face to indicate he was a veteran and as
such, was not required to pay a fare.

"Where are you off to at this hour, Granddad," laughed
a teenager dressed in blue jeans and a ski parka, "a cos-

tume ball?" He started to poke a finger in a moth hole, but backed away in mock fear when the old man brandished his cane.

A shabbily dressed older woman with an Army knapsack strapped to her back laced into the teenager. "It's the ones like him who fought off the Hitlerites before you were born," she trumpeted. Several of the older people in the bus nodded in agreement.

A pregnant woman stood up and offered Ivan her seat. He shook his head, but she pulled him into it anyhow. "Many of us know what those medals stand for," she whispered. "Many of us appreciate what you and your kind did for the Motherland."

Following the directions of the woman who had given him her seat, Ivan managed to negotiate a change of buses. When he spotted the toy store, Detsky Mir, he pounded on the door of the bus with his cane until the driver, muttering about the deterioration of public order, pulled up in the middle of a block and opened it.

Ivan emerged into clear, cold Moscow air and looked around. Not much had changed in the thirty-seven years since he had last set foot in Dzerzhinsky Square. There was more traffic, to be sure. And the people hurrying to work looked better dressed. But the massive structure across the street from the toy store still had the stately, impersonal look of an insurance building, which is what it had been before the Bolsheviks turned it into the headquarters of the secret police; into a prison that Russians called Lubyanka. Ivan remembered his last visit to the building as if it had taken place yesterday; he remembered looking back over his shoulder as he stumbled out of it, his fingers wrapped in gauze, his eyes filming over with fear.

Brandishing his cane to keep the cars at bay, Ivan cut diagonally across the street, marched directly up to the main entrance of the KGB headquarters and began pounding on the double door with his cane. The few people passing (Muscovites still avoided using the sidewalk on this side of the street) glanced curiously at the old man beating on the metal door. When no one responded, Ivan stepped back and studied the facade, then turned in a circle, all the while eyeing the building as if it were alive. Finally he returned to the door and started pounding his cane on it again. At length he heard the sound of a bolt being thrown. One of the heavy doors slowly swung open. A kindly-looking KGB officer with his uniform blouse unbuttoned and his tie undone looked out. He took in the old man with the thick stubble on his chin and the medals on his uniform blouse and the gleam in his deranged eyes.

The vision of the great metal door of hell opening made Ivan reel back a step. His heart started throbbing wildly. "The accusation against me is a fabrication," he managed to say. "How was I to know he was a White Russian, and an admiral?"

The officer had obviously seen people like Ivan at the door of the KGB headquarters before. "You have nothing to fear from us," he said very gently. "Go home, old man."

A point of pain stabbed at Ivan beneath his medals. His right arm turned numb. The cane slipped through his fingers and clattered to the sidewalk. "What do you say? . . . waiting all these years . . . not possible . . ." His knees started to give way. The kindly officer lunged forward to catch him under the armpits as he crumpled to the ground.

AÏDA BENT OVER THE SHRUNKEN figure of her father, lost in the large metal bed in the intensive care unit of the clinic. Four green Army blankets and a tattered quilt had been spread over him; the clinic had run out of coal the previous week and was no longer heated. Tubes spilled from the old man's nostrils. His mouth gaped open, sucking in air, creating clouds of vapor when he exhaled. Each breath sounded as if it would be his last. He must have sensed a presence because his eyes drifted open. He stared at Aïda, trying to place her. Then, suddenly, he succeeded.

He struggled to raise his body into a sitting position. Sinking back into the pillow, he tried to talk. His lips worked, but no sound came out. Then, slurring his words, he managed to ask, "Am I arrested?"

"You are in the clinic, Father," Aïda told him.

He searched her face to see if she were telling the truth. ". . . clinic?"

"You took sick on the street. They called an ambulance and brought you here."

"Right arm . . . right leg . . . no feeling."

"You had a stroke, Father."

His lips curled into a grotesque smile. Saliva dribbled from the corner of his mouth. Presently he asked, "Dying?"

Aïda nodded. "I think so," she said very softly.

"Oh!"

"Can I get you anything?"

The old man's head rolled from side to side on the pillow. "Worried."

"About what?"

Ivan sucked in air through his mouth. "Being buried alive . . . regaining consciousness . . . in coffin."

Aïda leaned closer so that her mouth was almost touching his ear. She could see the tufts of gray hair sprouting from his lobe. "I will not let that happen, Father."

"Promise . . . check, make sure . . . really dead before . . . before . . . buried."

"Of course I promise."

Incredibly wrinkled lids closed over the old man's moist eyes. He appeared to breathe more easily. A tired doctor with a soggy stump of a cigarette glued to her lower lip appeared in the doorway. Aïda went over to her. "How long does he have?" she whispered.

The cigarette bobbed on the doctor's lip as she talked. "An hour. A day. A week. Only God can say. Your father is suffering from an incurable disease called old age. If the stroke had not gotten him, something else would have. Is it true he was banging on the door of . . ."

Aïda nodded. "He was looking for an enemy."

The doctor tried to suck her cigarette into life, then

flicked it impatiently onto a pile of garbage in a corner of the room. "He will soon find an archenemy."

Gazing at her father, Aïda murmured, "So this is how it ends."

The doctor shrugged. "He has lived more than most."

A whimsical half-smile materialized on Aïda's lips. "Here, living more than most is synonymous with suffering more than most."

The two women exchanged a look of perfect complicity.

20

The rubber surgeon's glove attached to the lid of
Vadim's jar was completely inflated, evidence that the
process of fermentation had run its course and the Great
Helmsman's Greeting had aged sufficiently to drink.
Carefully skimming off the mold that had formed on the
peaches floating on the surface, Vadim scooped out
ladlefuls of his moonshine and, without spilling a drop,
filled to the brim the two long-stemmed wineglasses lined
up on the kitchen table. He slid one across the table to
Aïda. Holding his own glass up to the light, gently swirling
the liquid around in it, he inspected the home brew.
Then, muttering something about it having reasonably
good legs, he clanked his glass against Aïda's and took a
sip. Arching his eyebrows, smacking his lips, he raised his
voice so he could be heard over the radio, which Aïda had
turned up, and announced, "It is not nearly as bad as I
thought it would be."

Aïda left hers untouched. She had other things on her
mind. Leaning toward Vadim, she asked, "Are you positive our places are reserved?"

"After what I spent, they'd better be!"

"How did you find out about it?"

Vadim treated himself to another sip, rolling the moonshine around in his mouth before swallowing. "My mistress has a friend who is a doctor. This doctor has beds in the clinic where the operations are taking place, so she naturally heard about it when a doctor from the famous Mount Sinai Hospital in New York City started looking for suitable patients."

"It was a brilliant idea to suggest me and Saava."

"I did more than suggest," Vadim said with a dry snicker. He flashed a toothy grin, which usually indicated that he was quite pleased with himself. "I crossed palms with the nearest thing we have to gold, which is West German compact disks—the complete works of Dietrich Fischer-Dieskau." Vadim could tell Aïda was worried sick. She seemed paler than he ever remembered seeing her; she looked as if she got as much sunshine as the anemic mint geranium she kept on the floor of her apartment. "They say it is as routine as an appendectomy, both for the donor and the recipient," he reassured her. "Resist the temptation to be a Jewish mother." He decided to distract her. "Speaking of Jewish mothers, did you hear the one about the Jewish mother who gave her son two brand new shirts? When he came downstairs wearing one, tears appeared in her eyes. 'Admit it, you do not like the other,' she said. You get it? Because he was wearing one of the new shirts, she accused him of not liking the other one."

Aïda managed a faint smile. It was erased by a sudden thought. "You did not speak to anyone about this?" she demanded.

"I may be dumb," Vadim said, "but I am not stupid."

He started to explain the fine points of how he had arranged things, but Aïda cut him off. "Under no circumstance must word of this get back to the KGB—"

Vadim waved a hand. "I did not hear that," he announced. "I do not know what you are talking about, and I do not want to know." He glanced at his wristwatch and sprang up. "My taxi is waiting downstairs. My mistress is waiting at my apartment. A client is waiting in a restaurant. I have cornered the market in imported ribbons for computer printers. If you have a computer and you want to print out, you have to come to me." He screwed a plastic cap on the jar of moonshine and began fitting it into a large imitation leather satchel. "How is your father doing?" he asked Aïda as they started down the hallway toward the front door.

"He is still dying, but he is taking his time about it."

"If I were in his shoes I would drag my feet too. As a general rule, you should try to live as long as you can. That way you will be dead for as short a time as possible. Ha!"

At the front door Aïda planted a kiss on each of Vadim's cheeks. "You are the perfect ex-husband," she breathed into his ear. "We should have divorced long ago. We should have become friends sooner."

Vadim leered at his ex-wife. "Is friendship something you get to consummate?"

Aïda ducked away from his halfhearted attempt to embrace her. "How is your love affair with your mistress going?"

Vadim backed up until his back was against the wall. He no longer looked as if he was in a hurry. "You might have warned me, you know."

"About what?"

"About how a woman planes like a glider on youth, on good looks, on sexuality, on seduction; about how, somewhere around the age of forty, she finds it more difficult to find currents to fly on; about how she circles lower and lower, searching desperately for new updrafts. About how she panics and is driven to test her powers of seduction on a new man." He laughed through his nose. "It is me, that new man."

"Your formula is too neat to explain more than your own sense of disappointment."

Embarrassed at having revealed so much, Vadim tried

to change the subject. "Concerning Saava: Everything will work out," he growled. "It almost always does."

"Which means that sometimes it does not," Aïda observed worriedly.

"That is not what I meant," Vadim insisted. He pushed himself off the wall. "When this is over, I hope you will break off with the American. He has only brought you trouble."

Aïda studied her slippers. "I love him."

Vadim shook his head in disgust. "What does love have to do with life or poetry or Saava or you?"

"So." Cocking her head, she offered him a whimsical half-smile. "Everything."

SHE HAD RESISTED GOING there from the start of their affair; had resisted the suggestion when he brought it up after the amateur chamber music concert in a school auditorium; resisted it again as they wandered aimlessly through the Kuchkovo streets glistening from the first postwinter rain. "Where can we go, then?" Ben pleaded. "For God's sake, Aïda, I need to be alone with you."

Her apartment was out of the question. Nadezhda's husband's brother, a militia officer, had moved in temporarily while his apartment was being painted. It was impossible to rent a room in a hotel without showing identity papers. The room in the ramshackle hostel that Vadim leased by the year for his clients was being used by a cotton tycoon from Uzbekistan; he and Vadim were going into business manufacturing slivers of wood with wads of cotton on each end, which could be used to clean ears. Even the wooden *dacha* near Zagorsk was occupied—by a member of the Central Committee secretariat with whom Vadim hoped to go into the import-export business.

Reluctantly—she could feel the pull of his sexual desire, to which her own garden of lust responded—she gave in. Ducking into a booth, she made a quick phone call to check on Saava, who was sleeping over with a friend whose mother, to Aïda's relief, was a doctor. While she was making the call, Ben flagged down a taxi by waving an American ten-dollar bill (it was said that a Moscow taxi driver could spot foreign currency on a moonless night at a hundred meters). The driver let them off down the block from the Hotel Ukraine on Kutuzovsky Prospekt. Dodging streetcars going in both directions, they cut diagonally across the wide boulevard and headed for the compound in which Ben lived.

Aïda kept a tight grip on Ben's arm. "What if the militiaman asks me for my internal passport?" she asked worriedly.

"You are being irrational," Ben told her. "The Russians know all about us."

"I know it," Aïda replied, "without really knowing it."

The militiaman on duty, a tall, innocent-faced blond boy called Mitry, saluted Ben from his Plexiglas guard box. "Let me know if you are throwing out any more of those old American magazines," he called in Russian thick with a Ukrainian accent.

Ben waved and nodded, and pulled Aïda, who had wound her fox fur around the lower part of her face, into the lobby. He noticed that the elevator was on its way down and steered her into the stairwell before it arrived. Upstairs, Aïda stalked through the apartment like a caged animal, fingering curtains, straightening pictures on the wall, inspecting the furniture—it was used Danish modern, a hand-me-down from the previous owner. Ben switched on the radio. Aïda came over and turned up the volume. "Is it true that the apartments of diplomats are full of microphones?" Without waiting for a reply, she took hold of his hand and drew him into the bathroom and turned on the shower full blast. She talked with her lips pressed against his ear. "Dear Benedict, there is a way out!"

"What is it?"

Aïda told him about the operation. "A famous American doctor from Mount Sinai Hospital in New York has been invited to demonstrate the latest bone marrow transplant techniques to the Russians," she explained. "So: This is the miracle we have been waiting for. As my cells are compatible with Saava's, I am to be the donor. The American doctor will make three to five incisions in my pelvic bone and extract a liter and a half of bone marrow. He will give Saava an enormous dose of drugs, one that will kill the good cells as well as the cancerous cells. Then he replaces the killed good cells with the live cells in my bone marrow. Oh, Benedict, do you see it? If the operation is successful, Saava will not need Purinethol, and if he does not need Purinethol . . ." She let the sentence trail off.

Ben finished the sentence for her. ". . . we don't need them."

"*We—don't—need—them,*" she repeated, spitting out each word.

"When is the operation scheduled?"

"The American doctor is due to arrive at the end of the week. Vadim says he will need three days to prepare his equipment and train the nurses who will assist him. Also he will need to examine both of us. The actual operation could take place a week from today."

"That's fantastic news," Ben said. He pulled her to him. "We will live happily ever after, after all."

Still whispering in his ear, Aïda told Ben, "We must be careful not to speak of this over the phone. We must continue to give them . . . envelopes . . . as if nothing unusual was happening. If they get wind of the operation . . ." Again the sentence was left hanging.

High, for the first time in a long time, on hope, Aïda was able to concentrate on not concentrating. Ben stripped away her clothes and shed his own and pulled her into the shower and quenched his thirst drinking from the rivulets running down her skin. In his bed, it was as if the sex act—the act of sex—were being reinvented. Aïda arched her spine in a sumptuous stretch and fell forward across his chest, and they both drifted off into a coma-like sleep.

When Ben, finally stirring, nudged Aïda awake, it took a moment before either remembered where they were. Aïda padded naked to the kitchen and put the kettle to boil. Ben came in and wrapped his terry cloth bathrobe around her as she rummaged in the cabinet and started to make coffee. Waiting for it to drip through the filter, she rolled a thin cigarette and leaned toward Ben to light it from the match he held. Exhaling, she mused, "Pushkin has a wonderful line, something about how, if he were still able to believe in happiness, he would seek it here"—she nodded toward the coffee dripping through the filter—"in the monotony of worldly habits."

She found two chipped cups and carefully filled them and set them on the table. Ben blew on his to cool it. "Is happiness out of the realm of possibility for you, Aïda?"

"Until I met you I was convinced that happiness depended on how you came to terms with your dreams."

"And now?"

"Now," she said, "I am afraid I was right—but I harbor the faint hope that I was wrong."

STANDING AT HIS DARKENED WINDOW, nursing a scotch without rocks (the freezer compartment of his refrigerator had broken down; being a short timer in Moscow, he had not bothered to have it repaired), Manny Custer watched Mitry dancing an impatient jig in his Plexiglas guard box on the corner. It was five minutes past midnight and his relief had not turned up. Mitry looked again at his watch, then left his box and peered down the street to see if he could spot the bus that brought the next watch. Someone must have emerged from the entrance, just under Manny's window, because Mitry, glancing hurriedly in that direction, quickly retreated back into his guard box. Manny leaned forward until his forehead was pressing against the window. Two figures, one a man, the other a woman, came into view. The man was bareheaded, the woman wore a pillbox hat with a white feather spiked through it and what looked like a scarf wrapped around the lower part of her face—almost as if she did not want to be seen coming out of the apartment building that housed American diplomats. From his guard box, Mitry saluted the man, which meant that he was a diplomat.

The man waved back as he pulled the woman toward the street in search of a taxi. Mitry must have called something because the diplomat turned to answer as he passed under a street light. A thin smile etched itself into Manny's lips as he recognized Benedict Bassett, the erstwhile housekeeper who handled coded traffic on the side, who had attracted enough interest to be followed by the KGB when he left the embassy.

But who was the well-proportioned, wide-shouldered woman with him? If she were hiding her face from Mitry, it must mean she was married—or Russian! Surely Bassett was not imprudent enough to have an affair with a Russian woman. Or was he? Could that account for the Russians putting a tail on him?

Watching the woman plunge into the street to wave frantically at a passing taxi, Manny had the eerie sensation that he had seen her before. She had a way of plowing forward that reminded him of an icebreaker . . .

21

Nursing a cold (he had continued to dress for winter after the spring thaw), Ben collected his mail in the administrative section of the embassy and strolled over to the bulletin board to read the latest announcements. Someone being posted back to the States was holding a garage sale in an apartment in the New Office Building complex. Places were still available on a group trip to World War II battle sites around Stalingrad, now Volgograd. Tickets for an opera, a ballet, a play, a circus were on sale in the Community Liaison Office. Ben was reading the last announcement ("Now that snow is a thing of the past, Weight Watchers interested in bike riding around Moscow Sunday mornings put their John/Jane Hancocks below") when Sabine Harkenrider tapped him on the shoulder.

"You weren't hot under the collar for cross-country skiing," she remembered. "I don't imagine you're very enthusiastic about bike riding either."

Replying in a particularly nasal voice because of the

head cold, Ben said, "Sunday mornings I like to get a late
start and spend the rest of the day not catching up."

"Well," she said, smiling at the ground.

Suddenly an index card tacked to the bulletin board
caught Ben's eye. "Come One, Come All!" it said.

> *Cocktails and* zakuski *for*
> *Dr. Milton Zylberstein*
> *of Mount Sinai Hospital, NYC.*
> ———
> *Sam's Lounge, Monday,* 5 P.M.

Sabine Harkenrider read it over his shoulder. "Who is
Dr. Zylberstein of Mount Sinai Hospital," she asked, "and
what's he doing in Moscow?"

Ben suddenly felt as if he were peering down from the
edge of a great cliff. Manny Custer must have been right,
of course, about the embassy walls having ears. How else
could they have figured out who Charlie Inkermann's
"four fifteen" was? If they were listening then, it meant
that they were listening now. The thought sent a chill
through Ben. In his mind's eye he could see, far below, an
imaginary surf pounding against imaginary rocks. His
heart pushed upward in his chest cavity in a surge of
vertigo.

From somewhere a Teletype clattered, then was silent.
"Is something not right?" Sabine asked softly.

"No. No." For some reason his voice sounded even
more nasal. "I was wondering who this Zylberstein was
too. Ask in there."

Sabine poked her head through the window of the
Community Liaison Office. "Does anyone know who Dr.
Zylberstein is?"

"I heard he's a bone marrow transplant specialist," a
stenographer said. "He's going to do a couple of transplants to demonstrate the latest American techniques."

Sabine turned back to Ben. "Bone marrow transplants
are for people with leukemia, aren't they?"

Ben mumbled something about not knowing much about things like that.

Sabine gathered her courage. "I don't suppose . . ."

Ben smiled apologetically.

"Let me guess," said Sabine. "You have a previous engagement. You'd love a rain check." Smiling again, she turned away.

Ben watched her as she bent over the water cooler. She let the water splash over her face, then shook herself in a way that suggested an animal emerging from a lake. Without looking back, she disappeared through the door at the end of the corridor.

Heading for Charlie Inkermann's ribbon room, Ben caught a glimpse of his reflection in the glass door of the Community Liaison Office. For a split second he was completely disorientated. There was no one else in the corridor. The reflection had to be his.

Yet he didn't recognize himself.

What had he done to bring on this flash of visual amnesia?

VIKTOR'S SECRETARY, EVGENIYA LEONOVNA, carefully stirred a spoonful of her new lemon confiture into a cup of tea and set it on the desk so that the aroma wafted up to his nose. Viktor, catnapping in his chair, opened his eyes. "What is the time?" he asked.

Evgeniya Leonovna said defensively, "You told me to wake you when Captain Krostin got here . . ."

"Quite right," Viktor grumbled. He waved toward the venetian blinds. Evgeniya Leonovna darted over to open them. Brilliant sunshine stabbed through the windows into Viktor's eyes. Squinting, still only half-awake, he buzzed the outer office and instructed the appointment secretary to send in Section Chief Krostin.

Andrei Krostin placed a typewritten transcript on his boss's desk. He had been going through conversations picked up by a microphone buried in the wall near the bulletin board in the American Embassy's administrative section when he noticed something that aroused his curiosity.

Skimming the dialogue, Viktor at first did not see what Krostin was driving at. Only when he came across the sentence, "Bone marrow transplants are for people with leukemia, aren't they?" did the coin drop.

"I checked out the American doctor Zylberstein with Frolov's people," Krostin explained. "He is scheduled to perform two bone marrow transplant operations at the Kremlin hospital amphitheater next Wednesday, one in the morning, a second in the afternoon." Krostin's tone was even, but his eyes betrayed his excitement. "The first patient is aged eleven. His name is—"

"Not the boy Saava!"

Krostin nodded triumphantly.

Viktor reread the transcript. "Did you listen to the original intercepts?"

Krostin said he and Frolov had played the tapes half a dozen times. They had recognized several of the voices. One belonged to the grammar teacher, Sabine Harkenrider. The person who identified the American doctor Zylberstein as a bone marrow transplant specialist was a stenographer working in the Community Liaison Office. The third voice, which sounded extremely nasal through the distortions of the microphone buried deep in the wall, they had been unable to recognize, or match against known samples.

"The Zavaskaya woman must have heard about this doctor from the American Bassett," Viktor commented in annoyance.

Krostin pointed out that it would be very awkward if the KGB were to interfere with the choice of patients for the American doctor. Sipping his tea, Viktor thought about this for a moment, then issued his instructions: "Here's what you will do."

AFTER LUNCH, VIKTOR ATTENDED another of the old general's minisummits. The two analysts attached to the general's secretariat were going to deliver their initial findings on the latest Bassett material. "As usual," Olga Glebova began in her plodding manner, "we are working in the dark with respect to the origin of the documents." Fixing her bulging eyes on the general, she forged ahead. "The material breaks down into two groups. There are the ciphers themselves, which my colleague will deal with, and there is the text of the deciphered messages, which I will deal with."

N. Fillipov batted his lids as if he were dusting his eyes. "One is always thrilled to get one's hands on ciphers, on the condition that one can then use the key to unlock future messages. Unfortunately, the ciphers in question are one-time ciphers—"

Startled, Viktor leaned forward. "How can you be sure they are one-time ciphers?"

Fillipov's eyeglasses caught a ray of light from the window and turned opaque. "Even if one does not have the cipher key, the enciphered one-time message is distinctive enough so that anyone with a knowledge of cipher structure can distinguish it from a computer-made cipher. It contains what one might call a signature. This signature is the relative lack of randomness. Computer ciphers achieve near unbreakability through an almost, but not quite, absolute randomness. One-time ciphers are infinitely less random, but even more secure than computer ciphers because they are used only once before being discarded like disposable tissues."

"In other words, the cipher keys are completely useless to us," the old general muttered, casting a reproachful glance in Viktor's direction.

Glebova studied her hand-scrawled notes through the lower half of her octagonal bifocals. "As for the text of the deciphered messages," she said, "the seven examples we have been asked to analyze are extremely detailed. Each message is signed with a code name. Judging from the contents of the messages, these names can only refer to various members of the American Arms Control Implementation Unit. The messages are obviously reports from the American inspectors to the American Joint Chiefs on what they saw during their inspection tours. Take the message signed with the unlikely name Bergonza. It describes in elaborate detail a visit to a missile repair facility near Alma Ata. The American lieutenant commander Pierce inspected this facility ten days ago. Thus Bergonza—"

"—is obviously a code name for Pierce," Fillipov said impatiently.

Viktor stared impassively at Glebova's bird's nest hairdo. The fingers of the general's good hand beat out the passing seconds on the table. Glebova must have become aware of the sound because she skipped directly to her conclusions. "At first glance, the material you gave us looked like a windfall—enciphered messages with the plain language text, addressed to the Joint Chiefs. On closer inspection, it turns out that the information is for all practical purposes without value. Since our people accompany the American inspectors through the facilities and sites they inspect—"

"—we know what they have seen," Fillipov interjected, "and hence what they will report to their superiors, without having to read their deciphered messages. Let me say that it is precisely because one knows what they will be reporting," he added, "that they must use one-time ciphers. Working back from several texts, the contents of which one can roughly predict, it would only be a matter of time before one was able to break a computer cipher."

When the two analysts had collected their notes and departed, the general turned to his son-in-law. "You have no doubt seen the latest news," he snapped, as if Viktor was the one responsible. Emotion triggered a sinus attack and he started wheezing. "There is no limit to the man's arrogance. Not content with renouncing the leading role of the Communist Party, he has had himself elected president. He is presiding over the dissolution of the Party and the State and the empire. The *Pamyat* Directorate is meeting again at the end of the month. We must find a way to stop him before there is nothing left of seventy years of struggle."

The old general tried to go on, but his voice failed him. He produced a nasal inhaler from the pocket of his uniform blouse and sucked three spurts of a sickening spray into the back of his throat. Tears appeared in his eyes. He wiped them away with the back of his good hand. Gradually his breathing became more regular. "I am not pleased, Viktor," he announced when he found his voice. "You promised me gold, but you delivered fool's gold."

Viktor argued his case with fervor. "With all respect, General, I would like to invite your attention to a critical detail. Neither of your analysts has suggested that the material being passed to us is being *planted* on us."

"We are risking our necks for what? Reports that we do not need to read because we know what they will say."

"You do not abandon a harvest because the first grapes are disappointing—"

"I am not against gambling when the prize is worth—"

Both men took deep breaths. Viktor moved to a seat next to the general. "I ask you to bear in mind that we have never before penetrated the CIA station in the heart of the embassy," he said. "Even if the American Bassett has nothing in his safe but fool's gold, he is well placed to get his hands on the real thing. Think of the information that must be sitting around on desks—"

The fingers on the general's bad hand contracted. He straightened them one by one with his other hand. "I will give you ten days," he finally said. "If you are unable to come up with something that justifies the risk in that time, you will call off the penetration."

"In ten days," Viktor declared, "the American Bassett will give us the family jewels."

He tried to sound convincing. Only when he found himself back at his own desk did it dawn on him that the person he had been trying to convince was himself.

AÏDA DRESSED SAAVA in his best brown trousers and waist jacket with matching cap and took him down to Vadim's taxi, which was waiting, its motor idling, at the corner of the housing project. Saava loved riding in the taxi and always sat up front with the driver, Dmitri. This time he climbed into the backseat alongside his mother.

"What is it the doctor will do to me?" he asked nervously.

"I told you upstairs."

"Tell me again."

Aïda put an arm around the boy's shoulder and hugged him to her. "He is only going to listen to your heart with a stethoscope, and tap on your knees with a rubber hammer, and thump his fingertips against your chest. And ask you questions."

"What kind of questions?"

"About how well you sleep. About your appetite."

"You give me your word of honor he is not going to operate today?"

Aïda nodded. "I promise."

The boy sank into her arms, still worried. Aïda was anxious too. She wondered if she was expected to slip a packet of rubles to the American doctor the way you did to Russian doctors from whom you wanted special treatment. She wondered if there would be a last-minute hitch. She wondered if they were being watched.

Dmitri, following Vadim's instructions, was taking the long way into Moscow from Rechnoi Vokzal, weaving his way through traffic, then cutting away into a labyrinth of side streets before letting them off two blocks from the Kremlin hospital. As far as Aïda could tell, nobody was paying the slightest attention to them. She had started out early in order to leave plenty of time to cover her tracks. Pulling Saava along, she meandered through GUM, the vast department store across from the Kremlin, disappearing, at one point, into a stockroom (lined with metal shelves, all of them empty) and coming out through a second door into another part of the store.

At fifteen minutes to the appointed hour, she rang the small bell next to a back door of the hospital. After a short wait, the door was opened by a male nurse wearing the whitest uniform Aïda had ever seen during the hundreds of hours she had spent in hospital corridors.

"I am Zinaïda Ivanovna Zavaskaya," announced Aïda. She tried to find a tone that would indicate to this nurse with the sparkling white uniform that she was well connected, someone of consequence. "This is my son, Saava. We have an appointment with—" she pulled a slip of paper from her pocket and sounded out the name of the American surgeon—"Dr. Milt-oon Zyl-ber-stein."

The nurse appeared baffled. "The American doctor Zylberstein is not receiving individual patients—"

Aïda felt more than saw Saava take refuge behind her. She fought a sudden urge to kick open the door and push past the nurse, who obviously was not well informed. "It is about the bone marrow transplant. The American doctor Zylberstein wants to examine both of us before he performs the actual operations."

The nurse must have smelled trouble, because he took a firmer grip on the door. "The American doctor is only scheduled to perform two transplants," he informed Aïda.

"My son was selected for the first transplant," Aïda insisted.

The nurse was beginning to understand. "There were several candidates put forward by various people. In the end the hospital directors, acting on the suggestion of someone in the superstructure, selected two children of non-Russian minorities. One is an Azerbaijani, the other, Latvian." He could see the disappointment drifting like a dark cloud over the woman's enormous eyes. "I suppose they decided that letting the American doctor operate on minority children would look good in the newspapers. I am sincerely sorry if someone led you to hope . . ."

Aïda could feel Saava tugging at her skirt to leave. "There has been a mistake," she protested. "I will speak directly with the American doctor."

Aïda started to pull Saava through the door, but the male nurse eased it closed in her face. "That is not possible," he said.

"I do not need an operation," Saava whispered. He was clearly relieved that things were not working out the way Aïda thought they would. "Let's go home."

At that instant the door clicked closed. Aïda stabbed at the handle, but it was locked. Thinking irrationally that Saava's remark had decided the matter, she turned on the boy and slapped him hard across the face. Then, appalled by what she had done, she pulled him fiercely to her and started to rock him back and forth in a sobbing motion that lacked only tears, which remained dammed up inside her.

PERCHED IN SILENT ROWS on the tarnished bronze arms and shoulders and head of the poet Mayakovski, a dozen emaciated pigeons—Muscovites had taken to eating their stale bread themselves; the latest joke had them eating the pigeons too—regarded with sloe-eyed indifference the people queuing at the first *kvass* wagon on the streets after winter. At the far end of Mayakovski Square, Ben bought three greasy piroshki, each wrapped in a square of thin waxed paper, from a fat woman in a wooden kiosk and carried them back to Aïda and Saava, who were sitting on the statue's pedestal. Nibbling on his piroshki, Saava wandered off to watch a group of children stalk pigeons that, in a burst of strength, alighted on the sidewalk in search of the stray crumb. Aïda, who had not eaten anything since the episode at the hospital, fell on the piroshki. Her mouth full, she grimly announced, "This time they mean to kill Saava."

Ben watched the endless streams of proletarians, the vanguard of Lenin's failed revolution, flowing past on their way to work. "What did Vadim say?" he wanted to know.

Aïda appeared bewildered; discarding the waxed paper, lobbing the last crumbs of crust to a pigeon with disheveled plumage, she hugged herself as if she were holding herself together. Ben remembered the gesture; the first time he had seen it, they had been standing in the snowstorm outside the Druzhba Café just before he told her he hoped to Christ they would never meet again. "I was so crazy with worry," Aïda was saying, her eyes following Saava as he trailed after the other children, "that I slapped him, as if it were his fault the door had closed on us. So: Violence *is* a circle, and Saava has become my first victim. It is quite clear that I am going mad."

Ben shook her arm. "What did Vadim say?"

She leaned her head back and gazed at the thin trail of clouds steaming past overhead. "He said . . . what the male nurse said. That word had come down from on high. That for political reasons, Saava and the second boy had been replaced by two children from minority groups."

"When you went to the safe house yesterday, did they mention the incident at the hospital?"

"They were very polite. They brought me tea with cakes. When I had finished, one of them cleared away the cup and saucer and showed a film of me fucking like an animal."

Ben pulled her head onto his shoulder. "That was your first arrest," he quietly reminded her.

Running after the pigeons they did not quite want to catch, the children howled with laughter. Aïda shuddered and sat upright. "You are quite right," she said. "I must fight the urge to take refuge from the present in the past. The one with those terrible teeth stained with tobacco let me in. Lately he has taken to making small talk. Winter is a thing of the past, he would say. The buds have appeared early on the trees this year, he would say. In your poem 'Geography,' aren't the words longitude and latitude to be taken in their overtly sexual sense? he would say. But this time he got straight down to business. He instructed me to tell you that they were disappointed with the material you have been supplying. He instructed me to tell you that they were breaking off contact and terminating the operation. He instructed me to tell you that my residence permit to live in Kuchkovo has been rescinded. He instructed me to tell you that Saava and I had three days to pack our belongings and quit the city. There was no question, it went without saying, but he said it anyhow, of my obtaining additional quantities of Purinethol. As I was leaving, he instructed me to tell you to go to hell. So, dear heart"—Aïda's gray animal eyes, stripped of innocence, still capable of killing, but never for pleasure, were fixed unblinkingly on his—"go, please, to hell!"

Her words hit him like a slap across the face. In a vague way he understood that he had become Aïda's second victim. Wincing, he recoiled beyond arm's reach.

Aïda, appalled by the ease with which she slipped into violence, reached for Ben and drew him into an embrace in which they barely touched. "The first time I abandoned lucidity for lust," she whispered huskily, "my Polish lover betrayed me by dying. The second time was with you, and it too is ending badly."

Above their heads, on the tarnished arms and shoulders and head of Mayakovski, the emaciated pigeons cooed in what Aïda took to be an expression of empathy. If you have troubles, they seemed to be saying, use them.

ABSENTLY PICKING SUNFLOWER seeds out of a wedge of newspaper folded into a triangle, cracking them on an eye tooth, spitting the husks onto the sidewalk, Manny Custer squinted at the statue of Mayakovski, the flamboyant poet who had once invited the sun to have tea with him. At the age of thirty-six, Manny remembered, Mayakovski had composed a suicide note . . .

> *Life and I are quits,*
> *and there's no point*
> *in counting over*
> *mutual hurts,*
> *harms,*
> *and slights.*
> *Best of luck to all of you!*

. . . and then had shot himself in the heart. The suicide had been provoked by a profound disillusionment, Manny knew. But with what? The revolution that went astray? The light that failed? The love that failed? Or all of the above? Watching discreetly from a far corner of Mayakovski Square, Manny could make out the two figures sitting on Mayakovski's pedestal. The very lightness with which they clung to each other testified to the fragility of their relationship. Presently the man, in his early thirties with disheveled dark hair and the alert, watchful eyes of someone who was too rational to be passionate about anything, detached himself from the woman. He stood up and crossed the street to a pay telephone. Feeding a coin into a slot, he dialed a number. He spoke for a moment, listened, spoke briefly again and hung up. Standing at the edge of the curb, he watched the woman near the statue of Mayakovski grab hold of the hand of a boy and, plowing through the grazing pigeons, start toward the metro station. Only when the woman and the boy were lost to view did the man turn away and mingle with the crowd.

Item: Following Bassett from a safe distance as he left the apartment building earlier that morning, Manny had noticed the peasant woman, still dressed in the thick quilted Army coat despite the relative mildness of the weather, selling parsley to people queuing at a bus stop. As Bassett walked past her she had raised a bouquet of parsley. A young, clean-shaven Orthodox priest had detached himself from the bus queue and had fallen into step behind Bassett as he headed for the metro station. Inside the station the priest had lifted his hat and had run his hand through his hair and had peeled off in a different direction, to be replaced, if Manny's professional instinct was as sharp as it had once been, by a young man wearing faded blue jeans and carrying a worn plastic satchel filled with rolled-up posters. Now, watching from a corner of Mayakovski Square, Manny saw the same young man climb onto the pedestal of the statue and jab a rolled-up poster at the disappearing figure of Bassett. A workman in a pickup truck parked near the pay phone started his motor and pulled slowly into traffic after Bassett.

Item: The well-proportioned, wide-shouldered woman who had been sitting with Bassett on the pedestal had seemed tantalizingly familiar to Manny. It was only when she plowed like an icebreaker through the pigeons, frightening them into the air, that it came to him. She was the same woman who had been with Bassett when he came out of the apartment building late one night. She was the same woman who had plunged like an icebreaker through the crowd after reading her poetry to the Americans at Spaso House.

The woman in Bassett's life was the Russian poet Zinaïda Ivanovna Zavaskaya.

22

Confronting Viktor across a seedy kitchen table in the middle of a seedy room on the third floor of a seedy Stalin Gothic apartment house on the Lenin Hills, stirring cubes of sugar into a cup of muddy tea with a cheap spoon swiped, no doubt, from a neighborhood canteen, Ben thought he heard the stifled laughter of his grandfather reverberating through his skull. If you are figuring on dining with the devil, the old man cried in that peculiar half-cough, half-cackle he used when he was offering advice that had not been solicited, be goddamn sure you use a long spoon.

Too late for long spoons, Ben told himself.

"Get to the point," Viktor snapped from his side of the table. His gout had kept him awake part of the night. Imagining what his wife was doing in Kalinin had kept him up the rest. By morning he was an irritable wreck, a state of affairs his secretary, Evgeniya Leonovna, had noted when he griped about the weather and the contents of the overnight cables and the tea and the squeaking of his chair in one run-on sentence.

The man with the pear-shaped face and tobacco-stained teeth, standing in front of the double door as if he were guarding it, pushed back the frayed cuff of his thick hand-knit sweater and checked his wristwatch. "We are busy people," he remarked testily.

"The point," said Ben, "is . . ." He took a deep breath.

"Is?" Viktor prodded impatiently.

"The point is I am not what I appear to be."

Viktor, his gout suddenly forgotten, cast a triumphant glance at the mirror, then looked back at the American. "Are you telling us you are not a housekeeper for the famous Seven Dwarfs?"

Ben hesitated, then, reluctantly, nodded.

Viktor watched as Ben gnawed on his lower lip until a spot of blood appeared. Would he take the plunge?

"My being a housekeeper," Ben said finally, "is a cover story. I was sent to Moscow with a specific mission."

Viktor leaned toward the speaker, as if being physically nearer to him meant the words would reach him sooner. "And what is this specific mission?" he asked very quietly.

"I am eradicating all traces of a CIA operation called Ironweed."

The man with the pear face took a step in Ben's direction. "What is this Operation Ironweed?"

Ben shook his head.

"You do not know or you refuse to say?" demanded Pear Face.

"I do not know."

"How is it possible you do not know?"

Viktor waved off his chief of section. "Tell us what you do know," he instructed the American.

"I am what you call a sweeper," Ben said. "I am systematically going over the CIA station chief's backlist of enciphered Sensitive Compartmented Information cables. That is a category of cables so secret that the messages are enciphered on one-time pads and deciphered by the person they are addressed to. What I have been instructed to look for in Moscow is any message that bears the code name Ironweed."

"What do you do with these Ironweed messages when you find them?" inquired Viktor.

"I shred the enciphered message and put the strips in a burn bag. I destroy the corresponding plain language text. I doctor the station chief's cipher logs so that there is no trace of the message having been sent. If the reference to the Ironweed message comes at the end of a log page, I erase it and renumber subsequent entries for that day. If it falls anywhere else, I erase it and fill in the space with a log entry for a nonexistent message."

"What were you doing during the four months you spent in Prague?"

"The same thing. Only the operation I was eradicating was code named Silverweed."

"Are there any other embassies you are scheduled to go to?"

"No. Only Prague and Moscow."

Viktor said, "You must have some idea what Silverweed or Ironweed dealt with?"

Ben shrugged. "I do not have the foggiest idea."

The pear-faced man said from the wall, "You expect us to believe that you are erasing all traces of two operations, but you do not know what they were?"

Ben said, with conviction, "You can believe me or not believe me, as you like. That is the truth."

Viktor thought about this. "Do you know what it is about Silverweed and Ironweed that connects them to Prague and Moscow?"

Ben shook his head.

Viktor sat back on his kitchen chair. "Let us sum up. You are a sweeper, sent first to Prague, then to Moscow, to comb through the CIA's Sensitive Compartmented Information cables and destroy all messages and all log traces of the messages alluding to operations called Silverweed and Ironweed. You have no idea what Silverweed or Ironweed refer to. Do I have it right so far?"

Ben nodded once.

Viktor's section chief asked, "How far back do the Silverweed and Ironweed messages go?"

"For both Prague and Moscow, I was instructed to start with the 1967 cables and work up through 1985."

"At which date Operation Ironweed was presumably discontinued," Viktor ventured. His tone was extremely polite; he was clearly intrigued by Ben's story.

"It would seem so," Ben agreed.

Viktor folded his hands across his chest and let his chin droop until it was touching his tie. He closed his eyes. To Ben it looked as if he was catnapping. Presently Viktor emerged from his reverie. "Who is your employer?" he asked.

Ben shook his head. "I am not even sure about that."

"Somebody had to give you marching orders," the pear-faced man commented from the wall.

Ben responded to Viktor. "I was trained to work with one-time ciphers by Army Intelligence field agents," he said. "My specific instructions came from a nuts-and-bolts type named Marlowe. He showed me credentials identifying him as a State Department security officer, but I never really believed that. If I had to guess I would say he was from CIA, from operations."

"What made you think that?"

"He was very closemouthed. He said only what had to be said. Nothing more. It was ingrained in him. It had to have come from years of working in the shadows. State Department people are used to working in the light of day. They open up more when they talk to you."

Viktor asked for a physical description of Marlowe. Ben supplied it. He was in his late forties or early fifties, physically big bordering on fat, but he moved with incredible grace, almost like a ballet dancer. He had thin, prematurely gray hair and uneven teeth and talked with what Ben took to be a Texas drawl. He seldom smiled. When he did, he looked as if he were in pain.

The station chief Krostin, his blond beard vibrating with excitement, pulled a kitchen chair over to the table. "Let us get down to details," he said, settling into the chair. "Start with the tour in Prague. You erased traces of messages. How many? What do you remember of the contents?"

Ben looked at Viktor. "What about the boy? What about the seventy-five milligrams of 6-mercaptopurine he is supposed to take a day?"

Viktor nodded at Krostin, who removed a small brown paper satchel from his jacket pocket. Reaching across the table, he set it down in front of the American. Ben opened the satchel and stirred the pills with an index finger. "Once I give you the information you want, how can I be sure you will continue to supply the pills for the boy?" Ben wanted to know.

Krostin, frowning impatiently, started to say something about how you could not turn back once you started climbing the face of a cliff, but Viktor interrupted him. "It is a logical question and it deserves an answer," he decided. He scrutinized Ben in what he hoped was a fatherly way. "You impress me as a rational individual. Look at the situation from our point of view. You have alerted us to the fact that the American Central Intelligence Agency ran an operation in Prague with the code name Silverweed, and another operation in Moscow with the code name Ironweed. Now, for some reason that you claim not to understand and we can only guess at, the CIA is trying to erase all traces of these operations. The last thing in the world we want is for the Central Intelligence Agency to become aware that we know of the existence of Silverweed and Ironweed, or that the operations were important enough for the CIA to try to eradicate all traces of them; our knowledge will only be useful to us if the CIA does not know that we know. This leaves us with two possibilities with respect to you and the Zavaskaya woman and her son. We can eliminate all of you. I speak frankly; I do not mean to frighten you, only to educate you. Think about it: Even if your death appeared to be an accident, it would inevitably stir the Americans to suspect that we had discovered your secret mission and created the accident. The second possibility, by far the safest and surest from

an intelligence point of view, is to keep you happy. For
self-evident reasons, we can count on the fact that you will
not reveal to the Americans that you have become an
agent for the KGB. When you have finished eradicating
all traces of Ironweed from the CIA station chief's backlist of enciphered Sensitive Compartmented Information
cables, your handlers in Washington will find some credi-
ble excuse to recall you. At this point there is no reason
why we could not let the Zavaskaya woman and her son
emigrate. The Zavaskaya woman will accept emigration if
it means that her son can have an operation that will cure
his illness. What you do then will be your affair. You can
arrange to meet, as if for the first time, in Europe; you can
fall in love all over again. What, I put it to you, can be
more pleasurable than falling in love with someone you
already love? You could even marry."

"You sound very convincing," Ben remarked.

"The peasants have a saying," Viktor noted. "Truth con-
vinces by its own weight." He pushed back his chair and
got to his feet. For some reason he felt taller than he had
in ages; taller and younger. The adrenaline that had first
coursed through his veins the day he bayoneted the
Wehrmacht soldier was stimulating him again. Pretty soon
there would be no enemies left, and no Cold War to fight
—but until then the game was worth playing.

Viktor went into the kitchenette and returned with an
iced bottle of Polish Bison vodka and three tumblers. Filling each, he proposed a toast.

"To our enemies," he said, raising his glass high. "May
they always be there when we need them."

Krostin, who abhorred alcohol, touched his lips to the
vodka to be polite. Carefully setting down his tumbler, he
focused on Ben. "Start with the tour in Prague," he said
again. "You erased traces of messages. How many? What
do you remember of the contents?"

THE DAY HAD STARTED OFF overcast and gotten darker. By
noon impenetrable clouds loomed like a black canopy
over Moscow. Winds channeled through the city's boule-

vards sent the rain, when it started, pelting against the windows of the general's conference room. Inside, Olga Glebova, who had been caught in the storm during her lunch break, shivered. Her shoes, the hem of her dress, were soaked. Tufts of damp hair shot off in several directions from the bleached blond bird's nest teased up on her head, as if they had been charged with static electricity. Behind her octagonal bifocals, her eyes bulged more than usual from a face pinched more than usual.

The Second Chief Directorate had come clean; Viktor had given them the new material—as well as its source. Glebova had become so enthralled with the dossier that she had missed her period. "What intrigues me," she was telling the old general now in an agitated whisper, "is that the Americans are going to such lengths to muddy a trail, to eradicate all traces of the operation code named Ironweed—"

"Which would be one way of calling attention to Ironweed," the general noted in a gravelly voice. His instinct told him that every working group needed a devil's advocate. Viktor and his people clearly felt they had struck the mother lode, which narrowed the list of those who could play the role to him.

N. Fillipov's bushy white eyebrows fairly danced in disagreement. "One would have to be completely naive not to take that possibility into consideration," he said in a whine that reminded Viktor, following the conversation from his side of the table, of a wolf baying at the moon. Fillipov arched his back, pulled in his chin to indicate by his body language that naïveté was not one of his weaknesses. "Several things argue against the thesis. Most important, one has to remember that the American Bassett did not come to us, we came to him. Add to that his obvious reluctance to cooperate—"

"Getting information out of him has been like pulling teeth," Krostin interjected from his seat next to Viktor.

Noticing the old general's built-in frown grow darker, Viktor flashed a warning look in Krostin's direction. This is an analysts' show, his eyes seemed to warn.

Pursing chapped lips, massaging them with a pink tongue, rocking his head, Fillipov continued. "One must also put on the scales the fact that the American Bassett clearly does not know who or what Ironweed is. He is as much in the dark as we are. He is a lowly sweeper performing a technical task that he finds quite boring."

The fingers of the general's bad hand curled in on themselves, beckoning Glebova. She leaned toward him expectantly.

"About Ironweed," he muttered.

"About Ironweed?" Glebova repeated, mesmerized by the general's curling fingers.

"What is Ironweed?" the general asked.

Glebova corrected the general. "*Who is Ironweed?*" she said carefully. "If the American Bassett is telling the truth—"

"And so far we have no reason to suspect otherwise," Fillipov interjected impatiently.

"If, as I say, he is telling the truth," Glebova continued, "then we can conclude that the operation began in 1967 and terminated in 1985. Assuming, as seems likely, that the operation involved a Soviet citizen who defected to the Central Intelligence Agency but stayed on as an agent in place, the first question we can ask is why—"

"—why the operation was terminated in 1985," Fillipov picked up the thread of the narrative. "We considered the possibility that the agent in place died in 1985," he went on, "but downgraded that hypothesis for the simple reason that if the agent in place were dead, there would be no reason for the Americans to muddy the trail."

"We considered the possibility that the agent in place got what the Americans call cold feet," Glebova said. "We discarded that hypothesis because it is unlikely the Americans would allow him to retire; our feeling is that they would blackmail him into continuing."

"Our hunch," Fillipov observed in a funereal tone, "is they are wiping out all traces of the operation because Ironweed was promoted in the superstructure to a position of importance."

"One," announced Glebova excitedly, "where he had an influence on policy decisions."

"One," added Fillipov, "where he was far more valuable to the Americans than someone who merely supplied information."

"You do see what we are driving at?" Glebova asked the general. "In order to protect their agent in place they broke off contact with him in 1985. Then, as the agent in place rose still higher in the superstructure, they decided to eradicate all traces of those contacts."

Once again the general's fingers curled. "About Prague," he muttered.

"About Prague?" Glebova repeated, her eyes glued to the general's fingers.

"What is the connection between Prague and Moscow and Ironweed?"

Glebova tried to tuck some of the stray hairs back into her bird's nest, but only succeeded in creating more disorder. "The American Bassett claims to have eradicated between fifteen and twenty Silverweed messages during his four months in Prague," she said slowly. "Of these he was able to reconstruct for us the contents of eight messages. The Prague messages referred to someone code-named Silverweed. Silverweed would appear to be a Czech citizen. Judging from his ability to travel extensively in both the East and the West, he probably was a high-ranking Communist himself. Silverweed appears to have known Ironweed intimately for years; there is some suggestion that they studied together at university. It seems clear that both Ironweed and Silverweed were not betraying their countries for money. In one message there seems to have been a passing reference to a Swiss bank account. It is likely that the Americans were proposing to deposit funds in a numbered Swiss account. Judging from the apologies in another message—"

"Judging from the apologies," Fillipov cut in impatiently, "Silverweed was insulted by the offer and refused to pass it on to Ironweed."

"All very vague," the general said, waving his good

hand as if he were dispelling smoke. "Long on suppositions. Short on verifiable facts."

Glebova sniffed at the air, as if to say, we work with
what you give us. Fillipov, focusing on some middle distance, observed, "One is always eager for verifiable facts,
if only to lend support to the suppositions."

"Since we are relying on the memory of the American
Bassett," Glebova remarked, "we are, as the general sug-
gests, short on verifiable facts. But that will change. The
Second Chief Directorate"—Glebova almost but not
quite smiled across the table at Viktor—"has arranged for
the American Bassett to deliver copies of all the Ironweed
messages he finds and eradicates. From this point on we
ought to be able to deal in verifiable facts. To cross-check
them, as it were."

Fillipov, his mind, like his eyes, focusing elsewhere,
mumbled, "Bits and pieces. Pieces and bits." Sounding as
if he were talking to himself, he plunged on. "They are
not without a certain harmony. Take, for instance, one of
the very first messages between Silverweed and his control in Washington. Silverweed proposed trying to recruit
a Russian friend of his, someone he knew from university
—either he did not specify which university or the American Bassett did not remember the detail. According to
Silverweed, his Russian friend held a grudge against the
Party because of something that had happened to a close
childhood friend of his who was a Kalmyk."

Viktor asked, "A Kalmyk?"

"The Kalmyks," Glebova explained, "were a relatively
small tribe of Moslems who were deported by Stalin to
Siberia at the end of the Great Patriotic War for collabo-
rating with the German invaders. Before their deporta-
tion, they lived, for the most part, in the Stavropol
administrative unit, although there were enclaves
throughout the Caucasus. Either Ironweed got to know
this particular Kalmyk at university or afterward during a
posting to a city, or he himself may have originated from
the same Stavropol *krai*."

Fillipov focused on Viktor and his two associates as if

he were noticing them for the first time. He turned back to the general. "Silverweed visited Ironweed in Moscow during the winter of 1967. Several messages that the American Bassett remembered erasing dealt with the details of this and subsequent meetings. There was a safe house laid on. Silverweed and Ironweed talked through the afternoon and evening. It was at this meeting that Ironweed was apparently recruited to work for the CIA, using Silverweed as his cutout. A second meeting took place when Ironweed visited Prague during the fall of 1969. Once again the CIA arranged a safe house. A third meeting took place in Brussels, but the American Bassett did not remember the year. The Americans slipped Silverweed up a back staircase of Ironweed's hotel. The two talked through the night. Ironweed was instructed in the intricacies of dead drops. There was a fourth meeting on the Black Sea at a KGB sanatorium in Kislovodsk. Again, the American Bassett could not put a date to this meeting."

"That was the sanatorium that our late General Secretary Andropov used to vacation at," the general remembered. "I was invited to spend a weekend there with him once."

Glebova's head bobbed as if it were floating on a current. "The fact that Ironweed had access to the KGB sanatorium in Kislovodsk," she said warily, "could suggest that he was either a high-ranking member of our own organization—"

"—or a member of Andropov's entourage called in for consultations," Fillipov finished the thought for her.

"About the Moscow messages?"

"So far," Glebova said, "the American Bassett has worked his way through the station chief's backlist of enciphered Sensitive Compartmented Information cables covering the years 1967 through 1975. Once again he estimates having eradicated all traces of between a dozen and fifteen messages. Of these he was able to reconstruct the contents of five messages with a degree of accuracy.

Two of the five messages supplied Ironweed with technical support—"

Fillipov cut in. "Lists of dead drops in Moscow, code names for each, addresses in Western Europe where he could send innocent-looking picture postcards alerting his handlers that he was depositing something in a particular dead drop, that sort of thing."

"A third message," Glebova continued, "asked his handlers if they could get him and his family out of the Soviet Union in the event he felt that the KGB was closing in on him; apparently there is a wife, a child, on what Ironweed called his doomsday list, though there is no indication of the sex of the child, or its age. A fourth message, apparently sent in 1971, attempted to analyze the strengths and weaknesses of various members of the Politburo, and suggest who was likely to succeed Brezhnev as the General Secretary of the Party if he were to die. Once again Andropov's name plays a prominent role; Ironweed appeared to be convinced that Andropov stood a good chance of stepping into the number one slot despite reformist tendencies. Ironweed also appears to have believed that his star would rise within the superstructure as Andropov's star rose."

"Whoever Ironweed was," Fillipov asserted with vehemence, "he was known and liked by Andropov."

"Andropov knew hundreds of people," the general remarked sourly. "Of the hundreds, he may have liked half of them." He shook his head in exasperation. "You said the American was able to reconstruct five messages."

"The fifth message is very curious," Glebova confessed.

"Very curious," Fillipov repeated to himself.

"Up to this point the Americans had been careful never to contact Ironweed directly; everything was done through cutouts, like Silverweed, or through the use of dead drops. Then, during the summer of 1971, Ironweed for some reason insisted on talking to one of his American handlers. Someone was brought into the country as part of a delegation of environmentalists. Ironweed managed to pick him up in his car and take him for a long drive, during which Ironweed tried to convince his interlocutor that the Americans must increase their military expenditures year after year in order to force the Russians to keep pace. His point was that the Russians, unlike the Americans, could not afford both guns and butter at the same time—"

"—that the economy would crack," Fillipov explained, "bringing on the objective conditions needed to install a reformer as head of the Party."

"We have seen this analysis of the American motives before," the general observed. "Why do you characterize this message as curious?"

"What was curious," Fillipov answered for Glebova, "was an incident, described by the American author of the message, that took place while Ironweed was driving along a country road. They came across a tractor that had broken down and was blocking the road. According to his American companion, Ironweed got out of the car, rolled up his sleeves and proceeded to repair the tractor's engine —he removed a diesel filter and cleaned it, he purged air from a fuel line, he replaced everything and started the motor. The tractor driver laughingly told Ironweed that with such a skill, he could get a job running a tractor collective."

Fillipov's eyebrows arched in an agony of revelation. "You do see where this is going? Ironweed is clearly an *apparatchik*, a member even of the elite *nomenklatura*, working out of the superstructure. He wears a tie and a jacket when he goes to the office. He probably has a secretary, he probably has underlings. He knows Andropov, may even consider himself a protégé of sorts. Yet he can lift the hood of a tractor and repair the engine."

"Remember the Kalmyk who probably came from the Stavropol *krai?*" Glebova said, articulating each word.

The old general shook his head in frustration. "Probably this. Probably that. Ironweed probably went to a university, probably had a Czech friend who probably had an important Party post in Prague, probably was married, probably had a child when he asked the CIA to organize an emergency escape route, probably knew Andropov, probably was promoted (assuming he did not die) in 1985, probably had a friend who was a Kalmyk, probably was in Moscow in 1967 and in Prague in 1969, probably was in Brussels and a KGB sanatorium on the Black Sea at some point in his life, and probably had worked on a collective farm when he was young, how else could he have known how to repair a tractor engine?" The general's shoulders heaved. Turning to his son-in-law for the first time, he asked, "Tell me, Viktor, how many people were promoted to positions of authority when the government changed in 1985?"

"Several thousand, at least."

"Of these, how many do you think had a wife and one child? How many would have been acquainted with Andropov?"

Instead of responding to the general's question, Viktor addressed Glebova. "You have left out the business of Marlowe."

Glebova stiffened. "I did not omit it," she said in her plodding voice. "I was saving the best for the last." She studied her notes to refresh her memory, then looked up at the general. "Before being posted to Prague, the American Bassett was given his instructions by a person who pretended to be a State Department Security officer, and who went by the name of Marlowe. Bassett gave our colleagues from the Second Chief Directorate a physical description of the man. He was said to be in his late forties or early fifties, physically big to the point of being fat. He was said to move with incredible grace, almost like a ballet dancer. He was said to have thin, prematurely gray hair and uneven teeth and talk with a Texas accent. He was said to rarely smile. When he did smile he looked, according to the American Bassett, as if he were in pain."

Fillipov impatiently cut in. "The description fits the man who ran the CIA station in Prague from 1967 to 1975. He went under the name of Asher Spink. Spink, it would seem, was the case officer who ran the original Silverweed operation. When Silverweed recruited Iron-

weed, he ran both of them. Spink slipped into Moscow
during the summer of 1971 as a member of a group of
environmentalists. The Second Chief Directorate was
aware of his identity, but decided to let him into Russia in
order to see whom he contacted. He was followed every-
where he went. His room in the Hotel Ukraine was
seeded with microphones. On the third day of his visit he
disappeared during a conference with environmentalists
from the Forestry Ministry. He excused himself to go to
the bathroom, then wandered by seeming mistake into a
ladies' toilet. The operative who was assigned to him decided it would be too conspicuous to follow him. Spink
never emerged. It turned out that the ladies' toilet, unlike
the men's toilet, had a door leading to a storage room, and
the storage room in turn had a door leading to another
corridor."

"For how long did Spink drop from sight?" the general
rasped, for once openly intrigued.

"For seven and one-half hours," Glebova noted breathlessly.

"How do you interpret the significance of the disap-
pearance of the Prague station chief?" the general inquired. He managed to convey the feeling that he was
posing the question for the record; that he had already
glimpsed the response.

The rain hammered against the general's window.
Glebova's lips parted slightly as she sucked in air. "It is a
corroborating detail," she whispered emotionally. "It is
the first thing mentioned in the Ironweed file of eradicated messages that we can say with objective certainty
really happened. Ironweed asked for a face-to-face meeting. Spink slipped into the country. Then he disappeared
for half a day."

Fillipov pressed his eyes closed. "We think it can be
said with certitude," he announced in a voice that seemed
to take its cadence from the beat of the rain against the
window. "Somewhere in the upper echelons of the Party
the Americans have planted an agent in place, a traitor to
the Motherland known to his CIA handlers as Ironweed."

•   •   •

"YOU MUST HAVE HEARD THE STORY," the old general muttered to Viktor.

It was half past three in the morning. They were driving
back from the meeting of the *Pamyat* Directorate, which
had been held in an Orthodox church outside a small
village forty kilometers from Moscow. The church had
been used as a barn by the villagers for decades and only
recently was cleaned and disinfected in preparation for
restoration work. Despite this it still smelled faintly of
manure, and traces of the odor had clung to the clothing
of Viktor and the general.

Viktor worked the windshield wipers several times to
clear away the early morning humidity, which accumulated on the window like a film of tears. "By all means, tell
it," Viktor said to his father-in-law.

The old man's voice rasped out of the darkness. "It
seems that the Chekists had been interrogating some Yid,
but could not break him. When they reported this to Stalin, he posed the following question: 'How much does the
State weigh?' The Chekists were confused. They asked
Stalin what he meant by the question. 'I ask precisely
what I mean,' Stalin said. And he repeated the question:
'How much does the State—its buildings, its factories, its
sport stadiums, its highways, its trains, its trucks, its ships,
its tanks—weigh?' 'So much,' said the Chekists, 'that it
would be impossible to calculate.' And Stalin, who knew
how to break a Yid, who had broken his share in his day,
told them, 'Use it!' "

The old general laughed gruffly. The laugh transformed
itself into a hacking cough. He hauled an enormous handkerchief from his inside breast pocket and smothered the
cough in it. When he was able to talk again, he said, "The
higher you mount in the superstructure in your search for
Ironweed, the better it will be for *Pamyat*. Use the weight
of the State if you have to. Only find him."

23

The rough floor planks around the writing table were littered with crumpled sheets of paper torn from the lined grade-school notebook in which Aïda composed poetry. She was trying to work out a poem on the subject of schizophrenia. The theme had been in her head for weeks: Only someone with a split personality could cope with the schizophrenic aspects of reality. After a dozen false starts, a first stanza appeared full-blown behind her shut lids. She opened her eyes and wrote it down in the thick slanted script she used when she recorded her poems. Fingering Akhmatova's agate ring that had failed to banish fear, she read the stanza out loud.

> *Before the wave breaks*
> *a stillness . . .*
> *Drifts of water pile up*
> *against the crest . . .*

Ben, playing dominoes with Saava on the front porch of the *dacha,* heard her through the open door. "Sounds as if you are getting somewhere," he called.

Aïda was not at all sure she was getting anywhere; with her poetry, with her life. Studying the stanza again, she decided it perfectly described her mental state: The world around her was utterly still, things were in their place, her father was sinking slowly toward death in the unheated hospital room, Saava got his proper dose of pills, she had her lover in her bed. And yet . . . embracing Benedict the night before on the bearskin rug in front of the fire that had burned down to embers, her body glowing like the embers from the rough friction of their love-making, she had become aware of the mass of water piling up against the crest; she had sensed the shadow of the wave looming over her.

She had become, like her father before her, permanently frightened.

Without going into details, Ben had promised her that he had solved their problems. Twice a week he slipped her a sealed envelope thick with folded slips of paper, and she made her way to the awful street, to the awful building, to the awful room and delivered the envelope to the awful man with tobacco-stained teeth, and accepted from him the pills Saava needed to stay alive. "You will see," Ben had whispered, drawing her warm body against his warm body on the bearskin. "Things will end well. Saava will get his operation. And we will have a new incarnation in this incarnation."

"Swear it," Aïda had challenged.

Ben had raised his right hand. "I swear it. We will live happily ever after."

"The Romans put a hand on their testicles when they took an oath."

Ben had thought she was joking, but had seen from her expression that she was deadly serious. Smiling uncomfortably, he had placed his hand on his testicles. Her fingers had closed over his. "I swear it," he had repeated softly. Seeing the shadow of a doubt in her eyes, he had burst out, "What can I say to make you believe me?"

"I believe that you believe what you say," Aïda had told

him. "I am only afraid that you are deceiving yourself. And then there is the other matter."

"The other matter?"

"The Frenchman Camus somewhere wrote that it is better to suffer certain injustices than to commit them. I have always believed this."

"We are doing what we have to do in order to survive," Ben had retorted hotly.

"Concentrating on survival has its dangers," Aïda had told him.

"Name one."

"The instincts you develop to survive are not necessarily the instincts you need to live and love."

Come morning, Aïda's fears had ebbed; they had seemed like vague memories of bad dreams. Stripping to the skin at the edge of the lake below the *dacha*, she and Ben had scrubbed each other with sponges dipped in the still icy water, then had raced each other up the steep hill to the *dacha* to warm themselves in front of a roaring fire set to blazing with the addition of new wood on the previous night's embers. Aïda had boiled water over the fire and had prepared steaming bowls of oatmeal before waking Saava. After breakfast, Saava and Benedict had started a game of dominoes on the porch while Aïda had drowned her fears in poetry. Now, feeling as if she had come to a dead end, she glanced at the wristwatch that ran counterclockwise, recalled her Polish lover telling her that if time ran backward one could go back and undo the future. If only it were so! Smiling ironically, she interrupted the domino game and the three of them set off on one of their long meandering walks through the countryside around Zagorsk.

With Saava scampering ahead, they made their way past the first scarecrow of the planting season, past two ancient peasants hoeing in a vegetable garden, past birds beating up clouds of dust as they bathed in the dry dirt of the footpath, to the ruins of a church standing like a sentinel on a bluff overlooking the far end of the lake. Ducking under a tangle of vines to get inside, they discovered on one weathered wall the white trace of a large cross that must have hung there for centuries before the Bolsheviks decreed that religion was the opiate of the people. From somewhere outside the ruins came the sound of Saava testing an echo in his high-pitched voice.

"Ho ho," he cried.

"Ho ho," the echo replied.

Aïda, who was not religious in any conventional sense, who had in fact flirted with Tibetan Buddhism when she was younger, crossed herself with large gestures of her bunched fingers, then sank to her knees before the trace of the cross and, rocking forward, touched her forehead to the dirt. "Dear God in heaven," she murmured as Ben looked on curiously. And weaving the Buddhist concept of *chod* into her imperfect Orthodoxy, she offered up a prayer: "So: Give me the strength to embrace what I fear in order to better understand how all things in the world are related, and being related, divine."

VIKTOR WAS GOING OVER with his two section chiefs the latest nuggets, culled from conversations picked up by microphones recently planted in the Jewish speculator's *dacha* near Zagorsk, when the summons from his father-in-law reached him. Both Glebova and Fillipov were with the old general when Viktor arrived. Fillipov was contemplating his reflection in a window. He did not seem to be displeased with what he saw. Glebova had pulled a chair up to the general's desk and was stabbing a blood-red fingernail at sentences in a report that were already underlined. Her tight skirt had ridden up on her thighs, revealing two thick, knobby knees. She noticed Viktor noticing them and tugged at the hem of her skirt.

"Tell him what you have told me," the general instructed her.

"Silverweed," Glebova announced dramatically, "is a she!"

Fillipov lectured his reflection in the window. "They referred to Silverweed as 'he' to throw anyone who saw the Prague messages off the scent."

Viktor wanted to know how they had discovered that Silverweed was a woman.

Glebova abandoned a half-hearted attempt to iron out the wrinkles in her skirt with a palm. "The reference was buried in one of the Ironweed messages that the American Bassett passed to us last week," she said. She reached across the general's desk and pointed out a paragraph underlined in red. "Sensitive Compartmented Information Cable Delta Zebra one oh four of 4 March 1975. The communication is BIGOT listed, which means that the addressee controls dissemination and all copies are numbered. The CIA station chief is passing on a message from Ironweed retrieved from a dead drop. Ironweed is signaling that he has been selected to travel to West Germany as part of a delegation. He wants to see Silverweed when he gets there. Whenever Ironweed referred to Silverweed before, he always used the proper noun."

"Silverweed this, Silverweed that," Fillipov mumbled from the window.

"Now Ironweed slips up," Glebova explained. "He says, 'Ask Silverweed to bring her notes.' "

"*Her* notes!" Fillipov called across the room. He snorted with pleasure.

"What notes?" Viktor inquired.

The general fitted his eyeglasses over his ears and read the underlined passage. " 'Ask Silverweed to bring her notes from the Beetle's lecture on the psychological roots of free enterprise. Also the tract based on the lecture Silverweed published during the spring.' "

"It took us a while," Glebova said breathlessly, "but we managed to identify the Beetle."

"It was the nickname," Fillipov cut in, "students gave to the famous Professor Usov, Boris Sergeyevich, who was said to have resembled the singer John Lennon of the English pop group known as the Beatles. Usov delivered a series of guest lectures at Moscow State University in the fall of 1954 in which he expounded one of his pet theories. According to him, the efficiency of industrial enterprises should be measured by how much profit they make and not how many units they produce."

"At the time," Glebova picked up where Fillipov had left off, "Usov was considered to be a radical reformer, far outside the mainstream. Today he is seen as one of the gurus of the current leadership's economic policies."

Stretching his neck so that his Adam's apple protruded, adjusting the knot in his tie, Fillipov reluctantly turned away from the window to face Viktor. "The reference to Usov, and most especially the use of his nickname, would seem to place Ironweed at Moscow State University in 1954. His request for Silverweed's notes would seem to suggest that he and Silverweed were fellow students."

"Or lovers," Glebova chirped in exuberant discovery. "Remember how the two of them supposedly talked through the night in Brussels?"

Fillipov indicated with a frown that he was not convinced of his colleague's leap of imagination. "If one takes Ironweed's reference to 'the spring' to mean the Prague Spring of 1968," he continued, "one finds a tract on the subject of the psychological roots of free enterprise published by the Prague State Publishing House."

"The tract"—Glebova was whispering now—"bears the signature of Alexander Dubcek. An embassy report dated July 15, 1968, said the tract was ghostwritten by Dubcek's speech writer. And Dubcek's speech writer was—"

Glebova shuddered with nervous excitement. Fillipov finished the sentence for her. "—a woman named Martina Ilkiv. She was well known in Czechoslovakia during the Prague Spring as one of the architects of what Dubcek called Socialism with a human face. It was she who was said to have come up with this slogan."

Glebova found her voice again. "We have been going over the lists of students enrolled in the various disciplines at Moscow State University in the early and mid-1950s. So far we have been unable to find a trace of a Martina Ilkiv."

The general's deeply lined face screwed up in a sour grimace. It irritated him when pieces of a puzzle failed to

fit. Glebova said, "We have not been able to link the Ilkiv
woman to Moscow State University or a particular Russian, but we have been able to establish that she visited
Moscow during the winter of 1967, and again during the
summer of 1971, the dates Ironweed is supposed to have
been contacted by Silverweed. We know that she was in
Prague for most of 1969, the date of Ironweed's visit to
Prague and meeting with Silverweed. She was also said to
have been to Brussels at least a dozen times in the sixties
and seventies to visit her younger brother, who had emigrated there in the early 1960s. There is unfortunately no
record of her having been in West Germany in March or
April of 1975, although she was known to have been ab-
sent from Prague the last two weeks of March."

"The Ilkiv woman," Fillipov continued, "emigrated to
France in January of 1985, the year the CIA broke off
contact with Ironweed. She died of a burst appendix in a
Paris hospital in October of that year."

"What about the reference to Ironweed joining a delegation going to West Germany?" Viktor asked Glebova.
"That must narrow the list of possible Ironweeds consid-
erably."

Glebova shook her head carefully. "Ironweed unfortunately did not specify the date of the delegation's visit to
West Germany. There were five delegations dispatched to
West Germany in the two months following the date of
this message. One was cultural, one was political, three
were trade missions. There were one hundred and ninety-
seven men of rank involved in the five delegations—"

Fillipov, smiling slyly, interrupted his colleague from
the wall. "We have ruled out the possibility of Ironweed
being a woman on the theory that few women would be
capable of repairing the motor of a tractor."

"Of these hundred and ninety-seven men," Glebova
continued, "eighty-eight appear to fit the profile we have
of Ironweed." She began ticking off items on her fingers.
"Which is to say, they were married and had one child;
could have conceivably come into contact with Andropov
in the course of their careers and thus could have been

summoned to consult with him while he was staying at the
KGB sanatorium on the Black Sea; they were in Moscow
in 1967 and during the summer of 1971; they visited
Prague sometime during the fall of 1969; they had been to
Brussels at some point in their lives."

Fillipov was lecturing his image in the window again.
"We have decided that any man who ever owned or had
the use of a car or a truck might be capable of cleaning a
filter and purging air from a fuel line. Thus our profile of
Ironweed does not require him to have worked on a collective farm when he was younger."

"Which leaves the matter of his probable promotion in
1985, the year the Central Intelligence Agency broke off
contact with Ironweed," Glebova said. "Of our eighty-
eight potential Ironweeds, twenty-three rose in the ranks
that year."

"The bottom line is that you have narrowed the field to
twenty-three," Viktor said.

At the window, Fillipov nodded knowingly at his reflection. On the thick glass surface of the vast desk, the general's deformed fingers slowly curled in on themselves,
beckoning Viktor. With his good hand he picked up a
sheet of typed names and offered it to his son-in-law.

Viktor approached the desk and took the sheet from the
general. As his eyes ran down the list, his lips parted
slightly. An almost inaudible whistle seeped from between
his teeth. When he finally managed to tear his eyes away
from the list and look at the general, he appeared to have
stopped breathing.

MANNY HAD THE DEFTNESS of a virtuoso when it came to
basic tradecraft. His instinct for the street, nurtured during a childhood spent on the docks of Hoboken, honed
during his back-to-back tours as chief of station in Istanbul, was on a par with his appetite for the street. It was
where he felt comfortable; in his element. Which is why
he found himself taking certain precautions before he
made the conscious decision that precautions were in
order. He discovered what he was looking for in an open-

air flea market behind the central food market. Scores of poverty-stricken refugees who had fled Azerbaijani pogroms were selling their belongings out of open card-board suitcases to make ends meet. Now, decked out in an old worker's cap worn low on his forehead with the peak angled over his eyes, scuffed miner's lace-up boots and an old belted raincoat that drooped to his ankles, he trailed after the broad-shouldered, broad-hipped woman with a broken, badly set nose alive with freckles.

Manny had followed Benedict Bassett when he left the embassy on Thursday two weeks before to a workers' can-teen on Krasnaya Presnya, had observed him through the window meeting the poet Zavaskaya in the back room. Afterward Manny had followed her back to an apartment building at Rechnoi Vokzal. Acting on one of those hunches that had its roots in experience, he had decided to keep tabs on her (as opposed to him) for a week or so. Calling in sick to the embassy, he had picked her up as she left the apartment building in the morning, stayed with her through the day—there had been two poetry readings in factory auditoriums, there had been half a dozen trips to see someone in a clinic near the Kremlin, there had been a visit to the *Novy Mir* offices, there had been interminable hours spent queuing for food or, once the rains started in earnest, rubbers for the young boy who had been with her the day Manny spotted Bassett and the poet at the Mayakovski statue.

Zavaskaya and Bassett had met twice during the week Manny followed her: On Monday in a ramshackle hostel in a workers' section on the outskirts of Moscow, where they had disappeared into a room for two and a half hours; the second time late Thursday afternoon in a coffee house inside the Byelorussia Railroad Station. They met again the following Monday, this time in a vaulted base-ment restaurant inside the Economic Achievement Ex-hibition off Ostankinskaya Ulitsa. After each meeting Zavaskaya had done precisely the same thing: She had crossed the river and had started up the hill that led to the university. Halfway up the hill she had turned into a Stalin

Gothic apartment building. The second time this happened Manny had remained near enough to hear her
footsteps as she climbed to the sixth floor in stairwell C.
The third time he had been following her from in front.
Seeing that she was heading in the direction of the same
Stalin Gothic, he had raced ahead and waited for her on
the sixth floor. Concealed behind a foul-smelling plastic
garbage bin, he had watched as Zavaskaya crossed into
another wing of the building and started down another
stairwell. Listening at the top of the stairwell, he had
counted the flights as she descended. There were three of
them before a hall door slammed closed.

Sitting alone at a corner table at Sam's Lounge late
Wednesday night, nursing an Alka-Seltzer set on a felt
square advertising a Swedish beer, Manny retraced his
steps in his head. In his mind's eye he could see Bassett,
his arm around the woman's waist, steering her with sexual urgency through the swinging front door of the hostel.
He could see Bassett leaning over the small round table in
the coffee house inside the Byelorussia Railroad Station,
his head almost touching the woman's, talking intently—
as if he were trying to convince her of something. He
could see Bassett sitting next to her in the booth in the
basement restaurant, nodding earnestly as Zavaskaya, nervously toying with a ring on her finger, rambled on. At
one point Bassett had looked around quickly. Manny
could have sworn that Bassett's eyes lingered for a fleeting
instant on the bearded young man with an Army knapsack
drinking coffee at a table near the door. (Manny had noticed the same young man sitting behind the wheel of an
off-duty taxi parked down the block from the hostel three
days before.) If, as Manny suspected, Bassett had spotted
the KGB tail—a thin smile spread across Manny's thick
lips as he considered the possibility—he had certainly not
been put off by his presence. Reaching quickly into the
pocket of his raincoat folded over the back of his chair,
Bassett had—what? His hand had remained out of sight
under the table. Had he been caressing the woman's knee
or . . . passing her something? Did she then make a

beeline for what was probably a safe house on the Lenin Hills to report on what he had said . . . or pass on what he had given her?

Had the Russians penetrated into the heart of the American embassy? Had Bassett been pressured or blackmailed or bought? Forgetting the question of motivation, was he a Soviet agent?

As far as Manny could figure, there was one sure way to find out.

LATE THURSDAY AFTERNOON, the day, according to his calculations, that Bassett was due to meet Zavaskaya again, Manny was loitering in the courtyard behind the embassy, his back to the wall of the building that housed the incinerator. He had chosen the spot for a reason: It had been constructed by the same Seabees who built the communications bubble on the sixth floor as well as Inkermann's inner sanctum, making it the one place in the white-badge area of the embassy where the Russians had not planted microphones. Even if they had, the noise from the incinerator would drown out any conversation. And Manny did not want the conversation he planned to have with Bassett overheard by the Russians.

Manny had gotten rid of the wiry technician who tended the furnace and supervised the destruction of material brought down in burn bags. "Why don't you treat yourself to a long coffee break," he told him. "I'll mind the store." Now, glancing up from his folded copy of the Paris *Herald Tribune,* he watched the minute hand of his wristwatch click on to forty-five before the hour. He was beginning to wonder if Bassett might have canceled the usual Thursday afternoon meeting with his Russian mistress when he noticed someone pushing through a door from the embassy. Backing through the door, clutching the daily burn bag from the Arms Control Implementation Unit, one arm in his raincoat, the other struggling to find the sleeve opening, Bassett turned and came hurrying across the courtyard.

The mugging went smoothly. Manny looked up from

his newspaper and nodded, and Bassett, passing, nodded back. Then in one swift motion, Manny threw a hammerlock on him and pushed him roughly through the door into the incinerator room.

"What the fuck do you think—" Ben cried, his voice almost drowned out by the hiss of the incinerator. Manny's other arm pressed in on Bassett's neck, cutting off his wind and his words.

Keeping a tight grip on the hammerlock, Manny eased the pressure on Bassett's windpipe. Ben gagged. He sounded as if he might vomit. Leaning forward, Manny yelled into his ear. "What I'm gonna do is pound your head into the wall and give you a headache you will remember, after which I plan to strip you stark naked and search you. You can save yourself a lot of grief, Mr. Benedict Bassett, by handing it over."

"Don't know what . . . talking about," Ben gasped.

Manny took a grip on Bassett's hair and shoved his face into the wall. "The time for playing games is past," he announced.

"You're making a big mistake," Ben managed to get out. "What you're doing to me could ruin you."

Manny coughed up another of those guttural laughs that originated in some remote corner of his ulcer-prone stomach. His mouth close to Bassett's ear, he told him, "Hasn't anybody given you the news? This is Custer's last stand. I've been following you, I've been following the Zavaskaya lady, for weeks. You've been passing stuff to her." He cranked up the hammerlock a notch. "I want it."

Ben cried out in agony. "Call . . . Inkermann."

Manny pressed Ben's face into the wall and tightened the hammerlock another increment. Tears streamed down Ben's face. A stifled scream escaped from his mouth. Then he mumbled hoarsely, "It's taped . . . leg."

"What?" Manny yelled.

"It's taped to my left leg," Bassett cried.

"Whatever," Manny muttered. Keeping a grip on the hammerlock, he reached down and tugged at Bassett's trousers and peeled away the adhesive and came up with a sealed envelope thick with folded slips of paper. Snorting triumphantly, he released his grip on Bassett's arm. Ben slumped to the concrete floor. Manny inserted a thick finger in a corner of the envelope and slit it open in one motion. He pulled out the slips of paper and started to read them. "This is going to put you in a federal prison for several decades," he yelled at the figure on the floor.

Ben slowly worked the arm that had been behind his back around to the front and massaged it with his other hand. "Before you make a complete fool of yourself, go get Inkermann."

"What's Inkermann got to do with this?"

"For God's sake, call him. I'm part of an operation. He can confirm it. You risk ruining everything."

Manny gazed in disgust at the man crumpled on the concrete floor. He had been copying out BIGOT listed messages from Sensitive Compartmented Information cables and passing them on to the Russians. Yet lying there on the floor, rubbing his wrist and arm, Bassett didn't look like a man who had been caught in the act. Could he be telling the truth when he claimed to be an operation?

Manny yanked a wall telephone off its hook and, stabbing angrily at the numbers, dialed Inkermann's private extension. Inkermann came on the line. "Yeah?"

"It's me," Manny yelled into the phone.

"So it's you. So why are you yelling?"

"So you can hear me over the incinerator. How about you coming on down here."

"Now?"

"Now."

"Why?"

"I got an asshole here, claims you can vouch for him."

Manny imagined he could hear Inkermann thinking. Then the line went dead.

Four minutes later the door almost flew off its hinges as Inkermann burst into the incinerator room. "This better be—" he started to say. His mouth clamped closed as he took in Bassett on the floor, sitting now with his back to the wall, his clothes disheveled, his raincoat hanging off one arm.

Manny waved an envelope in Inkermann's face. "This was taped to his leg. He's been copying out BIGOT-listed messages and passing them to our friends at the Komitet Gosudarstvennoi Bezopasnosti," Manny yelled over the furnace. "He's a goddamn Soviet agent. Now he's saying you can vouch for him."

Inkermann's stubby fingers stabbed at the strands of hair plastered over his bald spot. "He's Army Intelligence," he told the security chief. "I was under orders to give him a sealed attaché case that was brought in in a sealed diplomatic pouch."

"Are you running him?"

Inkermann shrugged. "He's free-lancing. I was told he could do no wrong. In our line of work that means only one thing."

Manny looked from Inkermann to Bassett, and back to Inkermann. He shook his head in confusion. "You're telling me that he's an operation?"

"I'm telling you to give him back the goddamn envelope and mind your own goddamn business. Go back to looking for open safes. Put your nose into the wrong place, somebody's going to hack it off."

Bassett struggled to his feet and began dusting off his clothing. He stepped forward, a length of adhesive trailing from a trouser leg, and held out a hand for the envelope. Manny stared at him in disbelief. Inkermann snickered. "He can do no wrong," he shouted, "but you can. Give it to him or I'll hang your balls up to dry on a clothesline." He hiked his shoulders as if he were ready—even eager—for combat.

Manny hated to back down; hated the idea that someone was giving secrets to the Russians in *his* embassy, even if it was part of an operation; hated the impulse to be rational when what he would have liked to do was pound Inkermann's smug smile against the concrete wall. The two dozen or so times in his life he had resorted to violence he had experienced a surge of relief. Now, feeling sick to his stomach, he muttered "Whatever," and dropped the envelope into Bassett's outstretched hand as reluctantly as anything he had done in his professional career.

24

Manny's last bona fide binge had begun in a roadhouse near Langley, Virginia, two hours after his contract with the Central Intelligence Agency had been terminated, putting an end to his sixteen years with the Company. He had come to his senses three days later in a holding cell in a Norfolk, Virginia, jail. The charges against him (drunk and disorderly in a public place, lewd behavior in a public place, resisting arrest), filed by the arresting officer, one P. Duckworth, who had picked him out of the gutter behind an all-night bar in Virginia Beach, had included excerpts from Manny's drunken ravings. ". . . did menace the life of one Charles Inkman, whereabouts unknown, who subject claimed was responsible for his being unjustly fired from an unnamed company, in that he threatened to inject said Charles Inkman with monkey-gland extract, which contains adrenaline-like chemicals that cause blood pressure to shoot up and result in a brain hemorrhage and death, or alternately, force said Charles Inkman to drink a quantity of ethyl alcohol the temperature of which had been lowered to 50° below freezing, which results in the victim's insides freezing and death. The subject repeatedly boasted that using either of these methods, only the most experienced medical examiner would turn up evidence of foul play." Several of Manny's Company friends had gotten wind of the arrest. Flashing CIA credentials and mumbling about national security, they had convinced a local magistrate that Manny should be released in their recognizance.

Now, holed up in his Moscow apartment, Manny decided the time had come to purify his sinking spirits with a new binge. Kicking off his shoes, he lined up three bottles of cheap scotch on the folding bridge table next to the sofa. "Well, well, what have we here?" he said under his breath. Carefully filling a glass, he held it up to toast an imaginary drinking partner. "Here's mud or whatever in your eye," he grumbled, and flinging back his head, he drained the glass. Wiping his lips with the back of his hand, he refilled the glass and raised it in a new toast. "Here's to the miraculous power of alcohol to drown affronts, slights, insults to your intelligence, indignities, humiliations, assaults on your honor, whatever," he announced, and belching, he drained the second glass. "Ahhhh, this is getting serious," he told himself. Forming the fingers of his right hand into a pistol, he squinted along the barrel at one of the three bottles of scotch and pulled an imaginary trigger. "Bang, bang, you're anesthetized," he mumbled. He filled the glass again with a shaky hand and held it aloft. Scotch dripped onto his trousers. "Ahhhh! Don't want to waste any of this precious soon-to-be-bodily fluid, do I? Here's to monkey-gland extract and ethyl alcohol and whatever." He drank off the contents of the glass, then breathed deeply through his nostrils for several minutes. The world around him was beginning to blur. He felt the sofa move under him and began swaying from side to side to match the motion. He was on a boat, he decided, dragging anchor, pleasantly adrift in an alcoholic haze. Somehow he found himself raising another filled glass in toast. The scotch in it slopped from side to side. Some of it spilled on the floor, but he didn't care anymore. "Here's to the last of the cunts," he declared, "yours truly, Immanuel Custer, obsessed by the banality of evil, or whatever." He had difficulty closing the gap between the glass and his mouth. Wrapping both of his large hands around the glass, he managed the feat and drained off another glass of scotch without rocks.

The binge, he sensed, had gotten off to a reasonable start.

HE DRIFTED TO THE SURFACE, arriving in the pitch darkness of a Moscow night. There was a jackhammer working, which considering the hour surprised him until he figured out it was hammering away in his temple. Stumbling into the bathroom, he groped for a light switch, squinted in pain when the bulb came on. He found a jar of aspirins and spilled several into a wet palm and swallowed them. He found a clock and stared at it until it came into focus, trying to figure out why it did not say what day it was. He got his first clue of how long the binge had lasted when he spotted himself in the medicine chest mirror.

His gray face had a two-day growth of gray beard on it.

Peeling off his clothing, he maneuvered himself under the shower head and turned on the faucet. At first nothing happened. Then the plumbing screamed. Then rusty ice water trickled out. The trickle grew into a jet and he let it play over his hair and face and body.

It was under the shower that the word came back to him. He heard it inside his head. Iron. Iron whatever. Iron weed. Of course! Ironweed! That was what had been written on the slips of paper he had pulled from the envelope taped to Bassett's leg.

Wrapped in a terry cloth bathrobe, Manny set a pot of coffee to brewing on the stove while he shaved. Settling onto a high kitchen stool, he lined up five cups and filled each one with scalding coffee. He started blowing on the first one to bring the temperature down to where it was drinkable. Words drifted into his consciousness. Iron. Weed. Ironweed. A snatch of text from the slips of paper came to him. "Ironweed dead drop message reports that

Andropov's health seriously deteriorating, maneuvering for succession already begun." Which meant Ironweed was the code name of a person rather than an operation. If Ironweed knew that the health of Andropov, then the Secretary General of the Communist Party, was deteriorating, it meant he was important enough to have access to this kind of information. It might even mean he was one of those involved in the maneuvering. But assuming that the Company had a sleeper high in the Soviet superstructure, why was our side slipping his messages to the Soviet side? The Cold War and its attendant intelligence operations were winding down, so the world thought, so the newspapers said, but the American side was obviously still playing by the old rules. Another snatch of message came to him. "Ksenia," Manny remembered it saying, "must be added to the doomsday list." Who was Ksenia, and what was a doomsday list?

By the time he had finished the fifth cup of coffee, he had made up his mind. Better to go out with a bang than a whimper, he thought. Pulling on some clean clothing, he grabbed his car keys and headed for the parking lot.

IF THE TWO MARINES ON DUTY were surprised to see the security officer turn up at the embassy at half past three in the morning, the circles under his eyes as dark as bruises, his scowling face full of nicks where he had cut himself shaving, they masked it behind boyishly crisp nods. Manny made his way to his cubbyhole of an office. He had trouble opening his safe, had to try half a dozen variations of the combination before one worked. Pushing aside embassy security records and several new pairs of sweat socks, he retrieved a small wooden file box and began flipping through the cards until he found the one he wanted. Slipping it into his jacket pocket, he made his way to the ninth floor, where he found the marine on duty sitting alertly behind the table. "Your friends at the main entrance must have phoned up that I was in the building," Manny commented.

"What makes you say that, sir?" the marine asked with a straight face.

"Seeing you awake at this ungodly hour is what makes me say that. Whatever." Manny scratched his name in the log book and, under reason for visit to the embassy's green-badge area, wrote: "Surprise security inspection of restricted spaces." Then he walked up one flight to the tenth floor and made his way down the hall, past the defense attaché's offices, past the deputy chief of mission's office, to a door with only a number on it. To the right of the door was a small box and a blinking red light. Manny pulled the file card from his pocket, noted the door code and punched it into the box. The red dial stopped blinking. He turned the knob and pushed open the door to the CIA station.

Flicking on a desk lamp, Manny glanced around. He noticed a collection of lipsticks on Miss Macy's desk next to an unsigned interoffice memo on which was typed, "Your place or mine?" Snickering, Manny made his way to the door of the ribbon room, checked his file card again, then punched a number into the electronic door lock. The door to the ribbon room clicked open. Just inside the door Manny found a light switch. Two lamps, one on the small desk, one on a box of ribbons, came on. He walked over and crouched in front of the safe. He tried twirling the combination lock, but it spun freely. He noted the combination written on his file card, and rotated the dial past zero to thirty-three, then back past thirty-three to seven, then to eleven. He felt the dial catch. He pushed on the handle. The door swung open. Reaching up, Manny angled the desk lamp so that it illuminated the interior of the safe. Turning back, he memorized the position of a thin notebook on a shelf in the safe, then took it out. Settling down at the desk that Bassett worked at, he adjusted the lamp and opened the book.

On the inside cover someone had written, in ink: "In the event this book falls into the hands of anyone other than Benedict Bassett, it should be sealed, labeled 'top secret—eyes only' and expedited by special diplomatic pouch addressed to 'Intelligence Support Activity, Pentagon, Washington, D.C., attn: Marlowe.' "

Manny looked up. He had never heard of anything called an Intelligence Support Activity, but that of course did not mean much. He pulled a sheet of white bond typing paper folded into quarters from his jacket pocket and copied off the reference to an Intelligence Support Activity and Marlowe. Then he went back to the thin book and began working his way through its pages.

The book seemed to be divided into two parts. The first was labeled, in the same handwriting as the note on the inside cover, "Silverweed." The second part was labeled, "Ironweed." The Silverweed section was much thinner than the Ironweed section. Hunched over the desk, Manny read through the pages of the notebook, pausing from time to time to scribble notes to himself on his sheet of bond paper. There appeared to be extracts from eight messages concerning Silverweed. The gist of them was that Silverweed was planning to visit Moscow in 1967, and proposed recruiting someone he knew from his university days who held a grudge against the Party because of something that had happened to a close childhood friend who was a Kalmyk. A second meeting between Silverweed and Ironweed took place in Prague in the fall of 1969, a third in Brussels at an unspecified date. There was a fourth meeting, again the date unspecified, at a KGB sanatorium on the Black Sea.

Turning to the Ironweed section of the notebook, Manny skimmed the material on dead drops and addresses in Europe where messages could be sent activating the dead drops. Another of the messages caught Manny's eye. Ironweed was asking if his handlers could get his wife and a child out of Russia in case he was in danger of being caught. Two words leapt out of the notebook. Ironweed referred to his "doomsday list." Manny looked up, his face in the shadows, his eyes wide open in discovery. He was remembering what he had seen on one of the slips of paper in the envelope he had found taped to Bassett's leg. "Ksenia," it had said, "must be added to

the doomsday list." Manny licked the ball of his thumb
and rifled through the pages until he found what he was
looking for. It was an entry dated March 1973. "Ironweed
dead drop message insists Ksenia must be added to the
doomsday list."

Manny picked up reading where he had left off and
continued scribbling on his sheet of bond paper. He recorded the story about Ironweed repairing a tractor motor, caught the reference that indicated Silverweed was
female, made a note of Ironweed's visit to West Germany
in 1975, plunged on through the pages, reading and rereading the handwritten entries and extracting the pertinent details—places, dates, names. When he reached the
last entry in the thin book, he jotted on his paper, "Messages break off in 1985" and wrote the word: "Why?"

Back in his cubbyhole of an office, Manny locked the
door on the inside and flung his jacket over the back of a
chair and settled down at his own desk to read over the
notes he had made. After a while he pulled another sheet
of paper from a drawer and began to write:

"Item: Bassett's assignment as a housekeeper for the
Seven Dwarfs was a cover. On the surface he seems to
have been turned into a penetration agent by the KGB.
But he is an operation. He isn't delivering ciphers or deciphered messages to his KGB handlers; he is simply copying off items from a thin notebook in his safe on scraps of
paper and passing them to the Russians *as if they were
messages*.

Item: Bassett is slipping information to the Russians
that would tip them to the fact that the Americans were
running a high-level agent in place recruited in 1967.
Contact with the agent was broken off in 1985. The messages Bassett slipped to the Russians covering the years
between 1967 and 1985 were seeded with references to
places and people, almost as if . . ."

Manny looked up. Almost, he thought, as if the Americans were trying to narrow the list for the KGB; almost as
if they wanted the KGB to identify and punish the traitor.
The key to identifying the agent in place, Manny's in-

stincts told him, was the fact that the operation had broken off in 1985. "Why?" he asked out loud. Then he bent his head and spelled out the possible answers.

"Item: Ironweed died. Unlikely. If dead, why bother betraying him now?

"Item: Ironweed chickened out. Unlikely. Knowing my colleagues at the Company, they would threaten to betray him and those on his doomsday list to the Russians unless he kept nose to grindstone.

"Item: Ironweed became too important to run like an ordinary agent."

Completely baffled, Manny stared out over the lamp into the darkness. He remembered another of the scraps of paper he had seen in Bassett's envelope. Turning to the notes he had scribbled on the folded sheet of bond paper, he studied the original entry he had copied out of the thin book. "Ironweed dead drop message reports that Andropov's health seriously deteriorating, maneuvering for succession already begun." He stared at the words, shook his head, shrugged a heavy shoulder, tapped the point of his pen on the paper. How would Ironweed know the state of Andropov's health unless he, Ironweed, was a ranking member of the Party? Could Ironweed himself have been one of those maneuvering for the succession? Manny's thoughts again came full circle. If Ironweed was important enough to know Andropov, to maneuver for the succession, why was he being betrayed? If it served American interests to betray him, why betray him now? And why, in order to betray Ironweed, did Bassett have to copy handwritten messages out of the thin notebook that had been smuggled into the country in a sealed diplomatic pouch? Why didn't he copy the original messages?

Were there original messages to copy? Did Ironweed really exist? Or was he a figment of someone's Machiavellian imagination?

The answers to the riddle would fall into place, Manny suspected, if he could identify Ironweed. His eye fell on the reference to an "Intelligence Support Activity, Pentagon, Washington, D.C., attn: Marlowe." He would get an

enciphered message off to an old friend of his who
worked for the Pentagon's Defense Intelligence Agency, a
former CIA officer who, like him, had been kicked out of
the Company when his ideas clashed with the conventional wisdom of the in-house pessimists. Manny would
ask him if he had ever heard of an Intelligence Support
Activity, or someone named Marlowe. While he was waiting for the reply, he would pore over the State Department biographies of Soviet leaders on his shelf. He would
see if he could come up with someone who had been to
Prague in 1967, to Brussels some time in his life, to West
Germany in 1975, to Canada in 1983, to England in 1984,
to Paris in 1985, where (according to the last messages in
the thin notebook) he discreetly laid flowers on the grave
of someone. In addition, Ironweed would have a wife and
a child, and someone named Ksenia to whom he felt close
enough that he asked the CIA to add her name to his
"doomsday list," his background would have equipped
him to repair the motor of a tractor and he was probably
promoted to an important Party post in 1985.

Doodling on his sheet of typing paper, Manny wrote:
"Item: Silverweed, working for the CIA, recruits Iron-
weed. Bassett, working for who? betrays Ironweed.
Where is the thread of logic? Whatever."

FILLIPOV, WHO HAD BURIED himself in the KGB's dusty
archives for three straight days, came prancing into
Glebova's windowless office with the news. Glebova, with
Fillipov trailing in her wake, swooped through the halls,
her stiletto heels dispatching staccato echoes from its
walls, to the old general, who listened to what she had to
say, then asked her to repeat it twice before picking up
the telephone to summon Viktor.

"My analysts have narrowed the list of twenty-three
Ironweeds down to twelve," the general told Viktor when
he arrived, out of breath from having taken the stairs two
at a time (both elevators were out of order).

"Fillipov," Glebova announced, sucking air through her
nostrils after each noun to underscore the importance of

what she was saying, "has been prying Ksenias out of the woodwork."

"I found one grandmother, one mother, three sisters, two daughters, one granddaughter, one ex-wife and three mistresses with the name Ksenia," Fillipov triumphantly explained.

The general handed the typewritten list of twelve possible Ironweeds to Viktor. Once again he appeared to suspend breathing as he read it. Looking up, he reached into his pocket and pulled out the latest envelope thick with folded slips of paper. "We are approaching the dénouement," he declared huskily. "There are three messages in this batch that are particularly relevant. Ironweed was in Canada in 1983 and England in 1984. He met secretly with Silverweed on both occasions. In 1985, just before contact with him was broken off, he was in Paris. His CIA handlers were appalled to discover that he had visited a grave in Paris. His French hosts were left with the impression that someone he had known from his days at university had died in a Paris hospital. Ironweed stopped to buy a bouquet of chrysanthemums before wandering, alone, into Père Lachaise cemetery."

For a moment no one spoke. Then Glebova asked in a breathless voice, "What month was that?"

Viktor went through the slips in the envelope, unfolding each until he found the one he was looking for. "It was in October of 1985," he replied.

Fillipov drew himself up so that he was standing at attention, his fists pressed against his sides, his chin jutting. "The woman who was Dubcek's speech writer—Ilkiv —died of a burst appendix in a Paris hospital in October of 1985."

Glebova, looking like a ship of state, navigated across the carpet and docked at the general's enormous desk. "There is a question that must be asked," she declared.

The general nodded.

"Four of the names on our short list are in the stratosphere of our superstructure. Should our list narrow to one of these four . . ." Glebova was uncertain how to put her question. "What I mean is, if Ironweed turns out to be someone of extreme importance, can my colleague and I count on your protection?"

Viktor and the old general exchanged looks. The general heaved himself to his feet and contemplated Glebova across the desk. Because she was the taller of the two, his head was angled up. "In the eighteen years you have worked for me, have you ever known me to throw someone to the wolves?"

Glebova shook her head. "Never. But—"

"There is no *but*. You and your colleague will follow where the trail leads. We will deal with the consequences."

Glebova turned toward the door. "You will have to excuse us," she said gravely. "We have work to do." Followed by Fillipov, she plunged from the old general's corner office, headed for the dusty archives—and the solution to the Ironweed puzzle.

25

Aïda would have been the first to admit that Vadim, her ex-husband and guardian angel, had his faults, but forgetting birthdays had never been one of them. For Aïda's forty-second, he came up with an apartment where she could spend two nights running with her American lover. Located on the sixth floor of a dilapidated building behind the Puppet Theater on the peripheral boulevard, it belonged to a retired Jewish doctor who had gone off to take a mud bath cure at a spa on the Black Sea. Ben arrived at the apartment with French *bleu de Auvergne* and Swedish crackers and fresh fruit and two bottles of a relatively disappointing year of an excellent French Bordeaux named Montlabert, all bought at the diplomatic gastronome. The apartment had four small, dingy rooms and a kitchen with patches of linoleum peeling from the floor and a windowless bathroom with a toilet that never stopped running, but every inch of every wall, and both sides of every door, were covered with Russian paintings from the twenties and thirties. The Jewish doctor and his late wife had started the collection, Aïda explained, to

celebrate the death of Stalin in 1953. The rooms were
filled with canvases painted by Falk before his Paris period, still-lifes by Weissman, landscapes by Konchelevsky,
various paintings by Altmann and Pasternak père, and a
portrait of Lili Brik tossed off by Mayakovski between
extravagant poems glorifying the Bolshevik revolution.
"You are looking at what Russian art could have become,"
Aïda said with a sad smile, "if it had not been strangled by
Socialist realism. It is a wonderful place to make love,
don't you think?"

Ben eagerly agreed. They nibbled at the food and
sipped the wine and made love, and prowled naked
through the rooms gazing at the paintings, and made love
again. Both seemed to put behind them the tensions of
the past few weeks. Before sinking into a deep, dreamless
sleep, Aïda whispered, "It has not been this good between
us since the train to Leningrad."

Entangled in each other's arms in the early hours of the
morning, they were roused by the sound of trucks from
the collectives around Moscow hauling food to market.
Aïda tried to kiss Ben, but he turned his head away. "So:
Do the trucks remind you there is a real world outside our
private world?"

Ben propped himself up in the bed. Something was
obviously bothering him. "You told me I was in love with
you before I knew it myself," he reminded her. "Whatever happens to us from here on, I want you to know that
it is true. I do love you. God knows I didn't plan to fall in
love. God knows I didn't think I could fall in love." The
words spilled out with the same intensity with which Ben,
a lifetime back, had told Aïda, "I hope to Christ we do not
meet again!" "I bitterly regret getting you into this
mess—"

Startled by the burst of emotion, Aïda interrupted.
"Dear heart, it was not your—"

But Ben rushed on. "I am going to get Saava that operation," he vowed.

Aïda, annoyed with him for breaking the spell, reacted
angrily. "How?" she challenged.

"Espionage is a delicate game," Ben said. "Relationships depend on who has more to gain or lose at any given moment. Up to now I had more to lose by not doing what they wanted—I could lose you and you could lose the boy, and they knew it and used it. But that has all changed. We have reached a point where Viktor, or whatever his name really is, has more to lose than I do."

Aïda was regarding Ben strangely. "How do you know such things?"

"I figured it out."

"What does Viktor have to lose?"

Ben was thinking out loud now. "The information I stole from the embassy is valuable to him only so long as the Americans don't know the Russians have it. This gives me a card to play."

"I do not follow what you are saying."

"It doesn't matter whether you understand." Springing from the bed, Ben crossed the room and pulled an envelope out of the pocket of his sports jacket. "This is the last envelope you will have to give them," he announced as he dropped it in her hand.

"They will not believe there is no more information," she said worriedly. "They will cut Saava's dosage again."

"They *will* believe it when I tell them. When you give them the envelope, organize another meeting for me in the safe house. Thursday. At seven in the evening."

"So: If I permitted myself to believe you have a card to play, it would only raise my hopes, and raised hopes can only end in disappointment." The bittersweet half-smile appeared on Aïda's soft lips. "The truth is that I have more or less grown accustomed to living without hope. I take nothing for granted—not you in my bed, not Saava's medicine in my hand, not even the sun rising in the morning. I must feel its heat on my skin before I permit myself to believe it is there."

"This time you will not be disappointed," Ben whispered. He pulled her into his arms. "I love you," he said, discovering it, savoring it, believing it.

· · ·

THEY WERE DRINKING INSTANT coffee in the kitchen later that morning when they heard the knock at the front door. "Who knows we are here?" Ben asked quickly.

"Only Vadim." Aïda got up and called through the door, "Yes?"

"Zinaïda Ivanovna?"

Aïda recognized the voice of Vadim's taxi driver, Dmitri. She pulled open the door.

Dmitri, a round man who looked as if he might have been a monk at some point in his life, smiled nervously. "It's about your father," he said mournfully. "Vadim said for me to bring you straight off to the hospital."

Ben came up behind her. "I will go with you."

Aïda pulled a shawl over her shoulders. "It is better if we are not seen together," she said. She took his hand and lifted the back of it to her lips and kissed it, letting her tongue play quickly over his knuckles. Then she turned away and followed Dmitri.

At the clinic, Aïda found her father struggling feebly in his large metal bed to kick the tattered quilt off his legs. His eyes had almost disappeared into his gaunt face in the last few days. He looked at Aïda without recognizing her. "Come on, come on, damn it," he called, weakly waving his crushed, nailless fingers. Aïda massaged his calves and this seemed to calm him. His head sank back into the pillow. His eyes closed. He breathed heavily through caked lips.

An old woman wearing a pink bathrobe hobbled past the open door on two canes. She stopped to peer into the room. "How did he get like this?" she demanded in disgust.

"Old age," Aïda replied.

"That's no excuse," the old woman shot back and turning, hobbled on down the corridor.

Aïda's father tossed in the bed, babbling under his breath. "Books," he repeated again and again. "Books." When his eyes opened, she stroked his forehead. "Don't be frightened, Father."

"Not frightened," he said very clearly. Then: "Know who enemy is. Fighting. Not frightened."

These turned out to be his last distinguishable words. Kicking weakly at the quilt, playing with his penis, breathing with labored irregularity through his mouth, he sank into a shallow coma. The woman doctor, a stump of a cigarette glued to her lower lip, came into the room. She took his pulse, then gripped his hand. "Hello, Ivan, do you hear me?" she called. "If you hear me, squeeze my fingers."

When Aïda's father did not respond, the doctor examined his mutilated fingers, shook her head in pity and let his hand drop back onto the quilt. "It is almost the end," she informed Aïda. She touched her on the shoulder, one woman comforting another. "Holler if you need help," she said as she left.

Aïda reached for her father's hand. "Father, it's me, Zinaïda," she said quietly.

The old man's eyes suddenly flicked wide open. Aïda forced herself to smile into them until her father's lids drifted closed over his eyes. Some minutes later she detected a distinct rattle in the back of his throat each time he breathed. With infinite gradualness, his breathing became shallower. Finally it was reduced to tiny gasps. The old man's features relaxed. His mouth, open until then, sagged closed, his eyes slowly opened and stared at the ceiling, unseeing. Then, magically, he just stopped breathing. After fifteen seconds he took another weak gasp. Then a third. Then he did not breathe again.

"You did it," Aïda said softly. Still clinging to his hand, she reached up and pressed the lids closed over his eyes and kissed his forehead, and then sat back to memorize the dying.

AÏDA'S FATHER HAD BEEN fitted into a shallow open pine coffin that rested, now, on two chairs in a makeshift holding room on the first floor of the clinic. The window shades had been drawn. A scratchy rendition of some unidentifiable funeral music was being piped over a single

speaker set on a chair in a corner. The old man in the
coffin had been dressed in his uniform tunic and trousers;
his medals had been laid in rows on a small crimson cushion placed on his chest. There had been a fixed forfeit for
the funeral that included the casket and the cushion and
the hearse and the taped music and the wreath and, finally, burial in a plot set aside for veterans of the Great
Patriotic War. Candles had been extra and Aïda had decided to do without them. At the last minute Vadim had
turned up with two dozen church wafers. The flickering
yellowish light from the candles made the old man's skin
look waxlike. Aïda started to blow out the candles, but
Vadim, arguing that candles were traditional, pulled her
back to her chair.

Sitting next to Aïda on one of the folding chairs set up
in rows, Saava quietly sobbed his heart out. Vadim leaned
toward Aïda. "You might try crying too. Think of it as
therapeutic."

Aïda only fingered Akhmatova's agate ring and stared at
the coffin.

Aïda and Saava and Vadim piled into Vadim's taxi to
follow the hearse to the cemetery. The lid was nailed onto
the coffin, and the coffin lowered on worn ropes into a
freshly dug hole in the ground. Aïda, and then Saava,
picked up a handful of dirt and dropped it onto the coffin.
Vadim distributed generous tips to the gravediggers, and
signaled with a forefinger for his taxi to approach. Aïda
passed up the offer of a ride home in the taxi, preferring
instead to walk back to town with Saava.

They walked for a long while on a sidewalk that ran
parallel to a wide, pitted boulevard. Saava eventually
broke the silence. "It must have been the Cossacks who
finally got Granddad."

Aïda nodded.

"He told me once that we were the Cossacks," Saava
said. "What did he mean?"

A militia truck, painted dirty yellow with a blue stripe,
the blue light on top blinking frantically, sped past.

"So: I think it was his way of saying that the enemy is inside us."

"I don't get it—how can an enemy be inside someone?"

"Like many of his generation, your grandfather took the habit of having an enemy early in his life. It answered a deep need, I suppose. When he was confronted with the possibility that there were no more enemies, he became the enemy."

"How is it possible to become your own enemy?"

"It is difficult to explain to someone who has not lived through what your grandfather lived through."

"Every time I ask you something, you say it is difficult to explain."

"So: If it were not difficult to explain, you would not be asking."

"That is true." Saava slipped his hand into Aïda's. "When I think of Grandfather, I picture him sitting by the window through the night. Did he ever not sit by the window through the night?"

"Long ago," she said, "before he became afraid, he did not sit by the window through the night." And she added very softly, "Where he is now he surely does not have to sit by the window through the night."

GLEBOVA TURNED ASHEN WHEN N. Fillipov showed her the deciphered cable from Prague. She collapsed into the nearest chair to reread it. "This is the final piece of the puzzle," she whispered. "Now there can be no doubt."

Fillipov's bushy eyebrows twitched nervously. "Who in his wildest flights of imagination would have suspected such a dénouement," he muttered.

Glebova brought a hand to her breast. "My heart is beating so rapidly it is going to burst." She looked at Fillipov, who was gazing out a window, absorbed in his thoughts, then reached for the telephone and dialed an in-house number. "I must speak with the general," she insisted shrilly. "No, no. At once. I will take the responsibility. He will want you to break in on the conference."

Glebova kept the phone pressed to her ear. There was a long pause. Then she cupped a hand around the mouthpiece, as if the precaution would render the conversation more secure, and breathed into it, "General, Glebova here. I am calling to tell you that the list has been narrowed. To one."

Both Viktor and the general were standing when Glebova, followed closely by Fillipov, arrived at the general's office. The fingers of the general's bad hand contracted, beckoning Glebova. She stepped forward almost reluctantly and held out a typewritten sheet of paper. The general and Viktor avoided each other's eye. The general reached out with his good hand and accepted the paper. Viktor read it over the general's shoulder.

Twelve names had been typed on it. Eleven of them had been crossed out.

Viktor was the first to regain his composure. "Are you one hundred percent sure?"

Fillipov poked at an imaginary spot of dirt under a fingernail. "One can never be one hundred percent sure. But we are ninety-nine point nine percent sure. Remember how Ironweed repaired that tractor? The name on your list was born in the village of Privol'noye in the Stavropol *krai*. He was the son of peasants driven onto a collective farm during Stalin's forced collectivization of agriculture in the early 1930s. Thus he would have had a grudge against Soviet power, and a motive to betray it. In 1943, at the age of twelve, he worked as a combine operator at a tractor station. His best friend at the time was a Kalmyk who was subsequently deported to Siberia as part of a program to punish the Kalmyks because some of them collaborated with the German invaders. The man whose name is not crossed out has a wife and a child. In 1973, when Ironweed added the name Ksenia to his doomsday list, his daughter had a daughter named Ksenia." Shrugging delicately, Fillipov gestured with his chin toward the list in the general's hand. "He was a protégé of Andropov and was regularly invited to confer with him at the KGB spa on the Black Sea. Ironweed met

Silverweed in Canada in 1983 and in England in 1984."
Again Fillipov gestured toward the list. "He was in Canada in 1983 and in England in 1984. The CIA broke off contact with Ironweed in 1985, the year he"—Fillipov's forefinger, pointing at the single name on the paper not crossed out, trembled—"was promoted to his preeminent position."

Glebova's hand found its way to her breast again. "We have connected Silverweed to Ironweed," she solemnly announced, her moist eyes bulging, her breath coming in short gasps. "You recall the connection between Ironweed and the Dubcek speech writer named Martina Ilkiv? Ilkiv turned out to be her married name. Her maiden name was Dzur. There is a record of a Martina Dzur having attended the law faculty of Moscow State University when *he* was a student there. On her dossier there is even a credit for a course on economic logic taught by the famous Professor Usov." Like Fillipov, Glebova was pointing at the name on the paper in the general's hand; like Fillipov, her finger was trembling. "*He* attended the same class. We located two of her classmates who remembered that the young Czech Communist named Dzur had fallen in love with *him,* had for a time moved in with *him.* When the Ilkiv woman died, in Paris, in 1985 of a burst appendix, she was buried in Père Lachaise cemetery—three days before his CIA handlers spotted *him* wandering into the cemetery with a bouquet of chrysanthemums. One can even surmise that it was this blunder that pushed the CIA to break contact with him."

The general painstakingly folded the sheet of paper in half, and then in half again, and slipped it into his jacket pocket. His eyes clouded over as he slowly made his way to his desk and sat down behind it. "I want you to bring me your work sheets, your archives, your documents, your dossiers, your queries and the replies—everything associated with this case," he said huskily. "You are not to breathe a word of this to a living soul. Take some time off. Do not leave Moscow. Make sure my office knows where to reach you at all times."

The old general raised his chin and squinted at a painting depicting Lenin's arrival at the Finland Station. When he spoke again his voice seemed to echo through the room. "Know that you have done your country an extraordinary service."

Glebova glanced at Fillipov, then backed toward the door. Fillipov lingered, as if something more needed to be said. Thinking better of it, he followed her out of the office.

Viktor unbuttoned his jacket and settled heavily onto a chair next to the general's desk. The general pulled open a drawer and produced two small glasses and a bottle, and a covered tin. He undid the lid and pushed the tin across the desk toward Viktor, who leaned forward, selected a dried apricot and began eating it. The general filled the two small glasses and handed one to Viktor. "Cherry brandy. Georgian. Clear away the cobwebs." He nibbled at a dried apricot, brought his glass of brandy to his nose to smell it, then tilted back his head and drained off the brandy. Viktor followed suit. The alcohol seared their throats. Both men opened their mouths and exhaled deeply. The general began filling the two glasses again. "Where is my daughter these days?"

"She is filming a television series."

"You are a patient man, Viktor. I have always appreciated that trait in you. You have the quality essential in a good hunter—the ability to wait before going in for the kill. I admire that in a man."

He passed the filled glass back to Viktor and raised his in thoughtful toast. "Let us drink to *pamyat*, and going in for the kill."

Viktor repeated, "To *pamyat* and going in for the kill," and seared his throat a second time.

26

The pieces resisted falling into place for two days and three nights. Sometime after midnight on the third night, Manny ran out of scotch and rocks and stamina and despaired of finding an answer. He had come across too many Ksenias, too many people who had one wife and one daughter, too many who had been to the places Ironweed had been to at roughly the time Ironweed had been there, too many who had changed jobs in 1985, to do more than narrow the list of suspects. His head reeling with fatigue, he slumped back in his chair, his hands clasped behind his neck, to contemplate the slips of paper jutting from the pages of the State Department biographies of Soviet leaders heaped on his desk.

The sight stirred a memory. Manny's desk had been heaped with State Department biographies back in 1979 when he had prepared the written assessment of a new candidate member of the Politburo for his then boss, Charlie Inkermann. Slips of paper had jutted from the pages. Manny recalled that two of the slips had marked passages that seemed pertinent now.

Item: The subject of the 1979 written assessment had been born in the village of Privol'noye in the Stavropol *krai*, at the height of Stalin's ruthless program of collectivization in 1931. Sensing for the first time that he was onto something, Manny leaned forward and flipped through the pages of a State Department geography manual. He soon found what he was looking for. There had been Kalmyks living in a settlement thirty miles from Privol'noye; they had been deported en masse to Siberia in December 1943. Something else occurred to Manny. He reached for a State Department biography, moistened the ball of his thick thumb and skimmed through the pages until he found the reference. The subject had been raised on a collective farm, and sent to work on a tractor station at the age of twelve to replace the men who were off at war. He would have known how to repair a tractor motor. And he could easily have had a friend who was a Kalmyk!

Item: Manny's 1979 assessment for Inkermann (which had gotten him fired from the CIA when he refused to water it down) had called attention to an odd coincidence: The new candidate member of the Politburo had had a Czech intellectual for a mistress during three of the five years he attended the law faculty of Moscow State University. Manny's assessment had concluded that some of the radical ideas of the young woman, who later became a speech writer for Alexander Dubcek during the Prague Spring of 1968, would have had to rub off on the Soviet hick.

A Czech mistress who later became a speech writer for Alexander Dubcek during the Prague Spring! The pieces were falling into place. According to one of the messages Benedict Bassett had passed to the Russians, Silverweed was a woman. Could Dubcek's speech writer be Silverweed? Could she have recruited her classmate and lover from Moscow State University to work for the CIA?

Manny's eyes glazed over with elation. He had narrowed the list of suspects to one!

Meticulous to a fault, he went over the whole thing

again item by item. His prime suspect was the son of peasants who were forced onto a collective in the early 1930s, which meant he would have been raised in an atmosphere that was profoundly anti-Soviet. So much for motive. Ironweed had been to Prague in 1967, to Brussels some time in his life, to West Germany in 1975, to Canada in 1983, to England in 1984, to Paris in 1985. Ditto for the prime suspect. One wife, one child. Ksenia. Access to Andropov. The friend who was a Kalmyk. The ability to repair a tractor motor. His connection to Prague and Silverweed. A promotion of importance in 1985 that might have obliged the CIA to break off contact.

Peering through a haze of fatigue and incredulity, Manny realized he had come, unwillingly, grudgingly, to the only conclusion possible. The question was what to do about it.

PUSHING THROUGH THE CROWD of tourists and businessmen at the door, Manny waved a ten-dollar bill at the grinning Georgian with a pin on his lapel that read, "Maître d'Hôtel." "I reserved," Manny shouted over the balalaika music and the din. "Custer, Immanuel. From the American Embassy."

The maître d' checked a notebook, found Custer's name. "Table for two," he noted. "Follow me." Clutching the paper bag with the three bottles of Georgian wine (the restaurant did not have a liquor license, and encouraged clients to bring their own alcohol), Manny beckoned Bassett, and the two of them set off after the maître d' toward a table in the far corner of the private restaurant.

Depositing two of the wine bottles on the floor under his seat and the third on the table, Manny ordered up a small feast, and had the waiter uncork the first of the three bottles. He waved him away and filled the wineglasses himself. "To no hard feelings," he said, raising his glass.

"To no hard feelings," Ben agreed. They clicked glasses and drank their wine.

"I'm glad you accepted my invitation," Manny commented conversationally. "I treated you pretty roughly. I was off base. This is my way of saying *mea culpa, mea maxima culpa.*"

"You were only doing your job," Ben replied. "I appreciate the gesture."

"No grudges?" Manny asked.

"No grudges," Ben agreed.

Two musicians in Georgian folk costumes strummed their balalaikas and belted out a Georgian folk song. A young waiter wearing an impeccable tuxedo rested a tray on a stand next to the table, and began setting out the starters.

"It's a kind of Georgian smorgasbord," Manny noted. He pushed a dish toward Ben. "The things wrapped in grape leaves are very spicy. Try one."

Working their way through Georgian specialties, they finished off the first bottle of wine and started in on the second. Manny got Ben talking about his background—he had been born and raised in a railroad town in upstate New York called Hornell, and educated at Northwestern University outside Chicago. Well into the second bottle of wine, Manny introduced a more personal note into the conversation by telling him about the death, five years before, of his wife of twenty-five years. Halfway through the second bottle, Manny belched and refilled both glasses. Responding to a question, Ben told him briefly about his divorce, the subsequent custody battle that he lost and the son he had back in the States.

"Must have left you feeling pretty bitter about women," Manny noted.

Ben smiled in grim agreement.

Manny nodded sympathetically. Then, very casually, he remarked, "That lady poet of yours is quite a looker."

Ben glanced up. "Should we be having this conversation here?"

"Why do you think I took you to one of these new private restaurants? The folks tailing you can't afford to follow you inside and pay for a dinner. It's too expensive."

"What if the table was bugged?"

"I checked it out when I put the wine on the floor."

"You think of everything," Ben observed. The way he said it, it didn't sound like a compliment.

"I try to."

Ben took another sip of wine. He seemed to want to talk. "The lady poet is a looker, as you put it. My instructions were to get involved with a Russian woman. Nobody said I had to pick a dog."

"What's she like?"

Ben filled his own glass and drank some more. "She's the best that this godforsaken country has," he said with emotion. "She's all soul and guts and expects the worst and hopes for the best and keeps beating her head against a wall and coming back for more." He remembered something Aïda had told him in Leningrad. "She associates happiness with pain. She follows her heart until it breaks."

The waiter collected the empty serving dishes and returned with full ones. Some American tourists at a nearby table burst out laughing. The balalaika music soared. Manny loosened his belt a notch and spooned some mushrooms onto Ben's plate and then his own. "You don't need to tell me if you don't want to," he said over the noise. "I have a professional interest. I'm curious to know how they came at you. What did they do—threaten to send the lady poet away and break off the romance?"

Ben decided there would be no harm in answering now that the security officer was on his side. "She's got a kid," he said presently. "The kid's got leukemia. He needs Western drugs to stay alive. It wasn't only a matter of ending the romance. They threatened to cut off his supply of medicine unless I cooperated."

Manny whistled through his teeth. "Talk about operational bonuses! Any woman would have done. But what a stroke of luck to fall on someone with a sick kid." He eyed Ben. "What's going to happen to the kid when you leave?"

Ben leaned forward. "I thought about that," he confided eagerly. "Actually, I wouldn't mind having your opinion on something. I can tell you that the operation is

over. She's delivering my last envelope now. Which
means they'll soon find a pretext to transfer me back to
the States."

When Ben hesitated, Manny nodded encouragement.
"I spent back-to-back tours running operations like this
one out of Istanbul. If I can help you . . ."

"I asked her to set up a last meeting at the safe house."

"What for?"

Ben gulped down some more wine. The waiter
snatched away the empty bottle. Manny fetched the third
bottle from under the table and handed it to the waiter,
who opened it. Manny took the bottle back from the
waiter and filled Ben's glass. Ben ran his finger around the
rim for a while. Manny didn't push him. "I figure I have a
card to play," Ben said finally. "The KGB is convinced
that the Americans don't know I slipped them stuff. They
will want to keep it that way. I plan to offer Viktor—"

"Viktor?"

"That's the name my KGB contact goes by. I plan to
offer him a trade. My silence in return for an exit visa for
the kid and his mother." Ben explained about the American doctor and the bone marrow transplant. "What do
you think?"

Manny pushed away his plate. "Whatever."

"You don't like it?"

"It's not a matter of liking it or not. It won't work."

"Why not?"

"You've got to look at it from the KGB's point of view.
Once the kid and his mother are out of the country, your
friend Viktor will lose his hold on you. And you can't
outbluff Viktor by threatening to expose yourself as a spy.
He'll only threaten to cut off the kid's medicine if you
turn yourself in. It'll be a standoff. What do you do then?"

Ben toyed with his food. "You have a better idea?"

Cocking his head, Manny said carefully, "Maybe."

"What is it?"

"I'd need to know more about the operation. Like, for
instance, who's running you?"

Ben looked around to make sure nobody was within

earshot. "I was housekeeping for an Army Intelligence cipher unit in Washington. The CIA needed a fresh face and offered me a one-shot contract."

"What did they tell you about the purpose of the operation?"

"The guy who briefed me said the information I leaked to the Russians would discredit the opposition to *glasnost* and *perestroika*."

Manny angrily splashed some wine into his glass and downed it in one gulp. He snorted as he wiped his lips with the back of his hand. "You've been had," he announced.

Ben bridled. "What is that supposed to mean?"

"You sure you want to know?"

Ben wasn't sure. But he nodded anyhow.

Manny nodded back. "Okay," he said, and leaning over his plate, he told Ben that he had broken into his safe and read the thin notebook cover to cover. He told him about the tractor station and the one wife and one child and Ksenia and the Kalmyk and the access to Andropov and the connection to Dubcek's speech writer. He explained how the dates of the various trips abroad coincided. He told him about the promotion in 1985. "It fits like a glove. You leaked hints to your friend Viktor. Each hint narrowed the list until there was only one name left on it. You're not discrediting his opponents. You're discrediting Gorbachev himself. All the stuff you leaked to the Russkies pointed to him. You're supplying his enemies with phony evidence that the man who runs the country, the son of peasants who suffered under Stalin, hated the Soviet regime and worked for the CIA for years to undermine it. According to the phony evidence, when he became numero uno, the CIA, out of prudence, broke off contact with him, figuring he'd finish the job himself."

Ben's head was swimming. "It's not possible . . . you're making it all up to confuse me."

Manny shrugged his heavy shoulders. "Whatever."

Ben gazed at the table for a long time. He was thinking very hard. Manny nursed his drink. After a while Ben looked up. "Gorbachev's the one who's ending the Cold War. Why would the CIA want to kill him off?"

Manny snickered. "You're not being run by the CIA," he said flatly. "I spotted that notice on the inside cover of your notebook. If the book falls into the wrong hands it should be sealed, labeled 'top secret—eyes only' and expedited by special diplomatic pouch addressed to 'Intelligence Support Activity, Pentagon, Washington, D.C., attn: Marlowe.' "

"Marlowe is the guy who recruited me and briefed me. Marlowe is the guy who sent me the notebook."

"A big man in his early fifties who talks with a Texas accent, has thin, gray hair and uneven teeth that he hides by almost never smiling?" Manny massaged the length of his nose with the side of his wineglass. "Did you ever ask yourself what an Intelligence Support Activity was?"

"I assumed it was a mailbox for the CIA."

A scornful laugh rose to the surface from Manny's stomach. He pulled a folded message blank out of his jacket pocket and read it again before passing it across the table. "I cabled an old buddy of mine at DIA." When Ben looked puzzled, Manny said, "That's the Pentagon's Defense Intelligence Agency. Here's the answer I got back. The group in question is a Pentagon entity listed as a harmless Intelligence Support Activity. It came into existence during the Carter presidency to deal with the Iranian hostage crisis. When the crisis ended the Support Activity was disbanded, but like a lot of organizations that cease to function, it seemed to have remained on the books. According to my buddy, there were rumors circulating in the late eighties that the Support Activity had been resurrected by some middle-ranking Pentagon officers. If I had to guess, I'd say the thing that attracted them to this dormant Support Activity was that it was not associated with either the Central Intelligence Agency or the Defense Intelligence Agency, which meant it was outside congressional oversight parameters. The fact that it was also outside White House oversight parameters, inasmuch as it didn't need a presidential 'Finding' to set its wheels in motion, would have made it even more appealing. The secret to who controls any organization is its funding. The Intelligence Support Activity's budget, so my friend says, is buried in the Joint Chiefs' contingency fund under the heading 'Transportation, miscellaneous.' The person in nominal charge is a marine colonel attached to the long-term planning staff of the Joint Chiefs. The guy who runs the day-to-day ops goes by the name of Marlowe, but his real name is Asher Spink. Spink is a big man in his fifties, with thin, gray hair and uneven teeth that he hides by almost never smiling. He talks with a Texas drawl."

Visibly shaken, Ben handed back the cable. "Do you know this Spink?"

"We rubbed shoulders during one of my tours in Istanbul. He was a zealot, he loved the Cold War, he hated the Russians, he was obsessed with the idea that we could destroy Communism by outspending the Russians in the arms race; the pressure to keep up would run the Communist economies into the ground. In his distorted world view, everything that increased tensions, and therefore increased arms budgets, was devoutly to be wished. Spink moved on from Turkey to head the Prague station from the late sixties to the mid-seventies, where he may or may not have run an agent code named Silverweed. He must have come up with one harebrained scheme too many, because the CIA quietly pensioned him off. Last I heard of him he was making per diem consulting for some crazies in the bowels of the Pentagon. Now this Intelligence Support Activity thing turns up. Whatever."

The Americans at the other table were tucking dollars under a saucer and heading noisily for the door. The balalaika player was taking a break, smoking a Marlboro in a corner. The waiter came over to clear away the dinner dishes, and returned a few minutes later with the pastry tray and two cups of a thick liquid he described as coffee. When they were alone again Ben said, "What are you telling me?"

"I'm telling you you're a first-class sap. You're the field

hand for an illegal operation cooked up by a frustrated zealot named Spink and run out of the basement of the Pentagon by a shadowy Support Activity that doesn't have to account to anybody—not Congress, not the president —except the military." Manny was spitting out words now. "God knows how high in the chain of command accountability goes. Spink could be whispering in the ear of the Chairman of the Joint Chiefs. But he could just as well be whispering in the ear of some manic chicken colonel on the long-range planning staff, a Cold War junkie who's convinced it will damage American national interests, not to mention military careers and military-industrial profits, if Gorbachev is allowed to create the conditions for winding down the East-West confrontation."

Ben, suddenly very sober, helped himself to the last of the wine and drank it off. Manny signaled for the bill, and handed it back to the waiter without looking at it, along with his American Express card. The two men waited silently for the waiter to return. Manny scrawled his name on the receipt.

"Thanks for the dinner," Ben said ironically.

"My pleasure," Manny answered evenly.

Walking back toward the diplomatic compound across from the Hotel Ukraine, Manny muttered matter-of-factly, "You're being followed." When Ben looked around in puzzlement, Manny said, "Don't get nervous. You're always followed. That's one of the things that first made me wonder about you. In case you're curious, it's the young couple ahead of us. I recognize the blonde. She was tailing you that time we walked down Gorki together."

Concentrating on their thoughts, they turned right at the next intersection and walked without conversing for a long while. Manny finally broke the silence. "I want to ask you something."

Ben, chewing on his lower lip, glanced at him.

"What's really between you and the lady poet?"

Ben said very quietly, "Somewhere along the way I fell in love with her."

Manny responded very carefully, "That being the case, you may have a card to play after all."

Ben perked up.

"Here's the thing," Manny went on. "We're dealing with a rogue operation, run outside the mainstream of accountability. Blowing the whistle on it is out of the question—the world would never believe it wasn't official Washington policy to undermine *glasnost*. American credibility would be in shambles at a crucial moment in time. On the other hand, there is something you could do to stymie the plot and help the girl . . ."

Ben whispered, "I could go to prison for that."

Manny turned on him. "There are people on our side who don't want the Cold War to end. They're afraid of becoming warriors without adversaries, so they're trying to get the Russians who think like them to dump Gorbachev. Remember the conversation we had at Sam's? I told you I didn't think the Great Houdini could succeed, but I was all for giving him a fair shot at it. I still am." Embarrassed by his show of emotion, Manny shrugged. "Whatever."

They jaywalked across Kutuzovsky Prospekt and came within sight of the diplomatic compound. Suddenly Ben grabbed Manny's elbow. The two men stood facing each other on the sidewalk as traffic raced past. "Tell me about the card you think I can play."

27

When it came to mounting an operation, Manny had the instinct of a choreographer: The entrances and the exits of the dancers, as well as their movements between, had to be meticulously planned. Above all, the performance had to take place on his stage.

"Why?" Ben had asked when Manny insisted on this last point.

"The person who chooses the stage," Manny had explained laconically, "dominates the stage."

Which was why, when Viktor finally despaired of Ben turning up at the third-floor apartment in the Stalin Gothic for the rendezvous Aïda had arranged, he discovered an envelope on the floor outside the door. Pulling a sheet of white typewriter paper from the envelope, Viktor read the hand-printed message:

BY NOW YOU THINK YOU HAVE FIGURED OUT THE IDENTITY OF IRONWEED. IF YOU WANT TO KNOW THE REAL END TO THE IRONWEED STORY COME IMMEDI-

ATELY TO KOLOMENSKOE. THERE IS A
LONG TABLE WITH A RED TABLECLOTH
AND INKWELLS AND DOCUMENTS IN THE
CHANCELLERY ROOM IN THE GATE
HOUSE. ONE OF THE DOCUMENTS IS AN
ENVELOPE MARKED VIKTOR. INSIDE THE
ENVELOPE YOU WILL FIND A MESSAGE
TELLING YOU WHERE TO MEET ME. I
WILL BE THERE ONLY IF YOU COME
ALONE.

Manny and Ben, driving a Chevrolet from the embassy
car pool, were well on their way to Kolomenskoe, the
summer residence of the Tsars some ten miles southeast
of the Kremlin, by the time Viktor finished reading the
letter. Frolov and Krostin were all for surrounding
Kolomenskoe with militiamen and extracting whatever information the American Bassett had by intimidation.
Cooler heads (the old general's, Viktor's) prevailed. Viktor
issued instructions to his section chiefs while his limousine was being summoned.

"Kolomenskoe," he told Zenkevich as he settled into
the front seat of the Zil.

"Kolomenskoe?" Zenkevich asked in surprise. He had
never known his boss to spend an afternoon sightseeing.

"You heard me," Viktor snapped.

Gunning the motor, grinding gears, Zenkevich nosed
the car out into traffic. His eyes hooded and thoughtful,
Viktor reached into the glove compartment, removed the
Walther handgun he kept there and inserted a clip of
bullets. He checked to make sure the safety was on, then
dropped the gun into the pocket of his khaki raincoat.

FROM THE TOP OF THE Georgievsky Bell Tower at Kolomenskoe, Ben surveyed through Manny's binoculars the
hordes of tourists wandering around the residence
grounds. A steady stream of visitors poured into the Tsar's
residence from outside the front gate, where the tourist
buses and private automobiles and taxis parked. "There

he is," Ben exclaimed excitedly. He handed the binoculars to Manny. "The big man in the khaki raincoat just getting out of the car. The one leaning over and saying something to the driver."

Manny focused the binoculars on Viktor as he turned and started toward the gate. Before being posted to Moscow, Manny had leafed through a dozen photograph albums of known KGB officers. The face of the man whom Ben called Viktor was not familiar to him. As Viktor made his way through the crowds toward the Chancellery, Manny studied the parking lot. He noticed four private cars pulling up beyond the line of tourist buses. Two men got out of two of the cars and walked over to talk to each other. Manny passed the binoculars to Ben and pointed out the two men. Ben looked through the binoculars. "The pear-faced guy on the left is the one who was in the safe house the first time I went there," he said.

Manny took the binoculars and trained them on Viktor, who had stopped before the Chancellery building and was looking around as if he expected to meet someone. Manny checked the parking lot again. The two men were standing with their backs to one of the four cars, waiting. They were obviously under instructions not to follow Viktor onto the grounds of the residence.

"It looks like he's alone," Manny decided. "Come on."

IN THE CHANCELLERY BUILDING, Viktor joined a line of visitors filing through the exhibit rooms. In one of the rooms he spotted the long table with the red tablecloth. Inkwells and documents from the seventeenth century were scattered on the tablecloth. One of the envelopes was labeled, in red ink, "Viktor." As Viktor passed, he snatched the envelope from the table. When the *babushka* sitting on a folding chair started to protest, Viktor flashed his red identification booklet at her. Outside the Chancellery, he tore open the envelope and read the note, then turned on his heel and headed straight for the Church of John the Baptist at the far end of the grounds, near the Moscow River.

The church, which Ivan the Terrible caused to be built to mark his anointment as Tsar, was similar to the onion-domed St. Basil's Cathedral in Red Square. It consisted of a central section surrounded by four smaller chapels, each with its own entrance. Following the instructions in the note, Viktor found the chapel with the cord blocking the entrance and a piece of cardboard hanging from the cord on which was written "Closed for repairs." He ducked under the cord and pushed through the door into the chapel.

The inside was tenebrous. Thin beams of light stabbed through slits high in the thick walls. Coming out of the bright sunlight, Viktor was blinded for a moment. The odor of burnt candles and incense stung his nostrils. Gradually he made out a figure standing next to a lattice-work confessional. Walking up to him, Viktor said, "You must have something important on your mind to go to all this trouble."

Ben came straight to the point. "Ironweed is a disinformation operation," he announced. His tight voice ricocheted weakly off the icons covering the walls.

Viktor looked around to make sure they were alone, then inspected the face of the American Bassett. He seemed to be slightly out of breath, as if he had been running; as if he had been invoking a great lie or a great truth. A spectrum of possibilities flashed before Viktor's eyes. In his raincoat pocket, his fingers closed over the butt of the pistol.

"My four months in Prague, my transfer to Moscow, the love affair with a Russian woman that would leave me open to blackmail—it was all part of a carefully arranged plot. I was instructed to give you junk mail until you tightened the screws. When you were convinced that you had turned me into a penetration agent, I was to start feeding you material on Silverweed and Ironweed."

"Why are you telling me this now?"

"I want to negotiate a trade."

"What are you offering?"

"Proof that what I say is true. Proof that Ironweed is a disinformation operation."

"What is the nature of this proof?"

"The notebook from which I copied all the Ironweed and Silverweed messages that I was supposed to be eradicating from the CIA station's backlist of Sensitive Compartmented Information cables. Eventually I could take a lie detector test to prove to you that there were no messages to eradicate, that the notebook was the source of the messages."

"What do you want in return?"

"Exit visas for the woman and her son. When they are both out of the country, I will supply you with the proof."

Viktor took a step backward. He cleared his throat, then started to speak in a voice that sounded ominously brittle. "Did it ever occur to you that we might not want the proof? That we prefer to believe you were sent to Moscow to eradicate messages, which then fell into our hands? That we prefer to believe Ironweed was working for your CIA all these years? That we prefer to believe the CIA discovered you have been passing us the Ironweed messages and is trying to discredit the leak by having you claim you were part of a disinformation operation?"

Ben asked, "How can you turn your back on the truth?"

"Truth," Viktor observed, "is only useful if it is convenient." As he spoke his right hand drifted out of the raincoat pocket. Ben gasped as he caught the bluish glint of the pistol.

"I have been reading excerpts from your newspapers," Viktor said. "All of them agree that conditions in Moscow have deteriorated. The criminal element is bolder than ever. Your death will be attributed to robbery. A junior American diplomat visiting the Tsar's summer residence was shot dead by someone desperate for the hard currency he carried in his wallet. With a little ingenuity our detectives may even trace the bullet to a handgun owned by a known hoodlum, who will admit the crime when your wallet is discovered in his possession."

Viktor thumbed the safety back and scooped up the

hem of his raincoat and bunched it up against the muzzle of his pistol to dampen the sound of the shot. The adrenaline that had coursed through his veins the day he bayoneted the Wehrmacht soldier was again streaming through his body. The prospect of destroying an enemy was giving him a new high. "You are an amateur who has waded in over his head," he snarled. "Now you will lose your head." He started to extend the pistol when he heard a faint scuffing behind him. Suddenly he felt a hollow round object pressing into the back of his neck. The soft gruff voice of someone who was clearly not an amateur drawled in his ear. "Above all avoid sudden gestures. Do not drop the Walther. We would not want it to go off accidentally. Grip the barrel between your thumb and forefinger. Yes. Like that. Fine. Now slowly hold the pistol out to my friend. Very well done. I will take the weapon, Ben. Thank you."

Manny, who had been hiding in the latticework confessional, replaced the cap on his fountain pen and slipped it back in his pocket. Aiming the Walther at the back of Viktor's skull, he remarked, "And they say the Cold War is over." He snorted in derision. "It's just become more creative. Coming up with a hoodlum who will admit to the crime. Whatever."

Ben leaned shakily against the confessional. "I guess you were wrong," he told Manny. "I guess I didn't have a card to play."

"There was no way to know until you tried," Manny said. He slipped out of his sports jacket and carefully wound the sleeve around the Walther. Watching from the wall, Ben's eyes widened. "What are you going to do?" he whispered in alarm.

Reaching up, Manny deftly swiped the cloth-covered pistol sharply across the back of Viktor's head. He caught Viktor under his arms and eased him gently to the tiled floor. "What I am going to do," he calmly announced, "is get you out of Russia. For that you need a head start. Here, give me a hand."

The two of them maneuvered Viktor's limp body into

the confessional. "What if you killed him?" Ben breathed. He swallowed hard.

Manny shrugged his heavy shoulders into the sports jacket and dropped Viktor's pistol into one of its pockets. "The newspapers will say that a senior *apparatchik* working for the Komitet Gosudarstvennoi Bezopasnosti, better known by its initials, KGB, was mugged while visiting the Tsar's summer residence by someone desperate for the hard currency he carried in his wallet." He smiled down at Viktor for a moment, enjoying his little joke.

INKERMANN, WHO SUBSCRIBED to the theory that a good station chief didn't make waves, strode back and forth across his threadbare office carpet on his short legs, punctuating Manny's monologue with grunts of dissatisfaction. Every now and then he tossed a question over his shoulder as if it were a grenade, and waited for the muffled explosion.

"You're sure you're sure about the identity of Ironweed?" he asked at one point.

Manny described how he had narrowed the list down to one, and went on with his story.

"You're positive you didn't kill him?" he asked after Manny described how he had gotten his head start.

"It was a love tap," Manny replied.

"How did you smuggle Bassett out of Kolomenskoe?" Inkermann wanted to know.

"They close down the place at six," Manny explained. "We got lost in the flow of tourists crowding through the gate toward the buses. The pear-faced man Bassett recognized through binoculars was still staring over the heads of the tourists when we pulled away." Manny, sprawling in a seat, threw a quick glance at the CIA station chief. "The way I see it, Charlie, we've had our differences over the years, but this Ironweed business is another can of worms altogether. We've got to exfiltrate Bassett out of the country before the KGB heavies get their paws on him."

Inkermann continued pacing. "What I don't understand," he said, "is why this Viktor character would want to eliminate Bassett."

"I've been thinking about that," Manny said. "What I came up with is this: Some folks in the Pentagon have decided the world would be better off without *glasnost* and with the Cold War. So they mounted an operation to drop hints to the Russians that Gorbachev was a long-time CIA agent. The information fell into the hands of folks who are only too eager to believe this, because they also think the world would be better off without *glasnost* and with the Cold War. They plan to use the information Bassett slipped them to undermine Gorbachev and, when the time is ripe, dump him. So when Bassett comes along saying, 'Hey, fellas, I was only kidding about the Great Houdini being a CIA agent; what I passed you was part of a disinformation operation,' he's telling them something they don't want to hear. For all we know, Viktor and his friends may be *Pamyat* people. They couldn't care less if the messages Bassett slipped them are phony. The messages are a weapon they can use to get at Gorbachev. So what do they do? They kill the messenger and spare the messages."

Inkermann reached across his desk and stabbed at a button on his intercom. "Miss Macy, order me up some wheels from the car pool." Squinting at Manny in the murky half-light of his office, Inkermann asked, "Where did you stash him?"

Manny coughed up a guttural snicker. "I drove him out to a *dacha* near Zagorsk. Bassett said it was the secret hideaway of the Zavaskaya woman's ex-husband. We've got to assume that the KGB knows about it. But my guess is they won't get around to checking it until they've tried all the Moscow haunts first—Bassett's apartment, mine, yours, the embassy. Whatever. Which gives us three, maybe four hours to play with. The Zavaskaya woman and her kid are at the *dacha* for the weekend. Bassett will be waiting with them in an abandoned church near the *dacha*, as opposed to the *dacha* itself, on the off chance Viktor's people turn up in Zagorsk before we do. But he swears he won't leave the country unless she goes with him, and she won't go without the kid, so you have got to figure a way to get the three of them out."

Inkermann ran a sweaty palm over his scalp to slick back his hair. "I ought to be able to come up with something."

Manny corrected him. "*We* ought to be able to come up with something." When Inkermann challenged him with a dark look, Manny added sweetly, "It's me who knows where the *dacha* and the abandoned church are located."

Inkermann jerked his head in the direction of the door. "Tag along if it makes you feel useful."

"Whatever."

LOVERS DRAINED FROM SOMETHING other than love-making, they sat with their backs against one of the rough stone walls of the abandoned church on the bluff overlooking the far end of the lake. Their eyes were shut, their faces turned up to the sun. Farther down the slope Saava could be heard cracking open stones with an old hammer in search of fossils.

Aïda's voice, when she finally managed to speak, had grown hollow from listening to him. "So: Your Russian is more or less correct. The words you use are in my vocabulary. But I am not sure I understand what is in the spaces between the words. Are you telling me that everything that happened between us—on the train to Leningrad, in the hotel overlooking the Neva, here in the *dacha*—was part of someone's *plan*, was a figment of someone's *imagination*?"

Her sentence trailed off, as if what she had said needed digesting. From the slope Saava called up excitedly, "Aïda, I found a billion-years-old snail fossil!"

Aïda waved at the boy, who turned back to the stones and continued cracking them open with his hammer.

Her head, resting against the wall, rocked slowly until she was looking at Ben. "I feel as if I have been raped."

Ben touched her ribs with his fingertips. "I love you,

Aïda. Whatever else has happened has not changed that. I ask you to believe me."

She exhaled in frustration. "I do not know what to believe."

"At least believe me when I say you must leave the country . . ."

Covering her ears with her palms, Aïda turned her head away and spit out some lines of Akhmatova.

> I heard a voice call . . .
> 'Leave your remote and sinful country,
> Leave Russia behind forever . . .'
> I covered my ears with my palms . . .

"Do it for the boy," Ben pleaded. "He can have the bone marrow operation. His condition can be cured."

Her palms slowly dropped away from her ears. "That is the one note of your siren's song that reaches me."

"It's not only for the bone marrow operation that you must leave," Ben argued. "Viktor was going to kill me. If they kill me they will want to . . . eliminate you . . . eliminate Saava." He had to look away when he saw the expression of sheer terror in her eyes. He said weakly, "They are not the kind of people who leave loose ends."

Aïda watched Saava hacking away at the rocks. "You are trying to frighten me into going with you." She added softly, "And it is working."

"If I could undo what has been done—"

Aïda thrust out her wrist so that he could see the watch that ran counterclockwise. "So: If time ran backward," she told him bitterly, "you could go back in time and undo the future. You could fix things so that things did not need to be fixed."

Confronted with her bitter reproach, Ben couldn't bring himself to speak.

Below them the sound of hammering suddenly broke off. Saava was rising to his feet and staring at two men struggling up the slope through the high grass. Ben imme-

diately recognized them. "Help is on the way," he told
Aïda.

He stood and reached out to help Aïda up. Ignoring his
hand, she climbed to her feet and started down the slope,
past the two men, to collect Saava.

Inkermann, in his shirt sleeves, his jacket folded over
one arm, came up to Ben. Manny, still wearing his jacket,
sweat stains visible around the collar of his shirt, stopped
a few paces behind. Inkermann drew his forearm across
his brow to wipe away the perspiration. "Fucking hot
out," he commented.

Ben didn't say anything.

Inkermann patted the pockets of his jacket looking for
something, found it, pulled out a pair of handcuffs, which
he dangled from a finger. "I am sending you back to the
States under arrest," he informed Ben. Keeping his beady
eyes glued to Ben, he turned his head so that Manny
could hear him. "I figured it all out, Manny. If I arrest
him and send him back in irons, the Russians will assume
we caught him in the act, which will convince them that
the stuff he passed them is genuine."

Ben asked Inkermann, "What about her and the boy?"

Perspiration glistened on the station chief's scalp.
"She's not my problem. The kid's not my problem. You
are my problem."

Ben addressed Manny over Inkermann's shoulder.
"You gave me your word."

With a practiced flick of his wrist, Inkermann snapped
open the handcuffs. Behind him Manny mopped his brow
with his sleeve and then took off his jacket and wound it
around the metal object in one of the pockets. Stepping
up behind Inkermann, he deftly swiped the cloth-covered
pistol sharply across the back of his head. He caught Inkermann under his arms and eased him into a sitting position in the shade of a wall. Then he retrieved the
handcuffs and snapped them on the station chief's pale
ankles. "When he comes to he will be able to walk," he
told Ben, "but slowly."

Ben said nervously, "You are a specialist in head starts."

"This time I'm going to need it as much as you," Manny noted grimly. He stared down morosely at the CIA station chief. "The trouble is, without his help, I haven't the dimmest idea what to do with the head start."

Aïda, gripping Saava's hand in hers, had come up behind Manny. Speaking in English so as not to alarm the boy, she said, "I maybe know who can be helping us in the leaving of the country."

28

Vadim had been nipping moonshine most of the day, but the sight of Aïda's face as she pushed past him into the penthouse apartment had sobered him instantly. Now he cast haunted looks in the direction of the two Americans as his ex-wife, whispering intently, told him what had happened. "The big one there bunched up his jacket and hit the other one over the head with something and attached bracelets to his ankles so he could not follow us when he came to, and drove us back to Moscow in the embassy car, and here we are."

"And here you are," Vadim repeated without enthusiasm.

Aïda found it difficult to continue. Since the events on the bluff overlooking the far end of the lake, she had been plagued with bouts of dizziness. She pressed a palm to her forehead and fought to bring her breathing under control. After a while she managed to add, "Benedict says we must get ourselves out of the country before the KGB catches up with us."

The mention of the KGB really alarmed Vadim. "I don't see how I can help you."

Aïda darted over to an open door to check Saava, who had fallen asleep, fully dressed, on the waterbed Vadim had bought from a departing diplomat. The sight of the boy curled up in a fetal position provoked deep feelings of guilt in her. What had she been thinking of to put him at risk for her own carnal satisfaction? She turned back to Vadim. "So: If not you, who?" she asked gravely. "If you turn us away I will of course understand it, but you must know we have reached the end of the line."

"What about seeking asylum in the American Embassy?"

"The man whose ankles are bound in bracelets was from the American Embassy. They consider Benedict a traitor. As for Saava, as for me, they could not care less about our fate."

Vadim heaved himself out of his chair and started prowling around the living room, glancing from time to time at the two Americans sitting tensely on the couch, at Aïda slumped in a quilted easy chair. Stopping in his tracks, he began gesturing. Failing to find words to accompany the gestures, he continued prowling around the room, absently brushing his fingertips across his prized possessions—there was a Japanese hi-fi, there was a German video recorder, there was a French fax machine that switched automatically between phone calls and fax calls —as if he were weighing what he had to lose by helping her. He stopped in front of the picture window to study the pinpoints of light dancing on the surface of the Moscow River below, as if the pinpoints could tell him, in some sort of Morse code, what to do.

The two Americans exchanged looks. Ben tried, without success, to catch Aïda's eye. As for Aïda, she kept shaking her head as she tried to run time backward in her mind and discover at what instant she could have slipped free of the trap in which she now found herself.

Vadim, still prowling, trailed two fingers over a table, leaving parallel tracks in the dust. Then he touched the silver samovar he had bought only days before in an impromptu flea market set up on the ground floor of a factory dormitory. Scouring Moscow for a Japanese television camera, Vadim had spotted the samovar resting on a closed cardboard suitcase. A thin-faced, cross-eyed young Armenian refugee from Azerbaijani pogroms in the Caspian city of Baku had stared up at Vadim with his good eye. "I am practically giving it away," he had announced.

The samovar had reminded Vadim of the one his mother had polished every Sunday of her life until the day she traded it to a doctor in return for radiation treatments for her husband. "How much is practically giving it away?" he had inquired with studied disinterest.

"Make me an offer," the Armenian had retorted gloomily.

In the end they had dickered for a quarter of an hour before Vadim pulled out his packet of foreign banknotes, peeled off ten American dollars and ten English pounds and tucked the samovar under an arm. While they were dickering the Armenian had rambled on. "We packed our bags and ran for it," he had recounted with undisguised bitterness. "We left behind my three-room apartment and my Danish furniture and my Japanese TV, and my wife's French knitting machine and her German blending machine that makes carrot juice when you can find carrots." He had added Vadim's dollars and pounds to a meager wad in the breast pocket of a threadbare suit jacket. "You look like someone who recognizes opportunity when it knocks. You would not by any chance be interested in selling a Moscow residence permit or ration coupons or subletting a room in your apartment? Around here," he had added, gesturing toward the other Armenians selling silver and candlesticks and clothing and books from open suitcases, "people will do anything for these things."

The Armenian's "anything" had registered in a lobe of Vadim's brain.

Since his visit to the open-air flea market, Vadim had come across newspaper articles describing the plight of the Armenian refugees. There were roughly thirty thousand of them in Moscow, camping in hallways of public buildings and outlying shacks and factory dormitories and the abandoned hulls of scuttled river boats. The Moscow City Council, anxious to eliminate the eyesore, not to mention the strain in the ability of Moscow to supply food to its legal residents, had passed an ordinance requiring the refugees to move on by the end of the month. The Kremlin, meanwhile, had laid on free transportation back to Baku in an effort to get the refugees to return to their homes.

Sinking onto a chair, Vadim eyed the two Americans. He remembered the item he had read on one of *Pravda*'s inside pages: The first train carrying Armenians back to Baku was scheduled to leave Moscow at the end of the week. "Maybe I can help you after all," he heard himself say.

"You are a great man, Vadim," Aïda called from across the room.

"I am doing it for the boy," Vadim said gruffly. And leaning toward the two Americans, he described his meeting with the Armenian and spelled out the plan that had come to him. He even had an idea of how to dispose of the embassy Chevrolet so that it would never be found.

Manny liked the idea right off. "If you can get us to Rostov-on-Don," he said, "I can get us across the frontier. When I was running agents from Turkey my main contacts were two Cossacks, twin brothers who ran a smuggling operation out of Rostov. For a price they could get anything—or anybody—in or out of the country. Last I heard they were still in business."

An anxious Ben poked holes in Vadim's plan. "What if they scrutinize the internal passports at the railroad station?" he asked.

"Unlikely," Vadim said. "Who in his right mind would return to Baku if he wasn't obliged to?"

"What if some of the Armenians denounce us?"

"The odds are against that. The Armenians blame the authorities for what happened to them. If you told your average Armenian what you were doing, chances are he would help you out of spite."

"We will need hard currency, and lots of it," Manny put in.

"Some you can get from disposing of the car," Vadim told him. "I can give you whatever else you need."

Aïda suddenly said, "Come with us, Vadim." With a forlorn smile she added: "In America the beautiful the streets are paved with Sony Walkmans."

"What would I do in America the beautiful?" Vadim asked plaintively.

"You always wanted to work on Madison Street," Aïda reminded him.

Vadim shook his head sadly. "What would a Russian Jew like me know about advertising products that worked? I would run ideas up flagpoles and nobody would salute. Anyway, I have it made here—I have more money than I can spend, I can buy or trade for anything under the sun. And then there is Katya. She would be lost without me." He tried to change the subject. "Have you heard the latest about the Jew being summoned to the visa office to discuss his application to emigrate to Israel? 'I have two reasons for wanting to leave,' he tells the official. 'Every night my neighbor comes home drunk and starts cursing the Jews. He says that as soon as the Communists are overthrown, he and his *Pamyat* friends will string up all the Jews.' 'We Communists will never be overthrown,' the visa officer assures him. At which point the Jew says, 'That's my second reason for wanting to emigrate.' Ha!"

Vadim disappeared into the kitchen and emerged with a plate filled with salami and cheese and pickles and thinly sliced black bread. Working on his second cheese sandwich, Ben thought of another objection to Vadim's plan. "What if they won't let us leave the train at Rostov?" he asked. "What if the Cossacks Manny knew are no longer in business?"

"What if? What if?" Vadim repeated in exasperation.

"Your plan has flaws," Ben insisted nervously.

"It's not perfect," Manny admitted. "But like the man says, the perfect is the enemy of the good. Whatever."

WHILE AÏDA AND THE BOY waited in Vadim's taxi, Manny—following Vadim's directions—maneuvered the embassy Chevrolet through a labyrinth of streets behind the sprawling Exhibition of Economic Achievements. Turning into a pitted alleyway, he cut the motor in front of a run-down garage. Vadim took a quick sip from a silver flask, then reached over and honked the horn once. Seeing no sign of life, Ben said from the backseat, "Are you sure we've come to the right place?"

A bearded Kazakh in dirty overalls, his forearms covered with tattoos, the tattoos smeared with grease, appeared in a small door that opened in the garage door. He waved to Vadim and disappeared back into the garage. A moment later the garage door swung slowly open. Manny shifted into first and eased the Chevrolet into the garage.

He killed the motor as the garage door closed behind them, cutting off most of the light. Four Kazakhs in dirty overalls surrounded the Chevrolet as Manny and Vadim and Ben climbed out. "These guys are tough customers," Vadim said in English under his breath. "Stay close."

Another Kazakh, dressed in a rumpled black suit, appeared from behind huge drums of oil. Walking up to the car, he kicked at one of the wheels with a scuffed suede shoe. "Tires have bad treads," he sneered. "You never said nothing about bad treads."

Vadim smelled trouble. "We agreed on the price," he said. He backed up until he was standing between Ben and Manny. All three had their backs against the Chevrolet. The four men in overalls closed in on them. "Do not try to reopen negotiations now," Vadim added bravely.

"How can I be expected to fix a price till I see the car in question?" asked the man in the rumpled suit.

"How?" agreed the Kazakh with the tattoos on his forearms. He bent and picked up a large red monkey wrench, which he hiked onto his shoulder.

"Four hundred United States of America dollars, seventy-five English pounds, one thousand French francs is what we agreed on," Vadim said. "One kopeck less, we take our business elsewhere."

Another Kazakh scooped a tire iron off the concrete floor.

"I might see my way clear to paying two hundred United States dollars," said the man in the rumpled suit.

"Two hundred! You will get ten times that when you break the car up and sell the spare parts."

"Let's get out of here," Manny muttered. He reached for the door handle. Behind him he heard a sharp snap. He turned back. A rusty knife was in the hand of the third Kazakh.

"Look, fellas, I don't mind the occasional knife, but I draw the line at rusty blades," Manny said. "Cut somebody with that thing, he could come down with a fatal case of tetanus." He brought up a laugh from his stomach just as his hand brought up the Walther pistol from his pocket.

The Kazakhs backed off and looked at their employer. "Nobody said nothing about a gun," one of them mumbled.

Manny gestured with the pistol. The monkey wrench, the tire iron, the rusty knife clattered to the concrete floor.

Shrugging, the man in the rumpled suit kicked at the tire again. "The treads are maybe not as bad as I thought," he conceded.

THE SIGHT OF HER BOSS's head swathed in gauze had been too much for Viktor's secretary, Evgeniya Leonovna. Tears had welled in her eyes as she hovered over his hospital bed, stirring a second spoonful of her homemade confiture into an herb tea that she swore was good for dizzy spells, fingernails and bowel movements. "Nothing is sacred anymore," she had exclaimed. "To think you were attacked in a church. The hooligan who did that ought to be put up against a wall."

Viktor's wife had been more suspicious. Summoned to

the special KGB hospital where Viktor's head had been stitched up, Ekaterina had pushed him in a wheelchair to his limousine and had helped Zenkevich maneuver him into the front seat. "What were you doing in the Church of John the Baptist way out at Kolomenskoe?" she had asked as they headed back toward the airport and their apartment. Because of Zenkevich, she had refrained from commenting when Viktor trotted out the story about his having gone on the spur of the moment to offer up a candle to his dead mother at her favorite church. Back in the apartment, she had dissolved the yellowish powder the doctor had given her in tepid water and had handed the glass to Viktor, who was propped up on pillows in bed. "Now that we are alone," she had said, "you will tell me the truth. What is her name? How long have you been seeing her?"

"I swear to you—"

"Dear Viktor, you are such a lousy liar. You have not set foot in a church in fifty years. Are you forgetting that we have an arrangement? Your having a mistress will not change things between us. I only want to know about it."

"There was no woman," Viktor had said tiredly. "I was meeting an agent, if you must know. Obviously I am unable to tell you more."

Even then she had only half-believed him. "Obviously."

"I am very"—he searched for the right word—"*attached* to you, Katya. If there was another woman I would tell you. After all, you have your lover. There is no reason why I should not have a mistress."

"None," she had agreed. She had reached up and in a rare display of affection, had touched the gauze with her fingertips. "I would not like to be in his shoes when you find the man who did this to you."

"Nor would I," Viktor had agreed grimly.

At the office the next day the old general was extremely solicitous. "My daughter tells me you suffer dizzy spells," he said. "That is to be expected with minor concussions. You need time off. A week of fresh mountain air . . ."

Viktor blinked rapidly to keep the general in focus. "I would not want to miss the dénouement," he insisted.

Which explained why Viktor, his head wrapped in clean bandages (the stitches had been removed by the same KGB doctor who had put them in), his joints aching with gout, his lids blinking rapidly to keep the dizziness at bay, found himself taking part in the night-long meeting of the *Pamyat* Directorate devoted to Ironweed. Summoned by the old general for what was billed as "an extraordinary session," the eighteen high-ranking officers and former officers of the Komitet Gosudarstvennoi Bezopasnosti had descended from the four corners of the country on the dilapidated hunting lodge tucked away in a thick stand of white birches off the Moscow-Kiev highway. There was no preliminary banter, no refreshments, no anecdotes about past triumphs. "It was Stalin who formulated the rule of thumb that an enemy had to be eliminated politically before he could be eliminated physically," the general announced in his gravelly voice. "In front of each of you is a copy of a dossier with the word *Ironweed* on the first page. The contents of this dossier will ruin President Gorbachev politically. When that has been accomplished, we will see to his physical elimination. You all know the very talented head of our Second Chief Directorate, Viktor Prosenko. Viktor here will walk you through the dossier. When he has finished, you will understand why Gorbachev's days are numbered." The old man gestured toward his son-in-law with his deformed hand. "Viktor."

Swaying slightly, gripping the edge of the table to steady himself, Viktor rose to his feet. "The dossier before you contains irrefutable evidence that Gorbachev has been an active agent of American imperialism since 1967." Several of the men around the table gasped. Viktor waited for the murmur to subside before continuing. "You will see that he was known to the Americans by the code name Ironweed. When he became Secretary General in 1985, the Americans broke off contact in order to protect him. They were counting on the new Secretary General, who bore a lifelong grudge against our system, to 'reform'

Communism out of existence. In this he has almost succeeded. But our feeling is that it is not too late to set the
clock back. Once you have digested the information in
this dossier, you will return to your various constituencies
and spread the word. This dossier will create the ripple
that will drown Gorbachev. People who have supported
him up to now, once they learn of his treason, will abandon him. When we finally manage to depose him, the
West will conclude that he was devoured by the revolution he launched. They will say he was ousted by those
who were opposed to his economic program, who thought
he had proceeded with reforms too rapidly, or too slowly.
But those of us who belong to *Pamyat* will know the real
reason he was dethroned—because he is a traitor to the
Motherland."

Breathing deeply, Viktor flipped open his own dossier.
"The first inkling we had that the Americans had been
running a high-level agent in place came when . . ."

THE OLD GENERAL HAD BEEN CATEGORIC. It was preferable
that the American Bassett did not leave Russia alive. KGB
agents at the airports and the border crossing points had
been alerted to look for the American, thought to be trav-
eling with a woman in her early forties and an eleven-
year-old boy named Saava. The American was thought to
be armed with a Walther service pistol. An operational
code had been assigned to the alert indicating that the
American in question, along with anyone accompanying
him, was to be detained in absolute secrecy until receipt
of further instructions from the Center.

The old general cast the net wide. Tips came in from
various corners of the country. A man speaking Russian
with an American accent had been seen driving out of
Leningrad on the Vyborg road. A woman and young boy
were believed to be passengers in the car. An American
with a passport identifying him as Ben Bass had registered
at a hotel in Brest-Litovsk. A woman and a young boy had
been seen putting a man fitting Bassett's description on a
train at Lvov.

So it went. Each tip was checked out. Each proved to
be a case of overactive imagination or mistaken identity.
Three days passed. More tips accumulated. Each wound
up in a dead end. Then on Thursday, Viktor's section
chief, Krostin, phoned in. He had questioned the house-
wife who shared the flat with the Zavaskaya woman and
had learned that she had been asked to forward mail addressed to the poet's former husband, who now had an
apartment of his own. Krostin had the address and wanted
Viktor's permission to nose around.

Krostin called back later in the morning to say that one
of Vadim's neighbors had reported seeing a man fitting
Bassett's description, along with a woman and a young
boy, entering the building the night that Viktor was as-
saulted in the church. There had been another man,
heavyset, on the short side, with them. Krostin supposed
that it must be the man who sneaked up behind Viktor in
the church and hit him over the head. On the off chance
that the American and the Zavaskaya woman were still in
the apartment, Krostin had brought in two carloads of
agents and surrounded the building.

"Don't do anything until I get there," Viktor ordered.

Twenty minutes later Viktor, the gauze on his head replaced by now with a small bandage, found Krostin in the
lobby of the building. "I had one of my people phone
upstairs pretending he was taking a political survey,"
Krostin told his boss. His lips offered up an unaccustomed
smile. "The Jew is at home."

"I will see him alone," Viktor told Krostin.

Viktor tried the elevator, but there was no response
when he pushed the button. Breathing heavily, resting on
each landing, he made his way up nine flights to the top
floor. There were two apartments. He checked the name
plate under the first bell, then rang it. When there was
no response he rang more insistently. He could hear
footsteps approaching. The door opened as far as a safety
chain permitted. Vadim, bleary-eyed, pink-skinned,
peered out. He was wearing a crimson dressing gown, and
carrying a glass filled with ice cubes and some sort of thick

clear liquid. Thinking he was confronting a salesman, he quipped, "I am a seller, not a buyer."

Viktor held up a laminated card with his thumb covering his family name. Catching sight of the KGB logo on the card, Vadim put on a brave front. "I thought you people were all job hunting."

Viktor gestured with a forefinger. "Open it."

Vadim managed to tinkle the ice cubes in his glass insolently before slowly unlatching the door. Viktor brushed past him into the living room. He took in the view of the Moscow River, the furniture, the Japanese hi-fi, the German video recorder, the French fax machine; he took in the photograph of an exquisite-looking woman in a silver frame propped up on a mahogany table behind the couch. (He had the same photograph of the same woman, in the same silver frame, on the desk in his office.) Then he turned and took in Vadim.

Vadim could not miss the bandage on his visitor's scalp. "Hurt our head, have we?" he inquired with exaggerated concern. He sank onto the couch and crossed his legs and rattled the ice cubes again. "Have you heard the latest joke about the difference between the KGB and the CIA?"

Viktor seated himself on the quilted easy chair. "If it would make you feel more at ease, by all means tell it."

"The KGB has stolen from a CIA safe the blueprints for all American weapons systems developed during the past ten years. The CIA has stolen from the KGB safe the results of all Soviet elections for the next ten years. Ha!"

Viktor did not crack a smile. Vadim, his eyes pink from too much drink, said, "You don't get it?"

"I get it. I don't think it is funny."

"How about the one where a KGB officer denies a Jewish computer programmer permission to emigrate to Israel on the grounds that he knows state secrets. 'What secrets?' the programmer asks. 'Everyone knows the Americans are twenty years ahead of us in computer programming.' 'That's the secret!' says the KGB officer. Ha!" When Viktor still didn't smile, Vadim burped in annoyance. "You are obviously not in a good mood. Let's talk, as the Americans say, chicken or turkey. To what do I owe the dubious pleasure of this visit?"

"You are the former husband of Zinaïda Zavaskaya?"

Vadim nodded carefully.

"When is the last time you saw her?"

Vadim screwed up his eyes in thought. "We had lunch in the TV tower a few weeks ago."

"And you have not seen her since?"

Vadim shook his head.

"According to one of your neighbors, the Zavaskaya woman, accompanied by her son, Saava, and two men, one of them fitting the description of an American diplomat named Bassett, were seen entering the building four nights ago."

Vadim treated himself to a healthy drink, then rattled the ice cubes in the glass again to gain time. "If it was her, which is not certain, she must have been visiting someone else in the building because she did not come up here."

Against his will Viktor let his eyes drift to the photograph in the silver frame. The woman who gazed out with a thin, arrogant smile was breathtakingly beautiful. What could she possibly see in someone like Vadim? "The people who record history more often than not miss the important details," Viktor informed Vadim. "They tell you what a general said, but not what he had for breakfast. They don't describe the state of his bowels or nerves; they don't tell you that Napoleon had diarrhea before the battle of Borodino, that he did not sleep the night before because his anus itched."

"What has all that—"

"If some observer were recording this event, this encounter between a decorated veteran of the Great Patriotic War, a lieutenant colonel of the KGB in charge of the Second Chief Directorate, and an"—Viktor spit out the words—*"alcoholic Yid black marketeer"*—with an effort, he forced himself to speak normally—"what would he see? He would see a bandage on the head of the colonel covering five stitches that closed a wound caused when the same colonel was slugged by a Walther pistol wrapped in a suit jacket. He would note that the colonel had since suffered severe headaches that rendered him irritable, short-tempered, testy, a state not ameliorated when the colonel in question, interviewing the alcoholic Yid black marketeer in question, recognized a photograph in a silver frame." Viktor leaned forward. "How long have you been fucking Katya?"

"I do not have to answer that," Vadim said huskily.

"You do not have to answer because *I know the answer.* You have been fucking her for four years and four months. You met while she was filming a television series in Alma Ata. You were buying cotton on the black market and having it privately packaged and selling it to pharmacies at four times the price you paid."

Vadim gulped down the rest of his drink. "How do you know such things?"

"The woman in the silver frame is named Ekaterina Prosenka. She is married to Viktor Prosenko. It is, as they say, a very small world, Vadim. I am the cuckolded husband, Viktor Prosenko."

For the first time Vadim was really frightened. "She said you had an . . . arrangement."

"We did have an arrangement. She had her lovers, of whom you are the most recent. And I put up with it so that she would not leave me." Viktor smiled a cruel smile. "About the Zavaskaya woman and the American Bassett: Where did they go when they left here?"

"I cannot tell you."

"You mean you will not tell me."

Vadim made no answer.

Viktor said, "You will have seen in the newspapers that we are still punishing people for economic misconduct in what is left of our Soviet Union. The list of your economic crimes is as long as my arm. It is illegal to hire taxis by the year and pay the driver in dollars. It is illegal to lease river boats from the State under a new law intended for farmers who want to rent land. It is illegal to buy huge quantities of cotton and package it for sale to pharmacies at

exorbitant prices. You will be tried for black marketeering
and profiteering. You will be found guilty by the three
judges who preside over the court. You will be sentenced
to be executed. You will be shot by a firing squad. Katya
will mourn your death. In due time she will find another
lover to take your place." Viktor stood up and walked over
to the telephone and rested a hand on it. "About the
Zavaskaya woman and her friends: Where did they go
when they left here four nights ago?"

His knees trembling uncontrollably, Vadim slowly
raised his chin. "Have you heard the one about what
America the beautiful and the Soviet Union have in common? The ruble is not worth anything in either country is
what they have in common." And he added almost inaudi-
bly, "Ha!"

VIKTOR'S SECTION CHIEF brought Vadim's taxi driver, Dmitri,
in for questioning later that night. A meatball of a man
with a pockmarked face, he stood in front of Viktor's desk,
shifting his weight from one foot to the other, squinting
into Viktor's desk lamp, which had been angled up so that
it almost blinded him.

"State your name," Krostin instructed.

"Livshitz, Dmitri."

"State your occupation."

"Taxi driver."

"State your religion."

Dmitri mumbled something.

"I did not hear you."

"Israelite."

Viktor picked up the questioning. "Do you know a person by the name of Vadim?"

Dmitri threaded the sweat band of his cap through his
fingers. "I have driven him around Moscow from time to
time."

Viktor laughed under his breath. "In fact Vadim hires
you by the year. In fact he pays you in American dollars."

Dmitri started to deny the accusation, but Viktor cut
him off. "Let us be clear with each other. I am not con-

cerned with your black market activities. I am concerned with Vadim's black market activities. I am going to put some questions to you. If you answer them honestly and fully, you will walk out of here a free man. If not . . ."

Dmitri, thoroughly cowed, said, "I need to sit down."

Viktor motioned to Krostin. He pushed over a straight-backed wooden chair whose front legs had been slightly shortened. Dmitri collapsed into it, then tensed as he began to slide forward. Viktor said, "You are familiar with Vadim's former wife, Zinaïda Zavaskaya, and her son, Saava?"

Dmitri's head bobbed in reluctant acknowledgment.

"Four nights ago Vadim, the Zavaskaya woman and her son, as well as two other men, were passengers in your taxi."

It had not been put as a question, which indicated to Dmitri that the colonel already knew the answer. Again Dmitri's head bobbed.

"Where did you drive them?"

Dmitri tossed a nervous look over his shoulder at Krostin, then turned back to Viktor behind his desk. All he could make out was a silhouette. "Vadim left word for me to come by around ten at night. He and the ex and the boy came down, but they did not ride in my taxi at the start. They joined two men in an American Chevrolet. Vadim signaled for me to follow the Chevrolet. I parked on the main street near the Exhibition of Economic Achievements. Vadim dropped off the ex and the boy. They waited in my taxi. About fifteen minutes later Vadim and the two others came back. Vadim was counting money. It was then that they all squeezed into my taxi."

"Describe the two men with Vadim."

"I unfortunately did not get a good look at them."

"Describe them, Dmitri."

Staring at his shoes, Dmitri did as he was told. When he finished, Viktor addressed his section chief, "Now we know who hit me over the head." He wrote a name on a scrap of paper and passed it to Krostin, who read it and nodded.

On the paper, Viktor had written: "Immanuel Custer."

"What happened to the Chevrolet?" Krostin wanted to know.

Dmitri shrugged. "Vadim said something about having sold it to some Kazakhs for spare parts. He told the others it would be impossible to trace the car once it had been broken up."

"Where did you take them after they all squeezed into your taxi?" asked Viktor.

Dmitri looked down at his cap, then up again at the silhouette behind the desk. "How do I know you will let me go if I tell you what you want to know?"

"You do not know."

Dmitri chewed on a thumbnail. Finally he said, "I let them off at a dormitory behind a textile factory in the Lefortovo District, the one where they put up all those Armenian refugees from Baku. An hour or so later Vadim returned alone and I drove him back to his apartment."

"Armenian refugees," Viktor said thoughtfully. "That's how he is going to get them out."

AT THE AMERICAN EMBASSY, cables were flying back and forth between Moscow and Washington. Two members of the embassy were unaccounted for. The CIA station chief himself had disappeared for thirty-six hours; had turned up, the ends of handcuffs tucked into his socks so they would not rattle when he walked, with a tale of regaining consciousness on a hill overlooking a lake near Zagorsk, of breaking the chain on the cuffs with a rusty ax he found in a barn, of hitchhiking back to Moscow in the back of a truck full of pigs.

One whiff of his clothing was enough to prove that the last detail of his story, at least, was accurate.

Even before the handcuffs were cut off his ankles, Inkermann had enciphered a report to his masters in Washington. A barrage of replies was on its way back almost immediately. One came directly from the basement situation room of the White House. Deciphered, paraphrased, it said, Haven't you heard? The Cold War is over. And we do not, repeat, do not, want some inept embassy people reminding Americans who will soon be going to the polls that this might not be entirely true. In other words, do not rock the boat.

The story was accordingly put out to curious embassy hands that the two missing diplomats were not missing at all; they were said to be visiting Leningrad and were probably wandering around the ten thousand rooms of the Hermitage. Certainly there was no cause for alarm.

Inkermann, meanwhile, massaged the bruises on his ankles (the handcuffs had been cut off by the in-house plumber using an acetylene torch) and put out feelers with his web of subagents who were paid on a per diem basis and only too glad to find work. Pretty soon the station chief had picked up rumors that the KGB had gone to a full alert. Its people were reportedly combing Moscow hotels and brothels and airports, hunting for an American who bore a striking resemblance to Benedict Bassett. Inkermann even heard from a source inside the KGB that the Center's agents were under orders not to bring the American in alive.

Inkermann was not stupid. Custer, he understood, had gotten it right. Someone in Washington had leaked things to the Russians through Bassett that *some* Russians wanted to believe. Well, it suited Inkermann. Let the Russians dispose of Bassett and the asshole Custer at the same time. The bodies of the two of them would probably be discovered in a car that had skidded off a wet highway into a ravine and exploded. Autopsies would be performed when the bodies were returned to the States. But if the Russians turned out to be as proficient as they had been at the height of the Cold War, there would be no traces of the real cause of death.

At least that was how Inkermann would have handled the problem if he had been in their shoes.

29

Crammed into a narrow compartment he and Aïda shared with an Armenian family, Ben dozed, his head drumming lightly against the back of the slatted wooden bench in time to the motion of the train. He stirred when Aïda, puffing away on one of her hand-rolled cigarettes, returned from the toilet; she had had to wait three-quarters of an hour to use the railway car's only bathroom. "I almost threw up because of the odor," Aïda whispered as she squeezed in next to Ben on the bench. "I lit up to drown out the stench."

The Armenian husband and wife and the wife's two sisters jammed onto the benches with them, and the two teenage boys sleeping on the floor, rearranged their limbs. Outside the rain-stained window a gently rolling blur of wooded hills, illuminated by a sliver of moon darting in and out of dark clouds, flitted past. Ben glanced at his wristwatch. "We should be passing through Voronezh sometime this morning," he said.

The mere mention of Voronezh had an impact on Aïda. Her mouth fell open and she gazed out the window the

way she might have looked at a promised land. "So: It was
to Voronezh that our Mandelstam was exiled during the
last five years of his life," she whispered. "Akhmatova visited him there in 1936, after which she wrote four of the
most painful lines in a poetry overflowing with painful
lines." And pressing her lips against his ear, Aïda recited:

> . . . *in the room of the banished poet*
> *Fear and the Muse stand watch by turn,*
> *and the night falls,*
> *without the hope of dawn.*

The touch of Aïda's lips against his ear aroused erotic
memories. Ben remembered how, on the train to Leningrad a lifetime ago, she had fogged the compartment window with her breath and, reaching up, had written,
"Lucidity must yield to lust." Would lucidity ever yield to
lust again? It made his heart ache to think that it might
not. What a fool he had been to play a game with the
woman who had allowed him to live his wildest fantasies.
He slipped a hand under the rough khaki blanket draped
like a shawl over her and touched her thigh, but she only
turned to offer him a bittersweet half-smile, as if she too
were pondering what might have been.

It had been like that between them—his advances had
been fended off with ambiguous half-smiles—since they
had gone to ground in the prefabricated gray concrete
dormitory behind a textile factory in Moscow's Lefortovo
District. Stepping over the legs of Armenians sprawled on
straw pallets in the hallway, Vadim had led them to a door
with a card tacked to it that read "Social Club: Participa-
tion in the dormitory's monthly amateur night is invited
and required." Inside, rough khaki Army blankets had
been hung from electric wire stretched taut between the
walls, dividing the social club into a warren of small compartments. Vadim had scouted around to find the one he
had "rented," and the four of them—Aïda, Ben, Manny
and the boy—had camped on the tattered cushions and
straw pallets that came with the cubicle. Once and some-

times twice a day Vadim would turn up with something under his arm—a plastic shopping sack filled with black bread and margarine and several tins of sardines, second-hand clothing for them to change into so they would pass for Armenian refugees, a scissors to cut their hair short so they would be harder to recognize, round eyeglasses to disguise the two men.

Late one night, with hacking coughs and snoring and the unmistakable gasps of a woman making love coming from the blanketed compartments around them, Vadim had handed out internal passports that identified them as Armenians, along with official government affidavits authorizing them to travel, at the State's expense, back to Baku. Manny turned the documents over in his fingers. "Where did you get them?" he had demanded.

"I inherited them," Vadim had replied with a twinkle. "The person I inherited them from inherited some of my deutsche marks in return."

The morning they were due to start for the railroad station, Vadim had arrived lugging three cardboard suitcases. Setting them down on the floor, he had proceeded to pull his treasures out one by one. There had been a supply of Swedish biscuits and goat cheese and fermented goat's milk in a worker's thermos, and a sack of oranges and half a dozen Belgian chocolate bars for Saava. There had been more clothing and more hard currency—thick wads of dollars and pounds and francs and deutsche marks, which Vadim delivered into Manny's safekeeping. There had even been drawing paper and colored crayons for the boy. "You are a magician," Saava had exclaimed as he bit into a bar of chocolate.

"If I can make you disappear from Mother Russia," Vadim had replied grimly, "I will really be one."

They had pronounced their adieus then and there; Vadim had decided that they would attract less attention if they turned up at the station in the buses with all the other Armenians leaving that day. Aïda had hugged her ex-husband to her. "So: I am only good at arrivals," she had said. "I cannot bear the idea that we might not meet again."

Vadim had thought she would, at long last, burst into tears. The possibility had unnerved him; he had never seen her weep, and was not eager to cross that threshold at this late date. "What," he had demanded to head off the tears, "is the definition of a Soviet string quartet?"

Aïda had shaken her head.

"A Soviet orchestra that has come back from a tour of America the beautiful. Ha!"

The railroad station had been teeming with Armenians raging at being sent back—and frantic not to miss the train. People seemed to scurry off in all directions. The station, the waiting rooms, the quays, the corridors of railway carriages were littered with chicken bones sucked clean and crusts of bread and newspapers that had once enveloped sandwiches, and empty bottles and abandoned shoes and filthy blankets that had been folded and used as cots. The Armenians, carrying bulky radios, ironing boards, television sets, whatever they had managed to barter or buy in the relatively better-stocked stores of Moscow, had crowded past the single control point at the head of the quay. Ben and Manny, wearing eyeglasses and sporting four-day beards, had waved travel documents in the faces of the harried frontier policemen as they flowed with the river of humanity heading for the train. Aïda, draped in her khaki Army blanket, and Saava, tagging after a family with seven children, had slipped past the cordon without any problem.

Once the train was under way, the Armenians gradually settled down. The younger ones camping in the corridors broke out bottles of slivowitz and harmonicas and began singing folk songs. As a matter of professional prudence, Manny insisted they split up. Ben and Aïda found places in one compartment, Manny and the boy in another. The Armenians with whom Aïda and Ben shared the compartment droned on about the pogroms they had fled from and the possessions they had left behind and the uncertainty of what lay ahead. After a time they too grew silent.

The father, an elflike man with a pockmarked face, glanced briefly at the couple sharing the compartment with his family, then (after trying unsuccessfully to start a conversation with Aïda) produced a crossword puzzle and, adjusting his spectacles, began filling in the blanks. The women brought out knitting. One of the children produced a deck of cards and challenged his brother to a game of *melnitsa*, a two-handed card game similar to bluff. Slapping the cards on the floor between them, they played until both boys, their shoulders drooping with fatigue, collapsed into a fitful sleep on the blankets piled on the floor.

From time to time two young soldiers, wearing insignias of a KGB border police unit, could be seen stepping over the limbs of the Armenians sprawled in the corridor as they made their way from one end of the train to the other. Three times a day the train was shunted onto a remote siding to change crews, take on water and flush out the toilets. The Armenians, defying the shouts from the guards, took advantage of the stops to pour from the train and stretch their legs, pick wildflowers, or wade in nearby streams until the screech of the whistle announced that it was time to move on.

DURING ONE SUCH STOP, Manny and Saava stumbled down a steep embankment to the edge of a stream. Manny removed his jacket and rolled up his sleeve and splashed water over the seven-day gray stubble on his face. Pulling off his shoes and socks, he installed himself on the stump of a tree and dangled his feet in the still-icy water. Saava waved to Ben and Aïda, who were sitting in the shade of a walnut tree at the top of the embankment, then turned back to Manny. "Why is it I'm not supposed to talk to you when other people are around?" he asked.

"I'm embarrassed at how badly I speak Russian," Manny answered.

"That's not the reason," Saava said. "The reason is you don't want people to know you're not Russian." When Manny made no comment, the boy added, "You do make a lot of errors in Russian. You use the wrong declensions all the time."

"Look, sonny, I agree my Russian needs work, but it's better than your English."

"I don't speak English," Saava said. "I don't speak American either." He fell silent for a while, then tugged at Manny's shirt to get his attention. "I had trouble falling asleep last night."

"Try counting sheep."

"Counting what sheep?"

"You imagine a field full of sheep and then you count them."

"What good does that do?"

"It bores you to sleep."

"I'm bored without counting sheep. How much longer before we get to Rostov?"

"Depends."

"On what?"

"On how much time the train rolls, as opposed to how much time it spends on sidings." Manny noticed the anxiety on the boy's face and relented. "A day and a half, maybe. Two days at the most."

"What do we do when we get to Rostov?"

"You ask a lot of questions for a kid."

"You don't answer many of them for an adult."

Manny snickered.

Saava scratched a circle in the earth with the tip of a twig. "What kind of a name is Manny?"

"It's short for Immanuel. It's biblical."

"Why would parents give someone a name from the Bible?"

"Jesus. When do you turn off? They were religious, is why."

"In one of my textbooks it says that religion is the opiate of the people. What's an opiate?"

"Something that puts you to sleep."

"Is counting sheep an opiate?"

"You could say that."

Saava wandered off a few paces and started to fling

pebbles into the stream. "I have a knife," he called. "It has a magnifying glass in it. Vadim gave it to me for my name day."

"You don't say."

Saava came back and pulled the Swiss Army knife from his pocket. Manny took it and opened a blade. "At least it's not rusty," he remarked.

"It can't rust. It's stainless steel."

Manny glanced up the embankment at Ben. In the shade of the walnut tree, he was deep in conversation with Aïda. Her hands fluttered, as if she were batting away his arguments. "Under the stainless skin, everything rusts," Manny muttered in English. He switched back to Russian and told the boy, "I draw the line at rusty blades. They can infect you with tetanus." He smiled faintly at the memory of the rusty blade clattering to the floor in the Moscow garage.

"What's tetanus?"

"It's a disease that gives you lockjaw." Manny demonstrated. "T-h-e j-a-w o-c-k-s. Y-o-u c-a-n-'t a-l-k."

"There are injections for things like that."

"I'm afraid of injections," Manny said.

"Before I took pills, I used to get injections. It's true they hurt, but you get used to them."

Manny glanced at Saava. "I like your style, kid."

On the hill above them, the train's whistle shrieked. Startled, Manny yanked his feet out of the stream. "Come on, kid. And remember not to talk to me in front of other people. That way they won't suspect I'm not Russian."

AT DAWN THE MORNING after they had passed through Voronezh, Manny came awake with a start. Everyone else in the compartment was fast asleep. At first he could not figure out what had roused him. Then it hit him: It was the lack of motion.

He parted the soiled window curtain with a fingertip and looked out. The train had come to a stop in a deserted country station. A dark-skinned peasant woman was on her hands and knees scrubbing the tiles in the tiny waiting room. Pressing his face to the window, Manny could make out the stationmaster swinging a red lantern back and forth. The train jerked forward, then stopped, then jerked forward again and began picking up speed. As it pulled out of the station, Manny saw an empty truck parked along the side of the stationmaster's house. Feeling vaguely apprehensive, he sank back onto the wooden bench next to Saava.

Manny had difficulty dozing off. Staring at the window curtain swaying gently back and forth, he had the uneasy feeling that he was overlooking something. Then, suddenly, it came to him. Of course! The truck parked next to the stationmaster's house was an Army truck. And it was empty!

What was an empty Army truck doing at some godforsaken station? And where were the soldiers who had driven it there?

Manny bolted upright, awakening Saava.

"Where are you going?" the boy whispered when he saw Manny step over the man sleeping on the floor and start to ease open the compartment door.

"To stretch my legs," Manny whispered back.

Sliding the door closed behind him, he made his way down the corridor, stepping over the sleeping figures huddled in blankets on the floor. He hauled open the door at the end of the car and hauled it closed behind him and standing with a foot on each car, stared at the tracks rushing past under his feet before moving on to the next car. Threading his way over and around the sleeping figures, he worked his way from car to car back toward the rear of the train. Three cars from the caboose he spotted what he was afraid he would find. Up ahead, he could see six men, four armed with rifles and dressed in the uniforms and berets of KGB border guards, two in civilian raincoats and fedoras, making their way down the corridor, kicking awake the Armenians sprawled on the floor, flinging open compartment doors and reaching in to rouse those inside. While the border guards scrutinized identity papers, the two civilians compared the faces of the Armenians with photographs they held in their hands.

Manny turned and scrambled back to his own car near the head of the train. He scratched his fingernails on the glass door of Ben's compartment. Ben's eyes flitted open. Manny jerked his head sharply. Ben eased Aïda's head off his shoulder and came out into the corridor. "What's up?" he whispered.

Manny explained what he had seen. "They're waking everyone and checking identity papers."

"Oh, my God!" Ben exclaimed. He had a sudden vision of Aïda and the boy being marched off at the point of bayonets and clutched at a straw. "We have identity papers."

Manny shook his head. "The heavies in raincoats have photographs."

"Maybe they're not looking for us."

"Maybe they are." Manny glanced out the window, trying to judge the train's speed. He wondered how much trains slowed down on curves; he wondered if Aïda and the boy could survive if they jumped from it.

Behind Ben a door slid open and the elflike man who shared the compartment with Ben and Aïda stepped into the corridor. He took in the grim expression on Manny's lips and the wild look in Ben's eyes. "There is surely an alternative to jumping from the train," he said clearly. He smiled a conspiratorial smile. "If you please, when you do sums," he said, addressing Ben, "what language do you count in?"

"Russian," Ben answered.

The man reached up with a forefinger and pulled down on the skin under an eye, a sign that he did not believe Ben. "The Russians may have taken you for Armenians, but we Armenians did not take you for Armenians. We were on to you as soon as you walked into our compartment. My wife's sisters think the woman and the boy are Russian Jews trying to wend their way to Israel. As for you and your friend here, my wife thinks you are Turks, my sons say you are Germans or Hollanders. I myself have a ten-ruble wager with my sister-in-law that you count in English." He switched into English himself. "One, two, three, three and a half, three and three-quarters, and so forth and so on. I am a professor of algebra. I was correct about you counting in English, yes?"

This time Ben didn't deny it.

"Not to worry," the elflike man said quickly. "Nobody on this train will betray you to the Russians. On the contrary, we will help you if it is within our power. Explain me, if you please, where is the problem?"

Ben looked at Manny. With a shrug of his heavy shoulders, Manny turned to the Armenian teacher of algebra and told him about the border guards and the KGB agents in civilian clothing, and the photographs. The elflike man's two sons and wife and two sisters, hearing conversation in the corridor, came up behind him. Up and down the corridor, Armenians sleeping in blankets stirred. The elflike man repeated to his family what Manny had told him. Two older Armenians joined the group. Four more came up behind them. Soon all were babbling in Armenian.

The teacher of algebra turned back to Manny. "My wife, always practical, asks how long before the KGB whores arrive us?"

"At the rate they are going, maybe three-quarters of an hour. Maybe less."

The elflike man repeated this to his wife. There was another burst of conversation in Armenian. The wife, clearly strong willed, was insisting on something. One of the men who had joined the group pulled a large silver pocket watch from a vest pocket and made a short speech. The Armenians nodded. The teacher of algebra issued instructions to his sons. One set off toward the head of the train, the other in the direction of the advancing border guards.

Drawn by the commotion, Aïda appeared at the door of the compartment. "What is happening?" she called.

"Do not be frightened, dear lady," the elflike man told Aïda in Russian. "You will get to Israel yet." Switching to

English, he addressed Ben and Manny. "Please, this gentleman says me that he was born in Voronezh and knows the area like the palm of his hand. In fifteen minutes, maybe more, maybe less, the train will cross a bridge over a river. Immediately we have crossed, I personally will pull the emergency cord. My two sons are alerting people. When the train she stops, everyone will descend off the wagons to stretch legs, to excuse the expression urinate, to wash in the river. Prepare yourselves. Fill your pockets with food but do not take valises with you. There will be a disturbance at the front of the train. The KGB whores will be distracted. Make your way under the bridge and stay there when the whistle sounds. When the train has left, follow the river. The gentleman who was born in Voronezh says me if you walk for two days you will come to where the river empties into the Don. And the Don empties into the Sea of Azov, which in turn empties into the Black Sea. And the Black Sea empties into the Mediterranean."

Aïda brought a hand to her heart. "From our hearts, we thank you all."

The elflike man turned toward her. "If you please, there is no need to thank us. We are a people who trace our roots back to Noah. We believe in God. Go with God if you share our belief in God." Half-bowing in her direction, the elflike man added, "Go with Him even if you do not."

THE LOCOMOTIVE'S WHISTLE dispatched a plaintive shriek over the deserted wasteland in which the train had come to a stop. On signal, one family near the front of the train accused another of stealing food. Words, then blows, were exchanged. The women, screaming insults, joined the fray. The train's regular guards and the KGB border guards trotted off to see what the commotion was all about. But the two KGB agents in raincoats and fedoras hung back near the caboose, eyeing the Armenians suspiciously, waiting to make sure that everyone who had left the train got back on board.

The elflike professor of algebra and his practical wife conversed in urgent undertones. Then the wife, making her way back along the line of cars, marched straight up to the younger of the two KGB agents and slapped him sharply across the face. The other KGB man roughly pushed her away as she yelled something about the KGB having murdered her grandfather. Other Armenians drifted over and hurled accusations of their own. Backed up against the side of the caboose by the shouting Armenians, the younger KGB man panicked and tugged a pistol from his raincoat pocket. Near the middle of the train, the algebra teacher nodded at Ben. Manny grabbed Saava's hand and pulled him under the train and out the other side. Aïda and Ben scrambled under the train behind them.

"Quick," Manny called in a ruthless whisper as he scampered down an embankment and, moving with surprising speed for someone of his bulk, darted along a narrow drainage ditch toward the bridge. As they came abreast of the caboose, they could hear the furious shouts of the KGB men ordering the Armenians to back off. A dry crack of a pistol shot rang out and a high-pitched voice cried, "The next bullet won't be fired into the air."

At the bridge, there was a steep loose-pebbled incline down to the river. Anchoring himself with his left arm around the stump of a dead tree, Manny passed Saava to Ben, who was already halfway down the incline. Keeping a grip on Saava's hand, Ben eased him down the rest of the way. Then he skidded to the bottom after him. Aïda and Manny slid down the incline and the four of them, breathing hard, ducked under the bridge and flattened themselves against the wall.

Presently they heard the thud of boots on the ties over their heads, and the muffled voices of the KGB border guards taking a last look around. There was another plaintive shriek of the train's whistle. The KGB guards started back toward the caboose. Moments later several cars banged against each other as the train jerked forward.

With Manny leading the way, the group, moving paral-

lel to the river, started out across fields of crabgrass. They
skirted a large herd of sheep being shooed along by two
teenage boys riding ponies and, later in the day, made a
detour around a tractor station for a collective farm. The
first night they slept in an abandoned stone shelter that
had traces of previous fires in its makeshift chimney. Aïda
and Saava gathered dry twigs and lit a small fire. Manny
used Saava's Swiss Army knife to cut slices of bread and
goat cheese for everyone. Cradling Saava's head on her
lap, Aïda seemed mesmerized by the points of flame
dancing from the burning wood. Manny spread his raincoat over the sleeping boy. Aïda smiled her thanks. With
Manny snoring away in a corner, Ben settled down next to
Aïda. He touched her wristwatch with the tip of a finger.
"I would walk through fire if I could go back in time and
fix things so that things didn't need to be fixed," he whispered.

There was a forlorn half-smile on Aïda's lips as she
murmured, "I would walk through fire if I could go back
in time and fix things so that we never met. If anything
happens to Saava . . ." She turned away and shut her
eyes.

They were off again before dawn the next morning,
stumbling through woods in the darkness, clambering at
first light over crumbling stone walls glistening with dew.
Attempting to skirt a giant marshland where the river had
overflowed a bank, they lost their bearings. Manny was
sure the river was behind them, Ben thought it was somewhere off to their left. They turned in circles for hours,
meandering through an endless scrub, clawing their way
through fields of thick brambles, wandering into a wood,
finally sinking exhausted to the ground in a clearing.
Overhead, billowing clouds choked off the sun. Always on
the alert for omens, Aïda took it as an ominous sign. "We
will never reach the Don," she moaned. She pulled the
edge of her shirt out from under her belt and moistened it
with saliva and began to clean the scratches on Saava's
arms and legs.

Suddenly two shots echoed through the woods. Overhead, dozens of birds fluttered in fright into the sky. Manny rose to one knee. Aïda wrapped her arms around Saava and held him to her. The crack of dry twigs reverberated through the silent woods. Two figures approached. The man leading the way had a dark, hawklike face and was wearing a wide-brimmed felt hat, loose-fitting trousers and shirt, knee-length boots and a short green cape. A slender teenager dressed in a loose-fitting blouse and blue jeans and scuffed lace-up hunting boots trailed behind him. Each carried a shotgun slung under an armpit.

The man in the green cape stopped in his tracks when he spotted the four people in the clearing. "Who are you?" he called in a tone that made it seem as if he owned the woods. "Where do you come from?"

The teenager let the butt of the shotgun slide out from under his armpit so that he was holding the weapon loosely with both hands. He said something to the older man in a dialect.

Aïda whispered excitedly, "They are gypsies." She rose to her feet. "So: We are trying to escape from the Soviet police," she told the man in the green cape.

"For what crime are you being pursued?" the man called.

"For the crime of independence of spirit," she responded.

A thin smile appeared on the gypsy's face. He snapped a command in dialect. The teenage boy's shotgun slid back under his armpit.

Holding onto Saava's hand, pulling him along with her, Aïda took several steps in the direction of the man in the green cape. "We escaped yesterday from a train being guarded by frontier police with KGB badges."

At the mention of "KGB," the gypsy turned his head and spat on the ground.

"We were following the river in the hope of reaching the Don when we got lost," Aïda added.

"The river bends back on itself in a giant S at the marshland," the gypsy called. He raised a hand and

pointed off to his right. "It is there, beyond the woods. If
you walk like a gypsy and follow the river and cut across
the fields where it bends back on itself, you will arrive by
nightfall at the place where it flows into the Don."

Manny came up behind Aïda. "Ask him if there are
boats on the Don," he muttered.

Aïda repeated the question. The gypsy replied that, until the river froze over, maybe twenty, maybe twenty-five
flat-bottomed scows passed every day, almost all of them
heading for Rostov with cargoes that would eventually
wind up on freighters in the port.

Ben whispered, "The gypsy is the answer to our
prayers."

Slipping a hand into his inside breast pocket and fingering a wad of bills, Manny said under his breath, "Ask him
if he will guide us to the Don and arrange passage for us
on one of these scows."

The gypsy must have sensed that Manny was reaching
for a wallet, because he raised a palm in warning. "Tell
him money left in a pocket offends no one. Tell him there
is nothing we want that we cannot steal. Tell him also that
stealing from Bolsheviks is not a crime." Then, his eyes
flashing with pride, the gypsy announced that he and his
son would guide them to the Don. "We gypsies have a
proverb," he called. "The best of friends is the enemy of
your enemy."

ITS MOTOR THUMPING, its decks creaking under the load of
bales of cotton, the yellow-hulled river boat slipped with
the current of the Don past the vineyards on either bank
toward the city Aïda called Temerniskaya Tamozhnya, and
the captain of the river boat called Rostov-na-Donu, Rostov-on-Don. Late in the afternoon the roofs of buildings
could be seen in the distance. The captain eased the boat
against the higher of the two banks. "The customs house
is around the next bend," he called from the wheelhouse.

Clutching a line, Ben leaped ashore from the bow and
held the boat against the bank so the others could jump

off. Manny went aft and handed the captain three twenty-dollar bills.

"I have never seen such money before," the captain wheezed. "What country did you say it came from?"

"America the beautiful," Manny told him.

"In that case," the old captain replied, "you have given me far too much. On the black market, each of these pieces of paper is worth what I am paid for an entire month."

"Keep it, old man," Manny said. "No need to mention us to the customs people, is there?"

The captain tucked the money inside the sweat band of his faded blue cap. "No need at all," he agreed heartily. He pulled an old customs manifest from a cardboard box and, wetting the stub of a pencil on his tongue, wrote on the back, "Go to the palace of the circus off Budennovski Prospekt. Ask for Madame Sofiko, the tattooed woman." The captain handed Manny the paper. "Say Zurab sent you. If you give her some of those pretty bills, she will find a place for you to lay your heads while you do whatever it is you have come to Rostov-na-Donu to do."

Skirting the customs house, a blockhouselike concrete building on the edge of the river, Ben and Aïda and Manny and the boy picked their way through the maze of vegetable gardens and toolsheds north of Rostov. They waited in the shadow of a toolshed until darkness fell before entering the city. A cool breeze swept in from the river. The streets, set out in a grid, were wide and spotless, and lined with the usual assortment of rambling brick buildings that characterized Soviet rural architecture. Aïda and Ben and Saava, armed with some of Manny's ten-dollar bills, went off in one direction to find the circus "palace" and the tattooed woman, Madame Sofiko. Manny consulted a street-corner plan of the city, and set off toward the Sea of Azov Hotel on the corner of Prospekt Karl Marx and Pushkin Street, the last known address he had for the Brothers Karamazov, the Cossack smugglers who had run his agents across the Soviet frontier during his back-to-back tours for the CIA in Turkey.

The original Sea of Azov Hotel had been reduced to rubble in the violent battles of the Great Patriotic War, during which the city had changed hands several times. From the ashes of the old hotel had risen a Soviet monster, a building with a marble facade and Palladian pillars on either side of the main entrance and turrets at the four corners. Manny, who had never been to the hotel, but had described it in intimate detail to dozens of agents, ambled past the reception desk down a long corridor to the dark, stale-smelling saloon at the back. He walked over to the bar and plunked down a ten-ruble bill. "Vodka," he told the bartender.

When the vodka had been measured out and set before him, Manny waved away the change. "I am looking for the Kapitonov brothers," he announced.

The bartender shrugged; if he knew the Kapitonov brothers he was not admitting it. Manny coughed up a guttural laugh as he dropped a fifty-franc note onto the bar. The bartender, a slim young man with slicked-back hair and an insolent glint in his eyes, examined the bill. "Which of the brothers do you want, Gennadiy or Feodr?"

"Their names are Kirill and Konstantin," Manny muttered. "Either one will do."

"In the unlikely event I come across a Kirill or a Konstantin, what do I tell them?"

"Say a friend from Istanbul would like to see them. Say I used to go by the name of Pressman."

The bartender ducked through a door behind the bar. After a moment he reappeared at the door and gestured to Manny with his head. Manny came around behind the bar. The bartender nodded toward the interior of the room. Manny pushed through the door.

The room was thick with cigar smoke. Through the haze Manny could make out two men leaning forward, slapping domino chips onto a low table. When the door closed behind Manny one of the two players, a fat man crammed into a wicker wheelchair, let his gaze stray to the visitor. "Have we met before?" he asked, lazily sucking on the soggy end of a thick cigar.

Manny took a step toward the fat man in the wheelchair, but stopped when he saw the young man at the table half rise out of his seat. "We have not met," Manny said. "But our paths have crossed more than two hundred times."

"If you went by the name of Pressman, you will know by what name my brother and I were called, since you were the one to assign us the name."

"You were the Brothers Karamazov."

A benign smile spread across the fat man's fat face. He wheeled his chair around to face Manny. "You were a legend in your time. The few who came face-to-face with you said you had a habit of laughing when you were afraid. They said you hardly ever laughed. Who would have believed our paths would cross after all these years?"

"It's a strange world," Manny agreed. "What is your brother up to these days?"

"Kirill has been safely dead and safely buried since the summer."

"Did he die a natural death?"

"He died a death that for him was natural. A Turk and he were running guns across the border to the Shiites in Iran. When the time came to divide the profits, the Turk came up with a different count than my brother. The dispute concluded when the Turk planted his knife up to its very fancy hilt in Kirill's stomach."

"May he rest in peace," said Manny.

"My brother or the Turk?"

"Did the Turk die too?"

"In this part of the world it is not honorable to let the person who kills your brother continue living."

"Whatever," Manny mumbled in English. He settled onto a bench, leaned his back against the wall and studied Konstantin, who was neatly dressed in trousers and a double-breasted suit jacket and a white shirt buttoned up to the neck. "What is with you and the wheelchair?"

"My legs are paralyzed," Konstantin said, "the result of

a knife wound inflicted by the same Turk who killed my brother. But my spirit is willing."

"How willing?"

"Explain your problem and we will both of us see how willing."

Manny pointedly eyed the young man sitting at the table. Konstantin said, "He is Kirill's oldest son and my nephew. You can speak in front of him as you would in front of me."

Manny explained that he and three others needed to cross the Soviet border without going through the formality of having their passports stamped.

Konstantin backed one wheel of his chair and looked at his nephew. The young man pulled a small notebook from the breast pocket of his worn double-breasted jacket. He moistened a thumb and flipped the pages until he came to the one he wanted, and consulted a list written in a microscopic handwriting. "The Greek freighter *Thessaloniki* is due to sail for the Bosporus and Athens with a cargo of raw timber on tomorrow night's tide," he informed his uncle.

"If the *Thessaloniki* is carrying timber," Manny said, thinking out loud, "it could be loaded into the hold in such a way as to leave a hollow space in the middle of the cargo."

"It could be," Konstantin noted. "But such an arrangement would be expensive."

Manny spread his hands wide. "What about doing it for old times' sake?"

Konstantin wheeled his chair up to Manny. The two men stared into each other's eyes. "A person who performs for ideals can always be talked around to see the logic of a different idealism. A person who performs for money, on the other hand, is serving himself, and can therefore be trusted. This is something Mr. Pressman in Istanbul used to understand."

Manny brought up another laugh. "I still do," he said. "How much?"

Konstantin wheeled back his chair and studied Manny,

as if he were estimating what the traffic would bear. "There is my nephew here, who will approach the ship's captain on my behalf," he said, ticking items off on his fat fingers. "There is the ship's captain, who must organize with the Greeks to get you ashore. There are his two mates, who must be enticed to keep their mouths shut. There is the operator of the crane, who will load the timber in such a way as to leave a hollow space in the center. And there is yours truly, the last of the Brothers Karamazov, without whom nothing can be done. The total comes to twenty-five hundred dollars a head or its equivalent in any convertible currency for you and each of your friends. Payable in advance."

Manny knew better than to haggle; the price could always go up. He stretched out one of his hands. Konstantin, smiling, nodding, strained forward in his wheelchair to reach for it.

AT MIDNIGHT OF THE second night at sea, the captain and the two mates of the *Thessaloniki* heaved aside some of the timbers so that the four passengers could come up for air. They were taken to the first mate's cabin, where they showered and put on clean clothing provided by the captain. Cold chicken and glasses of grape juice were set out on a table. While the others were eating, the captain, with a jerk of his head, invited Manny to step into the passageway.

Kicking closed the cabin door behind him, the captain cleared his throat. "It is a matter of fact," he announced, "that we are clear of Soviet territorial waters."

Manny nodded warily.

"It is a matter of fact," the captain continued, "that even if the Russians knew you were aboard, they could not stop us and take you off."

"Whatever." Manny understood that the captain, whose name was Papavlachopoulos, had not taken him aside to pass the time of day.

Captain Papavlachopoulos slid his right hand inside his double-breasted blue jacket with faded gold stripes peel-

ing from the sleeves and scratched at his chest through a
black turtleneck sweater. "Which logically brings up the
matter of the second installment on your passage money,"
he said.

From the moment he set eyes on him, Manny had not
liked the looks of Captain Papavlachopoulos. He smiled
too often, and the smiles lasted too long, to suggest
friendliness. Two gold teeth glistened like fangs on either
side of his jaw when he smiled. (Manny wouldn't have
been surprised to learn that the captain actually stood in
front of a mirror and polished them.) On top of everything, his eyebrows didn't stir. They might have been
painted on his forehead for all the emotion they conveyed.

"What is your given name?" Manny asked politely.

"I do not understand . . ." There was another smile,
another flash of gold teeth, followed by a delicate shrug.
"I am called Epaminondas."

"Well, listen up, Epaminondas. You know there is no
second installment. And I know you know. So why would
I want to pay more for a ticket I already bought? Explain
me that."

"We are speaking man to man, no? We do not need to
dance around a bush. The second installment is for insurance. A man sneaking out of Russia would be a fool not to
take out insurance, no? A woman too. Accidents happen.
Especially on ships. It has arrived for passengers to fall
overboard and get chewed up in the screws. They yell for
help, but nobody hears them."

Manny shook his head, as if he were having trouble
believing his ears. "Insurance?"

The smile vanished from the captain's face. The eyebrows which never moved suddenly inclined slightly in-
ward. "Insurance. Yes."

Manny snickered. "If someone on board this tub needs
insurance, Epaminondas, it's you. An hour after your ship
ties up, a telephone had better ring in the back room of a
second-floor loft"—Manny named a street in Piraeus
where a CIA mailbox had been located for years, hoping it

was still there; hoping the address was familiar to the captain—"or you are a dead man. You have a wife? If we don't show up in Greece, take my advice, draw up a last testament giving her permission to remarry." Manny managed another snicker, this one colder, more deadly than the first. "If my colleagues in Athens don't get you, my friend in Rostov, Konstantin, the last of the Brothers Karamazov, will."

The captain studied Manny's face for some hint that he was bluffing. Finding none, his own eyes flickered to the deck. "You don't hold it against a man, taking the temperature of the water?"

"In your shoes, I would have done the same thing," Manny muttered.

The captain smiled. The two gold teeth flashed out a message of relief.

AFTER DINNER AÏDA SLIPPED out of the cabin and climbed onto a wing of the bridge. A fresh head wind was stirring up sheets of fine spray from the bow wave. Overhead a crescent of a moon knifed silently through wisps of clouds. The ship was navigating between the banks of the Bosporus; land was a long stone's throw to starboard and to port. From the stern of the *Thessaloniki* came the throaty squawk of gulls darting in and out of the ship's wake. Aïda, her hair hanging loose and tangling in gusts of wind, leaned over the railing to watch them. We are being squeezed out of Asia like dental paste from a tube, she thought. She stared at the phosphorescent wake, trying to imagine it stretching like a broad avenue all the way back through the Black Sea and the Sea of Azov to Temerniskaya Tamozhnya. She found herself toying with the agate ring that was supposed to banish fear. Her watch, she knew, might be running backward, but time was running relentlessly forward on the ship carrying her, with each passing moment, farther and farther away from her mother, her Russia.

.   .   .

AT MIDNIGHT OF THE third night at sea, the captain of the *Thessaloniki* hove to off Piraeus to wait for the boat that would bring the pilot—and take off his four passengers. When the red over white lights of the pilot boat's mast appeared, bobbing on the Aegean, Manny led the way down the steep ladder to the gangway. The pilot, a short man dressed in a white suit with wine stains on the lapels, vaulted onto the landing and saluted the four of them. "We do not get many Russians seeking political asylum these days," he said in precise Oxford English. "Welcome to the world where it is better to be in the black than the red."

It was the pilot who directed them to a small boarding-house on the outskirts of Piraeus. "The proprietor is the sister of my sister-in-law. Her rates are outrageous. But breakfasts and dinners are included. And more often than not she forgets to register guests with the police."

The boardinghouse, a stucco building bleached white in the Aegean sun, with purple patches of bougainvillea clinging like leeches to the walls, sat on a saddle of rocky land above Piraeus, which sprawled below in a tangle of streets around the port. White-whiskered billy goats foraged in a nearby municipal garbage dump. On the skyline, disjointed slivers of the Acropolis shimmered in waves of heat rising from Athens.

Ben and Aïda, worn out mentally as well as physically, slept late. Saava and Manny were up and about when the cock crowed. Saava went off to play with the billy goats. Manny went off to "negotiate" with the powers that be at the American Embassy.

He returned early in the afternoon, exhausted from the effort of dealing with the embassy. After a frustrating start, he had talked the ambassador into bringing Washington into the picture. Enciphered messages had been exchanged. The president's National Security Advisor had come on the line. Guarantees had been offered. The rogue unit in the bowels of the Pentagon would be quietly disbanded. There would be no publicity, no acknowledgment that it had existed, no hint that there had been a plot to topple Gorbachev lest American credibility be undermined. Could Custer and Bassett be counted on to cooperate? They could, Manny cabled back, for a consideration, which Manny spelled out. The National Security Advisor quickly cabled back his agreement. Inkermann would be retired out of the Service for permitting an unauthorized operation to go on under his nose. Manny would be pensioned off without prejudice. Bassett would be offered back his old job at Army Intelligence. Aïda would get the bone marrow transplant for Saava, after which she could settle in the country of her choice.

Manny explained all this to Ben and Aïda and then, excusing himself, retired to his room. He planned to sleep until the fall, he said. Do not disturb, he said. Ever again. He had had it up to here with Foreign Service officers motivated by an abstract concept of serving their country without having any real sense of what that country stood for. For many of them it stood for whatever the president of the moment said it stood for. Screw them. Screw the world. Whatever.

The sister of the pilot's sister-in-law, a former nightclub singer who piped tapes of her off-key performances into the dining room over a loudspeaker, packed a picnic lunch in a straw hamper and Ben, Aïda, and Saava hiked up to the hill from which Xerxes was said to have watched the battle of Salamis. "So," Aïda instructed Saava, pointing to the narrow strait between the island of Salamis and the mainland. "All this took place five hundred years before Jesus died on the cross. The Persian King Xerxes built a bridge of rafts across the Hellespont to launch Asia's first invasion of Europe."

"And did he succeed?" Saava asked.

"He sacked Athens," Aïda explained. "Then he set up a throne here on this hill, perhaps on this very spot, and watched while the outnumbered Greek fleet destroyed his ships in the strait at his feet. And that was the beginning of the end of his invasion of Europe."

"If he saw that his ships were losing," Saava wanted to know, "why didn't he call off the battle?"

"Even kings sometimes have trouble changing the course of history," Aïda noted.

"Maybe that's just as well," Ben put in.

Aïda nodded in fervent agreement. "Maybe."

While Saava scampered after butterflies, Ben and Aïda sat with their backs to a stunted olive tree, looking out at the tramp steamers and fishing boats crisscrossing the Aegean. At length Ben offered her a grin, but his heart wasn't in it. "History has a built-in echo," he observed. "My grandfather, the one who wound up, ancient before he was old, operating a projector in a Bronx motion picture theater, stowed away on a steamer bound for Istanbul one jump ahead of the Cheka hunting him as an enemy of the people. And here I am trailing in his footsteps, sneaking across the frontier one step ahead of the KGB."

"Your grandfather should have stayed in Russia," remarked Aïda.

"He would have been shot."

"Akhmatova said you should die *with* your country, as opposed to *for* your country." Aïda turned the agate ring on her finger. "When Saava has had his operation, he and I are going back to our Russia."

Ben studied the wakes crisscrossing the sea. He was amazed that they persisted in the water long after the ships that produced them had disappeared over the horizon. "What will become of us?" he asked Aïda.

"There is no longer an us," she announced in a hollow voice. Her jaw trembled. "I have betrayed poetry. In a manner of speaking you have betrayed prose. We are wandering, lost, on an endless steppe . . ."

Ben stared into her gray animal eyes, memorizing the pain in them. He remembered spiraling out of character on the steps of the Druzhba Café the day he first met her. He remembered the words that had gushed out. "I hope to Christ we do not meet again!" He remembered her talking about the incident later. "One day you will tell me a truth as intently as you did outside the café," she had said. "I hope I will believe you when you do." Now he needed to tell her another truth as intently as he could so that she would believe it; believe him. "In the beginning I went through the motions of being in love with you," he admitted. "But I am not going through motions now." His hand reached for hers, found it, cold and limp. "I am not acting. I love you, Aïda. I love Saava. I can't lose you both . . . again. I beg you to believe me, to trust me one more time."

She searched his eyes. The ever present lucidity seemed clouded by passion. "I believe you love me, Benedict. I believe you love Saava. And I will not deny that I love you. But lucidity has finally overpowered lust. There were too many betrayals, too many lies. Our past is rotting in our future. Under our feet there is a terrible carnival of dead leaves. So: I love you but I do not trust you. I can no longer be sure where our fictions stop and our love starts. I wish to God it were otherwise."

On an impulse Aïda picked up a rock the size of her fist and, in a sudden motion, smashed her wristwatch against it. She stared at the broken crystal, then held out her wrist so that Ben could see it. "Fate has offered us the gift of a curious coincidence," she said. "Remember the story of the friend who stopped the clock when Pushkin died? The hour and the minute hand had also stopped at two forty-five."

The shattering of the watch, the coincidence, caused a dam to rupture. Aïda pressed her eyes tightly shut to keep back the tears. " 'Life is finished,' " she whispered, repeating Pushkin's dying words. " 'It is difficult to breathe.' "

Her body shuddered with a quiet crying. Tears appeared from under the lids of her animal eyes and streamed down her face, leaving traces as persistent as the wakes in the sea.

Four people whose names would not have meant anything to the general public gathered around a table in a basement room in the Pentagon. The table was metal and covered with frayed green felt, the room windowless, stuffy, remote. If I know my man Spink, the former CIA station chief who went by the name of Marlowe, he would have produced a bottle of Jack Daniel's. Lining up four paper cups undoubtedly swiped from some water cooler, he would have poured a healthy shot into each and handed them around. I can see him raising his paper cup in toast. I can hear him saying, "Here's to us. We have dammed a river. We have diverted history."

According to a security log I was not supposed to see, this was the final meeting of a shadowy Pentagon organization listed innocuously as an Intelligence Support Activity.

Nursing his Jack Daniel's, the group's éminence grise would have asked the man he knew as Marlowe to bring him up to date on the principals.

"Once the boy Saava recovered from the operation, he

*and the lady poet disappeared back into Russia," Marlowe
would have reported. "I personally convinced Bassett that
Custer had gotten it all wrong—that, thanks to him, we
have discredited the opposition to glasnost and perestroika after all. He's been posted to Wyoming by our
friends in Army Intelligence, who promised to keep an eye
on him. As for Custer, he is depositing his retirement
checks in a small bank in Vermont. I understand he is
hard at work on a book about what happened in Moscow."*

*The éminence grise, who was something of an innocent
when it came to tradecraft, probably frowned. "How did
you find out about the book?"*

*Marlowe must have smirked with pleasure. "Walls, as
Custer liked to say, have ears. Custer was overheard saying he is going to try to get a friend who writes spy novels
to publish his book as fiction. That way the affidavits he
signed giving the Company prior review rights to anything he wrote would not come into play."*

*"Can we live with this?" the éminence grise would
have inquired.*

*Marlowe would have shrugged. "Who is going to read
fiction as disguised fact?"*

*"Who indeed," the former CIA Deputy Director surely
agreed with a grin.*

*At some point the marine colonel attached to the long-
term planning staff of the Joint Chiefs would certainly
have made a formal announcement. "I am authorized to
convey to you all a Bravo Zulu. In the Navy that stands
for 'Well done.' I am also authorized to remind you that it
is the only recognition you will ever get."*

*"Except that when we read the newspapers," I can hear
the former CIA Deputy Director remarking, "we will
know the reality behind the headlines."*

*"Here's to the reality behind the headlines," the Mar-
lowe I know and detest would not have resisted commenting.*

*"Whatever happens," the marine colonel is supposed to
have warned, "we must never speak of what we did in this*

room to anyone, never hint at it in our memoirs. We have every reason to believe the bait we planted was swallowed. We would be fools to put the operation, or ourselves, or American credibility at risk at this point."

The four men whose names would not have meant anything to the general public would have quietly polished off the last of the Jack Daniel's in the cups. Knowing how Marlowe operates, I'd bet the usual scotch on the usual rocks that, as the meeting broke up, he carefully collected the paper cups from the table, metal, covered with frayed green felt, so there would be no trace of anyone having been in the room, windowless, stuffy, remote.

AUTHOR'S NOTE

The publisher, acting on the advice of nervous lawyers, has asked the author to include the usual disclaimer; has made its inclusion (if I got the tone of the request right) a condition of publication.

For the record, fellas, the characters are figments of someone's imagination. Any resemblance to folks living or dead is pure coincidence. As for the story, it has obviously been invented; everyone knows that such things don't happen in real life. Whatever.

ABOUT THE AUTHOR

ROBERT LITTELL was born, raised, and educated in New York. A former *Newsweek* editor specializing in Soviet affairs, he left journalism in 1970 to write fiction full time. He is the author of ten novels, including the critically acclaimed *The Sisters, The Defection of A. J. Lewinter, The Debriefing, The Amateur, The Revolutionist,* and *The Once and Future Spy.*